*Hunter's
Moon*

Dear Readers,

Welcome to a new reality! Shapeshifters live among us, hidden in plain sight. The Sazi are wolves, bears, snakes, cats, and raptors. But they're also fathers and mothers, business owners and public servants, living and working beside regular humans. Tony Giodone is an attack victim, turned Sazi against his will. Since recovering from his injuries he's been forced to try to understand his new nature and to fight to fit it into his life.

People ask authors: where you come up with these ideas? The truth is that we haven't a clue! Usually we start with a question: What if? What would happen if werewolves existed? Would modern humans be tolerant of them? Would shapeshifters have to hide what they are in order to survive in society?

Absolutely. Rules would have to be strict. The secret would have to be clouded in smoke, hidden in shadow and wrapped in an enigma. Punishment of those who tell tales would be necessarily harsh, because discovery would bring the very real risk of slaughter. Sad, but true.

It's taken a lot of sweat and tears to bring Hunter's Moon to this final form, to create and apply rules for an entire society, and we're very proud of this wonderful new reality. We hope you enjoy visiting the world of the Sazi. We certainly enjoyed writing it!

Hunter's Moon

CATHY L. CLAMP
AND C. T. ADAMS

tor romance

A TOM DOHERTY ASSOCIATES BOOK
NEW YORK

HUNTER'S MOON

Copyright © 2003 by Cathy L. Clamp and C.T. Adams

Edited by Anna Genoese

A Tor Book
Published by Tom Doherty Associates, LLC
175 Fifth Avenue
New York, NY 10010

www.tor.com

Tor® is a registered trademark of Tom Doherty Associates, LLC.

ISBN 0-765-34913-2
EAN 978-0765-34913-2

First Tor edition: December 2004

Printed in the United States of America

0 9 8 7 6 5 4 3 2 1

DEDICATION AND
ACKNOWLEDGMENTS

This book is dedicated first to Don Clamp and James Adams, who have offered patience and unswerving moral support through the years. Then to our parents, families and friends for their love and willingness to read through version after version (really, *really* thanks for that!).

We would also like to thank those people who helped us make it this far: To Thia, Bonnee, Dara, Gina, and Trace for being wonderful and helpful. Special thanks go to our agent, Merrilee and the wonderful Ginger, and our terrific editor at Tor, Anna.

Lastly, but most importantly, our most sincere thanks to Laurell K. Hamilton and Darla for their steadfast encouragement and help, and just being all 'round terrific people.

Without all of you, this wouldn't have been possible. We know that words aren't enough, but they're what we do best.

Chapter one

Nick's Tavern is in the worst part of town. The front door opens onto a back alley and the back door dead-ends inside another building. The Fire Code wasn't in effect when the building was built. Nick's has been there that long. My Dad remembers going there after work for a schooner of beer— twenty-four full ounces—and a plate of cheese. A buck bought both in the 40s. It was big enough for lunch for two or dinner for one. They don't do cheese plates anymore. Pity.

One time I went around the back of the building just to see what was on the other side. It's an upholstery shop. Big frigging deal.

Most of the buildings that surround Nick's are vacant now. Multi-colored graffiti scars plywood-covered windows. God only knows the last time someone cleaned the trash from the sidewalks.

I'm known as Bob to my clientele. That's not my real name. I'm the kind of person you would expect to find at Nick's. Call me a businessman who works the wrong side of the street. All sorts of people have need of my services: high class, low class, quiet suburban mothers, good church-going men. At one time or another all of them give into their primal instincts and call me. I meet them here at Nick's to talk details.

I'm not a hooker or a drug dealer. Too many risks, not enough money. There are no drug deals at Nick's. You'd get bounced on your ear if you even thought about it.

I'm an assassin. A killer-for-hire. If you have the money, I'll do the job. I like puppies, kids and Christmas, but I don't give a shit about your story—or your problems. I'm the person you call when you want the job done right the first time with no sullying of your name. Yes, I am that good. I apprenticed in the Family.

Oh, there's one other thing I should mention. I'm also a werewolf.

Yeah, I know. Big joke. Ha. Ha. I never believed in "creatures of the night" like vampires, werewolves, or mummies. They're the stuff of schlock movies and Stephen King novels. I'm not.

The door to the bar opened and the figure silhouetted in the doorway almost made me laugh out loud. I stifled the laugh with a snort of air. Then I let my face go blank again. Talk about stereotyping. The woman wore an expensive black pantsuit, odd enough in a low-class part of town. But the part I liked was that she wore a dark wig-and-scarf getup like something you'd see in the 60s, and huge round black sunglasses. Oh yeah, she'll blend right in with the steel workers and biker babes. Sheesh.

My client had arrived—and she was early. No big deal. We'd only set the appointment a few hours ago. I hadn't even unpacked from my last job. The quicker we finished, the better I'd like it.

The woman in the doorway was forced to take off the sunglasses to look around the darkened bar. I got a look at her face. Nothing special. Deep, green eyes looked out from a relatively plain face. She stood about 5'5". I felt like I recognized her, but she was like me—a blender. She could probably get dolled up and look pretty but she would never be stunning. She was a woman that a man would fall in love with for her mind or personality. Or maybe her body, which was on the good side of average. She was probably a size ten—Maybe a twelve. She carried it well and comfortably. The suit spoke of money. Good. She could probably afford me. The rest of the get-up spoke of nerves.

She scanned the bar, looking for someone she had never met. You can't mistake the look. The person just stands there, hoping that someone will wave or pick them out. I let her feel uncomfortable for a moment, just long enough to size her up. She wasn't a plant or a cop. Nobody can fake that level of nervousness. She wasn't wringing her hands, but close.

I was sitting in the back booth—my usual table. I looked around the bar while I counted slowly to ten. It's a comfortable, familiar place. A Family hang-out. See, it hasn't been too long since the Mob ran this town. Nick's was one of the neutral taverns. Not upper-class. Nick didn't run "no hoitsy-toitsy gentlemen's club." His words, not mine. Nick's son Jocko runs the place now. Yeah, really. Nick actually named him Jocko. Poor guy.

The bar looks old. Not elegant old, just old. Dark wood covers the floors and walls and surrounds a real marble-topped bar. Remnants of old sweat and stale cigarette smoke cling to every surface. You can't see through the nicotine haze on the windows. Jocko doesn't do windows.

I finished counting, raised my hand, and caught her eye. She walked toward me, both hands clutching her purse like someone was going to lift it. A pleasant jingling reached my ears. Jewelry of some sort. When she reached the booth she looked at me, surprised. Apparently I wasn't what she expected.

I don't wear an eyepatch or have a swarthy mustache. I even have all of my teeth. I look absolutely ordinary. Collar-length black hair, blue-grey eyes the color of gun metal, and a build that shows I work out but not to excess. I was dressed in a blue cotton long-sleeved business shirt with the sleeves rolled up, grey slacks and black sneakers that look like dress shoes as long as I keep them polished. The jacket that matched the slacks was folded on the bench next to me. I look like I could be a lawyer, a writer, or a mechanic. I don't look like someone that would as soon shoot you as look at you. That's the idea. I gave her my best mercenary look; cold, uncaring. I wouldn't want her to think that I was just some guy hitting on her. She looked away, rattled.

Her scent blew me away. I notice smells more since the change. Nice term—"change". Her scent was stronger than it should be, but not perfume. This was just her. The woman smelled sweet and musky, with overtones of something tangy. I learned from Babs that means she's afraid. Fear reminds me, although Babs said I'm nuts, of hot and sour soup. Every emotion has its own particular scent. And lies! When someone lies, it smells like black pepper. I don't mind; it helps me interview clients.

Most scents are soft and not particularly noticeable. They rise off a person's skin like ghostly presences, only to disappear into unseen breezes. I have to concentrate to catch a person's real scent.

My client slid into the opposite side of the booth. I didn't stand. She didn't expect me to. Good thing. She sat with her back to the room. Another good indication that she wasn't a cop. Cops, like crooks, have a thing about having a wall at their back. Nobody can hit you from behind or pull your own gun on you.

"Um," she began when I just stared at her without saying anything. "Are you Bob?"

I nodded but still made no sound. It unnerved her and amused me. She was having a hard time looking at my face, whereas I looked straight into her eyes.

"I'm hoping you might be able to help me," she tried again. It required no comment, so I didn't make one.

My nose tingled. The client smelled like blood; like prey. But that's true of most people. Especially near the full moon. I never used to think much about the moon phases. Now I plan my life by them.

People didn't used to smell like food. Some days it pisses me off. But I didn't get a choice in the matter. A hit went bad. The woman I was stalking stalked me back. I wasn't prepared for a being with superhuman speed and strength. She ripped my throat out of my body and left me for dead. I should have died. She said so later. Guess I was too damn stubborn to die.

The wash of emotions from the client overpowered my nose. I could handle the fear and the blood. I was used to them. I don't meet with clients until after I've had a large rare steak for lunch. But this lady smelled of heat and sex. Heat, not sun—heat and something that I couldn't place that reminded me of a forest. Warm, dewy, sweet, salty. It was a safe, comforting smell unlike anything I've ever been in contact with. It was a smell that I wanted to soak into my pores. Breathe in, roll in. I had to blink and sneeze to clear my senses. Then I returned to staring quietly at her.

She couldn't meet my eyes but kept scanning the room. Her fingers tapped restlessly on the table, then on her lap, then on the table again while she bit at her lips as if looking for something to say or do. The hot and sour smell of fear, the burnt metal of frustration overwhelmed me as if they were my own. That was new. My muscles tensed against my will. Suddenly she stopped fidgeting, took a deep breath and looked right at me.

"Would you please say something?" she asked in frustration. "I'm drowning here."

That won her a quick smile. "Would you like something to drink? It's not much cooler in here than outside. That dark suit has to be hot."

She looked at her outfit and had the good grace to blush. "It's a little trite, isn't it? I didn't even think about the heat. I was trying to be inconspicuous." She smiled a bit as if she felt my amusement the way I was feeling her emotions, but she smelled embarrassed. A dry smell, like heat rising off desert sand, mixed with other things I didn't recognize yet. I don't know a lot of the emotions yet. Babs told me that I'd get the hang of identifying them. I'm in no hurry.

I didn't believe it at first. Didn't want to. But Babs followed me around for three days, and taped me with a camcorder. I avoided her like I avoid everyone, but she filmed enough to prove that she was telling the truth. Babs was a sadistic bitch about it, too. She made sure she immortalized all of the most embarrassing moments of a dog in living color. Pissed me off. I stopped returning her calls after that.

"I don't exactly blend in, do I?" The words brought me out of my musing.

Lying to save her feelings would be diplomatic, but I try to save lies for important things. "Not really."

I raised my hand to signal Jocko. He moved out from behind

the bar, wiping his meaty hands on a snow white bar rag. Jocko's a big 6'8". He looks beefy but it's mostly muscle—he was a pro wrestler for a few years. Jocko wears his waist-length black hair in a ponytail because of state health regs. A scar cuts his left eyebrow in half. He's second-generation Italian but he looks Native-American because of the hair.

Jocko smells like bad habits. Whiskey and cigarettes and sweat. He walked slowly toward the table—almost lethargically. Jocko moves slow because he threw his back out in the ring years ago and since there isn't any worker's comp insurance in wrestling he came home to run the family business. But he's hardly a cripple. Jocko can still throw a man through the front window if he puts his mind to it. Everybody knows it. Like me, he doesn't talk much. He just stood at the table waiting for our order.

"Draft for me." I turned to the client with a questioning look.

"Um—rum and Coke, I guess." Jocko started to walk away. She raised her voice a little bit to add, "Captain Morgan, please." He nodded without turning or stopping. "And Diet?" a little louder still. Anyone that didn't know Jocko would presume he hadn't heard her. I knew he heard her and that he was chuckling softly under his breath. The mild orange smell of amusement drifted to me. A rum and Coke is not the same thing at all as a Morgan and Diet. Not to a bartender.

She glanced at me. "Do you think he heard me?"

"He heard. Now, what can I do for you?"

"I want you to kill someone," she said calmly. "I can afford to pay whatever the cost."

Well, that was direct! I shut my mouth again, closed my eyes and reached my hand up to rub the bridge of my nose. It eased the tension behind my eyes.

"Is something wrong?"

There's a certain code in my profession. The client doesn't actually ask and I don't actually admit what I do for a living. It's just sort of understood. Money is discussed but only because both parties know what transaction is being, well, transacted.

I lowered my voice. "I would appreciate it if you could be a little more *discreet* about our business here."

That stopped her cold. She suddenly realized what she had said, and that she had said it in a normal tone, in a place of business. Her face flushed and her jaw worked noiselessly. The blend from the combination of emotions made me giddy.

"That was stupid, wasn't it?"

"Well, that sort of depends whether you *want* to spend the next twenty or so years in prison. It's called 'accessory before the fact'."

She shrugged. "Actually, for the job I'm proposing, I'd never see the inside of a prison."

"That might be a little overconfident," I replied, "There's always the chance of getting a very good investigator. I always make it clear to clients that there is risk involved. I'm good. I'm very good. But there is always a risk."

She shook her head. "You couldn't know since I haven't explained. But it's not an issue."

I believed her and I didn't know why. No black pepper smell of deceit, maybe. I shrugged my shoulders. "Fine. You've been warned." I drew a breath and began my list of conditions. "I'll need the name of the mark, a photograph, and home and work addresses. I work alone. I will choose the time and place of the job. Not you. If you want it public, I'll pick the time. You can pick the method if you want. If you don't specify, it could be by a variety of methods. I vary them to fit the situation and the mark. I don't do extras like rape or torture for the same money. There will be an additional charge for that kind of thing."

She listened intently and without comment. When I mentioned rape and torture, she grimaced slightly. I could feel her disapproval beat at me like heat from a furnace. I shook off the feeling and proceeded on.

"If the mark meets his end without my assistance, there are no refunds. I require payment in advance. Cash only, small bills. If the money is marked or traceable you will forfeit your life at a future time of my choosing. Don't presume that I can't find you. I can."

She nodded, as if she had heard my speech a million times. She leaned forward, eyes intent on my face—focused. Good. I like it when people listen.

Jocko arrived with the drinks so I stopped speaking. He put them on the table, then looked at me. "That'll be four-fifty."

I motioned for him to ask the lady. He turned his attention to her and she opened her little purse quickly. She extracted a ten dollar bill and held it out to him. "Keep it."

Jocko pursed his lips in approval and moved off silently.

"Go on," she said.

I tried to remember where I left off. I hate to get interrupted mid-stream. "If the police somehow get wind of me through you, I will make sure that you never live to testify. If there are family members involved and they get in the way, I will remove them. I don't charge for removal of witnesses. That's for my benefit, not yours. However, if there are potential witnesses that you do not wish removed, make sure they are kept out of the line of fire until after the job is complete. I won't be held responsible for mistaken identity, so if the photograph is not absolutely clear, or up-to-date, there could be a mistake."

The client sipped her drink as I spoke. It's a long spiel. Now's the only time I ask questions like whether she needed proof that the job had been accomplished. She smiled. "No, I think I'll know." That meant that it was someone close to her; possibly a husband or boyfriend. Her amusement smelled sweeter, more like tangerines than oranges.

When I finished, my beer was almost gone. "Do you have any questions?" I asked.

She had a mouthful of complimentary peanuts and she didn't respond immediately. Jocko puts out peanuts to increase drink sales. It works, so I don't indulge.

"No," she said when she'd swallowed, "That about covers it. When do I have to get the cash to you? And how much?"

"How much depends on who. Public figure or private? Who is the mark?"

She spread her hands out, showing her chest to perfection. It was a nice view but, "I don't understand."

"*I'm* the target. The mark. Whatever."

I raised my eyebrows. "Excuse me?"

"I'm hiring you to kill me. The time and place don't matter. But soon. How much will it cost?"

Alarms started ringing in my head. "There are a lot less expensive ways to do yourself in,"

She nodded her head once. "Probably. But this is the method I choose. Is there a problem?"

There was something wrong with this situation. I couldn't think of what specifically was bugging me. I really don't want to know a person's story but I was missing something. Something important. I needed to dig.

I leaned back in my seat. "Who are you and why do you need to die?"

Her eyes shifted. Yeah, there was something there all right. "Does it matter?"

"Normally, no," I admitted, "But this is a first for me and it's making me nervous. So, give. Why do you need to die in such a way that it *doesn't* look like a suicide?"

Intense emotions washed through my nose, blending and then splitting. I couldn't identify them all. I'm still new at this shit. I suppose a little part of me is annoyed that I haven't picked them up faster. It's been almost a year. But I'm not curious enough to contact Babs.

"I don't need to die. I want to. But you'd need to hear my story and you told me on the phone that you didn't want to hear it. I'm a nobody. No one special. Just take the money and do the job." Her eyes were bright, too bright, and her voice too intense. I didn't like it.

"What's your name?" In any event, I'd need it if she turned out to be the mark.

"Wh—" she began and then corrected herself. "Oh, that's right you need the name. Quentin. Sue Quentin."

Sue Quentin. That name rang a bell. I leaned forward and put my arms on the table. "Take off the wig," I ordered.

She looked around her nervously. Yeah, it probably wouldn't do to have her reveal herself in full view of everyone. That sort of thing is remembered.

"Fine," I crooked a finger and slid out of the booth. "Follow me." She stood and followed me down a hallway to the bathrooms. It was dark but my eyes are exceptionally good—funny thing. I knocked on both doors and waited. No response. I turned around to face her. "Take it off."

She slid the black wig with attached scarf from her head. Underneath were medium-brown permed ringlets that reached her shoulders. The hair changed the shape of her face. Even in the dim light of the hallway I instantly recognized her. The disguise was better than I'd credited. With the wig, I hadn't had more than a vague recognition. Fortunately, no one else in the bar would probably make her, either. I knew her but couldn't imagine why she would want to die.

I shook my head. "Huh-uh. No way. You're a *very* visible lady. I'd have to wait until the heat surrounding you dies down."

She stood very still, eyes closed. The hot blanket of sorrow pressed on me and tightened my throat. A single tear traced silver down her left cheek. "How long?" Her voice was barely a whisper.

I turned and walked back into the room, not able to answer right away. I had to get away from that distress. She got under my skin way too easily. That alone made me nervous. Some instinct told me if I didn't run from her, she was going to change my whole life. I didn't want this job.

I slid back into the booth. She followed me a couple minutes later, in control again. The wig was back in place and she had wiped the tear from her face. She looked relatively calm but her hands trembled a little. She folded them in front of her and held herself stiffly, as if hanging onto her control by her fingertips.

I'm not moved by tears. I've turned down jobs before. But she'd asked a question and I could at least give her an answer. "I don't know," I replied. "With all the publicity—a year, maybe more."

Her gaze was steady on me but the unshed tears made her eyes shine. "So I can count on that? A year from now you'll do the job?"

I held up my hands in front of me. "Whoa, lady. I didn't say that. I said, 'a year, *maybe more*'. I can't judge that. You could be in the papers again next week and it would start all over. I don't predict the future. No. I can't take the job."

"If you only understood," she began.

"Stop." She did. "You were right the first time, Ms. Quentin. I don't want to know. I don't *care* to know your story. I'm not a psychologist. I'm not a social worker." Except this time, I *did* want to know and I couldn't explain why.

Her eyes went cold for a moment, almost as though she could sense my thoughts. "Fine. How much?"

I felt my brow wrinkle. "For what?"

"To listen." She leaned forward a bit. "You're absolutely right. You're not a psychologist or a social worker. You're a mercenary. How much will it cost me for you to listen to my story?" Her anger bit at my nose. It smelled like coffee burning.

"It won't change anything," I said. "I don't want the job."

"So don't take it. There are other people out there with less *scruples*. I just want an ear. I just want you to shut up and listen to my story." Her voice tightened as she spoke— colder, harsher, more brittle. She was blinking back tears again. "You don't have to care. Just make the right noises in the right places. How much for a couple of hours?"

"It's not scruples that would stop me from taking the job, lady. It's self-preservation. Too many people know your name. Investigators would work a lot harder because you're newsworthy. And I'm not for rent on an hourly basis."

That was supposed to be it. The end. I don't know why I said the next. "But, fine. If you want to buy my ear for the night, it's for sale. A thousand up front and I'll let you know how much more when the story's over." I half-stood and half-slid out of the booth. "Let's go."

She looked startled. "Just like that?"

There I go again—being impulsive. I should walk out. My gut told me I should run. I've learned to trust my wolf instincts even when I don't understand them. And yet, I shrugged and smiled tightly at her. I had nothing better to do right now. I had no reason to fear this person. No logical reason, anyway. Money's money. It's just another job.

"Just like that. You're driving. But I have to make a call first. So finish your drink, go to the john or whatever. I'll meet you out front in a couple of minutes. What are you driving?"

Her eyes got wider. I could smell the hot tang of fear, the soured milk smell of disbelief and rising under both, the lighter smell of hope. She had been expecting me to walk out. Probably thought I was playing a cruel joke. Not a chance. For once I'd be able to indulge my curiosity. In my position, the less I know about a client or a mark the better. Except this time I wanted to know more. Maybe I'd find out how many people had walked out on her in the past. Or why she wanted to die. Maybe I'd walk out too. We'd see.

Chapter 2

I left her in the booth looking dazed. I went down the back hallway again. A payphone hangs on the wall in the corner near the door to the men's room. It's an old phone but it works.

I dialed a number and a man answered. "Plaza Hotel, how may I direct your call?"

I used my harried-but-professional businessman voice. "This is Anthony Giodone. May I speak to Max, please?"

"Good evening, Mr. Giodone. This is Max speaking. How may I assist you?"

I glanced at my watch and noticed a crack across the crystal. Damn it! I'd have to get it repaired. I like this watch. But still, not quite three o'clock on the 11th. Three more days until I checked in.

"Max, I know it's unusual but I was hoping my suite might be available."

"We always try to assist our loyal customers, sir," came the appropriate reply. "When did you want to book your suite?"

"For right now." Before he could continue I added, "I know it's unusual and short notice but I'm meeting someone on urgent business."

There was a hesitation. "No, it's not short notice, sir. When did you want to arrive?"

"Thirty minutes?"

"Oh!" his voice sounded relieved. "I understand now. Of course, we'll make the suite available immediately. We'll look forward to seeing you in a few minutes, Mr. Giodone."

I hung up the phone. The call had solved the *where*. Now to go outside and meet the *who*.

A bright yellow Mustang of this year's vintage sat purring

quietly by the curb. Well, I guess if I had won the state's largest lottery jackpot ever I'd probably splurge a little bit too. Two hundred sixty eight million dollars. Wow! I took in a little over a million a year, but even after she paid taxes, I'd have to live a hundred eighty years to accumulate what she had fallen into with a one dollar ticket. I guess that proves that money doesn't buy happiness. Susan Quentin was the least happy person I had met in some time.

She still had on the wig and scarf, which I was going to suggest anyway. I opened the door and slid onto the soft white leather seats. All the perks. A CD player played a soft rock ballad that I recognized from the radio. The wind blew her scent right at me. For a second I forgot to breathe. I could feel my nostrils flare as they willingly saturated with her fragrance. She watched me get in the car. It wasn't a casual look. Whatever was happening between us, she could feel it too. Her eyes were wide. I could smell her excitement—desire and fear. Heat, for lack of a better word.

When I was seated and closed the door, I looked at her. "Yes?"

She looked forward again and flushed. "Nothing. Sorry."

She blushed easily. This could be fun.

"Drive," I commanded. She put the car in gear.

"Where are we going?" she asked after we had traveled for a block or two.

I had already worked up a cover. "Head to the Plaza. Drop me off about a block from the hotel. Park the car. Wait ten minutes. No more, no less. You'll be Jessica Thornton, a broker."

The CD was still playing. I reached over to turn it off so it wouldn't be a distraction. She reached over at the same time. Our hands touched. She jerked back suddenly, as though burned. I felt it too. Electric, like when you scuff your feet and touch metal. But it was deeper inside, not just a surface shock. It felt good enough that parts of my body reacted forcibly.

I grabbed her hand, fast but gentle, and got the same reaction as before. Thrills of electricity up my arm that raised all the hair on my skin. It wasn't painful. The sensation was wild. It was scary but intoxicating. Almost addicting. The hand wore a small opal ring in a nice setting. Expensive and elegant but not gaudy. Probably new. The office-length nails were cared for, though not professionally.

I got glimpses of her mind as we touched. Since the change I can sometimes sense what other people are thinking. Only when I touch them, though. My hearing went berserk too. Some days if I stand real still, I can hear the neighbors talking two or three doors down. During the full moon, the humming of the refrigerator hurts my ears. I bought a stock of foam earplugs. Why is he doing this? Is he going to hurt me? Stop. Don't stop. I'm not supposed to like this. What's happening to me?

She glanced at me. It wasn't fear—not exactly. I turned her hand over and looked at the palm. I forced my voice to remain cold and rational. "I won't specify stock or real estate. It's none of the hotel's business. I'll ask at the desk whether you've arrived. Then I'll head to my suite and ask that you be directed to the room when you get there."

She drove silently, listening intently while I traced the lines and the callousing on her palm with my thumb. Her mind couldn't come up with a complete thought. Even in the heat I saw her shiver.

I wanted to raise her hand to my mouth. Kiss the skin, roll the taste of her in my mouth. Shit. This is too weird. I released the hand and she pulled it away slow, like she had just started to enjoy it. I shook my head once to clear it and turned off the music. "When you go into the hotel, ask the desk clerk for Anthony Giodone. That's not my real name so don't bother to remember it. He'll either direct or escort you to Room 935. It's on the top floor. I'll have dinner delivered from room service. How do you like your steak?"

She didn't respond for a moment and I looked at her, waiting for an answer. "That was impressive," she finally said.

"What was?"

"You said all that in one breath. I'm impressed. And I like my steak well done."

I almost laughed but held back. "I'll let room service know."

It was about twenty miles on the freeway to the Plaza Hotel. It's very nice and comfortably furbished. It's also extremely expensive. When it was first built I met with the owner to discuss renting a suite on a permanent basis. It was about five months after the change occurred that I realized I needed somewhere to go for three days that was absolutely safe. I'd tried to lock myself in my house, but I always managed to get out. I would wake up and find a window broken and bloody feathers or fur littering my bed. Any idea what that stuff feels like coming out the other side? Once I found the refrigerator hanging open and groceries scattered through the house. It was a pain in the ass to clean up.

The client suddenly shifted into fifth gear and I once again heard the delicate jingle of metal. It must be a bracelet. I just couldn't see it under the jacket sleeve.

The hotel was in sight. I needed to go shopping soon. I always bring food with me for my visit. Then I lock the door and stay in the room for three days. They leave me alone; no maid service, no calls, no nothing. When I come back to my senses I clean up the mess, or pay for anything I've damaged. It's worked well so far because I've never told anyone I go there.

Except now I was bringing this client to my hideout. Go figure. Weirder still was that I was glad that the room could be ready.

I heard her swallow and noticed the nervous tapping of her fingers on the wheel. She was shifting back and forth in her seat restlessly.

"So, how did you get my number?"

She relaxed back into her seat. The tension drained from her like air from a balloon. She smelled of gratitude. Warm and slightly musty like air from a dryer's vent. "You would not *believe* how difficult it is to find someone in your profession."

I said nothing. It's not supposed to be easy. That's how we stay out of jail.

"I mean, it's not like you can just look in the phone book." She put her hands on top of the steering wheel, resting her wrists on it and pretended to be flipping pages. "Let's see, here we go, *assassins*. See *hired killers*." Amusement edged her voice.

I chuckled. So much for my fear she'd get maudlin.

"I remembered reading a few years ago in that magazine from Colorado . . . oh, you know the one. I can't remember the name."

"I know it," I responded, "Go on."

"Well, I remember they got into real trouble because they were running ads for mercenaries."

I nodded. "I read about that. The people who put in the advertisements weren't real bright, either."

"Well, I hoped that maybe even though they got busted they might still be doing it."

I raised my eyebrows. "And were they?"

"Sort of," she conceded. "There weren't any actual ads but when I called the magazine and talked to the classified department the clerk had a list of people who *couldn't* put ads in."

A back door approach. I like it. I grinned.

"It must have been a private list. He started to tell me but I guess his boss came in 'cause he hung up. I tried to call back later but he wouldn't take my call."

"So what did you do?"

"I went to the library and looked up some back issues. The ones that *did* have the ads in them."

"Attagirl."

She blushed and smiled. She was bright. It won her a few more points. It almost made up for the '60s spy movie get-up. Smart, with black humor. And hey, she wasn't bad-looking. I looked her up and down. Decent figure, great hair under the wig, nice smile. Not bad at all. Yeah, I could do her. Happily, if that little taste earlier was accurate. She glanced at me and must've seen something of what I was thinking. Her eyes widened and her head snapped forward again. Her knuckles whitened on the steering wheel. I smelled the sharpness of her sudden fear and the musky heat of desire.

"So, anyway," Her voice, now, was just a little shaky, "I

called two of the numbers I found but they were both on 'extended leave of absence'. I presumed that meant they were in jail."

"Or on the run."

"Either or," she agreed. "But one woman gave me a number of someone that she said was good. That her 'man', as she phrased it, respected."

"And that's how you called me?"

She shook her head. "No. I got the number of another person. *That*.was the weirdest meeting I've ever had in my life." She shivered. "I got a message to meet him at this little video arcade that has a lunchroom. I sat down at the table that I was told to, and up comes this kid wearing baggy blue jeans and a striped T-shirt. Dark blonde hair cut long on the front so it covered his eyes and shaved in the back. You know, typical teenager."

Ah. Him. I nodded, unable to suppress a smile.

"Anyway, I figured that the kid was going to try to sponge money. So I ignored him, hoping he'd go away. I mean," she looked at me somewhat pathetically, "I was supposed to *meet* someone."

"Not realizing that he was who you were coming to meet?"

She looked at me, shocked. "You mean you know him!?!"

"Go on."

"Well, apparently, he *was* who I was coming to meet." Her brows were buried under the bangs of the wig, as if she was still startled. "He sat down at the table and asked if I was Sue. He was very professional. Very business-like. It was incredibly unnerving."

"Scotty has that effect on people," I agreed.

She looked at me again, newly surprised. "You really *do* know him."

I nodded.

"He's a baby!!"

I laughed out loud. "Lady, Scotty wasn't a baby when he was born!" She smelled sour-sharp with disapproval but at the same time oozed wet, fog-bank sorrow.

"He can't be more than, what, twelve?" She gestured with

her fingers while controlling the wheel with the heels of her palms. She was agitated enough about the kid that she couldn't sit still.

"I mean, he's only a few years older than my nephew who still plays video games and is shy around girls."

I nodded agreement. "He just turned thirteen. He's already had two strikes so he'll have to keep his head down. Next time, they'll charge him as an adult. And he *does* still play video games and *is* shy around girls."

"You mean he's been *caught* before? Killing people? Then why is he still out and . . ."

"Talking to people like you?" I asked with a smirk. "Because he's a minor. He got the maximum five years in juvie hall for the first one. They had to drop the case on the second one. Witnesses kept disappearing."

She glanced at me in horror. "But if he was in juvenile hall for five years, then . . ."

I completed the thought, "He did his first job, sloppily, at the tender age of six."

Her eyes went wide. "The poor baby!"

I shook my head. "Don't feel real sorry for him. He's the way he wants to be. I checked him out. There's no history of abuse. The kid's just a psychopath. He doesn't look like anything other than a normal kid. It's his trademark. Nobody expects him, so he can sneak up on people." I thought I knew but asked anyway. "Why'd he turn you down?"

She shook her head with a small laugh. "He said that it wouldn't be any *fun* to 'do me', because I'd know he was coming. He said he does 'close in' work, whatever that means and he couldn't sneak up on me."

"That's with a knife or other arm's length weapon. A blade, a golf club, whatever. For Scotty, it's a visceral pleasure for him to watch a person die. He actually gets a physical high. Maybe even a sexual high." I shrugged. "To each his own."

"That," she said with a shiver, "is just so . . . bizarre! He really scared me."

I looked at her with a questioning smirk. "And I don't?"

She paused. "Not in the same way," she said thoughtfully. "He gets his kick out of pain. You can see it in his eyes. You look like you'll do it, but it's just business."

Not at the full moon. I nodded in agreement anyway. I stared hard at the side of her face for a minute and abruptly decided she needed a dose of reality. I admire the kid's work. He's talented. I wouldn't want her to go all socially conscious on him and turn him in "for his own good."

"You know, you should be happy that he does this for a living."

"Why in God's name would you say that?" Her eyebrows climbed high on her forehead. She spared a horrified glance before returning her attention to the freeway traffic.

"Because as long as he does it for a living, it satisfies the need and he doesn't do it for *fun*." She glanced at me, stunned. "Understand? A lot less dead people. Scotty's damn smart. He won't get caught easy. He'll be a serial killer if he ever stops being an assassin."

A sign whizzed past. The next exit was ours. She flipped on her turn signal and changed lanes. Her eyes blinked in time with the sound. "I guess."

I rested my elbow on the car windowsill. "You still haven't said. How'd you find me?"

Silence for a little while, then she took a deep breath. She shook her head and straightened in her seat. "From him. He wouldn't do the job but he gave me your number. Said you were the best, if I could afford you."

Huh. Didn't know the little bastard even had my number. Maybe I'd return the favor on the next blade job.

As instructed, she stopped the car about a block from the hotel and parked at the curb. All the reasons why this was a bad idea came rushing back to me. I had never invited another soul to the suite. Too late now. I was actually enjoying talking to her—looking at her. That worried me. My voice was harsher than I had intended when I steered the conversation back to business.

"Before we go any further—a thousand up front. Remember?"

"Oh!" It seemed like she had truly forgotten and wasn't just trying to burn me. She opened the clutch purse. My eyes opened wide. Inside the little black bag was a huge wad of cash! That explained her death grip on the purse.

She pulled the roll of currency out of the bag, in full view of whoever was walking by and counted out ten one hundred dollar bills. I shook my head wearily as I accepted the money. I carry around a lot of cash, but get real! She was a robbery waiting to happen.

"I wouldn't flash that wad of money around, if I were you," I warned. "You've already got a target painted on your back from the car. No need to advertise."

She looked mortified and hurriedly stuffed the money back in the bag. "I wasn't sure how much you would charge but I figured you would want cash."

I smiled. "You wouldn't have enough there. Not unless those are thousand dollar bills. My base price is fifty grand and goes up from there."

She cleared her throat. "Fifty. I see. I've only got ten here."

"Like I said, not nearly enough. But it would have been enough to show good faith. I would have accompanied you to the bank for the rest. *If* I had agreed to the job."

She looked at me slyly. "You haven't actually refused, you know."

"Close enough." I pocketed the money and got out of the car.

As I walked to the hotel, I heard the rhythmic beat of soft-soled shoes behind me. Seconds later, a jogger passed me by, headphones drowning out the world. The muscles in my legs instantly tensed to run—to start the chase. I forced myself to keep walking. I could hear the pounding of the man's heart over the music feeding into his ears. The light dew of sweat on his forehead and trickling down his back from the heat was like some intoxicating perfume that turned my blood to fire. I fought down the desire to snarl and take off after the runner; to bring him down. To quench the hunger.

I have this problem a lot. It makes jogging in the park tricky. People seem to resent it when you chase them. Go figure. And I *have* to run. I *have* to chase. It's part of me now. It gets harder and harder to control the closer it gets to the full moon.

When I reached the hotel, the doorman quickly moved to open the door for me. "Afternoon, Mike," I said cordially. He'd worked here since the place opened.

"G'day, Mr. Giodone," he responded with a grin. Mike is Aussie, right off the boat. He always smells like eucalyptus and mint and the citrus smell of happiness, penetrating and bright as his smile. The smell cleared out the musk from the client and the prey-smell of the jogger. I slipped him his usual tip. A crisp twenty keeps his smile genuine.

Max Holcomb met me halfway across the room with a slight bow. He's the Concierge; tall, thin, and always immaculately dressed. In another time, he would probably have been a butler or a gentleman's gentleman. He has the temperament for it. Obedient and dependable, the smell of a well-tended lawn with overtones of cookie spice. It's a comforting smell. Another deep breath calmed me down the rest of the way.

"Good afternoon, Mr. Giodone."

"I've told you before, Max, you can call me by my first name."

"Now, Mr. Giodone," he said somewhat reproachfully, "That would hardly be proper."

I smiled. The same game every time I came in. "No, I suppose not." I looked around the room, as though searching for someone. "I was to meet my broker here. Has she arrived yet? Her name is Jessica Thornton."

He pursed his lips as though concentrating. Yeah, right. He knew each and every person in the building and their location. "No, sir, nobody by that name has come in. Would you like to wait for her in the lounge?"

I gave it a moment's thought. "No, just have her shown to my room." He nodded and handed me the key card. I started to walk to the elevator but then stopped and turned briefly. "Oh, and have a bottle of Captain Morgan and some Diet Coke delivered to the suite for the lady. Is there draft on tap?"

Max raised his eyebrows and the scent of his surprise drifted to me. "Of course, sir. You asked that the room be ready. It is." It made me smile. "Will there be anything else?"

I remembered to order dinner before I took the elevator to the top floor. There was a bellboy already waiting for me at the door with the requested items. I slipped him a five. He accepted the proffered bill and left quickly. That's the way I like staff.

Once he was gone, I opened the door and tossed the key card on the marble-topped table inside the door. The blast of cooled air greeted me like a welcomed friend. Exactly as I remembered it. The stone fireplace with the natural gas logs stood ready if the need arose. The drapes had been opened to reveal the excellent view. Clear blue skies stretched to the horizon and the mountainside looked just ready to begin to turn colors. Next month this time, it'd be stunning.

I kicked off my shoes and padded to the wet bar opposite the fireplace. There were two taps available. Guinness Dark and whatever was on sale. Today it was Bud. That suited me.

I removed one of the mugs from the small freezer below the bar and filled it. A slight layer of frost formed on the outside of the mug and I took a grateful sip. It really was hot outside. I hate heat. I've always been a cold weather person. Give me a forty degree day anytime, no coat, no sleeves, and I'll be happy. Heat is even worse since I became a wolf. It's like I have fur even in human form.

I sat on one of the two recliners across from the couch and put up my feet. Not enough sleep for a couple of days now. It's been a rough week. I glanced at my watch again. My brow furrowed when I saw that it hadn't changed since we left Nick's. I tapped on the crystal. The second hand grudgingly moved a second forward and then stopped again. Damn! I'd not only cracked the crystal, I broke the whole watch! When had that happened?

I closed my eyes and sighed when it hit me. Oh, yeah. I knew *exactly* when I'd done it. It was during that second car theft, when I'd had to roll the hot Mustang into a ditch and high-tail it before the cops arrived. I'd forgotten to grab the portable police scanner from the front seat after I got out and the door had slammed into me when it started to roll. Yeah, this last job in Atlantic City had gone very, *very* badly.

If Carmine had given me the mark's real name instead of his current alias, I would have refused the job. I'd gambled with Jeffrey a couple of times. He knew me on sight and would see me coming. Granted, the guy had to go. He'd tried to slice a piece out of Carmine's pie. If that wasn't bad enough, he'd taken out one of our guys in the process. Under the circumstances, it didn't matter that he was the son of a cooperating family in Atlantic City. Nobody, but *nobody* invades Carmine's turf. The minute Jeffrey spotted me, he knew what was coming and ran home to daddy. I had no choice but to follow.

Carmine had called ahead. Vito, the daddy, had said he'd handle the situation. But Daddy wasn't my client. Carmine was, and he wanted the job done anyway. A strong message needed to be sent. That's when Jeffrey decided to go to the police for protection. Not his best plan and not what Daddy had in mind, either. They went to stop him and bring him home.

My one and only chance to avoid Daddy's goons and to get the job done was when the kid was walking up the police precinct steps. Granted, I would have preferred *any* set-up over that. Atlantic City's so hot for me now that I may *never* be able to go back. It's going to take some serious negotiations for Carmine to repair the damage with Vito.

The police threw a dragnet around the city in record time from sheer embarrassment. My only option was to steal cars and take forgotten back roads. It took a lot more time than I planned—how long had it taken me to get back? Shit. I'd lost track of what day it was.

Speaking of time . . .

I started to glance at my watch and swore again. I walked to the bedroom and checked the digital readout on the clock radio. Nearly eighteen minutes had passed since I got out of the car. She should be here by now. I sat back down in the recliner and reached to my left to pick up the telephone and dialed an extension I knew by heart. It and room service were the only two numbers I ever dialed.

"Concierge," came Max's voice. "How may I be of service?"

"Max, this is Tony Giodone. Has Ms. Thornton arrived yet?"

There was a pause that I didn't like. "Could you describe her for me, Mr. Giodone?"

"She's about thirty-five, 5'5", dark hair, black Chanel pantsuit. Seen her?"

"Yes, sir. She's arrived but hasn't checked in at the desk yet. She's in a rather odd conversation with another woman."

The devil, you say. Why hadn't I listened to my instincts?

"Odd, how?" I asked, as I grabbed at my shoes. The phone wouldn't reach and I had to lean back in the chair and stretch to drag them over with my feet.

"It appears that a woman is insisting she knows your guest. Ms. Thornton is trying to ignore her but the other woman keeps stopping her to talk to her. Would you like me to intervene?"

"No," I replied, holding the phone with chin and shoulder as I hurriedly tied a bow in the second shoelace, "I'm on my way down. Don't let either of them leave."

I hung up the phone and raced to the door.

Chapter 3

I realized that I'd forgotten the key card as the door slowly swung closed behind me and snaked my arm between the double doors to grab it before the lock latched. The heavy oak crushed my arm. White flowers erupted in my vision for a second and I bit back a curse.

Key card safely in pocket, I closed the door and headed for the elevator. I got out at the second floor. Old paranoid habits die hard. This could still be a set-up. I'd rather not have the elevator door open in the lobby to a waiting group of police. I turned the corner and entered the stairwell. I took the steps two at a time. When I reached the ground floor, I peered through the small rectangular window in the stairwell door.

Susan was trying, without success, to escape a blonde woman who kept grabbing her arm to stop her. The blonde bore a strong resemblance to the client. She was taller and slimmer; with a sharp angular face. Each time, Susan would back away. She wasn't making a sound. My guess was that she did know the woman but didn't want to be identified, and since she wasn't very good at lying, she didn't speak. That won her a few more points.

My payment for listening to the story included ensuring that she had the opportunity to tell it. I opened the door and entered the lobby.

"I don't know what kind of game you're playing, Suzi Quentin, but you're not going to get away with it," I heard the blonde say as the door quietly latched behind me. "I don't care if you talk or not—you're my sister and I know you. So just give it up. You might as well stop and talk to me. And," her hand shot upward, "take off that ridiculous wig."

I quickened my step and just as the blonde's hand reached Susan's shoulder, I reached out and grabbed her wrist.

"Who the hell are you and why are you bothering my friend?" I asked, with quiet menace that wasn't faked. The smell of this woman made me fight down a growl: rotten meat, like a buzzard. She set off alarm bells. It made no sense. I turned to Susan, still holding the wrist. "Jessica, are you all right?"

Susan didn't have a chance to answer. The blonde tried to pull her arm out of my grasp but I merely tightened the grip. A part of me wanted to hurt her badly. "Let go of my arm!" she exclaimed. "Who do you think you are?"

"I'm a friend of the woman that you're accosting," I explained. Quiet was useless, but I was determined to keep this confrontation as low-key as possible. "You seem to have mistaken her for someone you know." My eyes were steady on the woman. She finally stopped trying to escape my hold. She glared at me.

I turned to Susan again. "Jessica," I stared hard at her, hoping she would take the hint to play along. "Do you know this woman?"

She shook her head, trying to look confused.

"You see? You've simply mistaken her for someone. I would appreciate it if you would just leave us be."

The woman gave me a look that said she didn't buy it for a moment. The conversation had started quietly, but her voice kept raising. "I don't know who you are but this has nothing to do with you. I want to talk to my sister." She started to move closer to Susan, but I snapped her wrist backward, stopping her abruptly.

"This woman is not your sister," I hissed. "Her name is Jessica Thornton and I've known her for years. She doesn't have any sisters." My voice was steel cold. "You've made a mistake." I saw Max out of the corner of my eye, mock-casually walking toward our little group. I was surprised it had taken this long. Security should have arrived some time ago. Then I glanced over his shoulder and saw the matching charcoal suits standing right near the check-in. Max had apparently hoped I could handle the situation without intrusion.

"Please don't force me to become... *insistent*." I tightened my grip until she gasped. Her eyes stared into mine and slowly lightened from defiant to anxious. A part of her clearly understood that I *wanted* to injure her. I smelled it and saw it in her eyes.

We continued to stare at each other until Max reached us. "Mr. Giodone, Ms. Thornton, is there a problem here?"

Susan was still frozen, gazing with something approaching wonder at my confrontation with her sister. I spared him a relieved glance. "Yes, Max, there is. This woman is bothering us. Would you please escort her out?"

The blonde looked at Max in surprise when he addressed Susan as Ms. Thornton. Max follows a lead well, whether or not he believes it.

"Madame," he said, "I would appreciate it if you would please leave this establishment. I'm afraid you're creating a disturbance."

The woman's anger escalated and she yanked her wrist out of my hand. She winced at the effort and rubbed it with the other hand briefly. I raised my brows when she glared. No apologies. That's what you get for being a bitch.

Then she pointed a finger at Susan. "This isn't over, little sister! Don't forget I was with you when you bought that pantsuit. You can't hide under some fake hair and silence. I don't know why or how you buffaloed these two into protecting you, but I *will* get the truth out of you. You have no business leaving her alone. If anything happens to her, I hold you responsible!"

I grabbed Susan's arm and led her toward the elevator. The moment I touched her, a little electric breeze sprang up. The fear of discovery and guilt flowing from her nearly overwhelmed me. "Max," I said pleadingly over my shoulder, "take care of this."

Max raised a finger in the air and the two security guards

appeared on either side of the woman. They each gently took an arm.

She stopped short and looked from one to the other. "I am a customer here!" she exclaimed in outrage. "You can't do this."

"We can carry you out, ma'am," said the man on her right, who was built like a linebacker, "But it might embarrass you. Could you *please* come with us?"

The elevator dinged. Susan and I stepped in through the opening doors. I watched as she suddenly realized that we had escaped and that the entire lobby was looking at her as though she had grown a second head. She tried to regain a little dignity. She squared her shoulders and raised her nose.

"Very well. If you insist, I'll go. But you will never have my business again," said the blonde.

As the elevator doors closed, I heard Max say, "I'll make note of that in my records, madame." A chuckle escaped me.

Chapter 4

I hit the button for the seventh floor. When the doors opened, I gestured for Susan to follow me. I didn't touch her again. The flow of emotions every time I did set me on overload.

Susan looked confused. "I thought you said the top floor. Which room are you in?" I just walked away from her and she eventually followed to the stairwell and up. If the woman watched the elevator, she wouldn't know what floor we were really on.

We arrived at the room with her a little out of breath from climbing stairs in three-inch heels. I used the key card on the door and waved her inside. I took off my jacket and automatically checked the weapon concealed at the small of my back in a specially made holster.

I removed my billfold, counted out five hundred dollar bills and offered them to Susan. When she didn't take them, I reached down, grabbed her hand and stuffed the bills into it.

She looked down at the money, then up at me.

"What is this for?"

"I just bought your pantsuit," I explained. "You don't own it anymore. You sold it to a consignment shop three days ago. You can leave out the date, if you don't lie well. If the issue is ever brought up, you can honestly say that you sold it."

The startled look on her face gave way to a look of relief. "That never would have occurred to me! I can do that. It's not a lie. Not really."

I walked back to the wet bar. I could see in the mirror behind the bar the moment when she noticed my gun. A flicker of fear disappeared in quiet resolve.

I picked up my beer, then turned to face her. "Were you followed, or was that little scene an accident?" Self-preservation and professional pride made me ask. I hadn't noticed a tail and she'd already proven she couldn't lie worth shit.

"I don't think I was followed." Worry edged her voice and thick fog rose from her. "I tried to be careful. I know her car, unless she rented one like I did." She began to pace in small circles. "This was a stupid idea! Stupid, stupid, stupid! I should have known that I couldn't have even a few moments of peace. Are you *sure* that you can't kill me right now?" Her cheeks were flushed with embarrassment, voice thick with frustration.

A burst of bitter laughter escaped me. "Here? After *that* scene? You've got to be kidding."

She looked chagrined, as she should. Low-key was a distant memory. All I could hope for at this point was polite embarrassed silence from the gossip pages. I was just glad that I have a good enough relationship with Max that he didn't call the cops. One particular homicide detective has it in for me. He'd loved to run me in, even on a "disturbing the peace" charge.

Time to change the subject. "I had the bar send up Morgan and Diet. Help yourself. You look like you could use one."

She looked from me to the bar and back again, brightening. "That was *nice* of you." She smelled surprised, a shock of scent but warm. Warmth?

"Don't look so shocked," I said in reproach. "I can be nice."

She flushed again. I seemed to have that effect on her.

"I mean . . ." she stammered. "In your profession . . ." She stopped, biting her lip as if she didn't know how to finish the sentence without insulting me.

I let it go. Not important enough to make an issue. I ended the silence with, "Don't worry about it. Grab a drink and sit down."

She moved a little too quickly to the bar. She mixed a Morgan and Diet in one of the beer steins. It was a pretty large glass for a mixed drink. She sat down on the couch but couldn't get comfortable. She restlessly shifted in her seat, body rigid. She wouldn't look at me.

"Why death?" I asked as I turned and walked farther into the room. I faced her and then sank into the overstuffed leather recliner.

She didn't appear surprised by the quick questioning. "Mind if I get comfortable? This will take a while."

I waved my hand at the empty couch and took a long draw of beer.

She pulled off the wig and flipped her hair several times to get the sweat out. It gleamed softly in the light. She gave her scalp a quick scratching. I hid a sympathetic smile in my beer. I know how wigs itch.

Then she unbuttoned and removed the top part of the pantsuit. Underneath was a white silk shell. The chiming sound was from a small silver charm bracelet with tiny bells and little bunny rabbits. I suppressed a chuckle and let my eyes keep roving. Small circles of sweat were beginning to form under her arms. The cool air hit her bare skin and raised goosebumps. My eyes automatically rose. Yes, she felt the cold there too. She stretched and arched her back, outlining the hardened nipples against the thin silk. Definitely enticing. She ended the stretch abruptly and stared at me in shock as if she'd heard what I was thinking. Her scent was embarrassed but a little turned-on. The musk was a very nice touch.

The air blower stopped just then and I could hear her heart beat in the sudden silence. I didn't turn my gaze. She did.

When she sat down, she slumped slightly as if to hide her figure. She looked as though carved in stone. Drink in one hand, legs tight together and crossed at the ankle. Gaze anywhere but at me. My psych professor in college would have said that she had "closed" body language. I'd say more like "slammed shut."

I shook my head and smiled. "Would you please mellow? I won't bite." I paused, allowing myself another good look. "Unless you want me to, of course."

She glanced at me and saw the hungry look in my eyes. I

heard her heart rate increase and could smell heavier musk with overtones of hot and sour soup brush my nose. She flushed again and looked away. Yep, definitely interested, but timid. Fine with me. If she didn't turn out to be an absolute basket case, we could have fun. But I didn't want to make her a wreck. "You wanted to talk. So talk."

She looked at me then. I leaned back into the sofa and put one arm across the back. See, completely relaxed. Just two friends chatting. Except one was a hired killer and the other a multi-millionairess. I sipped the beer. "Well? Why death, Susan?"

"My name's not Susan."

"You're not Susan Quentin?" My hand tightened on my stein but I kept my voice calm. "That's who the papers called you."

"They got my name wrong," she replied angrily. "It's not Susan. It's *Suzi*."

I took a deep breath, shrugged and allowed myself to relax again. "Same difference."

Burned coffee filled the air, thick and pungent. I was a little surprised at the intensity. "No. It's not the same at all."

She hesitated a moment. "My parents named me Suzi. It was supposed to be cute. Suzi Quentin. Suzi-Q. I've spent most of my life being called SuziQ. Makes me sound like some fluffy-headed cheerleader. I hate it."

Her voice vibrated with that hatred. I could smell it too— jalapeño pepper, strong and hot, had joined the burning coffee. There were some other emotions roiling underneath. Too many smells. I couldn't concentrate. I fought for control.

I took a deep whiff of the beer in my hands before I took a drink. Hops. Barley. Alcohol. The emotions faded in the sharp smells. Good. I swallowed deeply. "So what should I call you?"

"Anything but that." She hesitated. "Actually, nobody's ever asked me before what *I* wanted to be called. I don't know."

"What's your middle name?"

She wrinkled her nose. "Lynette. Why?"

I looked her over head to toe then nodded. "You look like a 'Lynette'. How about that?"

She repeated the name to herself several times. Then she shook her head. "Nah. I've never liked it. Just call me Sue."

I nodded in approval. "Sue it is." I stood and walked to the bar to get another beer. She took a swig of her own drink.

"So, *Sue*, you still haven't answered my question. Why death?"

She hesitated not as though she didn't know but like she wanted to collect her thoughts. Trying to give an honest answer. Finally, she looked at me very intently. "Have you ever been used?"

I smiled at that. "I spend every night being used. I'm in a . . . *service* industry."

She shook her head. "Not like that. You have a job. You get paid for your time. I mean really used. Forced to do something you don't want because of duty or obligation or even guilt. With no payment and no thanks?"

My brows raised. "No, using that definition—never."

Her face hardened and she held her glass tight in both hands. "Well, I have. I've spent my entire life being used."

"Why would you want to do that?" I was honestly curious.

She laughed. It was sharp, like broken glass. "I didn't want to. I was born with no backbone. I can't say no. People ask me to do things and I can't think of a polite way to refuse. Or the person sets it up so that I can't refuse without hurting someone. My family is famous for that."

I shrugged. "Tell them to go to hell."

"You don't understand." She sat deeper into the sofa.

I didn't. I mean, why would a person do something just so they wouldn't hurt someone? "So explain it to me."

She thought for a moment and then nodded. "Okay, an example. Years ago, I worked at a fast food place. Just part-time while I was getting on my feet." She looked up and I nodded. "I started at the bottom. You know, cleaning the floor, making fries, that stuff. The boss found out that I could do books and keep money straight, so he started to ask for little favors: 'Could you help me with next week's schedule? I can't get it right', or 'Would you mind dropping off the deposit on your way home? I can trust you.' It made me feel important at first and I was flattered that I'd be asked to help with important stuff but then it became part of my assigned duties. Pretty soon, I was doing all the managerial stuff and he was taking off more and more time. Just not showing up. So I would have to open the store and count the cash and make sure everything was closed properly. . ."

I held up a hand to stop her. "*Why* did you have to?"

She swallowed another large mouthful of her drink and tried to answer. Another wash of emotions—burnt coffee, burnt water, anger and bitterness and the heavy fog of sorrow all mixed together. It almost took my breath away. I took another whiff of beer.

"Because although he was a jerk it wasn't the fault of other employees whose hours would be screwed up without a schedule, or the customers who expected the business to be open even when he didn't show up. I felt an obligation to them, if not to him."

"But every time you did that, you saved his butt from being fired. He deserved to be canned if he wasn't doing his job."

She sighed, like my words were old news. "But then I would feel guilty because it also wasn't his wife's fault. She was confined to a wheelchair and depended on his salary. Who else would give the jerk a job?"

I chuckled. "You weren't born without a backbone, sweetheart. You were born with an overdose of guilt. But that's nothing to die for. You can fix that."

She jumped at the endearment, then plowed on shakily. "If that was the only problem it wouldn't be so bad. I eventually quit, which was my way of solving the problem without confrontation. I don't like confrontation. It's why I say I've got no backbone. Which leads me back to my family. More specifically, my mother." She paused and stared at me, like I was going to walk out on the conversation. Fat chance. It was just getting interesting.

I raised my eyebrows, encouraging her to proceed.

"I'm the adult care-giver for my mother."

I've known a few of them. Tough life. Watching your parent become a child again, less and less able to provide for themselves. It explained the comment from her sister about leaving "her" alone. "That's a rough job. Is she terminal?"

Another dose of burned coffee. "Some day she will be," she said matter-of-factly and then her eyes narrowed with fury. Thick coffee boiled on the breeze. "But not now. Right now, I'm the adult care giver for a perfectly healthy manipulator."

My surprise must have showed because she smiled bitterly and continued. "Oh, she's good. She's very good. The rest of the family believes that she needs full time care. You only see the truth when you live with her every day. The problem is, I can't get anyone else to believe it. And I can't get rid of her. She possesses my every waking moment. *Demands* my every waking moment."

She finished her drink in a three-gulp wash and stalked to the bar for another.

"She moved in with me two years ago. Back then I truly believed she was failing fast, just like everyone else. She looked like death. She had lost a lot of weight and was having trouble remembering things. Of course, I'm the youngest with no husband or children so it was *decided* that Mom would come to live with me. My input wasn't sought. It was *DECIDED*." Her voice seethed with bitterness. "Everything has always been decided for me." She paused. "But you probably don't want to hear me whine." She took a long draw on the new drink. She was going to get toasted if she didn't slow down. But maybe that was the point.

I took the opening anyway. "I want to hear anything you want to say. Whine or not." She looked at me with surprise. Like even for money I wouldn't want to hear it. Actually, since I had given back half the retainer, I was operating solely on curiosity.

The drinks were starting to take effect. She sat down on the couch and swung her legs up, kicking off her shoes in the process. She grabbed a pillow from the other end and stuffed it behind her back. She had to turn her head to look at me. I felt like a psychiatrist sitting in the chair while she reclined on the couch.

She was silent for a little while before speaking again. She was thinking. Working out where to start. "When Mom moved in with me, I was like everyone else in the family. I believed that she was going senile. The first thing that happened was that she failed her eye test and lost her driver's license. Everybody felt sorry for her. Sorry for the loss of freedom; of independence. We all took turns driving her around to doctor's appointments and the grocery store and other places."

I nodded. Not having a car is a bitch.

"Then, one by one, the rest of the family started getting too busy. I still felt sorry for her and I really did have more time than anyone else. So I guess it sort of made warped sense when they decided for her to move in with me. She just showed up on my doorstep one day; my sister dropped her off. They sold her house and she had nowhere else to be. See what I mean about setting up situations?" She looked to me for agreement.

"Pretty sneaky trick."

"Oh, twice as sneaky as you think. But not on my sister's part; on my mother's. I found out later that Mom had known full well what was happening. She told them that she'd discussed it with me. But she didn't. I had my own life. I had a nice job and a comfortable apartment. I even had a long-standing relationship." She looked sad for a moment. "But they're all gone now. God, I miss it."

"Miss what?"

"My life! She got me fired, and then had me evicted. She even alienated my boyfriend." I could smell it again—the seared caramel that coffee makes when it scorches, muffled under the rising foggy smell of sorrow. Tears came to her eyes and she took another swill.

Oh God, I hoped I wasn't in for a crying jag.

"I don't make friends easily. Relationships are even harder. I knew when she drove Robert away from me that she'd never let me have another. She set it up so *slick*." She glanced at me to see if I was uncomfortable having her talk about a former lover.

It didn't bother me and I said so: "I'm not bothered by much. There's not a lot you can surprise or embarrass me with. Talk away." She blushed and looked away again, then she shifted uncomfortably on the couch and switched subjects. "When she moved in it started innocently enough. I let her have my bedroom. It was only a one bedroom so I took the couch. I figured that she would only be there for a few weeks until she found a new place. But she had no intention of leaving. My neighbors hated her. She made so many complaints against everyone that eventually I got evicted."

Wow. That takes effort. I've lived next to some real annoying people, but could never get them kicked out.

"Once I found my current house she started making requests. Just little ones, you know, like 'Oh Suzi, could you help me with my medicines? I can't remember which ones I've taken today.' I figured if her memory was failing, it would probably be best for me to take control of her medicine. You know, so she didn't overdose."

I nodded.

"And little by little, she just *infringed* into my space. 'Oh, no, Suzi, you can't buy *that* soap. I'm terribly allergic to it.' And, 'Suzi, dear, must you play that rock music? It's so difficult to concentrate.' I tried to make her feel like a guest but she didn't want guest status. She wanted to run the show. No, that's not right either," she said, shaking her head. "She wanted to run the backstage, and have *me* in front of the camera running the show."

The beer had run through me. I excused myself to the bathroom. She nodded politely and sat staring into space running a slow fingertip around the lip of her glass.

I didn't waste any time. I wanted to get right back. I was enjoying her company, despite my better judgment. I even liked her. I spent the minute or two trying to figure out what it was. She had a certain—I don't know, maybe *stamina* that was refreshing. A "grin and bear it" attitude. But if she wanted to die then things had taken a turn for the worse. I wanted to hear chapter two.

I returned to the living room. Her glass was full again. A glance at the clear bottle of rum on the bar confirmed that it was another full strength job. Nearly a quarter fifth gone in three drinks.

I walked over and took the drink out of her hand. She looked at me, startled. "Slow down a little," I said. "If you pass out, you can't talk. You're plenty relaxed now." I put the drink on the bar and poured a second glass of just Diet Coke. She took the glass, nodded, and sipped the soda. Then she began talking again as if she hadn't stopped and I had missed part of the conversation when I left the room.

"Becky was the pretty one. Tall and athletic with blonde hair to her waist. She could have anyone she wanted. I wasn't born pretty. I'm not tall or blonde. I got reminded of it every day. That was Becky downstairs."

"Well," I responded glibly, "At least you have manners."

She smiled at that. Smiled at me. A fog of spiced tangerines drifted to my nose. Happiness stronger than gratitude. "Becky's never had to be polite. She's pretty. People excuse bad behavior in pretty people." I shrugged. I couldn't disagree.

"Becky thinks that I'm just being selfish. That I want to have this wild life or something now that I've got money. She's just sure I want to throw Mom into the street."

"Do you?"

"Honestly? Sometimes. But I can't. And I probably wouldn't, given the choice. After I won the money I bought a big house, way larger than I needed. I figured that Mom could have space and I would have a room or two where I could be alone. I've always liked being alone. But Mom can't be alone. Actually *can't*. It drives her nuts. I sit down to take a bath and she's knocking on the door, wanting to come in to talk. It drives me insane!"

"Well, if she really can live alone, why don't you buy her a place of her own? Move her out and be done with it."

She shook her head so hard that her hair whipped with the

force. The alcohol, I thought—her movements were getting bigger, stronger, as if overcompensating.

"Don't you think I tried? That was the *first* thing I thought of. I have two doctors on my side and they're very well respected. When I got the money, the first thing I did was hire a team of doctors to give her a full exam. I mean a *full* exam." Her arm swept the air and almost knocked the drink out of her other hand.

"X-rays, CTs, blood tests, the works. I got a neurological specialist because she said she was losing feeling in her fingers. She swore she was growing taller so she had an MRI to see if she had a tumor. All negative. Oh, and her eyes are just fine. But if she had a license I wouldn't have to drive her. The doctor confirmed that she is as healthy as a racehorse. Healthy for someone half her age. More healthy than *me*. She called them quacks and demanded we see some Chinese herbalist that a friend told her about. I couldn't imagine what *friend* told her that. She doesn't have any friends. I wish she did!"

She shook her head wearily. "I thought the money would help. But things are even worse. I finally convinced the family to let her try to live alone. I bought her an apartment. I even offered to pay for a full-time nurse." She sputtered angrily. "You know what she did? Huh?"

"I can't imagine."

"She broke her hip!"

I raised my eyebrows. "Not intentionally, I'm sure."

Her eyes were cold but calm. "She *absolutely,* intentionally broke her hip. I was finally going to be free and she just couldn't stand it." She said it as if it was a fact, not merely suspicion.

I began to understand.

Chapter 5

"How do you know she hurt her hip intentionally?" I asked.

"She was taped." She waited for a reaction. I carefully leaned forward and set my stein on the table. Then I leaned back and put up the footrest. The slow movements were meant to cover surprise. This was getting even more interesting.

"You videotaped her?"

She smelled embarrassed. "Not on purpose. When I bought the house, there were six months left on a security contract. You know, a burglar alarm company?"

I nodded knowingly.

"Part of the contract is to replace tapes in the hidden monitors around the house every few weeks. It's a real expensive house, but I have them set on pretty low-resolution and on the longest run time since I don't really have much to steal. I don't even think mom knows they exist. Anyway, I was out making the final arrangements on the apartment. She helped pick the colors and the wallpaper. She seemed excited about having her own place again. Something that didn't remind her of Dad. When I got back, she was nearly unconscious on the floor. I couldn't move her. I called an ambulance."

Sue was quiet for a moment. Her scent shifted again. The burned coffee of anger twined with the sour, bitter smell of guilt.

"I felt horrible," she said at last. "Just horrible. I really did feel selfish. When I was out that morning I had been feeling so smug. I was going to be free of her. Then I found her on the floor with her leg bent wrong. She was whimpering."

"When did you get the tape?"

She ignored the question at first. She was in her own little world. Another dose of emotions. Too many to sort out. Time for another long sniff of beer.

"She looked so helpless. I couldn't help. Not even a little. She's a big woman. I couldn't even move her. I was afraid to. So I waited for help. I sat on the floor next to her and tried to make her comfortable. I felt so guilty. I wondered if I had imagined all of the mind games. Whether I really was the selfish one for wanting my own space when she needed me." Tears came to her eyes and she didn't bother to wipe them away. They ran down her face unchecked.

She snuffled and then coughed. I leaned over to the table next to my chair, rummaged a moment, then tossed her a box of tissues. She missed the box but it landed on the floor within reach. She set her drink on the table, grabbed a tissue, and blew her nose. Unlike most people, she actually cried well. Her face flushed and looked better than normal, even with red-rimmed eyes.

"I got a call from the insurance company months after her fall. I had been acting so apologetic. She just ate it up. I bought the apartment anyway; I had a contract. But I never finished the decorations. I stayed home all the time in case she needed something. She had to have a hip replacement. It took months to heal. I literally put my life on hold for three months."

"What did the insurance company tell you?"

"I guess they routinely investigate accidents like this. They saw the monitor in the hallway when they came to the house and checked with the security company. They said they were denying the claim because it was faked. Not the injury. It was real. But the accident was set up. I didn't believe them. Not at first."

She hesitated and I prodded gently. "But they convinced you, didn't they?"

"They showed me the tape. There was no mistaking it. In clear black and white. She knelt down at the top of the bannister and removed the screws from the handrail. She jiggled it to make sure it was loose. Then she calmly climbed the stairs and started back down. When she got to a certain point

right near the top she pushed her whole body weight sideways and went right through the banister. It was so cold and
calculated. She said something when she was wiggling the
banister. Even though it's not the kind of system that picks
up sound, her face was clear on the camera. It showed her
lips moving."

She looked up at me, very intent. "I never told her that the
monitors worked. It never came up. I haven't told her since.
I took the hit on the medical. Luckily, I can afford it now.
Then I took a copy of the tape to a deaf school. They read
her lips." Her eyes were tearing up again. She smelled of
anger and heartbreak. Like she wished it never happened.

"What did she say?"

She pursed her lips angrily but her eyes were pained. "She
said, 'Now let's see her kick me out.' Is that cold, or what?"
Crystal tears glittered at the edge of her swollen lids.

I tried to absorb that. Tried to fathom a family member
doing that. My mind rebelled. Family just didn't do that. I
spoke before I thought. "That sort of makes me glad I don't
have parents."

"They're dead?" She wiped at her face with a handful of
tissues. Her voice was already more steady.

I nodded. "When I was ten. Well, my mom anyway. My
father died before I was born."

"Who raised you?"

"My father's people. He was a small-time courier for the
Family." I said it to imply the capital F.

She dropped her tissues in the wastebasket and shuddered
visibly. "I'm really glad they were run out of town."

That made me glare at her with a surprising amount of
venom. "I'm not! I had a home with them!" She winced and
looked away again.

I took a deep breath and tried to explain. It was probably
better if she didn't know about my past but the odds were
good that I'd do the job for her, especially if she knew too
much. That's what I told myself. And hey, I felt talkative.
"They didn't have to take me in. My father was a two-bit
hood, a wanna-be. My mom was a whore." She didn't say

anything but I could hear her stiffen on the couch and smelled the sharpness of her shock, underlain with the dusty smell of shame.

I shrugged in response to the scent. "Prostitutes are moms too, you know. The Family didn't have to do anything. I was nothing to them. But my father got killed on a run. They felt responsible. He had told someone high up about this real lady that he was seeing. He was one of her regulars. He told everyone how beautiful she was and how he was going to make 'an honest woman' out of her and that they had already started a family. Patrone took him at his word. Gave me a home when she died of syphilis. Treated me like blood."

Her smell shifted again; wet, foggy, but not sorrow. Not exactly. "You're right. They didn't have to do that. I'm sorry for what I said. Is that why you do what you do?"

I shrugged again. "It's what I know. It's what I was raised with. Like, the boys in the Appalachians who don't know that they're not supposed to sleep with their sisters until they get into the outside world and find out it's considered deviant. It's the same in the Family. It's the way things are."

"But," she said, looking truly confused. "How can you take another person's life?"

I smiled coldly. "It's supply and demand. If there was no demand for killing, there'd be no supply. I don't wish anyone ill, but others do. I only carry out other people's bad intentions."

She shifted position again, tense, disapproving. I didn't have to smell it to sense it and it made me uncomfortable. I shifted the subject away from me. "The Family had standards." She gave me a disbelieving look. "No. really. Before two years ago, did you ever see a drive-by shooting of a little kid? Or graffiti sprayed on street signs?"

She thought briefly and shook her head. "Not really."

"Exactly!" I held a finger in the air to accentuate my words. "We kept our business internal. Our fights stayed within our factions. The general public saw few, if any, signs of our presence. These new gangs have no respect for anything or anybody. Before, if someone was killed, there was a reason. Now it's open season on little kids and the elderly. The gangs are scavengers; they take down the weakest. Anyone they can get. We allowed the weak and the innocent to pass by unharmed. We concentrated on our equals. It was the Family that kept the gangs under control. They feared us; respected us." I leaned forward in my chair again, my gaze intent on her.

"I know that most people wanted them out of town. But right or wrong, they were my people. I'm sorry they went to jail. They're family. You stand by them even when they do wrong. I'll stand by them again when they get out."

She nodded, accepting that without question. "I wish I had family that would stand by me. I want them to like me, to love me. But they just don't."

"Oh, I doubt that. I'm sure they love you."

"No," she disagreed, "they really don't! They have no respect for me. No empathy for me; no desire to know about me or my life. You can't feel love for someone if you're not even interested in them." She said it very matter-of-factly. "They don't care. All my life they've told me I'm worthless. Not smart enough, not talented enough, not pretty enough. I'm apparently just not enough of anything to make them love me. My only purpose in life is what they can use me for."

Tears glittered again in her eyes and she stood and walked to the bar. Even without the wolf senses, I could feel her hurt at saying those words. She made herself another drink, ignoring the one from earlier. I watched her in the mirror as she took a healthy swallow. I didn't feel pity for her. She intrigued me, even broken like this.

Then she abruptly began talking again. "It was hard when Robert left me. Harder still when it was Becky he left me for." *That* made my eyebrows climb.

"He said he was sorry but he just wasn't attracted to me anymore. It was understandable, of course." Her voice trembled. There was a sing-song quality to it as though she'd repeated the justifications over and over, trying to believe. "Given the choice, why would he pick me over her? I'm just absolutely insignificant. She's breezy and funny and gorgeous. But it still hurts that he would believe Mom's lies."

No. I stood and walked up behind her.

"I'll never be anyone that a man lusts after. I know that." She took a deep, quavering breath. "But every time I see him, the few times I can't avoid it, he feels so guilty that he has to remind me. He apologizes and then says he hopes that we can be *friends*."

She picked up her glass again just as I stopped behind her. This close, I could hear the catch in her voice.

She raised the glass to her lips once more. "I always wonder—if I had been prettier, would he be married to me instead? I'm rich now. I could have plastic surgery." She turned and found me standing there nearly touching. There was pain in her face that didn't need to be there.

I met her eyes and said softly, "I think you're just fine." She didn't speak but just looked at me.

I breathed in the tang of fear's hot and sour soup. The smell made my jaw tighten. It rolled over the summer forest of her own smell and the musky hot scent of desire. This time, the wolf inside wanted something that was against my better judgment. I needed to taste her. I took the drink out of her hand and set it on the bar. Then I leaned forward and braced one hand on either side of her on the bar to brush my lips to hers. Her lips were supple and her breath had a hint of vanilla.

Dear God! The sensation that passed through me as our lips met was incredible. Heat flowed between our mouths and thrills of electricity spread along the skin of my face; then across my scalp. I felt her rear back in surprise and apprehension. The power of the first meager brush of lips raised every hair on the back of my neck. A brilliant flash awakened each nerve along my spine until I shivered. Oh, I wanted more of this! I wanted to reach for her and pull her against me until I pulled her inside my skin.

Instead, I leaned into her and opened her mouth with mine. My jaw worked slowly against hers. The kiss was soft and gentle until I pressed my body forward and pushed her against the bar. Tingles slid up and down my body, centering in my groin, until I could barely think. My tongue slid into her mouth to tease hers. After a pause she kissed me back. I don't think she could help it any more than I could.

When she gave in, it was complete. She wrapped her arms around me and slid them up my back. I moved one arm around her shoulders and tightened it. The other hand stayed on the bar for balance. I hardly remembered doing it. I felt her heart flutter where our chests touched. I could feel the hard press of her nipples through my shirt. I wanted to lie her down on the floor, tear off her clothes, and run my hands over her; taste every inch of her skin. But I knew better than to push. She accepted this, needed it—but too much and she'd run.

I ended the kiss as gently as it began, and when I moved away, I put the drink back in her hand. Damn! I walked back to the sofa, my knees unsteady. My heart raced like I'd been running. My lungs were heaving almost painfully for air. I checked the thermostat on my way back to allow me to collect myself. I'd never felt like that from just a kiss. I let out a slow breath and closed my eyes. I felt hot but it was probably just the heat of attraction. Because I was attracted to her.

Bad plan, Tony. Then again, what was one more risk?

Chapter 6

I fought to get my voice back. I cleared my throat. "Why do you think your mom had anything to do with your man leaving?" My voice was still a little shakier than I liked.

She walked to the window and looked out over the city. I followed her with my eyes and watched her stare at the setting sun. It would be time to turn on the lamp soon.

"Robert knew Becky the whole time we were together. He said he thought she was annoying. I found out things Mom said one time when he was a little tipsy at a Christmas party. It was after he and Becky were married. He wondered why I had never told him I thought he was boring and why I *told Mom* that he'd be better suited to Becky. She apparently told him that I thought they were both superficial and egotistical." She laughed harshly. "I never said any of those things. I never talked about Robert with my mom. But he wouldn't believe it. After all, why would my mother lie? That's when I knew. That's when it became crystal clear." She glanced back at me over her shoulder, then returned to staring out the window.

"The rest of the family is all the same. My other sister, Mitzi, brings her dogs over and just leaves them at my door."

"Mitzi, Becky and Suzi?" I shook my head in amazement. "Well, at least Becky is semi-normal."

"Sure," she replied sarcastically. "If they would have spelled like sane people. But it's B-e-k-k-i."

I rolled my eyes. God save me from cutesy parents! Mind you, I've heard worse. I knew a Candy Sweet in school and once worked with Jett Black. She had a brother—Cole. Sad. Truly sad.

"Some days I walk outside and there they are. But at least the dogs are always glad to see me and they keep the geese away."

I smiled. "Geese?"

"I used to like geese. They're so pretty in the air." She wrinkled her nose. "On the ground, they're disgusting. Apparently, the previous owners of my house encouraged a whole flock to live by the swimming pool. Built boxes and stuff for nests. Now I can't get rid of them."

I stifled a smile. "Let me guess. It's not the geese's fault that they were invited in the first place, and you can't just kill them." Again that sense of *noblesse oblige*. This quirk of hers seemed to be the root of all of her problems.

Her smile shone brilliant in the window's reflection. "Exactly. But Mom doesn't like them either, so sometimes I can hide from her outside. She's afraid of them." She paused as she gazed out, shifting restlessly to one side. "The sky is pretty tonight. You can see the full moon while the clouds are still colored."

I looked beyond her and saw the pale, almost full moon rising in a blood red sky. My heart started pounding uncontrollably. I must have screwed up my calendar when the watch broke. Did it really take me three days to get out of Atlantic City? No wonder Max was confused when I asked to have the suite tonight. I already had it!

I had to get her out of here. Already I felt hot, the unnatural heat of the change. It might be too late already. I bit off a curse but my voice was harsh. "You have to leave. Get your things and go! Now!!"

She turned back to me, startled. "What? Why?" Smells, emotions, eddied over me. The thick tang of fear spiked with the even sharper smell of worry. Too much, too much—

I grabbed her jacket and threw it at her. One of my legs gave out and started to spasm. "Go! Get the hell out now, or you'll die *tonight*, instead of a year from now."

My vision started to go. Flashes of black and white flowed back to color with a red haze bleeding into everything. Still she stood there gaping at me, as if unable to understand what was happening. She would understand in a minute. Too well. *I'm sorry,* I thought and staggered toward the bedroom. *Give her . . . a chance—*

I got the door shut before I totally collapsed, nearly screaming with the pain of the transformation. Even through the soundproofing I heard her pounding at the door, asking if I was okay. "Get out!" I screamed but she couldn't hear.

I threw the lock and then the change had me.

Chapter 7

I woke up sprawled across the bed. It hurt to move—but then, it always did after. Human limbs don't willingly bend into the shape of a dog.

I stood and stretched. As always, I was naked. I don't know how I get my clothes off. Don't remember. It was odd that I hadn't destroyed the room. I had on other occasions. That and the fact that I wasn't hungry had me worried. I didn't want to go out into the main room. I suspected there was a chewed up millionairess out there and I wasn't looking forward to cleaning it up. My gut turned taut and hollow. For being a part of my life for such a short time she was already leaving a large dent. Damn it!

I walked to the closet and retrieved underwear, a T-shirt, and a pair of shorts from a secret drawer that only me and the owner knew about. The few items are all that would fit in the space but are enough for me to be decent in public. I put on the underwear but not the rest. I needed to take a shower. Makes me feel human again. I twisted the doorknob but stopped short. I really didn't want to go out there. I've seen what I've done to a human being in the past. Only once but it was enough.

I grabbed my gun from the dresser, took a deep breath, and quickly opened the door. Light shone in from the open drapes, highlighting surfaces and creating shadows on the clean floor. No bloody body. The coil of nerves inside my gut released slightly and I let out a slow breath.

A sound caught my ear suddenly. I wasn't alone.

The tumult of running water came from the direction of the bathroom. I moved quietly toward the door. Warm steam,

fragrant with eucalyptus and cloves, curled under the closed
door and licked at my bare legs. The aroma overpowered the
scent of the person inside even when I concentrated.

I counted silently in my head as I flipped off the safety.
When I reached three I raised up my foot and kicked in the
door.

The flimsy lock gave way immediately and the broken
door bounced against the wall with a bang. A shriek came
from inside the room. I moved through the doorway, crouched
low, gun leading me.

Sue raised frightened eyes over the lip of the marble tub.
My head reeled from the sultry combination of her forest
scent, the sudden piquance of her fear, and the bath oil hanging thick and strong. When she sat up I got a clear view of
her body to the waist, adding visual stimuli to my already
aroused body. I couldn't stop a wolfish smile.

She suddenly realized that she was naked and blushed
furiously. She quickly grabbed a royal blue towel to pull
around her. The towel sank heavily into the hot water and
darkened to nearly black. The cloth enhanced her curves and
made her eyes seem a much more vivid green. Nice.

"You're back," she said.

Well, that certainly made me nervous. "Have I been
anywhere?"

I'm what Babs calls "A three-day dog". That's the day
before a full moon, the full, and the day after. I'm not sure
how much time I spend human when night arrives. I don't
remember the stuff I do when I'm in wolf form. It's not like
I have human thoughts. Since I can't control the change and
don't remember it, I lock myself away for the whole three
days, even though I'm human for part of it.

She seemed comfortable suddenly. Spiced citrus and baking bread rode the steam to my nose. "Physically? No. But
mentally? Let's just say you weren't a real great conversa-
tionalist. On the plus side, you listen well that way and that
is what I was paying you for." She gave me a short grin that
showed her amusement.

I didn't know how to respond to her. She was happy?

Comfortable? "What happened?" I asked. I needed to know how she survived.

She looked surprised. "You don't remember? Really?"

That was none of her business. "Just tell me your version."

She leaned back in the tub, keeping the towel in place as she moved. She was absolutely sober now and looked more in control of herself. I shut the door to keep in the warmth and the incredible scent and set the gun on the sink. She'd never reach it before me if it came to that. I moved further into the spacious room and sat down on the edge of the tub, near her knees, facing her. It made her a little nervous but it was either that or sit on the stool. If I sat there she'd have to twist her head the whole time. She tightened the towel a bit in unconscious response.

"Well, you threw my coat at me and told me to get out."

"Which you didn't do," I admonished.

"You looked like you were in pain and you screamed." Her voice was calm, as though it was sufficient reason.

I gave an annoyed shake of my head. "That room is supposed to be soundproof."

She shrugged. "You screamed before the door shut completely. After that, it was. You wouldn't let me in and I didn't know what to do. So I went downstairs."

The sudden panic of discovery knotted my gut.

"You didn't tell anyone? Tell me that you didn't say anything!"

She gave me a withering look, completely unafraid. "Do I look like a complete idiot? I just asked the concierge—Max?—if there was a separate key for the master bedroom because I had accidentally locked up my jacket. He offered to come up but I told him that you were in a foul mood and it wouldn't be a good idea. You apparently have a reputation. His eyes went real wide and he agreed."

Smart man.

"Anyway, he gave me a master key that I have to give back before I go. He said it would open anything in the room. It does, by the way. I got bored and tried all the locks."

That's why everything smelled like her. "And you got up the nerve to open the bedroom door?"

"I had to. I thought maybe you had a seizure or something."

"Or something," I said wryly.

"It was something, all right. I unlocked the door and there you were, in full glory! Black and white and teeth all over." She looked impressed but not frightened.

"This is supposed to bother you, ya know. It's not a real normal thing."

She shrugged again and the towel slipped. She caught it before it showed anything interesting. When she saw me watching she flushed, sending a burst of desert-like scent into the room. You'd think that was impossible in a steam filled room, but that's what embarrassment smells like.

"It probably would if it was the first time. But I've seen it before."

"What?" I exclaimed. "Me, personally?"

"No. Not you. Someone else. I don't even know his name. Probably never will. I had completely forgotten about it. When I opened the door and saw you sitting on your haunches ripping off the rest of your shirt with your teeth, it reminded me."

"Then what?"

"You turned to me and whatever is human inside you wasn't home. The look was all animal. Have you been this way your whole life?"

I shook my head. That was all the information she was getting about me for now.

"What then?" I'd never had a blow-by-blow narration before. Mild burned coffee rose to me. She was getting irritated by my interruptions.

"I didn't know what to do. I backed up and you followed, stalking me. I think you thought I was dinner."

I had a flash of memory just then. I'd never had one before. Visions in black and white, of seeing Sue and having to look up at her. Of being a wolf. I saw her wide eyes, smelled her fear. But she smelled like me. She had my scent on her and I liked the combination of smells. She didn't smell like food, she smelled like . . . a mate. I knew why I had stalked her. I couldn't tell her that I hadn't wanted to eat her, I had wanted to screw her. That's way too weird, even for me!

Sue's voice cut through the memory. It frayed at the edges, then fell away from my mind. "I had no choice but to accept what I was seeing. Then there was a knock on the door. You growled and backed into the bedroom. I shut the bedroom door and answered the knock."

"That was stupid." I was annoyed more at myself than her.

"I asked first! Give me *some* credit. The man said he was room service with dinner. You told me you were going to order."

Oh.

"There was no one at the door, just a cart with covered dishes. So I wheeled it inside. The food smelled great. I heard you snuffling at the door like you could smell the food and I figured that if you weren't hungry, maybe you wouldn't be so...aggressive. So I took the plate with the rare steak and moved it close to the door. You snuffled louder so I opened the door a little, slid the plate inside and backed up."

"Thanks for the dinner."

She shook her head. "You wouldn't eat it. You sniffed it and gave the steak a lick but your eyes went right back to me. I didn't like that look so I closed the door again."

I coughed to hide a smile. Yeah, I am a little single-minded. I probably would have eaten the steak without her there. "Why didn't you leave?"

"I didn't know how long you'd be like that or what would happen next. I couldn't just leave you trapped in the room. You couldn't open the door. You might starve or die of thirst if I just left."

I sighed and shook my head. "That soft heart is going to get you killed."

"That's the plan," she replied smoothly. It made me smile. I like black humor.

"So why didn't you let me make you dinner if that's the plan?"

"Because how would you explain it? It'd be a horrible mess."

She wasn't lying. "So you weren't afraid of me?"

She shrugged her shoulders. "As much as I am of any dog, er—wolf. I like animals."

"You said you've seen it before. When?"

"Oh, God, a long time ago. It's just bits and pieces of memory. I'm not even positive that it was real."

"Tell me," I ordered. I need to know if there are others like me. Other than Babs. She hasn't exactly been a fountain of information and it's not like I can sniff them out or something. At least, I don't think I can. Maybe I should have let Babs give me some instruction like she wanted to.

"I must've been about four years old." She scooted down further into the water, reaching up with a toe to turn on the hot water spigot. She spoke louder although she didn't need to. "My parents took us all to the woods. Mom was really great back when Dad was alive. Sweet and thoughtful and just wonderful." She smiled. "I remember Mom made a special trip to the grocery store to buy me bologna for the trip. My favorite sandwich back then was bologna with ketchup on white bread."

She giggled, really giggled. I'd never heard one that wasn't faked. It was cute and I smiled at her. The smile reached all the way to my eyes. She blushed again and averted her eyes. Musky desire rose from her. Her toe stretched again for the faucet but I beat her to it. My hand brushed her bare foot and electricity raced through us both. She gasped and glanced up at me in shock. Our eyes locked briefly but then she looked away uncomfortably. Her foot dropped back into the water.

Sexual tension crackled in the air.

Not yet, I told myself sternly. Business first.

"So, you were camping?" I prompted, after her sudden fear tickled my nose.

A relieved breath exited from her lips. She nodded. "We had just eaten and I was playing near the edge of the woods with my favorite doll. Her name was Jessica. Strange, huh?"

I raised my brows slightly in agreement. I've always liked the name. It's why I picked the fake name for her to use.

"She was one of those dolls that had adjustable hair, you know?"

I didn't. I shrugged and shook my head. "Sorry, dolls aren't my thing."

"Well, she did," she said firmly. "My sisters decided to tease me. I think it was meant as a tease. I try to remember it that way. They took my doll and threw it into the woods. They told me that Mom would be mad if I lost my doll and I'd better go get her. They were right. They wouldn't get in trouble for throwing the doll; I'd get in trouble for losing her. It was the way it was in our family."

"Kids can be cruel."

"Yeah. But they're supposed to grow out of it. Bekki and Mitzi didn't." The anger that she still felt all these years later surprised me again. There was no mistaking the scent.

"Sorry." It was the only thing I could think of to say.

She shrugged. This time, she didn't catch the towel in time. Yes, I watched. I waited for the blush. She didn't disappoint me.

She quickly tightened the towel around her body. "Anyway, I went into the woods to find Jessica. It was hours later when I did. If my parents called me I never heard them. When I found my doll and turned around to head back, I didn't know where I was. I was absolutely lost and the sun was setting. I wasn't a Girl Scout or even a Brownie. I didn't know directions. I knew I'd get spanked for running off so I started to cry."

Sadness and fear rose from her in a sudden burst, engulfing me in her memory. The emotions shadowed her voice as she spoke. "I still had part of my sandwich in my pocket and my doll for company so I sat down under a tree and waited. But nobody came."

"What happened then?"

"I heard a sound and thought it might be Mom or Dad. I called out but it wasn't them. It was a big dog, white as snow with blue eyes. It was beautiful. I didn't know a wolf from a dog. I did remember that Dad always told me a doggie without a collar doesn't like people so I shouldn't pet it. But it was a pretty dog and I was lonely."

I closed my eyes and sighed. "That wasn't real bright."

"Hey!" she retorted. "I was *four*! What can you expect?"

"Okay, yeah, I know. What did you do then?"

"I thought the doggy might be hungry because I was. I shared my sandwich with it. All dogs like bologna."

I wrinkled my nose. "Don't *ever* feed me bologna. I know what's in that stuff." I was startled that I said it as though it would come up again.

"Said by a man who just ate a raw turkey," she replied snidely.

I didn't understand the apparent dig. "So I guess the 'doggie' didn't eat you."

"The wolf was very sweet." The ground clove smell of pride; self-satisfaction burst into the air. Maybe the cloves weren't in the oil.

"He stayed with me all night. Kept me company. That's what reminded me. When you laid down on the couch and just stayed with me. Warm and just, well, *there*. It's hard to describe." Cinnamon and sugar blended with the cloves in the air.

"So why did you think the dog was a man?"

"I didn't. Not that night. The next morning I finally heard the search party. I found out later that they'd been looking for me all night. When I heard Mom's voice I ran off, forgetting about the dog. I was halfway to the voices when I remembered the nice doggy and went back to say good-bye. But when I got there . . ."

"It was gone?"

"Sort of. I saw a bright flash of light and then saw a man—a naked Hispanic man with long black hair. He dropped to his hands and knees and collapsed on the forest floor. I tried to wake him but he was unconscious.

My brows raised. Maybe she really had seen one of us.

"I knew," she continued, "that I'd get in trouble for being with a strange *man* a lot more than a strange dog. Somehow

I knew that he was the dog. But my folks were calling. I left Jessica with the man so he wouldn't get lonely. I've never told anyone about that night."

I smiled and she stared at the water, looking shy. "That was sweet of you. But I doubt he'll remember you. Not if he's like me."

"What else could I do? I was four."

"So, what did you do with *me* after I started to stalk you?"

Cloves dusted the steam once more. She warmed to the new subject. "I decided that you wanted raw meat, not cooked. Even rare is cooked. So I went downstairs and snuck into the kitchen." She started to grin, "And I found the perfect meal."

"What did I have for dinner? I don't exactly recall."

"I told you! Turkey! There was a nearly raw turkey in the oven. It was bloody and warm, hardly cooked at all. I put it on a silver platter and covered it with one of those domes and snuck back into the elevator. I should have taken a cart. I almost dropped it twice. It weighed, like, twenty pounds and once it started to bleed, it got really slippery on the tray. Nobody saw, thank God."

I nodded admiringly. Impressive.

She smiled. "You were so cute!" That made me frown. I don't like to be thought of as cute.

"I put the platter on the floor next to the bedroom. I opened the door just a bit then backed up. You looked at me first, then the turkey. You were real suspicious. You sniffed it a couple of times and then picked it up in your mouth and came here into the bathroom with it. I followed you to see what you would do. You jumped into the bathtub, lay down, and ate the bird. Bones and all. Hardly left a scrap."

Damn! No wonder I wasn't hungry. Twenty pounds of turkey had better fill me up!

"Thank you." I'd only say it once.

"After I fed you, you were real nice. I took the flowers out of that big bowl on the coffee table and filled it up with water. You drank almost all of it. I sat down and stayed on the couch so you'd have room to move around. But you jumped up on the recliner and just watched me. Like you're doing now. Interested in me. I've never had that. So I kept talking and you listened. I got a lot out of my system. I appreciate it."

She blushed and it reddened not only her face but her neck and chest, as well. "I'm sort of glad you don't remember some of the stuff I said."

"Now I'm sorry I missed it." My smile was genuine.

I looked at her; really looked at her. Her hair was wet and tangled and her face was still blushing. Our eyes locked and the flustered smile on her face slowly slid away, replaced by nervous anticipation. The sultry musk that rose from her was stronger now. The scent of her desire filled me completely.

The soft lighting in the bath turned her eyes an even deeper green. She wasn't stunning, but she was pretty, even without makeup. Her eyes went dark and bottomless while I stared into them. Like earlier, the wolf roared to the surface. Before I could stop myself I leaned over and kissed her. It started slow, like last time, but deepened and grew. I snaked a hand behind her head to pull her closer. The tingles where our lips touched nearly scalded but it didn't hurt. It felt incredibly good. I couldn't breathe past the sensations that engulfed me.

My other hand slipped into the water and I helped the towel float away. I stroked a hand down her naked body and she made little noises in the back of her throat. I tried again to remind myself that she was off limits but my body didn't care. It hungered for something that has no name, something beyond logic right at the edge of sanity.

I pulled back and asked for a third time, whispered it into her mouth because I needed to know. "Why do you want to die, Sue?"

She answered this time. Maybe the time she spent talking to my wolf form allowed her to come up with the answer. "To deny them. To escape everybody that has used me."

She gave a harsh laugh. "I've worked when I was delirious with fever; worked when there was no pay, no thanks.

There's never any appreciation. Never a reward. I keep setting aside my own dreams for someone else's. Even the money isn't a reward. It's a curse." A single tear caught the light in flashes as it rolled slowly down her cheek.

"I've been drained of everything independent and useful by a bitter, hateful family. I've been used and used until I'm all used up. I have nothing left to give and it will only keep hurting to give more. It will only end when I'm gone. Because I can't stop them. I can't escape them. I don't know any other way."

"You're wrong. You *could* escape them," I said strongly. A rotten family is no reason to die. "Set up a trust. Disappear in the night. Go to Argentina, Brazil—even Switzerland. You can buy a new identity and be someone else."

She shook her head again. "They'd find me. They would spend all the money and they would track me until the day I died to get the rest. So I have to die."

The next words were whispered with eyes closed. Her voice trembled. "But I'm not even strong enough to do it myself. I figured if I hired someone and paid them it would just happen. Sometime when I wasn't looking." More tears joined the first. They flowed down her cheeks unchecked. I ran fingers through her hair and wiped the tears away with the back of my hand. She shuddered from the electricity as our skin touched.

"Why don't you pay me to hit her instead? Then you could go on."

She smiled but shook her head. "Because she's family, and no matter how bad they screw up, you stand by them. Remember? I can't kill her but I can eliminate myself. Then she'll be forced to move on. Be forced to grow up. I know she's lonely and scared of being by herself. But I can't give any more of me. There's no more to give. She's made me bitter and cynical and not able to love or be loved. I hate her for that. I hate them all." Peppers, strong enough to burn my eyes, made me believe it.

"And I hate myself for allowing it." She shook her head sadly. I couldn't smell the sorrow over the fog-filled room but I knew it was there. "If all that's left inside of me is hate then I don't want to live. I'd rather die."

"Well, I don't want you to die. Not today." I reached into the water and placed my arm under her bent legs. I lifted her out of the tub, and her arms closed around my neck. A mild burning sensation quickened my breath. She still wore the delicate silver charm bracelet. Each movement brought pain as the silver singed my skin. Did she somehow know that silver prevents the infection? How?

Back when I was still speaking to Babs, she mentioned, with a smile, that sex would be a whole new experience—as long as the woman wore silver. There was no problem with damage to me. I'd heal and not infect her as long as I didn't draw blood from her. Probably a good idea for Sue to keep the bracelet. Wish I would have had one when I took on Babs. I wouldn't be what I've become.

Chapter 8

I looked into Sue's eyes. Water streamed off her body and soaked me. I tightened my arm around her shoulder. I turned to take her to the bedroom. The sudden sour ammonia of her panic and the frantic pounding of her heart struck me full in the chest. It stopped me where I stood. I looked into her eyes, trying to decide whether to end it here. She held my gaze with wide eyes but she made no move to stop.

I brushed my lips against hers. She pulled me into the kiss deeper and accepted my tongue hungrily. Hot musk. Enough to drown in. Then the fear hit me again. Still so afraid. So very afraid. Why?

"We can stop." I said quietly. I set her back onto her legs but continued to gently trace the curves of her waist with my hands.

"It's just that . . ." Too many emotions rose from her to sort out so I gave her time to respond. I moved a hand up and brushed her cheek. She shuddered and moved into my touch but couldn't look me in the eyes.

She stared at my chest. Her fingertips traced electrifying patterns on my skin. She tried again. "I mean, someone like me with someone like . . . *you.*" She dropped off again.

Ah. I understood now.

A one-night stand with an assassin wasn't in her plans. It wasn't allowed. Not in her world. Or maybe it was the whole supernatural thing. She couldn't know that it only worked if I broke skin *and* she wasn't wearing silver.

"You're allowed to want this; to enjoy this. Nobody has the right to tell you otherwise. If you want to stop, I will. But you can't become like me doing this. Just keep your bracelet on.

It'll protect you." I lifted her chin until her eyes met mine. "As for being an assassin, if we go on, no one has to know. That's up to you. I'm pretty good at keeping secrets." My eyes reflected humor. A quick smile played across her face.

"I really shouldn't," she said weakly, without conviction.

I brought my lips closer to hers, drawing her body against me. "But you want to." The words lowered to a whisper that breathed into her mouth, "And so do I." Our lips met just as her body pressed against me. The sudden spasms in my groin from the combined contact almost dropped me to my knees. It was difficult to pick her up and carry her into the next room.

I laid her on the bed and she released my neck. I bent down and removed the water in her navel with a quick pull of my tongue. A sudden gasp made her chest move heavily as she became aroused. I fought back the desire to have her as my body wanted, fast and furious. God! I wanted to wrestle with her until we were both sweat-soaked and exhausted. But no. I decided instead to move slowly.

It's easy to be aroused by a gorgeous woman. But a beautiful woman is accustomed to being admired. It'll be good sex but not memorable. On the other hand, if you spend the time to make a plain woman feel desirable, she'll reward you with enthusiasm. It will become more than sex.

Sue's musky scent was stronger now. It blended with the bath oil to create a smell that ignited every desire I'd ever had in my life, and several that I'd never even imagined.

I started by licking the tiny droplets of water and tangy oil from her skin. Not the obvious parts where most men start, but the less common erotic spots. I turned her over and licked her shoulders, the small of her back, the backs of her legs. Light, delicate flicks to barely move the hairs. She tasted salty, like grass and woods. The smell and the taste and the electric charge that ran between us made me moan and nearly lose control. Her breathing grew heavier as I bathed her with my tongue. As I had wanted to earlier, I rolled the taste of her in my mouth and a new part of me realized that I was marking her as my own. Her mind was awash with uncompleted thoughts, but all of them were urging me on.

Next, I blew lightly along the skin I wetted with my tongue. She shivered and whimpered. I blew cool air down her spine and watched goosebumps form as she squirmed on the bed. I flicked my tongue behind her knees and down her smooth calf. I picked up her foot and gently blew air onto the sole. She clutched the pillow in tight fists.

By the time I turned her over, she was panting and so was I. When she looked at me she gasped and her eyes went wide.

"What?" I asked in a husky voice.

"Your eyes . . . they're glowing."

I'd never made love to a woman before during the full moon, but the wolf part of me knew that this was normal, natural. "Is that okay? Does it scare you?"

She looked at me and I could smell surprise when she answered. "Actually, no. It sort of turns me on."

I smiled and listened to the thoughts running through her mind. *It really does turn me on! I don't know if this is such a good idea or not. I'm scared but, oh, God, I want this.*

I stared into her eyes as I again started at her feet. She watched me lick her legs slowly and deliberately, and her thighs spread almost involuntarily. The rush of musk to my nose was almost too much to stand, but again I ignored the invitation and moved higher to trace slow circles with my tongue on her stomach. She made low sounds in her throat. Her eyes closed and her mouth moved but no sound emerged.

"You have a beautiful body," I said softly.

Her voice was sad. "No, I don't.

I raised up on my arms and stared at her. "Are you calling me a liar?"

"N-n-no. I didn't mean . . ."

"Either that, or you're insulting my taste. I like what I see. Do you have a problem with that?" *Sometimes you have to be aggressive to get it through their head. A lot of women have a hard time taking compliments.*

She smiled then. "No problem." She lay back and closed her eyes. "Thank you."

I slid my body up hers, fast and hard. Her eyes opened to find me staring at her. Her hips writhed where I was pressing against her. "Just checking," I said and lowered my mouth to hers. My tongue filled her mouth forcefully and she shivered and ran her hands along my spine. Strong fingers dug into my back and she wrapped her legs tightly around my hips. I forced my arms under her and locked her against me. The tingling was driving me insane and I craved more of it. Needed to go further, faster.

My mouth moved to her neck and I kissed and nipped the skin gently while I ground myself against her. I needed more. My teeth sunk deeper into her neck. Her breath started to erupt into short shallow pants. What I wanted next wasn't at all like me. I had to, *had to*, master her. Make her submit. I moved my hands up her arms until they rested on her wrists and lowered her arms to the bed. I nipped at her skin harder, then even harder, but stopping just short of drawing blood. That was a no-no.

Her smell was still only of desire and hunger. No fear at all. She liked what I was doing. I read it in her thoughts and in her scent. I stared at her. She stared back into my glowing blue eyes and accepted me. I bit her again softly. She seemed to know what I needed from her. She cried out even though I didn't bite hard.

I knew that whatever I felt she felt too. It scared her; exhilarated her. It was a closeness that she'd never had before. Hearing her submit settled the part of me that needed mastery.

I wasn't ready to go farther. I could hold out for some time yet. She had satisfied my hunger earlier. I wanted to do the same for her.

I rolled until I lay beside her. She started to roll to face me but I stopped her.

"Just relax," I said. I pressed her shoulder down so she remained on her back. I touched her with light fingertips to stimulate the nerves on her skin. Across her collarbone, between her well-formed breasts and down her stomach. Muscles contracted where I touched and her breath was shaky. She fidgeted, nearly frantic for me to touch where she needed to be touched. She hungered to feel that electric caress inside her body. Somehow I knew it was all she could think of.

I moved my fingers slowly up the inside of her thigh while I nibbled her breast with my lips. Her hands moved to my face as though to push me away. Her fingers trembled on my cheeks as I suckled her, pressed teeth into her flesh. I ran my hand across her stomach and toyed with the nerves near her hipbones. As a small cry escaped her, I felt her suddenly tug at my hair, pulling me tight against her. Her legs spread as if by magic. Already I could see wetness on the tips of the hair.

She tried to raise her hips toward my hand. No, not quite yet. I traced lazy designs all around the area without actually touching anything. She was whimpering in earnest now, and mumbling incoherently. I kept just out of reach. I teased her and took her even higher.

Minutes later my fingers brushed her dark curls and found them slick. It was enough to turn my mind to fire. Enough to remind me that I needed release as much as she.

When I finally eased a finger inside her, it was actually three. It was more than she could stand. Her back arched and she cried out. Her hands clutched at anything and everything and strong muscles contracted around my hand, pulled on the current of electricity. I moved with her, pulling when she pushed, and then she actually screamed. Leaving my hand where it was, I kissed her breasts and then her mouth, muting her cries.

She grabbed at me. I winced briefly as her fingernails tore at my back and then her bracelet scorched my skin in long lines through the blood. I didn't think it was intentional. That's okay. I could take a little pain. It didn't interfere with my pleasure at all. I was a little unnerved that I was enjoying it. A lot.

She abruptly broke away from the kiss. She moved her hands away from my back and looked at her fingernails with wide eyes. Small bits of bloody flesh were lodged under them. She moved on the bed in such a way that I realized that she had felt my pain in her own back. I saw it in her mind. Her breathing sped up in a moment of panic.

I smiled lightly. "Go ahead. You can't hurt me and it won't hurt you."

Her eyes widened even more and a shock of surprised scent rose from her. The smile reached my eyes and she let out a little nervous laugh. After a heartbeat's pause she closed her eyes and accepted the connection. Her hands returned to my back and relaxed slowly. I butterfly-kissed her cheek and neck as I prepared to indulge my own enjoyment. I slipped off my briefs as I caressed her body.

"I want you. Now. Please . . ."

"And you'll have me," I promised softly. "So hold that thought for just a second."

I eased off her and knelt on the bed. She watched as I reached to the night stand and retrieved the pale blue foil pouch from my wallet.

She moved up onto her elbows. "Let me." I want to touch him eased into my mind.

A half-smile came to my face. One of my favorite things. I handed the square to her with one hand and stroked one of her calves with the other. "Be my guest."

She sat up, bringing us face to face. She carefully set the condom on the bed and stroked the front of my thighs gently. Tingles went through me and an appreciative "mmm," escaped me.

Her hands traveled across my hipbones and up the taut muscles of my stomach. Spasms wracked my groin. I lost my willpower to be the seducer and agreed to be seduced. "Just relax, lover." she said.

The way she said the word made it more than just seduction for today. I looked at her sharply and she looked back, confidence growing in her gaze. "Say that too often," I replied, surprisingly serious, "And you might not be able to get rid of me."

"That might be nice." She eased toward me. I moved my

mouth to meet hers but she dipped her chin and found my chest. She planted slow lingering kisses in a line across my collarbone. I reached up and ran my hand through her drying hair. I separated the tangled curls with my fingers as her hands caressed my lower back and then gently squeezed my buttocks. Nice.

My chest was starting to heave as the kisses descended lower. She adjusted herself on the bed to travel downward. Her hands reached around my body and moved up and down my thighs as she licked and kissed my nipples. I jumped as I felt the gentle pressure and resulting tingles from her hand between my legs. My breath fell out in a shuddering sigh. I sat back on my heels so I wouldn't fall over. I placed my hands gently on her shoulders, caressed her skin and allowed her to tease me.

When her kisses reached my navel, I tightened my hands on her shoulders and stopped her. I didn't want her to stop. In fact, I couldn't think of anything I wanted more. I couldn't even imagine what it would feel like, considering. But I wanted to take her over again before I reached my peak. Wanted to please her; not just me. I reached for the foil packet again. "You'd better stop now or I won't last long enough to use this." I handed her the packet and she smiled. She ripped the foil and eased the sheath over me, taking her time. It made me groan.

I reached for her waist and laid her down gently. I felt her hot, exhaled breath on my cheek; shallow pants that increased as she opened to me. I entered her slowly and then thrust a second time, hard. The feeling of her body, still slick with oil, as she writhed under me was almost too much. I'm a little better than average in size, but at that moment it felt as though I was too large for her. She was swollen and wet but all that I could think was that her fragile body shouldn't be able to contain the swell of magic that filled me. A blaze of blue light burned behind my eyes and threatened to fill the room. It sparkled and danced in my vision as my hips moved against her, faster and harder.

My mouth closed over hers. Small, hungry sounds

climbed out of her throat to exit in my mouth and I responded in kind. We ate at each other's mouths, tongues tangling desperately. I felt her nails in my back again, digging deeper into the previous wounds. I dug my hands into the bed sheets to keep from digging them into her skin. The hunger that I had been suppressing since I met her consumed my mind. The need was driving me onward. It was hard to concentrate. I didn't want to concentrate. I didn't want anything more than my body plunging inside her. I lapped hot musk and sweat from her skin almost deliriously. I rolled the sharp, sweet scent in my mouth and lifted her legs to wrap around my waist.

I drove into her more frantically, seeking the phantom of the release I knew must exist, but couldn't quite imagine. I wasn't sure I could last long enough to take her back over the edge. But I wanted to make sure she would remember today. I didn't think I was going to be able to forget it. It was too intense. Every movement built the tension, built the magic. The moon itself seemed pressed against my back.

Every woman can be multi-orgasmic if you take the time to get them back there. We had the time. Her face flushed a second time, her back arched and she screamed soundlessly. Her every nerve tingled and sang with effort and I watched. Finally, it was too much.

As I neared the top, she rode the wave of sensation with me. I'm no innocent, but I'd never felt *anything* like this. The intensity was incredible. Bursts of silver light exploded in my vision and passed through me in waves of mind-numbing pleasure so great that I couldn't breathe. I could feel the moon call me, entice me. I poured my magic into her like a great roll of liquid. It welled through her, filled her, until the silver blaze filled her eyes, too. Distantly, I heard screams and realized that they were mine.

My senses were saturated by the light, heat, and the scent of fulfilled desire. The orgasm was like a spiral. When I flew over the edge she went with me. I felt her climax and my own increased, which intensified hers leaving us both exhausted.

I rolled off and out of her and lay beside her. I pulled her to me and expected to doze to sleep as I normally do. My body would have none of it, though. She stroked a hand across my chest with a sigh, nails curving in just enough to lightly scrape the skin. The electricity wasn't gone. The appetite hadn't been quelled. It lay just under my skin like a great hungry beast. Her nails awoke it a second time and it flowed through my skin. Every muscle was suddenly invigorated. I drew in a sharp breath and looked down at her with desire again filling my eyes. She caught my gaze and held it. Her eyes held the same need but surprise was there too. Not so soon, surely.

I started to turn her over to take her again but stopped. I wouldn't without protection. Not on a bet. I'm not that stupid. With reckless hope I reached over and opened the drawer of the night stand, silently willing some previous tenant to have left an extra. When I opened my eyes I laughed. I couldn't help it. A brand new box of condoms lay in the drawer— the only occupant. I could only imagine what Max had thought when I told him I was meeting someone in the room. I'd never brought *anyone* here. I'd have to remember to thank him.

The daylight hours passed by without notice as we sated each other over and over. It was probably the longest lovemaking session I had ever been involved in. It was definitely the most intense.

Chapter 9

I woke in semi-dark with Sue curled around me. I pulled her against me and watched her sleep. Somewhere in the middle it stopped being just sex for me. It became something deeper, something I had no name for. I realized that I hadn't gotten close to a woman since I lost my humanity a year ago. I've been afraid to let anyone get too close in case I accidentally mangled them.

But I hadn't. Given the chance, I hadn't killed her. Hell, I hadn't even bruised her during sex. It was like I *couldn't.* Something inside pulled me up short. It gave me hope. But it also caused problems for me. I'm a loner. I like my space. As much fun as this time had been, I didn't know what tomorrow would bring. I did know one thing. I didn't want her to die. I have never believed in love at first sight. Maybe it's real, maybe not. I didn't even know if I felt love for her but lust? Oh, yeah.

I realized that I wanted to wake up beside her tomorrow and the next day. The problem was, if I didn't kill her, I would be just using her like everyone else. I couldn't change her past. If she wanted to die, I should let her. Help her. Keeping her alive for my own needs would make me as bad as the others.

I rose and went to the bathroom, then walked naked through the living room and poured myself a drink. Something stronger than beer. I sat in the late afternoon sunshine just thinking.

I could feel her sleeping in the other room. In some part of my insides I could feel her. I didn't know if she could sense me in return but I knew when she woke. I felt her lying in the dark. Conscious; thinking. Somehow I knew that if I concentrated I could read her thoughts. But I didn't know if it flowed both ways. I needed a few minutes alone and it seemed like she did too. I had an overwhelming fear that if I tried to increase the connection between us, even as an experiment, I wouldn't be able to reverse it.

Paranoia isn't logical.

So, alone—as the night of the true moon neared—I contemplated this woman. What was happening between us? My brain should be flashing lights and blaring warning sirens at the thought of having a bond like we seemed to have formed. But it wasn't. Did that mean there was a future? A future with someone who could accept me—my profession—*and* what I had become? Could she survive in my world? Would I want to be part of hers? Then I imagined the rest of my life without her. None of the options seemed a good idea in the long run.

An hour or so later she made an appearance but kept her distance. She lingered just near the doorway. Her body was clothed only in sunset's crimson, cut with shadows thick as ink. She tilted her head as she watched me. One eye disappeared into darkness.

"Are you all right?" she asked tentatively.

"Fine." I could feel the moon trembling at the edge of the horizon. Warmth flared over my skin as I waited for the rush of energy.

She padded toward me, footsteps silent in the thick carpet. I watched the light and dark play across her skin in sultry patterns as she moved. I lifted my glass to my lips and she suddenly became two, then three, through the thick crystal as I took a sip. Each movement of her muscles as she walked, every breeze that stirred her scent toward me tightened my body with desire. I wanted her again. I closed my eyes until the feeling passed. It was too near to true darkness to risk it. This was only day two and it would be time soon.

She sat down next to me on the couch and I automatically put my arm around her and pulled her against me. Scary.

"I've been thinking," she said as she snuggled into the

curve of my arm. She slid a slow hand across the hair of my chest and tucked it around my waist.

"Me too. Will you be here when I wake up tomorrow?" I looked down at her.

She seemed startled. "I don't know. I should probably go home." She didn't sound like she wanted to. "Nobody knows where I am. And Mom's alone . . ."

I didn't comment on that. It was her decision. "I'd like you to stay, if you want to. I won't force you. If you have to go, you have to." I shrugged but I wanted her to stay. "What were you thinking about?"

"What just happened between us? There's something there even now." She lifted her hand and again touched my chest with gentle fingertips. A nervous energy rose from her. Her heartbeat quickened as she thought about it. My body responded again but I fought it down forcibly. We needed to talk.

Why lie? "I don't know."

"Will it go away when we leave here?" The curiosity blended with sadness, as though she already knew the answer.

"You're the first woman that I've let get this close during a full moon. I assume it has something to do with what I am. I've been with other women but it's never been like this."

That made her happy and she hugged me. Every woman wants to think that she's special. This time, it was the truth. There was a pause. It was filled with the clove scent of pride, the light tangerine of happiness, and determination mixed with a healthy dose of fear. She took a deep breath. My stomach clenched. I wasn't sure I wanted to hear what she was about to say.

"I've got this big house," she said abruptly and continued quickly so I couldn't interrupt, and probably so she wouldn't lose her nerve. "They put a full apartment in the basement. A real apartment with a kitchen and bath and a separate entrance. I can't put Mom down there because she can't handle the stairs. The door to the main floor can be locked so you can come and go and nobody can bother you. There's a fenced estate and a pool." The fear faded as she finished the speech she had prepared. It was said. The implication was clear.

She didn't move even a muscle as she finished. She was frozen against me, waiting, nervous. I let the silence grow for a moment as I thought about all of the consequences.

"And geese," I said lightly. She let out a relieved breath.

"And geese." Humor edged her voice. Then she hurried on. "Anyway, if I paid you in advance, I wouldn't want you to wander off with my money and not do the job."

"Naturally."

"So I was thinking that maybe you could sort of, maybe, take the apartment. It's huge. Really. It's the whole lower level."

I didn't know what to say. Her words echoed my thoughts from a moment ago and I still didn't have an answer. "And do what? I'm not the Ozzie and Harriet type, Sue. This has been great. Incredible, even. But I don't want to move in with anyone."

"I know you don't. Neither do I." Part truth, part lie. I didn't know which was which.

"I was thinking more of . . . well, a bodyguard. There have been some threatening calls. Mom stupidly promised some man money to *protect* us. He said that no *accidents* would happen as long as we paid every month. Even *I* know what that means."

I laughed at that. "A combination bodyguard/assassin. Sort of an oxymoron, don't you think?"

"You'd keep me safe until it was time. When the heat died down. I could pay you a salary in addition to the fee. You could help me with things around the house."

"Like keep your mom in line and the money suckers away? Is that it? A hired gun?"

She looked up at me, hope plain on her face. The light, dizzying scent of it made my head swim. "I'd let you poach the geese. . . "

I smiled and leaned back into the sofa with a laugh. "Couldn't be any worse than half-cooked turkey." She laughed with me.

Then she looked at me very seriously. "Yes. I'll be here tomorrow."

I grinned without intending to and felt a little foolish in the darkness. I leaned over and kissed her deeply. I opened my senses and let the moon in. Power crawled over my skin but it wasn't strong enough yet to turn me. Maybe there was still time. If we hurried . . .

Chapter 10

Sue wasn't in the suite the next morning. I found a note from her saying she hoped I made it back okay.

Made it back from where?

There was a sack on the dresser with clothes. Khaki Dockers and a black T-shirt with a pocket. She even remembered socks. A second note in the bag said, "Look in the fridge." I went to the bar and opened the refrigerator door. I found a whole prime rib, bone in. It barely fit inside the small space. She had to remove the shelves and bend it nearly in two. I thought about eating it for breakfast, but no. That would be overkill. Still, her thoughtfulness really took me by surprise.

I started a pot of coffee while I took a shower and brushed my teeth and then settled down to read yesterday's newspaper—better than nothing. As always, room service knocked on my door without calling them promptly at 8:00. The trays filled with eggs over medium, toast, fried potatoes, and a rare t-bone were on a cart in the hallway. I wheeled it inside. I pay tips through my room account.

The day was starting grey and gloomy. It was a welcome change from the summer heat but I wasn't sorry that I was indoors. I closed the curtains and turned on a lamp after I saw rain pattering gently on the glass.

Several minutes went by before I heard footsteps moving down the carpeted hallway toward the suite. They stopped in front of the door. I couldn't smell through the thick oak so I grabbed my Sig and quietly stepped to where the door would hide me if it opened. There's a peephole but I never use one. That's a real good way to get a bullet in your brain. I know.

I heard paper rustling and the key card slip into the lock. Even though I was expecting Sue to return, I remained cautious. I'm not without enemies. The door opened fully and I saw the back of a black wig and Sue's well-shaped body. She looked terrific in a hot pink T-shirt tucked into tight blue jean shorts, but it wasn't exactly *incognito*. I sighed. We'd have to talk about the concept of low-key.

Her bare arms wore tiny droplets of water that shimmered and moved as she walked. The scent of her, dewy and laden with moss, mingled with the scent of the rain. It affected me like a drug. I would have a hard time pulling the trigger even if someone dangerous were with her. That's not a good thing.

I slammed the door behind her—just in case. It latched and locked with a sharp crack. Sue turned quickly, eyes wide and panicked. She saw the gun and the bags in her arms dropped to the floor with a soft thud.

One hand went over her chest and I felt her heart race for a moment. "Don't *do* that," she exclaimed. She smelled slightly annoyed but relieved. Tangerines blended with coffee and with the musty scent of anxiety.

"I'm really glad you're back. I was worried," she said.

We'd deal with that in a minute. I put the Sig in the waistband of my pants so it rested at the small of my back. I stepped closer and eased my hands around her waist. I couldn't seem to help it. I needed to touch her, run my hands along her bare skin, drink in the scent and taste of her. I raised a hand and took off Sue's dark sunglasses. Her eyes were greener than yesterday. I saw those eyes smile at me, comfortable, possessive. I ran the back of my hand down her cheek and she leaned into my touch with a sigh.

"Good morning," I said and pulled her the rest of the way into my arms. The sunglasses dropped to the carpet as I kissed her slow and easy. Her body was damp and warm against my artificial chill. The kiss deepened and her arms moved up my back and tightened. She was more aggressive this morning and took what she wanted. Her tongue found mine first. I moved my hands down her back to those tight shorts and lifted her up until her legs were wrapped around my waist. She dug her nails in again but it didn't sting. In fact, I hadn't realized it earlier in the shower but my back had healed completely. Very nice.

Even this morning, our bodies were charged with energy. It rolled across my skin and made me shiver. Whatever was between us wasn't temporary. I knew that if I took her now it would be as intense and fierce as yesterday.

I pulled back from the kiss, leaving her breathless. She let out a little laugh. "Good morning to you too!" she said as I gently lowered her feet to the floor.

"Now, what did you mean, you're glad I'm back?"

"I was worried." She stopped when she saw my expression. "You don't remember, do you?"

I shook my head with a frown. "What happened?"

She smelled embarrassed and couldn't meet my eyes. She stood and walked toward the fireplace. "I feel just horrible. I didn't mean to let you out. . ."

"Out?" A buzzing filled my ears. "What do you mean, out?"

She glanced at me, still anxious. She chewed on her lower lip for a moment. "Last night. I went downstairs after we . . . well, you know. While you were sleeping. I got back to the room a little after dark. I thought it would be okay. But when I got here, you'd already changed."

I was starting to feel butterflies in my stomach. "When I opened the door, you sprang past me, faster than I could move."

Oh, shit! I sat down heavily on the sofa. "You mean I was out all night?"

She turned then and looked at me. "I honestly don't know. When you bolted I tried to follow you. I swear I did. I thought that once you found that you were confined to this floor you'd come back to the room with me.

I had a flash of memory, just like yesterday. I stalked the hallway, feeling trapped. There were walls all around me. They led in a circle. I remember one man exiting the elevator as I walked past. I bared teeth at him and snarled. He backed into the elevator before the doors shut. I felt his fear as I passed and it was good. Fear was a good thing. Sour and sharp. It made me hungrier, though.

Sue's words sifted through the memories of grey walls and black carpet; where scents were visible in the air like faded watercolors. They were recollections of a world sharply focused and alien.

"You slowed down when you heard my voice," she continued. "But something else caught your attention. I don't know what. You headed toward the window at the end of the hall. It was almost faster than I could see. But I could feel it." There was an odd edge to her voice. I looked at her. She hugged herself and shivered.

"I could literally feel you move. Experience your anxiety. You felt trapped. Before I could react, you took a running leap and went . . ."

"Right through the window," I completed softly, distantly. I remembered it now. I saw the moon through the window and needed to reach it. Needed to touch it, let it touch me. I leapt and I soared through the air. The window glass felt like tissue paper. It was nothing to me.

Sue nodded. "I was terrified. We're nine stories up!" She walked toward me and drenched my senses in the clove-scent of pride with a healthy dose of fear. "I rushed to the window. I couldn't believe it. I saw you jump into space and then land on the roof of the hospital across the street. Across the street!" Her voice held amazement but her scent was still pride.

I knew that it should be a big deal. Really. But it didn't feel like I was straining at the time. It was just an average jump. Nothing special.

"I *felt* you jump, felt my muscles react and my breathing increase. It was incredible; wonderful. Like flying but better."

I nodded, still lost in the dream of it. I felt free. So trapped for so long and I was finally free. It was my turn to shiver.

"You ran to the other end of the roof and then I don't know where you went. I could feel you go but I lost sight of you."

I knew where I went. I needed trees. I needed meat. I picked up the story where Sue left off. I could hear my own voice from a distance as if I were narrating a movie. "I needed the night. Too trapped for too long," I heard myself say.

Sue nodded in agreement and hugged herself again. "I felt that too." She smiled suddenly and it was beautiful. "God, it felt so good to *run*. I could feel your muscles stretching, your body moving and it felt so incredibly . . . *incredible*." She looked at me then. Her smile was radiant. Tangerines blended with the cloves, buoyed by her own summer forest. As scents go it was a serious turn-on.

"Why do you coop yourself up in this room? You loved it out there. In the night. The fresh air, the scent of trees and rocks . . . I didn't even know that rocks had a smell until last night. But I stood there at the window after I couldn't see you anymore. I could feel you, sense you. Smell through your nose, see through your eyes. Well, actually, that's not quite true. I couldn't actually *see* but I could feel you react to what you *did* see. What kind of duck was it?"

I remembered that too. The image was so strong it sucked me back inside. The pond at the city park; the cattails where I lay in wait. Even now I could smell the musty scent of rotting vegetation. I saw the bloated body of a small-mouth bass float by as I watched the birds move closer. It was a male duck. He separated from the group and moved toward shore. I could feel a small line of saliva drip from my lower jaw as I watched.

I moved closer, each paw settling quietly into the moistened undergrowth. And I could feel Sue there. Knew she was with me. It felt *right*. My mate should be with me in the hunt.

"Pintail," I finally said.

"The taste exploded into my mouth when you caught it. I felt like I should bite down, like there was something there to chew on."

I didn't know what to say to that. It had never happened before. Not with anyone.

"Why did you leave the hotel?" I knew somehow that she had.

She shrugged. "I thought that if I could feel you I could

find you. But I couldn't. I knew that you couldn't get back into the hotel as a wolf and you wouldn't have any clothes if you woke up outside. So I went after you. I left the door ajar just in case you came back. I guess you got back in."

I tried to recall how I got back to the room. I had awakened on the bed. How did I get back upstairs? I felt my brow furrow as I fought to remember. Nope, not there.

"I have no idea. Maybe the same way I went out?" I suggested.

Sue shrugged. "Maybe. I didn't check to see if they fixed the window."

"And where have you been since then?"

"At the park mostly. But I had to buy some stuff too."

Sue told me that she drove to just outside the city and called her house to say she was staying out of town with a friend. She used a calling card so it would show up as a long-distance call. I nodded in approval and cloves dusted the air again.

She told her family that she wouldn't be back until the following day. Her mother and sister gave it to her with both barrels for leaving without a word. They apparently tag-teamed on two extensions in the house, accusing her of the fiasco in the lobby. She kept up the confused story, claiming to not understand what they meant. She looked at me hopefully, fishing for a compliment.

"I'm proud of you," I told her. "Good job."

"But I'm worried. When you move in, she'll know I was lying about not being in the hotel."

I looked at her sharply. I was afraid of this.

"I *might* be willing to *look* at the apartment, Sue." Her cheeks flushed with embarrassment and her scent changed to match. She nodded.

I'd never lived with anyone before. Not even a roommate. I like my privacy. But this . . . felt somehow natural. Like I was meant to be with this person. All by itself *that* made me tense.

"Let's go have some breakfast and we can talk about it some more."

The spring tightened in my gut again. Ever one to change the subject, I wiggled my eyebrows at her. "I actually had something else in mind. I've already eaten," I said, pointing toward the empty trays.

She pouted a little bit and it was cute. "But I really *am* hungry." She flashed a smile designed to melt me. It did, damn it.

"Okay. We'll order some more room service."

"Nah. I'm feeling restless. Let's go to the dining room."

I shook my head. She didn't understand. "I can't leave the room until tomorrow."

She cocked her head to the side, questioning. "Why not? In the daytime you're fine."

"No! I'm not. I *look* okay but I'm not fine. There's still shit inside of me boiling around. I can't be around other people. I tried it after I became—well, what I am. It doesn't work."

I turned from her and walked to the window. I looked around me as I stepped. The fireplace, the leather furniture, even the wall of tinted glass with its gorgeous view remind me that I'm a prisoner. Locked away from the rest of humanity. Caged like the animal I've become. A night in the park only reinforced that. I stood with legs spread slightly, arms crossed against my chest. Gazing at everything and seeing nothing.

"When it first happened. I didn't know what it was. I just felt real aggressive, plain mean for a couple of days a month. I thought I just woke up on the wrong side of the bed. Until I met you I'd never *remembered* turning into an animal. But I feel like one." Sue came to stand behind me. I caught the misty smell of sorrow, laced with an unknown spice. Concern, maybe? It's not one I've smelled often. She put her arms around my waist from the back and I hugged her. The memory was easier with her there.

"The third month, some guy cut me off on the road. Not intentionally. He just didn't see me. But I started to growl. Right there in the car. That sound coming out of my own mouth . . . it was eerie."

Sue's eyes were wide in the reflection of the window and her arms twitched as though she knew what I was going to say next. I could tell that she thought about pulling away but she didn't.

"I saw red—literally. My vision had this weird-ass pink haze and all I could think of was blood. His blood. It made my stomach growl if that's sick enough for you."

This story was hard to tell. I don't like how badly I lost control. Babs thought the story was funny. Big surprise. She thought killing me was funny too. It wasn't so funny to her when I showed up alive.

Babs is still around somewhere. That's a thorn in my side every day. I tried to kill her—twice. Put a bullet through her head once, but she got away. That was the first time she knew I'd survived. The second time I tracked her down, I blasted her chest open with two rounds from a twelve-gauge. She stayed down but by the time I got to my car, she was fully healed. She bent my shotgun into a pretzel. Tough lady. Supposedly, I'm just as tough, but I haven't had the occasion to test that theory. We made a brief truce that lasted until she betrayed me.

After the second attempt, Babs learned the identity of my client. Then she took him out. I had no sense of humor about that. I may still go after her again someday with some silver rounds I'm working on, but other things have concerned me more lately.

"Anyway, I tracked the guy down and ripped his throat out." Short, sweet and to the point.

She did pull away then and came around to face me. She watched my eyes as I spoke. I couldn't tell from her expression or her scent what she thought. She was sorting. I looked her squarely in the pupils. I wouldn't hide from what happened. I couldn't hide from it. But it still gives me nightmares sometimes.

"Again, literally. With my bare hands. But even that wasn't enough. I didn't just kill him, I mangled him. Bathed in his blood." I looked down at my open hands; palms up. It was too familiar, too close. My mind's eye saw the crimson blood, slick and shiny on my hands and arms. My shirt was soaked; my pants as well. I looked down and visualized again the face of the victim, eyes wide with surprise, mouth open in a scream that never reached air. My heart pounded like a caged animal and bile seared the back of my throat.

"Let's just say that I had a hell of a time cleaning it up." I turned from her and walked back to the bar and poured a glass of water. I downed it in one gulp. It chased the bile back down. "No, it's just not safe."

"Are you going to hurt me if I stay?" Fear now in her voice.

"No." My head shook as I said it. I knew the truth of the statement. I didn't understand why. "If I was going to hurt you it would have been last night. But your average jerk on the street? I can't say. Some months are worse than others. Someday I might get a handle on this and be able to control it but right now I can't."

She nodded her head, trying to grasp the concept.

"You can leave if you want." My hand tightened around the water glass. I stayed turned from her. "I'd understand. It's a bit much to start a relationship with."

I felt her eyes on me. She was startled, surprised. She walked toward me. She stopped just behind, not touching. I smelled her and it was like earlier, sweet enough to drown in. Parts of me tightened but the coil of fear remained. Except now the coil was a snake—writhing, sinking fangs inside my gut again and again.

"Do we have a relationship?" Hope mingled with fear in her scent.

I faced her. I wanted to see if there was horror in her eyes. The green eyes were just the same, warm with concern. There was no fear. No hate.

"I think we might have the beginnings of something," I replied quietly. "You tell me."

"Can I ask you a question first?"

I nodded, even though I didn't want to hear the question.

"Why are you so affected by this?" It was my turn to be

startled. I mean, how could I not be? My surprise must have shown on my face because she responded to the unasked question.

"You kill for a living. Why does this bother you so much? It's not his death." She touched her own chest and then mine. "I can feel it. There's something else inside you that is *horrified* by this."

I took a deep breath and let it out slowly. How could I explain it so it made sense? "I do a job. I'm not Scotty. I don't kill for pleasure." But I did. God help me but it made me happy while I was ripping his skin open. The bile returned, hot and burning.

I groped for the right words. "It comes down to standards. Humans don't eat their dead. It's what separates us from the real animals. We kill without remorse, torture without regret, but we aren't cannibals. We have standards."

I really believe that. Often personal standards, morals, are all we have against insanity. His death had been too . . . participatory. Sue nodded in agreement but still looked confused.

"Some things are still beneath us. It's why *Silence of the Lambs* scares us and Jeffrey Dahlmer was front-page news for weeks instead of hours."

"I understand that." She crossed her arms and shook her head. "So you lost control." She shrugged and gave a little laugh, meant to lighten the mood. "But it's not like you ate him afterwards."

I didn't answer. I just looked at her. Our eyes locked and I willed my eyes alone to tell the story. Some part of me didn't want to admit it. I couldn't quite voice the reality.

The look was enough. Her eyes went from confused to alarmed and then the slightest trace of horror set in. Her jaw dropped slightly and her arms dropped to her sides almost unconsciously.

"Did you?" It was a whisper.

I held her gaze for as long as I could but I broke eye contact first. "I don't know for sure." But I suspected.

"When I came to and started to clean up there were marks

on him. Marks that didn't match up with finger gouges; marks with ragged edges. I couldn't find some of the pieces." Ah. *Now* there was horror settling in at the back of those emerald eyes.

"When the smell got to me from the ruptured intestines, I threw up." I can't forget the smell. Rancid thick gas that churned into the air. The blood was sweet and coppery but when I laid open the gut... Half digested food, partially formed feces. My stomach threatened to repeat. I swallowed hard and forced the bitter acid back where it came from. I left the conclusion unspoken.

Her voice shook ever so slightly. "Did you find the rest of the pieces?"

I shrugged. I hadn't looked. I didn't want to know. But I could still remember the taste of sweet, warm blood that lingered on my tongue as I knelt over the body.

She nodded her head. I looked at her but she couldn't meet my eyes. She just kept nodding. Her gaze was on the carpet at my feet. I reached out to touch her shoulder and she flinched, pulling her arm back. I let her. I dropped my hand to my side and waited.

I started kicking myself almost immediately. Why did I tell her? What did I hope to accomplish except to chase her away? Then again, maybe that was it. I wanted to frighten her away. There was something about Sue that I wanted to keep near me. Maybe this was my subconscious way of making her leave. If my buddy, John-Boy, knew about the whole werewolf thing, he would probably tell me that I was exhibiting self-fulfilling behavior. I think I'm an animal and don't believe that anyone could want me so I'll tell her what an animal I am so she won't want me.

"Like I said, if you want to go I'll understand." I meant it.

"You'd just let me go? Even knowing what I do?"

"Well, actually, no. It'd just mean that I'll take the job you wanted to hire me for. But it would be hard. Know that. Really hard."

She almost smiled but she didn't come any closer, didn't touch me. Her scent was a blending of everything I knew and a few I couldn't sort out. "Can I think about it? This is all happening so fast. It's not what I planned."

I smiled. "If life was only what you planned, it'd be pretty dull."

She smiled back but it was shaky. "Maybe that's why my life has been dull. But I really need some time to assimilate all this."

Suddenly, I was annoyed. I didn't know why. Her reaction was what I expected. Then again, maybe not. I think a part of me hoped she would laugh and call me silly for worrying. Stupid and romantic. But it's what I hoped for even though reality isn't like that. Some things can't be gotten past.

Another part of me wanted her to run screaming from the room; leave me to my misery. Let me drown in my fears and my curse and never move on.

"Go then," I said harshly. I turned from her and walked to the couch. I sat and picked up the paper. "Come back if you want. Don't if you don't." The words sounded cold, unfeeling. I didn't look at her, couldn't watch the fear in her eyes. "If you don't come back, bring a case with fifty grand back here and leave it with Max to put in the safe. I'll see you in a year or so. I can find you."

I glanced at her briefly where she stood immobile. I could smell her discomfort. Her sympathy and fear were almost equal. She gestured with her hands helplessly not sure what to say. I certainly wasn't going to help. I don't need pity. I tried to concentrate on the front page story but the words only swam through my brain. They didn't form sentences.

"Can I take the key card with me?"

I let out a short, bitter laugh. "Might as well. *I* won't be needing it. If you decide not to come back turn it in at the desk. If it's there when I check out I'll have my answer."

She picked up the white, credit-card sized square of plastic and turned it slowly in her fingers. I tried to ignore her but she slipped into my peripheral vision. She opened her mouth and then shut it again. Tears were close to the surface. I could smell them. I didn't want her to cry. She was digging too far under my skin. I knew that if I saw tears I would go to her; hold her; try to make it better. I went back to staring blankly at the paper.

After a moment I felt her gather dignity around herself like a cloak. She took a deep breath, released it and then slipped the key into the pocket of her shorts. She picked up the bags that were on the floor. I tried not to watch. Tried not to think.

"I'll see you later." Tentative hope edged her voice.

I nodded without looking at her. "One way or another."

She left without saying good-bye.

Chapter 11

The longer I sat alone the easier it was to forget the look on her face when she left. Confused, helpless, scared. All rolled into a last lingering look that I knew that I would be regretting for years. The smell wasn't so easy to ignore. It stirred something deep in me and I wanted it back. Wanted her back. But I didn't expect it. If the tables were turned, I wouldn't. I know it's hypocritical but I expect more of other people than of myself. Isn't it always the way?

I needed a distraction so I turned on the boob tube. Daytime television is a joke. There isn't any football and the game shows have been replaced by what I call 'controversy shows'. Jerry Springer and the like—not talk but confrontation. Soaps are fiction, but the controversy shows rival them for content and are disturbingly real. Whoever said that "truth is stranger than fiction" knew their stuff.

I clicked through twenty-four channels before I finally stopped in the middle of *Casablanca*. I like old black-and-white movies. *African Queen*, *Ship of Fools* and *In Cold Blood* are favorites. I did watch the colorized versions that Turner did, but it's just not the same. Chocolate syrup that looks like real blood turns back into Hershey's finest even after they change the color.

I felt restless. I should be doing something. Usually when this is planned, I bring along my laptop or pay my bills. Last March I did my income tax returns after getting all the forms off the 'net.

I tried to think about work. I had three other jobs to plan; jobs that I've already been paid for. But all the detail—the maps, photographs, and itineraries were at my house. I also started cursing myself for not laundering a case of cash in Atlantic City before I screwed up my free pass. I'd decided to wait until after one more job. Just my luck that the next job happened to be Jeffrey. Now I wouldn't be able to use any of the casinos there friendly to my type of transaction.

I can run a lot of money through the security company, but I'd taken too many jobs in too short a time. The plan was to take a vacation for a year or so. I hadn't had one in awhile. I was swimming in cash and needed to have it appear legit, so I could bask in the sun in Hawaii or Monaco. A rigged gambling game is best for that. But it would mean I'd have to go to Vegas. Shit.

Thinking about some of my least favorite characters didn't improve my mood. I checked my broken watch, then shook my head in annoyance and finally took it off. Useless piece of crap. It was only 1:10 p.m. by the clock in the bedroom. I went to the fridge and removed the prime rib. I opened the package over the sink in the bathroom and left it to warm to room temperature. Dinner was ready. I supposed that I should eat lunch.

I called room service and ordered a Monte Cristo sandwich with raspberry jam and homecut fries. It's one of my favorites. I considered trying to get drunk, going so far as to pour a double Maker's Mark, neat, but then poured it back in the bottle. It wouldn't improve my mood. It'd probably make it worse. I can't seem to get drunk anymore and the effort makes me grumpy.

It shouldn't matter whether she came back. One night of fairly good sex and I get these lofty fucking ideas of some imaginary romance. Worse still is a romance that I don't have the time or the inclination for. I've had enough women in my life that it shouldn't matter.

I was probably just pissed that I'd gotten my calendar messed up and I was stuck here. On the plus side, though, now I could go to the poker game. I had cancelled because of the job. But with the job over and the change over . . .

That brightened my mood considerably. Yeah, getting together with the boys for an all-nighter would get my disposition back to normal. I started to call Carmine to tell him that I'd be at the game with bells on but remembered that the calls are tracked and put on my bill. No, tying this room number with Carmine's private line wouldn't do at all. I got my nerve together and went downstairs.

When the elevator door opened on the main floor I headed straight for the pay phones. I did my best to ignore the smell of people moving around, their blood flowing thick and heavy under paper-thin skin. I smelled their joys, their sorrows, their fears. It was too many smells. Too many emotions. Another reason I lock myself away—sensory overload.

Only one phone was working. I called and heard the sultry recording of Carmine's wife, Linda. I left a message and then called Jocko and asked him to check up on my car. I hadn't intended to leave it for days.

"I wondered why you hadn't come back," he said. "Found a new lady? I noticed the way the brunette was looking at you."

"Keep your mind out of the gutter," I snarled. "Is the car okay?"

He was silent for a moment. "Yeah. I let Sweetboy know it was yours and both gangs are keeping away from it. Unilateral decision. They know what you'd do to them. It's probably the only thing they've agreed on this year."

"Damn straight." For a moment my vision started to redden as I imagined pounding one of those street punks into a bloody pulp. The thought of his screams as I tore him apart made me smile. I could almost smell his sweat and mouthwatering fear. My stomach growled and I shivered.

"You okay?" Jocko asked quietly. "You sound rough."

I took a deep breath and let it out slowly. Calm. Stay calm. No bloody rampages in the lobby of the hotel. I felt a tap on my shoulder and I turned. A woman with dark hair and a tailored business suit looked impatient.

"Will you be long?" she asked. "I need the phone." She wore too much perfume and it masked her underlying scent.

I ignored her by turning back to look at the phone bank. "I'll be okay. Things haven't gone as planned this week."

"Okay." He sounded uncertain. The broad behind me tapped again and I fought back the urge to turn and grab her throat and slam the receiver into her face again and again and then lick the blood off the black plastic.

Whoa! Definitely time to get back upstairs.

I shook my head hard to clear it. "Hey, I've got to go. I'll be back in a day or so. Keep the word out that my car is off-limits." I turned and looked right into the eyes of the brunette when I allowed my voice to drop an octave and take on a heavy Italian accent. "Anyone touches my ride and I'll rip off their dick and feed it to them. *Capisce?*"

I smiled evilly and the brunette's eyes grew wide. I watched the pulse in her neck move faster. A light dew of sweat began to form on her upper lip. I wanted her pulse between my teeth. I scrutinized the prey intently. Her eyes darted back and forth quickly as she looked to escape. Fear turned quickly to ammonia panic. Excellent. I bared teeth at her, then brought my lips together and blew her a kiss. She backed slowly away, nearly tripping over her own feet. I struggled not to follow, not to pounce.

Jocko chuckled over the phone line. It startled me. I flinched abruptly and then laughed with him but for a different reason. There was a high edge to my laughter that I didn't like.

"I'll let them know," he promised.

I made it all the way back to the room before I remembered that Sue had the card key and I was locked out. I stood in the hallway fighting the beginnings of panic. I didn't need this shit today. I kicked the door hard and felt the force of it sing through my leg. The heavy oak cracked sharply and I watched a hairline fracture swim up the grain of the wood. Oops.

"Mr. Giodone?" came a voice from the hallway. I turned to see Tim, one of the kitchen staff, rolling a cart toward me.

A wave of relief passed through me. "I locked myself out."

He laughed and produced a pass key. He reached past me and opened the door. I entered and he wheeled the cart in after me. "Can I get you anything else?"

I shook my head, not trusting myself to speak. They'd miss him; I know they would. But I could smell him. His aftershave only partly masked the scent of his skin. My stomach growled agonizingly and I fought down a snarl as I looked at his smiling face and thought of him only as food. Another part of my brain questioned what kind of wine went with red meat and I almost laughed. Just call me Hannibal. My tongue slipped out to catch a thin line of saliva that was creeping down my jaw.

I shook my head, clearing the thoughts. He had to leave. Now! I reached into my pocket and removed my wallet. I peeled off a twenty and handed it to him.

He looked at the bill in surprise. "They'll put the food on your tab."

"As they should. Thanks for letting me in."

His smile was brilliant against his dark skin. "Hey, wow! You need anything else, you just let me know!" I nodded and turned my attention to the cart. It was his cue to leave.

Sadly, the build-up of the prey smells left the sandwich incapable of satisfying my hunger. My nose led me to the bathroom. The bathroom still smelled like Sue. Trees and musk and sex. My body reacted to the smell and I slapped the thought out of my mind.

The scent of the meat, warm and bleeding in the sink was too much. Everything was too much today. Fine. If not sex then blood. Sweet, metallic, heady. Even as my mind screamed its disapproval I bit a bloody hunk of prime rib and chewed it slowly. The tension dissipated as I chewed the raw beef and I accepted what I was for these three days.

A wolf. A carnivore. So be it.

At least for today I wasn't a cannibal.

Chapter 12

Darkness came and went. As I woke to the daylight the room was silent as a tomb. I toured the room and found the remains of a gnawed bone in the tub. One end of it was cracked and ragged. The marrow had been removed as far as, I presume, my tongue would reach. Maybe it's better that I don't remember the things I do.

I didn't find any sign that Sue had come back. Not unexpected but still disappointing. I took my shower and dressed again in the Dockers and T-shirt.

I called down and asked that a newspaper be brought to the room along with breakfast. After I finished eating I put the cart outside in the hallway along with the one from the afternoon before.

When I heard the lock release nearly an hour later I didn't even reach for my gun. I could sense who it was—thick moss, musk, and sex. I actually felt my heart stop as the door opened. I watched the silly sunglasses and wig enter the room ahead of Sue and fought back a grin. She could just be returning long enough to say good-bye. I wouldn't get my hopes up. Shouldn't even have hopes.

"Hi," she said softly. She was worried; nervous. She stood at the edge of the room but wanted to come closer.

"Hi. What's up?" Might as well get it over with.

"Can I come in?" Her expression made it clear that she didn't know the answer.

I couldn't seem to stop the reply. I even meant it. "Always."

She stepped into the room. She looked delectable in a purple cotton short set with pansies embroidered across the neck of the spaghetti-string top. Her breasts were unfettered and made the cloth tent out far enough that the bottom of the shirt didn't touch skin. Another pair of jelly sandals matched the outfit. She must be buying as she went. I wanted to take her right now whether or not she planned to leave me, and that scared the shit out of me.

She took off the wig and glasses. Her hair was damp and tightly curled from the heat and humidity. I smelled the sweat and it still smelled of herbs. I remained seated but leaned forward and rested my arms on my knees. I hoped I looked interested and not like I was waiting for the other boot to drop. Although I was.

She sat down across from me. She looked at me, then away, then back. Her polished nails tapped a nervous pattern on her bare legs. "I've been thinking."

"So have I."

"You first," she said quickly, anticipatory. Her whole body moved forward on the couch several inches.

I shook my head. "This is your decision, not mine."

She nodded and scooted back in the couch. Her eyes dropped again and she suddenly looked as she did when we first met, uncomfortable and set in stone. She couldn't meet my eyes. Her foot began to tap lightly on the thick carpet.

I jumped in with both feet. "You're leaving. Right?"

Her eyes shot up and locked with mine. She looked surprised. "No!"

The heady scent of spices rolled off of her. Too many to sort, but over the top, the comfort smell of baking bread reached me. Then why the nervousness?

She continued, a little flustered. "I mean, not unless you want me to." She looked at the floor. With her legs crossed, head bowed, and hands folded in her lap, she looked like a little girl waiting outside the principal's office. She expected to be rejected one more time. I could feel it in my chest. She didn't even dare hope that I might want her. Odd that we were both thinking the same thing.

"Look, let's just be open here. You said you've been thinking. Do you want to stay or go?"

She took a deep breath. "Stay. If you want me to."

I fought not to grin. I motioned with my hand. "Then why are you sitting over there?" I patted my knee. Sue looked up, watched my face, to see if I was mocking her. I did smile then. With my face and with my eyes.

She smiled shyly and stood. She walked around the coffee table, turned sideways and then sat down on my lap. I put my arms around her waist. She snuggled against my chest and laid her head on my shoulder. A small sigh eased out of her and her arms went around my neck. I felt her fingers glide over my scalp. I rested my face against her hair. The honey-colored curls smelled of salty sweat, soft musk, and herbs.

The scent did more than turn me on. If only it was that easy. I would kill, or die, for the scent of her. God, I shouldn't ever want anyone this much. It's too dangerous.

"You're sure about this?" I asked after a few moments of silence.

"I really did go stay at a friend's last night. I used to have lots of friends. We hadn't even spoken for over a year!" She moved her head so she could look at me. "I missed you. I spent the night wondering about you; wishing you were there, wishing I was here. I could feel you pace around the room looking for me. I felt you eat the prime rib. I laughed when you got frustrated that your tongue couldn't reach the marrow in the center of the bone. I wanted to be here to help." She was silent for a moment. "A part of me wanted you to come look for me. Find me. Take me. Another part of me was really scared that you would."

"I can't say that I missed you last night. But this morning was a bitch. Yesterday too." Tangerines dusted my nose and blended with the herbs.

"So? Now what? What's next? I've never done anything like this, felt anything like this before. I don't want to leave without you but I'm sure you've got a life. I don't even know if you're married. I don't even know your real name. Is it really Bob?"

I shook my head. "My friends call me Tony. Only clients call me Bob." I ignored the "real name" question. Too soon. "And no, I'm not married."

I paused as I thought briefly, then I nodded. "You're right. We do need to get to know one another. When are you due back at your house?"

She shrugged. "Whenever I get there. Bekki is staying until I get back. So Mom has someone around. I'm sure there'll be hell to pay but I told them I'd be gone a couple of days. I don't have a job so as long as Mom's covered . . ." She grinned suddenly, "Oh God, Bekki will be mad! Heaven forbid something should intrude on *her* life!"

I chuckled. My lady was starting to grow a backbone. Good. "Then let's check out and we'll go on a trip. When's the last time you were in Vegas?"

"Las Vegas? I've *never* been there. You mean that we're just going to pick up and leave town?" She seemed startled at the suggestion.

I shrugged, which rubbed my arms against her breasts. "Why not? I have some business, but it'll only take a few hours. We can take an afternoon flight and make it back in the morning. Hell, we can stay a week if you want."

"Oh! I can't be gone *that* long! I don't even have any clothes."

I shrugged again and felt the urging of the hunger under my skin as she pressed against me. "We'll buy new. I only need to stop at my place for a second to pick up some stuff." No need to bring up what sort of stuff I needed. Even if we were getting together, the less she knew, the better.

"We're going to be stopping by *your* house?" The question seemed loaded and I didn't know why.

"Is that a problem?" Her scent was suddenly tense.

"No. No, not at all. I'm just trying to imagine where you might live and I'm coming up blank."

"Well, in a little bit, you'll see. But for the next few minutes," I said and tightened my arms, "you won't be having any time to imagine much of anything."

She was smiling as I kissed her and our teeth clicked together for an instant. The thick, heady scent of her desire made thinking impossible. So I didn't bother to try. I just let the hunger have its way.

Chapter 13

After I checked out she drove me to Nick's so I could collect my car. It's a '67 Mustang Fastback. Black with white interior. It'll overtake almost any other car off the line or on the stretch. Not only had nobody bothered my car, they'd waxed it. I could smell residual sweat blended with the fresh paste wax. It's nice to be feared.

Sue was amazed that nobody had touched my car in that neighborhood so I told her about my conversation with Jocko.

"You'd really do it. Wouldn't you?" Burned coffee, burned water, with the slightest hint of cloves.

"Absolutely," I said firmly. "A threat has no teeth if you're not willing to follow through." It was a lesson she needed to learn if she wanted to be able to stand up to her family.

"Okay..." I couldn't smell her mood.

We stopped at her bank first. She was amazed when I suggested that she take about a quarter mil. She finally agreed to take five thousand. What a waste of a good gambling trip.

I took the lead and she followed to my house to drop off my car. I live in a large ranch-style in a quiet, suburban neighborhood. The house is huge. It's bigger than I need but I like space. The suite is half of the top floor of the hotel but even that feels cramped. As I parked the car I wondered again what was possessing me that I kept letting her further and further into my life. Only the boys have ever been to my place. We take turns hosting the poker game. It's only once every five months, so the neighbors don't bitch. Much. Bodyguards and unconcealed carrys make folks nervous.

I unlocked the door and ushered her inside. "Look

around," I said. "I'll just be a minute. I really want to get out of these clothes."

She smelled like I had hurt her feelings. "You don't like them?"

I smiled and gave her a quick kiss on the cheek. "Actually, I like them a lot. But I've been wearing them for two days."

"Oh!" came a relieved comment. Her fragrance was sunny again. I was going to have to watch what I said around her until her skin thickened a bit.

I went into the master bedroom and as I stripped, she called to me.

"This is really nice! Did you decorate it yourself?"

I turned on the shower for a quick rinse. "Mostly. Some of the paintings were gifts from my dad."

I turned to see her standing in the doorway of the bedroom. "I thought you said your dad died before you were born."

"No, I said my *father* died before I was born. My dad is the man who raised me."

She gave me a questioning glance.

"Dad was a bodyguard for the *Patrone*," I explained, using the Italian pronunciation. "You've probably heard him called the Godfather. *Patrone* doesn't actually translate to Godfather. Literally, it's 'patron'; figuratively, 'grandfather'. The head of the family, a protector. Anyway, Dad didn't have any family and when I moved into the big house, I didn't either. Dad felt sorry for me and he always wanted a kid. So he asked and *Patrone* let Dad raise me."

She smiled at me and smelled of warm cinnamon rolls. "That's nice. It's nice that you found each other."

I stepped into the shower. I spoke louder to be heard over the water. "It's a family of choice, rather than a family of blood. Both are important."

I heard her voice move closer. I could sense that she was standing just inside the doorway.

"Do you have any blood family left? Did your mother or father have any family?"

"If they did they've never come forward. I didn't know my mother's real name. She just called herself Amber."

I stepped out of the shower and joined her in the bedroom. The towel I wore around my waist was to finish drying off. I'm not real modest.

I could feel in my head that she was hoping I had a picture. I did, but it was old and tired-looking from riding in my wallet for years. Still, I sorted through receipts and business cards until I found it. I pulled it out so she could see it.

Sue stared at the photo as I scrubbed my hair with the towel.

"She's beautiful!" she exclaimed in surprise. I glanced at the picture. I don't look at it often. Mom had thick black hair, which I inherited and sapphire blue eyes I didn't. Her pale skin and delicate features put her in the model category. The body matched the face. She could have been more than just a whore if she had tried, but I didn't know her long enough to ask her story. It's not something that a ten-year-old thinks of.

Sue pointed to the young boy smiling out of the cracked and faded wallet print. "Is that you in the photo with her?"

"Yeah. I was five when that was taken. It was right before she got the syphilis real bad. She didn't look so pretty when she died. It wasn't anything that a kid should watch."

She looked at me and watched the brief flash of pain appear then disappear from my eyes as the memory slipped through.

"I'm sorry." She really was. The feeling made my chest tight.

I shrugged. "Oh, well. Can't change the past. It's what happened."

"Yeah. I understand about pasts not going away." She stood there staring at the picture of a woman long dead, a person she didn't even know and felt sorrow. Hot tears shimmered just below the surface. She handed me back the photo without a word.

I wanted to go to her and hold her; make it better. But I couldn't. Instead, I hurriedly put on clothes suitable for Vegas. She watched me dress with a proprietary air. As I would walk from place to place she would reach out and touch a leg or an arm. Like it still wasn't quite real to her. I smiled at her once and she smiled back.

Once I was dressed and packed for a day or two, I reached into the closet behind the clothes and the shelves. My finger found a small indentation in the wall and I pulled sideways. A small panel opened and blind fingers found the handle of a briefcase. It was a typical hard-side case made of black leather, with twin dial locks set into the top. I didn't open it. There was no need. I knew what was in it. There was a hand-cuff attached and I snapped it closed around my wrist.

Sue watched with interest. Curiosity sparkled in the back of her eyes. "What's in the case?"

"Something I need to deliver to someone. It won't take long." My voice was light but neutral.

She shrugged but I could smell her curiosity. I was pleased that she didn't ask any questions I didn't want to answer.

We dropped off Sue's rental car at the airport lot. Plane tickets were easy to come by. The next flight boarded in only twenty minutes.

We went to the airport stores and found several outfits for Sue. I was a little surprised when she selected size fourteens. I'm usually better at guessing than that. We also bought her a travel case, new cosmetics and toiletries.

"I can't believe I'm doing this!" she exclaimed, as we paid the cashier. "This is so . . ."

"So . . . what?"

"I don't know! Wicked? Extravagant?"

Still that sense that she wasn't entitled to be happy. I turned her to face me right at the cash register. I put a hand on each shoulder and held her gaze. I repeated something I said the first day. "You're allowed to enjoy this, Sue."

Her eyes thanked me with words she couldn't say. A smile spoke the rest and she hugged me.

When we arrived at the security gate, I accompanied a guard to a separate room after flashing a card that identified me as a high-security courier. It hadn't been an easy I.D. to obtain and I was proud of it. I was fully bonded and could transport large sums of cash and jewels all over the country as carry-on. I had to check my gun but I could keep it as concealed carry when I landed. I just make sure that my carry piece isn't what I use for jobs. My carry piece is either the Sig or a snub nose Taurus .38. I had the Taurus today. Sweet shooting gun. It'll put five rounds in a one inch group right out of the box.

The drug dogs were a trip. They completely ignored the case and sniffed me all over. Then they went to their bellies in submission with tails flipping madly. A female beagle flipped on her back and howled. Apparently I'm a big dog now. I've seen it before, but the guards didn't know what to make of their reaction. They finally had to drag the dogs through the crowd of laughing passengers and then hand searched the bag.

Sue was waiting for me on the other side of the x-ray machine when I returned. My briefcase now had a security seal taped across the opening. She looked at it with undisguised curiosity but didn't ask any questions. Smart girl.

We had to scramble a bit to reach the gate, two concourses over. She was out of breath but laughing happily when we slid through the door and handed our boarding passes to the flight attendant.

The flight attendant tried to tell me that I had to stow the briefcase. When I showed her the handcuff and the security tape, she relented but wasn't happy. Oh, well. Her attitude wasn't my problem.

The weather was perfect for flying. I'm used to flying, but it was obvious that Sue wasn't. Her scent changed to nearly abject terror. Terror goes beyond the ammonia smell of panic. It's like a week-old cat box—it could peel paint off the wall if humans could smell it. Her knuckles were bloodless on the chair arms as we accelerated toward take-off. I could hear her heart beat faster and faster until it was hummingbird quick.

"Don't like to fly, love?"

"Never have before," she said, eyes closed. "The thought of being suspended in a tin box ten thousand feet in the air just came home to me. I think I might be sick."

I thought it best not to mention that we'd be significantly

higher than ten thousand. I tried to take one of her hands to hold it and comfort her, but she refused to let go of the arm-rest. So I settled for resting my hand over the top of hers, and stroking the skin gently. Take-offs are usually the worst for non-flyers. I could feel her pulse race where my fingers touched her wrist. She whimpered slightly. The sound made me want to nuzzle her, comfort her.

"It'll be over soon," I said instead, and patted her hand.

Her eyes opened suddenly, and she glanced at me in panic. "Why do you say that?"

I chuckled softly. "I didn't mean we were going to crash. Once we're at level flight, you'll see that it's not so bad."

The acceleration decreased, and I could feel the flight level off. The pilot came over the speaker to welcome us and tell us that weather conditions were perfect for the short hop to Vegas. It would only be an hour flight. The plane was packed, and the flight attendants were at a dead run. They came around and offered us coffee or sodas. Sue turned a lit-tle green when I ordered orange juice.

"This really doesn't bother you, does it?" she asked.

"I really like to fly," I admitted. "I've even got ground school under my belt, but never had the time to finish get-ting my pilot's license. There's lots of air time involved. Life has just been too busy."

The trip was nearly half over before Sue relaxed her hands on the chair arms. I suggested that she might want to get some blood back into them. They were stiff and rigid at first, and I helped rub them to get the circulation going again.

"You must think that I'm some sort of wimp," she said ruefully.

"Not at all," I said with a gentle smile. "Thousands of people don't like to fly. You're not the first. You won't be the last. I've known some real tough guys that turn into jello in an airplane. We all have our phobias."

"What are yours?" she asked. Curiosity filled the pres-sured air and then disappeared through a vent.

I chuckled. "You wouldn't believe me."

"Please?" she pleaded. "It'll make me feel better to hear about someone else's."

"Okay," I said, "But it's stupid. I'm afraid of needles."

Her eyebrows raised. "Needles? Like shots, or sewing?"

"Like shots," I repeated. "Now, understand. I know that they have beneficial uses, but all the stuff inside looks the same to me. Could be medicine, could be poison. Get a needle near me, and I'll beat the person holding it senseless. I almost got tetanus once because I wouldn't go to the hospital. Dad finally had to hold me down—with the help of three interns, so they didn't have to cut off my foot."

She gave a crow of laughter. "Needles! That's wonderful! A big, strong . . . ," I could sense that she nearly said the word, *assassin*, but stopped short. "man, like you."

I gave her a sarcastic smile. "Glad I could amuse you. I didn't laugh at you, ya know."

That sobered her right up. "I'm sorry," she said, with humor still in her voice. "I guess you don't get flu shots, huh?

"No," I responded, "That's not high on my priority list. I figure if everyone around me gets one, I should be safe. But tell you what, I'll roll up my sleeve for you if you'll go flying with me. Just you and me in the wild blue. We can do barrel rolls and Immelmans." There was a sparkle of teasing in my eyes. At that precise moment, the plane hit an air pocket, and we dropped a foot or two. She went slightly white and her panic tickled my nose.

"Okay, I give," she said quickly. "Sorry I laughed. Really, really sorry." I laughed, loud and hard until she finally joined in.

We talked more about our likes. It turned out that we both could live on Italian food forever, but that neither of us liked veggies on our pizza. She doesn't like scallops, but enjoys calamari—which I detest, and we both adore shrimp.

"You will *love* the shrimp cocktails at the casinos," I commented.

"Good, huh?" she asked.

"Even better. Free."

Her eyebrows disappeared under her bangs. "They *give away* shrimp cocktails? Cool!"

"Food's cheap," I said with a shrug. "Free food keeps people spending money at the tables."

Sue kept glancing out of the window nervously so I reached over and shut the blind. She smelled startled but it really did calm her down. We talked about books. Turned out that we had major differences in taste.

"Mostly I like real life stuff," she said. "Not biographies, but like true crime."

"Ah. Joseph Wambaugh and such?"

She nodded her head. "Yeah, that sort. And drama about people who have done interesting things. What about you?"

"Nope. I like escapism. I've already got enough drama in my life, thank you. Real events are traumatic enough without borrowing other people's problems. Sci-fi, good mysteries— the ones that make you think about whodunit—and thrillers are good, too. I read a lot of Asimov, Cussler and Clancy."

All in all, I managed to distract her enough with conversation that she didn't even remember most of the flight.

But when we started to descend into Vegas, we ran into turbulance. We were racing down the runway before I could forcibly remove her bloodless knuckles from my arm. If she'd lost much more circulation we'd have had to amputate.

After we arrived I had to check in with Security to get my piece back, have the tape removed and get the money counted a second time. I snapped the case around my wrist and locked my fingers around the handle.

Sue was waiting for me at the luggage carousel. The bags were on the floor next to her and she was smiling broadly.

"Happy?" I asked, even though it was obvious from her scent.

"I've never done anything like this. I am having so much fun."

"The fun hasn't started yet."

She opened her mouth to speak when my cell phone rang. I have it set to actually *ring*. It sets it apart from all of the chirps and inane songs from other phones. I glanced at the display. Damn it. I might as well take the call. Sara would dial constantly until she reached me. I held a finger up to stop Sue's reply, pressed a button and held the phone to my ear.

"Tony here."

"Tony, it's Sara. I've been trying to reach you!"

"I've been in a plane, Sara."

Panic suffused through her voice. "Does that mean you're out of town?"

"Yes, Sara. I'm out of town for a few days. What's the problem?"

"But I need you to come over. The security system isn't working."

I sighed. The security system is *never* working when Sara is managing the store. I don't think machines like her.

"What's it doing?"

"It's those damn door sensors! They beep at the customers every time someone goes out the door."

"*Every* time, Sara?" It helped to get enough information about the problem to be able to fix it.

"Well, no, not every time. But it's gone off six times in the past hour! See, there it goes again!" She was right. In the background I heard the characteristic tones of the shoplifting sensor.

"Did a customer go through? Or an employee? Tell me what's happening, Sara."

"It was a customer. The man had just gone through the register line and it still beeped at him."

"Did he buy something that needed to be nullified? Did the clerk remove the tag?"

"Yes, Tom's the clerk on that register."

Okay. I know him. He's pretty careful. So, maybe it was the sensors. "Is the customer still in the store?"

Her voice sounded hurt. "Of course. I'm standing right here next to him. What do I do?" I heard her cover the mouthpiece with her hand and explain to the customer that she was talking to the security repair company. Then she started chatting with the customer and forgot I was on the phone.

I didn't have the time or inclination to play with her today. "Sara? Sara!"

"Oh! Sorry, Tony. What do I do?"

"Take the customer's bag and stand away from the sensors. Then swing the bag through the sensor and tell me what happens."

"Okay. Hold on." I could hear her set down the receiver and ask the customer for the bag. The male customer objected, which perked my ears. I listened closer, focusing in with my wolf hearing.

"This is stupid!" said the man. "I don't have time to help you fix your equipment. Now, give me my bag. I have other things to do."

Ah, ha. I got an idea.

"Sara! Pick up the phone!"

There was a scrambling sound and then I heard her voice. "Yes, Tony?"

"Do you have the bag?"

"Yep. Right here." Her voice muffled again. "I'm sorry, sir. This will only take a moment. I get a reprimand in my file if I don't report these errors when they happen."

"Sara? Did you wave the bag through?"

"Yes. It didn't do it this time."

"Do me a favor and ask the man to walk through the sensor again. But this time, *you* hold the bag until after he goes through."

"But . . ."

"Just do it, Sara. Trust me." The customer didn't want to walk through and I knew why.

"Tony? He doesn't want to walk through. I can't force him to. What do I do?"

"Call security, Sara. The guy's shoplifting."

"No, really, Tony. I've got the bag right here. I watched him check out."

Sue was watching me closely with furrowed brows. I knew that she was listening. Even if she could only hear part of the conversation, she found it interesting.

"He bought some things. He just didn't buy *every* thing.

Don't let go of that bag, Sara. If the guy bolts, follow him out to his car and get a plate number. I'll bet that whatever is hidden in his pocket or under his shirt is worth a lot more than what's in the bag. But he probably won't leave without what he paid for. Call me back after security's checked him out."

I hung up without waiting for a reply.

I held up one finger aloft for Sue to wait and didn't even look at the display when the phone rang a second time.

"Tony here."

"Oh, my God! Tony, you were right. The guy had pockets sewed all up and down the inside of his pants. There were those real expensive cell phone batteries, some pricey women's perfume and a couple of CDs. Do you think that all of the other beeps were thefts, too?

"Maybe a couple of them. But the unit probably does need to be adjusted. I'll swing by when I get back. Until then, have a couple of the stockers stand at the exit and carry people's bags through. Then you'll know if it's the person or the bag. It'll get you by until I get back."

"Thank you *so* much, Tony! No wonder Carol insists on using your company!"

"No problem, Sara. I'll be by in a couple of days."

I hung up to find Sue looking at me curiously. The thick, sweet scent of antifreeze filled the air. At least that's how it smells to me.

"How could you know the customer was shoplifting over the phone?"

I shrugged. "Most people consider the security devices annoying, but they're pretty good about understanding the need for them. When he didn't want to give up the bag, I figured that there was something wrong. It takes one to know one."

"So, you run a security company? Is that what you do for a living?"

I chuckled. "It's what I do to keep busy. You already know what I do for a *living.*"

But, having the phone out reminded me of something. I picked up my bag and motioned for Sue to do the same. I punched the menu button on the phone and scanned down the list of names. When I reached Sal's number, I dialed.

"Talk to me." It's how Sal always answers.

"Sal? Tony. How's business?"

"Hey, Tony! 'Sup, buddy? You in town?"

"Yeah. I'm hoping we can do business. I've got money burning a hole in my pocket." It's the truth and it's also innocuous enough that it didn't matter if anyone overheard. Sal knew what I needed to do.

We'd reached the car rental booth and I handed them my membership card with all the pertinent information, so I didn't need to talk to the girl.

I was disappointed at Sal's response. "Sorry, Ton. It's audit week. Can't help you out."

Shit. "Any suggestions?"

"Not really. The gaming inspectors are running all over the city. Oh, wait! They've already finished at the Lucky Strike. You can probably take care of it there."

I grimaced. "Not my first choice, Sal."

"It's the *only* choice right now, Tony. Unless you want to come back next week."

No. I'd already screwed this up once. If I didn't take care of it this time, I was going to be stuck with the cash. That damn cop has been watching me like a hawk. I wouldn't be able to run it through the business. Without the cash, I couldn't afford the vacation I wanted.

But truthfully, I wasn't really looking forward to going to the Lucky Strike. Leo Scapolo may be Family, but isn't a friend. He *is* high on my list of enemies. But it was necessary.

"Okay. Well, thanks anyway, Sal."

"Stop by anyway, Tony. I'll comp you a room. That much I *can* do."

"I'll take you up on that. We'll be by in a few."

"Ah. You have a guest." He chuckled. "I can guess the gender. Mixing business with pleasure, are we? I'll get you set up in a nice suite."

"Always a pleasure working with you, Sal." I hung up

and grabbed the keys that the clerk had slid across the counter with a smile.

"Where are we going? Sue asked.

"Down to the strip for the night. But then we're going to have to spend some time downtown. Is that okay?"

She shrugged and the bright scent of tangerines filled the air. "I don't care where we go. I'm along for the ride."

Once we arrived at the hotel, I suggested that we do some touring of the strip casinos since the car was already parked. Sue was suitably awe-struck staring at the lights of the strip. They're impressive even in the daytime.

We checked in. Sal greeted us warmly and then personally delivered my case to the safe for the night. I didn't worry about it. Las Vegas casinos have some of the tightest security in the world. If a hotel ever got a reputation for valuables disappearing, it would go out of business in a heartbeat.

The lobby had been all muted light and quiet conversation. But I was completely unprepared for the assault on my senses when we walked through the doors of the casino.

I'd been in crowds since the change. I'd even been in bars with live music. But the high pitched tones of the bells and buzzers that only a year ago were a pleasant background became a frenzied cacophony that gave me a splitting headache almost immediately. I also hadn't planned on the variety of extreme emotions that put my nose on overload. Joy. Fury. Grief. They were all too intense and each one was penetrating and thick as liquid hanging in the air. For a moment my heart raced and I couldn't breathe. I couldn't think; couldn't move. I needed to leave. I wanted to run from away the emotional bedlam. Sue watched me with near panic on her face. Her eyes darted this way and that, trying to find the source of my discomfort but it wasn't from one source.

I fought back into control and slowed the pounding of my heart. I stood quietly and took deep careful breaths. I let the smells pass by me and didn't fight to sort or categorize them. That was the trouble. I was trying to identify everything and I couldn't. The sounds were still too loud so I reached in my pocket and stuffed in a pair of earplugs. Better. Much better. The high end of the noise muted. The din faded and I could think again. I gave Sue a shaky smile but she continued to watch me like a dog watches a nervous master.

We walked around but didn't play much. The headache was still right behind my eyes. My nerves were starting to get edgy the more places we went and Sue was beginning to notice.

"You feel tense," she said. I *feel* tense? That was a strange way to phrase it but I couldn't disagree.

"Let's get out in the sun for awhile. Maybe that'll help. I thought we'd go see Hoover Dam," I said, when she finally turned back around.

"That would be fun," she said and we headed for the parking garage. Once outside, I could remove the earplugs. The further we got from the center of the Strip, the easier it was to relax. The dam is a ways out of town. We started to talk again about whatever struck our minds. Movies, into politics, and then religion. Our views were more alike than not, but there were some significant differences. We disagreed on the ethics and legality of photo radar that the cops are using now, since we saw one parked on the side of the road on the way out of town. I generally travel the speed limit so it's not an issue, but I think that the inability to confront your accuser violates certain personal rights.

Sue believed that the deterrent is the visibility to *other* drivers of the pulled over car. Hence the bright, multi-colored lights that can be seen for miles.

"So you think that the flashing lights aren't just about safety and visibility for the stopped car, but for the sheer spectacle to others?"

"Exactly." she replied with a burst of citrus and clove scent. "So the photo van's strobe is the same deterrent, or even better. People always "resume illegal speed" when a parked police car doesn't follow, but with photo radar, you aren't sure whether you got hit until you get the ticket in the mail. They stay slow because they're nervous."

I thought about it and then waggled my head slightly.

"Sorry, not good enough. That may be the rationale they try to push, but the whole concept still reeks of constitutional violations on a number of fronts. It's just revenue enhancement to me." I said with a shake of my head.

A smile played across my face as the beginnings of burnt metal frustration drifted to me. A glance told me I was right. Her jaw had set slightly and her arms were crossed tight.

When she noted my smile, she rolled her eyes and tangerines replaced her frustration. She laughed and I soon followed. We agreed to disagree, since both viewpoints had merit. She proved that she had a mind, and was willing to stretch it, which is real important to me. Debates, as long as they don't degrade into personal attacks, are a lot of fun.

We had to wait for a few minutes for the first tour to start. It occurred to both of us that we had forgotten to eat lunch. We had only gotten a snack on the plane. No matter. After the lecture, we'd go back into town. I've been on the tour several times. It was as informative and interesting as always. Sue was fascinated by the tunnels under the dam, and asked some real intelligent questions about the construction. Like I said, she's got a mind.

It was nearly sunset when we arrived back at the strip and Sue got to see the full spectacle of daylight at night. When the moon rose through the warm desert air, I could feel the pull of it, but it was only a tease. A few times, though, I found myself standing motionless, staring at the sky. Sue touched my arm and warm tingles flowed through me. God, that sensation was addicting.

We spent the night wallowing in each other's bodies. I couldn't get enough of the taste of her, the scent of rich soil and growing things—the feel of magic as it flowed between us. The sound of her cries as I brought her to climax over and over took my breath away.

But even so, the next morning I woke really early, tense and fidgety. I had planned on this being a nice relaxing trip.

Visiting Leo's place would keep me watching my back for the rest of the visit.

"Are you okay?" asked Sue as she stepped out of the bathroom from her morning routine. I'd given her first shot. Her scent changed to the sharp, tangy scent of worry.

I grabbed my travel case and headed in to shower and brush my teeth. "I just need to get my business taken care of. I didn't mean to ruin your mood."

She shrugged and smiled. "Then let's get your delivery made so we can go back to having fun. I returned the smile.

It was only about 6:00 a.m. when we drove downtown and parked in the Lucky Strike's lot. Downtown isn't as brazenly flashy as the strip but there's still plenty of lights and activity. The cowgirl and cowboy neon signs are still there and the old Union Plaza still has the huge canopy of lights with the train in the background.

I thought seriously about putting the earplugs back in. But no, they'd be viewed as a sign of weakness by Leo. I needed to be on top of my game to see him. I knew he'd be awake and already working. He only sleeps a couple of hours a night and sometimes not at all. He calls people who sleep a full eight hours "wusses." I only sleep about six myself, so I partially agree.

I took a deep breath and braced myself but my head was pounding by the time we walked up to the desk. The briefcase was once again attached to my wrist.

The clerk was a kid. Lately everyone seems like a kid. Thirty-seven years into life and I'm already feeling old. I took an instant dislike to him. I had to fight not to growl. He smelled like blood and death and worse things. It didn't fit with the boyish face.

"Could you ask Leo to come to the desk? I need to speak to him." I used my best polite voice. Sugar might be better than vinegar. We'd see.

His back went up immediately. The smell of black coffee and dry heat rose from him in a cloud. Pissed him off, I did. Touchy little shit.

"The General Manager is very busy right now. I can't interrupt him."

That was bull and I knew it. No business is more important to Leo than money. I was in no mood to have a snot-nosed kid tell me whether or not I could see him.

"Sue, wait here. His office still in the same place?" I glanced at the clerk as I headed for the hallway next to the front desk.

The clerk moved to step in front of me. "You can't go back there, sir. It's for employees only."

I started to push him to the side when Sue touched my arm. "Tony, please," she said. "Let's just go somewhere else. It's not a big deal."

I would have loved to comply. But I turned to her and put a finger to her lips. "It's okay. I don't plan to make a scene." I turned and scanned the room and my eyes fell upon a tall black man that I knew. He wore a white shirt with a name badge. I smiled.

I walked toward him. "Bobby," I said jovially. He turned and when his eyes focused on me his dark face lit up with a smile. It was brilliantly white against his dark skin. Bobby is from somewhere in South Africa. His skin is almost a blue black. He smelled of expensive cologne, Chapstick, and old cigarette smoke—not his. But as for his underlying smell, the cologne overpowered any sense of it. His hand shot out and I shook it. He still had a grip like a full-grown bear, but this time I was able to give as good as I got.

His eyes flickered oddly for a second when we shook, but it passed quickly. I guess I surprised him.

"Hey, there, you old reprobate!" he said heartily, "How you doin', man? You've been working out! What are you going by now-a-days?"

"Still Tony. Life's so-so right now," I fingered the white shirt. "Pit Boss? Getting up in the world."

He pursed his lips and shrugged. "It's more trouble than it's worth most days. But the money's good."

The smile dropped off my face. "I need to see Leo."

Bobby's smile also faded and took on a look that was similar to my own. Blank, expressionless.

"You sure that's a good idea?" His face showed a level of discomfort that I couldn't smell.

"It's business. I've got no choice."

He turned and walked back toward the desk with me. "There are always choices in life, Tony. Always." I could tell he believed it.

"Obligations frequently overpower choices, Bobbo. You above all people know that."

He stopped and glanced at me. He licked his lips, a quick flash of pink on his dark skin. A cloud passed over his face and pain slid through his eyes. Bobby and I had a history that involved some pretty nasty things done in the name of obligation. Maybe I had lied to Sue when I said I had never been used. He nodded briefly.

The clerk smelled surprised as Bobby walked toward the desk. "It's okay, Ben," he said on his way down the hall. "Leo will want to see these folks." The clerk shot me a dark look. His anger hit me like a hot breeze. I blew him a kiss.

Sue smelled nervous, so I took her hand and pressed it to my lips. "Just let me lead," I instructed her.

Bobby came out of a door down the hall and a second man followed. Leo Scapolo is a big man. Most of it is muscle but a little has turned to fat around the waist. A lot of people mistake him for Jewish because of his dark curly hair. Over the years, the hair has become just a fringe around a bald pate. He has a big nose and small nearly black button eyes. They're always shifting, always thinking. Always dangerous.

As he approached the counter I got a whiff of him. Not surprisingly, Leo smells like someone else's pain. It was a wet thick smell that oozed out of his pores. He smelled of lies and hate and menace. He reeked of dead things, like raw meat that's sat out for too long. One particular odor made me look at him sharply. He smelled of fur. Fur like mine. It made me want to growl. Sue could feel the tension between us. Her fingers trembled on my arm.

Bobby's tongue flicked out over his upper lip again. He looked a little nervous too.

The smile that was on Leo's face was for show only. It never reached his eyes. He stared at me with a dangerous look that made me think somehow he knew who I was—*what* I was.

"Tony, good to see you." Yeah, right. And I believe in the tooth fairy.

"Leo," I said with a false smile of my own. "How's business?"

"Good, good," he said, nodding. His voice warmed a notch for a flickering moment. "How's your dad?"

That question was actually an honest one. They really did like each other. "Dad's doing well. He's retired now. Living the life down in Florida. Whiling away the hours playing boccie and canasta."

"He always was a sucker for a good boccie game." Leo's laugh was deep and genuine. He sobered so suddenly it was like someone hit pause on a video. "What can I do for you?"

I raised the briefcase slightly and it caught his eye. "I've got some business with you."

He stared at me menacingly for long seconds. I didn't flinch. Sue looked back and forth from me to Leo. She nibbled her lips nervously. Without a word, he turned and walked down the hallway. I started to follow when she grabbed my arm in a panic.

"I've got a bad feeling about this, Tony."

I touched her arm lightly and winked. "Don't worry. Everything's fine. Why don't you wait for me in the restaurant? Order me a beer and a steak. Rare. I'll meet you in a couple of minutes. Bobby, would you show her the way?"

Bobby nodded and moved to stand next to Sue. "Okay," she said hesitantly but followed Bobby. She looked back to me more than once.

Leo was standing at the door of his office waiting. I followed. He opened a door at the end of the hall. A placard on the door read, 'Private—No Admittance'. Leo's inner sanctum.

I entered the room, scanned for bodyguards and cameras

and then closed the door behind me. He was a confident little asshole. Nobody was in sight. I listed for a moment with my wolf hearing but I didn't hear any mechanical sounds other than the slight hiss from the blower. I shifted my leg and felt the ankle holster press into my skin. Good enough.

He went behind a carved oak desk and sat down on a black leather executive-style chair.

"Well, well," he said snidely after he was seated. "Tony the Nose. You realize that I'm only seeing you out of deference to your dad."

I reached into my pocket and withdrew the key to the cuff. "Yeah, I know. It's the only reason that I'd set eyes on your ugly puss too."

All hints of the polite smile were erased. "What do you want, *sazee*?"

Huh? Must be new slang for something really bad. Leo wouldn't address me with anything less. "I've got business. You want it or should I go elsewhere?"

I opened the case and turned it to show him the neatly stacked bills.

"How much?" he asked.

"A million. What's the house cut?"

He pursed his lips and I could see his beady eyes sparkle. "Ten percent."

My eyebrows shot to the roof and I snorted. I closed the case again with a shake of my head. "You've got to be kidding. Fuck this. I *will* go somewhere else." Audit or no, someone else in town had to be doing business.

I closed the case, set the locks, and was just about to snap the cuff around my wrist. He tapped all of the fingers of his left hand on the desk. It sounded like a muted woodpecker. Finally, he spoke.

"Fine. Five percent. Plus an hour with your lady."

Whoa! Where the hell did that come from? I didn't think he'd even glanced Sue's way.

"The hell you say!" The cuff snapped closed. I wanted to reach across the desk and rip out his throat. But I didn't. Say 'thanks', Dad.

"No dice. You don't want my money? Fine. But you even *talk* to my lady and you'll be breathing out of a new hole in your skull."

He quavered his hands in front of me. "Ooo! I'm so scared." He wasn't. His eyes were cold and dead.

His mistake. He should be.

I flipped him a one-finger salute and pocketed the key. He exhaled a sharp breath and I could hear him counting slowly under his breath. I walked toward the door. The knob was in my hand when he said with annoyed acceptance, "Six percent. It's the best offer you'll get in town."

I stopped where I was and thought about it. Yeah, six percent was at least equal to what I'd get elsewhere and it'd make me points with Dad. God, the things I do for family. I turned to face the piece of scum.

"Done." I repeated the performance of unsnapping the cuff and handed him the case. "I'd like a receipt."

"Don't trust me?" he asked with a sneer. The sharp, unpleasant smell of his hate oozed through my brain.

"Not as far as I can throw you and I can't even pick you up."

He wrote a house receipt for the cash and accepted the case. He told me what table to be at and who the dealer would be.

I was surprised that he never mentioned that he could smell my fur like I could his. But then again, I didn't mention it to him. Maybe that's the way it works. But I learned I could smell others like me. Or, maybe I'm nuts.

I left Leo's office with the receipt and no case. I had some cash to get coins and the table would be set up for me soon. So I joined Sue in the restaurant. I raised my eyebrows as I saw her digging into a half-eaten rare steak. Another rested on a plate across from her.

"I thought you like your steaks well done."

She raised her eyes to me in confusion. "I do. Why?"

I motioned to her plate. She looked at the piece on her fork as though she had seen it for the first time. Horror filled her eyes and she set the utensil down shakily. "That's weird."

I shrugged my shoulders. "Ask the waitress to send it back."

"But it's half eaten!"

"So? It's none of their business. You're not asking for a new one."

I was almost done with my steak when hers returned. But she had a hard time eating the thoroughly cooked slice of meat. I got the distinct impression that she preferred it rare. The wolf inside me was pleased but I didn't say anything.

We went downstairs and while she was looking at the quarter slots I set her up on a machine.

I called to her and she sat where I directed. She looked up at me as I started to leave. "Aren't you staying?"

"I'm going to go play the tables for a bit. Gambling is kind of a solitary activity. You won't be real social when you get involved in the machine in front of you."

"Okay," she said with a shrug, "If you say so. Where will you be?"

I directed her attention to the blackjack table at the edge of the pit. "See the table with the red-headed woman dealer? That's where I'll be. If you run out of money or want to leave, just come get me." I pressed the button to start her reels spinning for the first time. A single cherry came up and she won two credits.

"Ooh, look! I already won! This is fun!" She pressed the button again but nothing hit. She was engrossed but twenty credits down by the time I left.

I knew the dealer at my table. A single chair was open and waiting when I arrived. Marge smiled at me and I smiled back. "Good to see you again, Mr. Giodone," she said softly, as she removed the small placard labeled 'Reserved' from the spot in front of my seat.

Marge smells nice. Sweet and soft, like a fluffy blanket just out of the dryer. She's sort of the 'Mom' on the floor. She's older than she looks and smells. Meaner too.

"New hairdo?"

She smiled and smelled warm and fuzzy. "Nice of you to notice. Are you in for this hand?" I nodded.

An hour later, I was ten thousand up and going strong but I needed a break. The table had attracted a crowd while I played and there were groans from the group when I stood and stretched. "I'm going to take a break, Marge. Cash me out."

She handed me a tray and I stacked the multi-colored, paper wrapped tokens in it. I glanced toward where Sue had been playing and she was still sitting at the same machine. When I came up behind her, she started in surprise. "You scared me," she said with a giggle.

I looked at the display. It read 407. Not bad. Two hundred up from when I left her.

"You're doing well." I nodded in approval.

"Okay, I guess." She smelled a little disappointed. "I was higher earlier. It'd be more fun if it was *big* money." I looked at her and my brow furrowed. She didn't consider this big money? Then I realized what the confusion was and I smiled.

"Sue, what's 500 multiplied by two?"

She looked at me and shrugged. "A thousand. Why?"

"Then 200 times five is the same?"

"Duh," was her reply. "So?"

I pointed toward the number on the face of the machine. "Then I guess that you've won about a thousand dollars, huh?"

The look on her face was worth the wait. I didn't need a smell to know her thoughts. She looked again at the front of the machine and then to the machines to the side of her. "This is a *nickel* machine, right?"

I shook my head. "A five dollar machine." There was no dollar sign in front of the large number on the face of the machine. She had thought she was playing nickels.

"Five dollars a pull!?" She looked at the display once more. "Oh, my God! I won a thousand dollars! Aahh!"

I chuckled as she exploded into laughter. Her happiness gave way to delight and citrus burst into my nose. She leapt up and hugged me hard enough that I almost dropped the tray in my hands. The tingles were even headier from her excitement. I had to smile. All of her millions and she's still enthused by this small win. She stood in front of the machine just looking at it, not sure what to do next.

"Do you want to cash out?" I asked. "I thought about taking a break."

She looked at the machine again. "I don't know how." She appealed to me with glittering but confused eyes and I grinned. I reached across her and pressed the 'Cash/Credit' button. The machine began to ding wildly as the oversized, copper-colored coins exited into the tray noisily. I winced slightly. The headache was back.

We took a break and walked around the casino watching the other players. We stood back from the gaming tables while I explained each game in a whisper so we wouldn't distract the participants.

"Are you going to play again?" she asked, after she thought she understood how the games worked.

Well, I sort of have to. I didn't want to be here for days to "win" back my money. "I had planned to. Want to watch?"

She nodded eagerly and she started to pull out a stool at the table where we stood. I shook my head and steered her back toward Marge's table.

Sue leaned in to me and whispered, "Why this table?"

I shrugged. "I was winning here. Call me superstitious." She mused about that for a moment and then smiled. She believed me.

"Are you both in?" asked Marge with a calm face. Her question actually was, "Are you both supposed to win here?" I thought about it for a second. It would look better overall for both of us to win but I didn't want Sue to get sucked into this too far. She's a bright girl. I figured she'd understand the concept and why I needed to launder the money, but I didn't think she'd want to be involved in the process.

Money laundering is a necessary part of my business. Large amounts of cash are hard to account for, even with a couple of businesses to run it through. Capone and Gotti never got busted for murder or racketeering. They got hammered on tax evasion. So I dutifully pay my taxes even if I have to break secondary laws to do it. But the less people involved in deals like this the better. I don't know how the casino works it into their books. Nor do I care.

I shook my head. "Just me." Sue looked at me in dismay. "Oohh," she said with a pout. I probably should have let her in on the plan, but it was too late now.

I lifted her hand to my mouth and kissing it gently. "You're my good luck charm. I don't want to play against you and risk losing."

She smiled. "Flatterer." Cookie spice and citrus licked at my nose. She tucked an arm through mine.

I anted and the game began. Sue watched the game and the people as well. She tried to whisper things to me but it was sort of distracting. Even when the odds are stacked to win, I still have to pay attention to the game. I put a finger to my lips and she shushed. I could tell that she wanted to play. After about an hour she started to get bored. She shifted in her seat constantly and kept looking around her.

"Can I go play the machines again?" Frustration edged her voice.

I nodded. "Don't go far. I don't want to have to track you down later. Try playing the keno machines. I think you'll like them." She nodded happily and wandered off toward the slots again.

Another hour passed and I looked up from my game and stretched. Marge took a sip of water from a glass, which was my cue to lose the next hand. Can't win every hand. It would be noticed. But I was already thirty thousand ahead. The crowd around the table was sizable. I glanced around the room to find where Sue was sitting. She should be very visible considering she was wearing bright yellow. I didn't see her. Oh, well.

There was a smattering of annoyed sounds from the crowd when I lost the hand and Marge gathered the chips from the table. I jumped slightly when a heavy hand landed on my shoulder. What now?

"We need to talk, Giodone," Bobby's voice hissed in my ear. "You've got trouble."

I glanced at Marge without giving any reaction to Bobby's warning. I stood up smoothly.

"I've got a call, Marge. Hold my chair." She nodded and raised one finger. A guard moved over to her side. She whispered to him and he sat in my place to keep the crowd honest. Another grey suit widened his coverage of the area in response.

I moved away with Bobby and said in a low voice, "What's up?"

"Like I said, you've got trouble." His voice was still low and strained. I couldn't catch his scent to see if he was lying or if he was worried. He *looked* worried. He kept scanning around us and checking the mirrors on the walls to make sure that we weren't followed.

When we reached a semi-private spot—not that there are many in a casino—I stopped him. "I'm not going any further until you tell me what's going on."

He crossed his arms over his chest and stared at me with angry eyes. "Does the name Jeffrey Prezza ring a bell?"

Ah, shit! "You heard about that, huh?"

"Hell, Tony! *Everybody's* heard about that. Well, anyone who matters. Anyway, I just overheard a conversation. Leo's setting you up. He called Vito Prezza and a couple of his boys are on their way over to collect you. That's why you haven't been winning so fast this time. They're stalling you. You need to get out of here."

Yeah. I did. But I started to wonder who was setting up *who*. Was I going to run right into their arms if I went with Bobby?

"Why would you care?" I asked with narrowed eyes. My instinct told me not to trust anyone I couldn't smell. I'd worked with Bobby before, so I knew he was capable of a double-cross.

He let out an exasperated noise. "Christ, Tony. I'm the good guy here. I still owe you my life from Panama. Other than that, you're right. I don't care. Granted it took a big pair of *cajones* to off the kid right at the precinct steps, but it was pretty stupid, too."

He was right about Panama. That had been another really bad week. "Okay, let's say I believe you. How long do I have?"

"Not long. Leo's getting ready to leave for a meeting so that he's not here when it goes down. I know a back way out. But you'll have to get your lady and get moving."

"Not before I get my money back, Bobby. Leo's got a case full of it."

"Leave the money, Tony. Let it go. I'll get it for you if I can, but you need to high-tail it out of here right now."

I saw Bobby's face harden as he looked over my shoulder. I turned to see one of Vito's goons walking toward the table where I used to be. Shit! How long ago did Leo call them? How could they be here already?

I was trying to figure out how to find Sue when she found us. The hallway where we stood wasn't on the way to anywhere. It couldn't been easily seen. But that damn wolf intuition told me it was how it was supposed to work.

"What are you doing here?" asked Bobby with a startled look.

She shrugged her shoulders and a confused blend of scents rose from her. "I don't really know. I just got the feeling that I should come over this direction, so I cleared out my machine. But here you are! Wasn't that lucky?"

Yeah. Lucky. That weird, eerie sort of lucky.

"We have to go." I grabbed her hand and started to lead her in the direction that Bobby and I had started.

She pulled her hand back and soured milk disbelief burst from her skin. "But we just got here! Where are we going?"

Good question. I turned my attention to Bobby. "Where *are* we going?"

"The garage. Let's go! Now!"

I followed without a word pulling Sue along behind me by the hand. When we reached a doorway near the end of a hall, Bobby used his keys to open it. Inside was a stairwell that was narrow and steep. This wasn't for the public to use. That was obvious.

"What's going on, Tony? I don't want to go down there." Her fear was back and it struck me in the face like a brick.

I had to tell her. I hoped she could handle it. "Look, Sue. There are some men back there that are looking for me. If they catch me, I'm toast. We have to leave. You have to trust me."

Her breathing stilled and her voice was quiet. Her scent was a rising anger that caramelized the tiny room. "Are the police after you?"

I snorted as Bobby darted down the stairs to try to find a vehicle for us. "I wish! No, I won't have to worry about the police if *these* guys catch me. And they've seen me with you. You can't afford to stay, either." I stared at her long and hard. "What's it going to be, Sue? What am I worth to you?"

Her jaw set as she made her decision. "Let's go. But what about our stuff?"

"Leave it. We'll buy new." I turned and headed down the stairway with Sue at my heels. I quickly pulled away from her so I could get to Bobby to help him find a car. I bounded down two flights of stairs at a good clip. I was halfway across the garage level when I heard a commotion behind me. I turned to see that a doorway had opened on the next landing up and the kid from the desk had emerged behind Sue. He grabbed at her and was trying to cover her mouth with a cloth. She pulled away and swung her denim purse at him. It hit the side of his face with a thud and staggered him. Good purse. I started toward them with a burst of supernatural speed.

He quickly grabbed her arm and ripped the purse from it. It dropped to the stairway like lead. She screamed once as he pulled her through a doorway, the cloth once again over her face. I felt fuzz try to cover my brain and I stumbled against the wall for a moment. What the hell? I shook my head and blinked a few times as the door latched behind them.

Bobby only caught a glimpse of me as I growled and headed back upstairs.

Chapter 14

I opened the door where the kid had gone. I dropped to the ground and sniffed. Bingo! Dead things in a summer forest. Something inside me went berserk. It ripped away the last shreds of haze clouding my mind. Bobby had reached me and tried to slow me down. He grabbed my arm with a grip of iron. I knew in that instant that he was like me, like Leo, but I didn't have time to dwell on it. I moved through the door with supernatural speed. I heard the sleeve of my silk shirt rip with a wet sucking sound. I left Bobby holding a swatch of cloth.

I followed the trail of Sue's scent, nose up, nostrils flared. Her fragrance hung in the musty hallway like mist, laced heavily with ammonia panic and the chemical scent of whatever drug the kid had used. I could feel something building inside of me as I tracked her down. Something dangerous. When I heard her first moan I re-doubled my speed and found the shaft of dim yellow light from the doorway at the end of the third hallway. I smelled gun oil and the kid's confidence. I smelled Sue.

He stood inside the small room with gun aimed at the door. He held a semi-auto 9mm in a comfortable knowledgeable grip. So young, so self-assured. So stupid. A single, bare bulb hung from the ceiling of the grey concrete chamber. The room had the scent of multiple deaths. Too many to sort. Some had been quick, some slow and tortured. The scent hung like a pall and made the room seem small and close.

Sue was in and out of consciousness, crumpled on the floor in the corner. She hadn't gotten a full dose of whatever the drug had been and was trying to shake it off.

I smelled Ben's pride at catching Sue; his lust, sweat and then his terror as he saw me race toward him. He moved quickly, tried to get a shot off but I leapt at him before he could fire. I ripped the gun away from him. It skittered across the floor to disappear into the shadows. New muscles flexed and I felt him raise off the floor. My fingers convulsed around his neck. He flailed at me with fists and got me with a kick between the legs that would have dropped me to the floor a year ago. I hardly felt it.

I casually held him before me by the throat for a moment. I tightened my hand until I could feel the elastic skin start to give. He clawed at my fist, gasping for air. While I held him I saw his thoughts. Heard his conversation with Leo where they nonchalantly decided how to torture Sue once Vito's boys had taken me. Decided what acts would hurt me the most. I was supposed to die but not until after I knew what they'd done to her.

It didn't win him any points. I might have only hurt him. Not now. With one violent movement I snapped his neck. Sue didn't see what I had done. But I felt her tolerance of my act as well as a dark pleasure that surprised and frightened her. I saw the light in his eyes go out with a final surprised look. It pleased me.

"Jesus!" exclaimed Bobby from the doorway. He was breathing hard and stared with open horror at the scene. I held Ben's limp weight with one hand. His legs dangled above the floor. I turned and looked at Bobby. My lips were pulled back from my teeth and a nasty snarl erupted from me.

My stomach growled angrily and I battled the hunger again. What the hell was wrong with me? The moon was long gone. Why did I have the urge to rip out his throat?

Bobby swallowed hard but didn't back up. I had to give him credit.

"What the fuck *are* you, Tony? Ben was one of the best I've ever known."

My eyes flashed blue. "Better than me?"

He paused and considered. "Better than you *used* to be. What's happened to you? You're scaring the shit out of me here." He looked scared but didn't smell scared. In fact, he didn't smell at all, which was still confusing.

I dropped the kid to the floor with a thud. I turned and got a flash from Bobby as I brushed by him on my way out the door with Sue in my arms. I figured that he would be worried about Leo's wrath when he came back and found his plan ruined, whether or not Leo thought that Bobby helped. But that wasn't it. I sensed something else instead. A strength that was new to me. He wasn't afraid of Leo. He was higher somehow, more dominant. Dark images. Anger. Bobby had plans but they now must be changed. That was the worry. Everything was spoiled. Because of me.

"We've got to get you out of here," said Bobby, the anger rising into his voice. "Before they find us."

"I *want* Leo, Bobby." I had plans for him. I wasn't going to run anymore.

He was suddenly in front of me. His determination bit at my nose. His eyes were cold and hard. He stood right in my face. "No! That's not your decision."

I growled but he didn't back down. He sighed in frustration. "Look, Tony. I know he's got it coming. But there's shit going on that *you* don't know about. Don't get involved in this mess. Just take your lady and go. I'm serious here. Just go."

Sue was coming around. She rose to her hands and knees and shook her head.

"No! I want my money and I want Leo's head. He was going to hurt my lady!"

"I told you before. Walk away from the money, Ton," he said quietly. "I'll get it back to you if I can. But you've got to trust me on this. I'll clean up this *mess* you've left as best I can. Don't start a war you can't win. Let us take care of Leo. I promise you that he'll pay for this. I swear to you, man. My word."

I stared at him. There was something that Bobby was withholding. But then I looked at Leo's protégée lying at wrong angles on the floor, his eyes still open and startled. I sighed and Bobby took a deep shaky breath.

"Get us out of here in one piece and we'll call it square. But if you don't do him I *will* come back."

He nodded curtly. "I owe you nothing as of now. Right?"

I returned the nod.

"The only vehicle I could find is Leo's private limo. I took care of the driver. It's running. I was going to drive you, but now I've got to clean this up. Do me a favor and find another car before you get out of the city. I don't want to give him any reason to chase you."

I nodded. Sue could stand on her own. She shook her head again and blinked her eyes.

"What happened?"

"Let's get going. I'll explain on the way."

Chapter 15

I picked up Sue's purse at a run. Jeez! The thing must weigh twenty pounds! I handed it to her and she slung it over her shoulder with considerable effort as we flew down the stairs to the waiting car. I put on the chauffeur's cap and sunglasses that were lying on the dashboard. I couldn't hide the torn sleeve on my right arm. I had to hope that the guard wouldn't notice. Sue ducked down in the back. I put a finger to my cap as the gate raised, kept my arm tight to my body and smiled. The attendant did the same. The dark windows hid Sue's form in the back. Boy, would he hear about it for letting me out!

"It was nice of Bobby to give you back your case." Sue said after a few minutes. I glanced into the back in surprise, almost hitting another car in the next lane.

"He did?" Sue held up the case and damned if it didn't look like mine.

"See if you can open it up for me, will ya? The combination is 2192." I heard metallic clicking as she moved the dials and a snap as the latches opened.

"Is it all there?" I asked.

"I guess I don't know what *all* is," she replied.

"There should be about a million dollars in there. It's mostly twenties and hundreds."

Her scent from the back seat was surprise and disbelief. "No. There's no money here. It's all just documents and maps." I heard rustling paper.

I was getting annoyed that I kept hitting green lights. There was nowhere to park but I couldn't afford to anyway. I needed to ditch this car quick. I headed toward the suburbs to try to pick up a car from a grocery store lot. I really hate stealing cars. It's beneath me. And the second time in a month! Poor planning like this is a serious blow to my pride.

"There's a blueprint of a house and a bunch of things about some guy named Carmine Leone."

"What?" I turned my head again but snapped it forward when a horn blared beside me. I reached out my right hand. "Give me that blueprint."

"You can't look at it while you're driving!" Her voice matched the shock of soured milk.

"Just do it, Sue. This could be important."

She handed me the blueprint and I glanced at it while I drove. It didn't take much concentration. I knew the design immediately. It was the schematic of Carmine's house, all right, down to the security system. I had helped design it. What the hell was Leo doing with it? And why was it in my case?

The sound of screeching tires returned me to the car. I glanced in the rearview and found a black sedan quickly pulling up on our tail. Damn! There's nothing as conspicuous as a black limo in this town. They're *meant* to be noticed. I hit the gas hard and winced a bit as I heard Sue get thrown onto the floor from the force.

"Ow." She moved her head from side to side and I heard the joints crack back into place.

No time for sympathy right now. "Put everything back in that case and lock it up!" I ordered. "I need to look at everything in it. And see if there's any other paperwork back there, too."

"We can't take this!" Her anger bit at my nose. I'm getting really sick of the smell of burnt coffee. But at this point, I didn't care if she was angry or not.

"It's my case, Sue. There's got to be a reason why *my* case with *my* fingerprints all over it is holding documents showing how to break into *my* boss's house. Doesn't that seem a little suspicious to you?"

Her eyes widened in the mirror and she looked down at the papers in her hand. "Do you mean this Leo person is trying to frame you for something?"

"Looks that way. But I won't know *what* until I look everything over."

The anger scent slowly dissolved, to be replaced by thoughtful confusion. I glanced back at her in the rearview. She slipped inside herself. I didn't go with her. I was too busy weaving through traffic. I ducked through a cold red light before the oncoming traffic made it past the crosswalk. That did it! The black sedan did a nosedive as the brakes locked up to avoid getting creamed. I turned a wide corner and then pulled into the nearest alley. I just about had to hit the car on the other side of the street to make the turn. The doors barely opened far enough to exit in the narrow space between dumpsters. I removed the key and bent it in two. Then I tossed it on the seat. Like Bobby said, no reasons to follow. Leo probably has another key somewhere. I took the case from Sue's grasp and tugged her hand. She had a death grip on her purse with her other.

"Let's go!"

Her voice had a thoughtful edge and she stubbornly held her ground. "Why does Leo hate you enough to do all this?"

We didn't have time for this! I could hear squealing tires not too far away. "If I promise to tell you later will you get a move on?"

She nodded and we took off at a run.

We entered the next block and found ourselves in the middle of a group of elderly tourists. We tried to get around them, but they wouldn't be hurried. We tried to turn around to find another group of gamblers filling in behind. The casino in front of us was likewise packed with people. We were stopped cold. I looked back down the alley. With the limo in the way and the key useless, the pair of thugs had to struggle to get around to reach us. We had only a few seconds of respite. I sneezed suddenly as multiple scents assaulted my nose from the crowd. The primary scent was pineapple. God only knows why. I sneezed a second time and tried to edge us through the group.

"Slow down and enjoy the day, you two!" said a smiling woman with a cane and a bright pink sun visor that read, "Born to Gamble!" over thinning silver hair.

"Oh, look, Leonard!" said another elderly lady. "Let's take the shuttle." I glanced at the goons again. One of them was crawling over the roof. I turned at the old woman's words. Perfect! No grand theft auto for us today!

We waited in the crowd as the bus slowed and then stopped. When the bus door opened with a hiss, I noted that another one was just about to depart across the street. That's the one! It was heading in the direction I wanted to go. I grabbed at Sue's hand and pointed. She took another look behind at the commotion from Vito's boys. Her eyes got wide and we darted across the street. The bus was just pulling away from the curb and I had to rush to bang on the door with the briefcase. It stopped with a lurch and the doors opened. Fortunately, they hadn't gotten back into traffic yet. Sue was breathing hard as we stepped up the stairs. I was reaching for my wallet, hoping I had a couple of singles when Sue produced a bus pass from her bag. She handed to the driver with a flourish.

I glanced at her in surprise. She shrugged. "They were for sale in the casino store. I thought it would be easier to get around."

I grabbed her face with both hands and planted a kiss on her lips. "Good job!" She beamed at me as the driver handed her back the card with a shake of his head at our antics.

I turned to look behind as Sue settled into a seat beside me. Her heart was still beating fast and I realized that the pineapple scent was coming from her. I don't know that particular emotion yet. Or maybe it was the drugs. I looked at her closely. The edges of her nostrils were red and she was squinting a little.

"You doing okay? I don't know what the kid gave you. You look a little rough."

She turned to me. "I'm fine. I didn't get much more than a whiff," she replied. "I've got a little headache, but it'll be gone soon." I couldn't detect any pepper. Just pineapples.

The two men had finally reached the street and watched as our bus pulled out into traffic. One of them took off his baseball cap and threw it against the wall in frustration.

Sue was busily tucking the bus pass back into her purse.

"What the hell's in that thing?" I asked. "It weighs a ton!"

She looked sheepish. The scent of hot sand was edged with cloves. It blended with tangerine and the remaining pineapple. Fruit salad in the desert. Weird.

"I didn't have a chance to turn them all in." She reached into her bag and pulled out a large stack of oversized copper coins. I remembered her heaving it into the kid's head. I laughed—a sudden burst of sound that caused people around me to turn.

"You're a dangerous woman, Sue." My eyes sparkled with humor and pride.

It wasn't funny for long, unfortunately. I was angry with myself for going to the Lucky Strike. I'd nearly gotten Sue captured and I'd lost the whole damn million. Still, I'd replaced it with a case of dynamite. I just didn't know what the package was going to blow up.

Chapter 16

Renting a car didn't take much time. We used Sue's name for it. Leo probably wouldn't be able to trace us that way and she had more cash than I did right now. We didn't dare take a flight. Leo would already have someone posted at the airport.

By the time we reached the outskirts, Sue was finally relaxing. Ozone filled the rental from both of us as relief replaced adrenaline in our system. Hmm. Maybe pineapple is a rush of adrenaline. I'd have to do some investigating. I would have thought it would smell more bitter.

"So, are you going to tell me about Leo now?"

"Hadn't planned to." I said flatly. The question reminded me that I was still pissed at myself.

She looked at me with confusion at the strength of my statement. Her head cocked sideways a bit and she turned in her seat. The seatbelt cut into her neck.

"I want to know. Why does he loathe you enough to want to frame you?"

A burst of brittle laughter escaped me. "He isn't trying to frame me, Sue. He's trying to kill me. Whether Carmine does the job, or Vito's boys do it instead. He wants me dead."

"But *why?*"

"It's a long story." My voice went cold and empty. I stared at the road.

"It's a long drive," she replied tentatively, a small attempt at a joke to lighten the mood. When it failed, she shrugged. Emotions bled from her. Soured milk, just-burning coffee, burned metal and antifreeze. Annoyance edged her voice. Not quite anger. "If you don't want to tell me, fine. It's your business. But I think I've sort of earned the right to know."

True. More true than she knew. This wasn't over yet. I'd had a chance to look through the case while we were waiting for the rental to be brought around. I didn't know where he'd gotten them, but the papers documented a series of intended hits on Carmine's various businesses. There were names, addresses, as well as photographs and schematics. The case held payrolls for Carmine's legit businesses, along with schedules for material shipment for the under the table stuff.

The problem was, I didn't know what the hell was being planned or who was planning it. Was Leo planning a take-over of our town? Was the case intended to go to Vito—or to the unnamed person Leo was planning to meet? Or was it even more sinister? Was the case going to be delivered to *Carmine* along with photos of me walking through the casino with it? My prints were all over the outside and inside. I just didn't know. But I knew that Leo would want it back. I just had to get it to Carmine before that happened. I was hoping that someone's fingerprints, other than mine and Sue's, were still on it. It wouldn't do much good to just tell Carmine that the papers *smelled* of Leo.

Sue was sitting with her arms crossed. The nose-tickling scent of her annoyance filled the car. I sighed. I *had* promised.

My hands flexed rhythmically on the steering wheel more than once. Where could I start? I leaned back in my seat, trying to get comfortable. A little tough, given the circumstances. "Leo wanted my mom."

Sue smelled surprised, like she hadn't expected me to tell her. Hadn't expected her appeal to matter to me. It sort of annoyed me that it did.

"He wanted her bad. Rumor was that he went so far as to actually court her. She couldn't stand him. *That* was from her own mouth." I looked sideways. Sue was watching my every movement, hanging on my every word. I looked back at the road. "He was a little perverted even then. Wanted to do strange things and my mom said no. Repeatedly. At first. he'd just back off and go. But over the years he got more insistent." I never saw Mom and Leo together. She'd always send me to my room when he would show up at the door. But I wasn't deaf.

"Early on, he never went so far as to beat her or rape her but he was loud. She had to threaten to call the police more than once." Sue continued to watch me intently as I drove. She really was interested in Leo's rationale.

"When Mom hooked up with my father," I said, then interrupted myself to add a disclaimer, "Keep in mind that most of this information is third hand since I wasn't born yet." I glanced at Sue and she nodded.

"Anyway, Mom told Leo that she wasn't on the market anymore. She really went for my father and he for her. She started tapering off her clients and intended that by the time she married him, she would be a proper wife." She always phrased it that way whenever she talked about it. "A proper wife." My hands tightened on the steering wheel. Part of me is glad that I never witnessed most of this. Part of me wishes that I had been there at my present age to break Leo's skull open.

"Leo went insane when she told him that she was going to get married. Leo called my father a lot of names—then he started calling her names. Joseph—that was my father's name—got to her place just as Leo had started to slap her around. He really believed that hitting her would change her mind. Joseph jumped Leo and pulled him off. Then he punched Leo in the face. Leo threatened them both. Said they'd never reach the altar." I paused, letting the hate wash over me. "They didn't."

My fingers started to drum on the wheel as I remembered the story I was told by Jocko. He was around for the end, a teenager when it happened. "Only a couple of months after that, Joseph was killed. There was gossip that Leo had a hand in his death. Mom suspected it. She told me as much when I was about the age in the picture you saw. She could never prove it, though."

I'll always wonder if anyone tried to help her pin the murder on him. Leo's an asshole but he's got a lot of pull.

"After Joseph died and Mom started to show with me, Leo came sniffing around again. He tried to convince her that she needed a man around if she was going to be a mother. Mom told him to shove off. Said she knew he had Joseph killed. Said she hated him and would die before she would ever let him touch her." I flipped on the left blinker and switched lanes to go around a slow-moving car. Sue's eyes were focused on me. I knew that she was creating a picture in her head to go with my story.

"If the Family hadn't been at her back, I think Leo would have just killed her right there. But they were being real attentive and apologetic to her for Joseph's death. There were flowers all around the house months later from the top dogs in the Family." Mom had always been proud of that. Proud that Joseph had been respected. That's a big deal in the Family. She kept all of the cards they sent. I found them after she died.

"Leo couldn't have helped but notice. So he left her alone. But I'm a constant reminder of what he couldn't have. What he never had."

I laughed, a harsh sound in the closed car. Sue flinched at the ugly sound. I heard a snarl in my voice as I continued. "And he's a constant reminder of what he deprived me of. I could have had a real family if not for him, instead of a whore with a broken heart for a mom and no father. It was only luck that I ended up with a dad. It's the only reason that I've never killed him outright."

Sue was silent for a moment. I could feel her discomfort, smell her concern and sympathy. "Wow. That's quite a story. I see now why you reacted like you did." Her voice continued with a note of confusion. "But is that all there is?"

I looked at her sharply. "Isn't that *enough*?"

"For you to hate *him*, sure," she said. "But for him to try to kill *you* all these years later? Just because your mom wouldn't sleep with him? That is just really out there." Her eyes blinked and a blend of confused scents muddied the air.

"People are strange, Sue. Look at Bosnia and Serbia. Those guys are fighting for things that happened *centuries* ago, between people that are long dead. This isn't nearly as strange. All I know is that the first time he saw me at Dad's house, when I was eight, he swore that he would see me dead."

Sue was open-mouthed. So was I when it happened. He had laughed at my expression and walked out. I never told Dad what he said. Leo was my battle, not his. I paused for a second, and then amended.

"But first he has to ruin me. Those were his words. *I'll ruin you, kid. Then I'll dance on your grave like I danced on Joseph's.*"

As soon as I said the words, it hit me. I knew which scenario he was planning. I shook my head angrily as the picture cleared.

Vito's boys would take me back to New Jersey and rough me up for a few days. Then Leo would hand over the case to Carmine, saying he "found it in my room." Sal would be able to back up that I'd gone to see Leo. Vito would turn me over to Carmine as a gesture of good faith. It would be Carmine who would finish the job. Like I said, *nobody* crosses him—not even me. Vito would be satisfied, Leo would be satisfied and both would have clean hands. I would be the bad guy. Torturing Sue was probably just a pleasant bonus to him. Clever. Very clever.

"I'm having a hard time even imagining that level of hate," Sue said with still-wide eyes. "I guess you're right. I've heard of things like that. I've just never encountered it first hand."

I shook the scene out of my mind. Fortunately, Leo's plan was blown out of the water now. I had the case. I was in control. Carmine would be able to do a little housecleaning—find out the leak in his organization. I was confident he would think of a suitable demise for Leo.

I just wished I could have *thanked* Leo personally for his clever plan. Hell, the whole thing had to have been on impulse. He couldn't have known I decided to go to Vegas or that I'd end up at his place. Or could he? When's the last time I checked the hotel room for bugs?

A jackrabbit hopped across the road and I blinked suddenly. I swerved to avoid it and just barely succeeded. It brought me back to myself and threw a question into my mind. Now there's a segue for you—from a nearly squished rabbit to a purse full of copper.

"By the way," I said. "Why did you fight so hard against the kid? He would have killed you just fine and you wouldn't have owed me a dime."

The question startled Sue. She stared at me open-mouthed and her jaw worked noiselessly for a moment. "I—I don't know." Her eyes darted from side to side as she tried to think through the logic.

"Why did *you* save me?" The best defense is a good offense. Fortunately, I was expecting it.

"For the money. I lost a million bucks today." I left my voice flat and looked at her with raised brows. Then I returned to looking at the road.

She studied the side of my face for a long moment. I kept it straight. No good. I heard her mind whispering doubts.

She raised her nose in the air and tried to appear haughty—baiting me. "Well, I hired *you* to do it clean and neat. I didn't know him at all. He probably would have messed it up and left me alive."

Okay, good one. A chuckle escaped me. I looked at her, with her eyes sparkling humor, and then made a quick decision. I flipped on the right blinker and pulled over to the side of the road. The tires locked and skidded slightly in the thick blown sand. The road was nearly deserted; not surprising considering the heat and the fact that it was the middle of a workday.

I unhooked my seatbelt and turned to face her. The intensity of my gaze made her suddenly nervous.

"I couldn't turn anyone over to Leo. *Especially* not you.

You've become surprisingly important to me in a real short time." Scary but true. I picked up her hand and held it in both of mine. The rush of power grew with each passing second. Sound roared in my head.

"God knows I didn't plan it. There's something between us that I don't understand. It's deep and overwhelming and scary as hell." I felt her thoughts swim by me as I touched her. Scary. But I want it; need it.

"I'll promise you something." I said.

I became very serious. Because this was serious. I released her hand and she drew it back. I didn't want to be distracted. I locked my eyes on hers and spoke to the person behind them. "I don't make promises lightly and I keep them." She sat quietly, hands in her lap, listening to my words.

"I'll keep you safe. And I'll try to keep you out of the bad parts of my life. But, Sue, it's who I am. I won't change for you. I'll shield you from the danger and from the law as much as I can. But, it may not be enough. So if you want to walk away, do it now."

I could feel the fear rise off her like heat. Yet there was something else there too. An affection, more than desire but less than love. She shook her head. Then she reached out for my hand and I let her take it.

"I've never known anyone like you, Tony. Your life scares me. I can't deny it. But *you* make me happy." She smiled more brilliantly than the sun. Warm, baking bread filled the car. "Even when I was terrified in the garage I was happy 'cause I was with you. So if I have to live in your life to have you then I'll do it."

I sighed. The snake coiled tight inside me relaxed. It was what I had hoped she'd say. Funny, I didn't realize it was what I wanted until she said it.

A semi drove by at top speed and the wash of air rocked the car. It moved me forward slightly and I kept moving on my own after it passed.

I closed my mouth over hers gently. I braced a hand on her door. A pulsing warmth passed through me along with the familiar tingles. This close, I could hear her heart beat and heard it speed up until the beat matched mine. We stayed like that for a time, mouths together, jaws still and quiet. Tongues dancing together in warm wetness. Just tasting each other. I loved the taste of her. I wanted to be near her. Wanted to drown in the scent of her.

My right arm was balanced on the top of her seat and I moved my left arm until it rested on her lap. My bare forearm and hand pressed against the skin of Sue's thighs. Nerves tingled where they touched her skin. I moved my hand slightly and caressed her skin. Her reaction was strong enough to that brief touch that I felt a frantic surging in my groin. It didn't start out to be sex but I wasn't adverse to it progressing that way. Her scent changed to the deep musk I was getting addicted to.

I eased my hand underneath her cotton shorts, then inside the second layer of silky cloth until my fingers rested against her. Her breathing increased and I felt her heart skip a beat as another semi passed by, sending us swaying. I twisted my body until I could get my right hand behind her head and bury it in her soft curls. A roll of power grew between us. It raised every hair on my body. The longing inside of me wanted to pull on it but I fought it down and concentrated on her pleasure. I thrust the silvered power back into her and felt her whole body tense as it swept through her.

My mouth locked over hers as I rubbed her slowly. Her arms were trapped between our bodies and the seatbelt kept her tight against the bucket seat. The only part of her that could move was her hips and she wriggled and squirmed under my touch. My jaw ate against her mouth in time to my hand motions. My tongue teased her as well. Slow then fast, until she could take no more.

A startled sound escaped her when she fell over the edge. I felt her body tense under mine and then go slack as she floated on a hazy cloud. I moved back from her to watch her face. Her eyes were in that half-closed position that only occurs after. Not quite sleep but not truly awake.

She laughed shakily after a moment while I feather-kissed her cheeks and lips.

"On the side of a highway in Nevada! Life is never dull with you."

I chuckled.

She never opened her eyes before she drifted to sleep.

Chapter 17

It took almost eight hours to drive to an airport big enough to have a direct flight to our town. It had been a long day at the end of a long week.

I can't sleep in a car so I was nearly dead when we arrived. I offered to let Sue stay to sleep off the trip but she wanted to get home. I thought I should probably go into the office, or stop by to see Sara, but screw it. I needed rest. However, I did try to call Carmine about the case. He wouldn't be home until the game. I told Marvin I'd see him then. It wasn't something to be discussed with an employee.

I gave Sue my home number and she gave me hers. I suggested maybe doing lunch the next day or something similar. I remember mumbling something like "See you later. Love you." I wasn't sure that I was in love with her yet but I was definitely in lust. They're different things.

The shrill ring of the phone woke me up with a start. I squinted at the clock across the room through sleep-filled eyes. It said 7:10. The bedroom curtains weren't quite closed and a shaft of fading sunlight highlighted my feet, lumpy under the covers. It wasn't even night yet. Ooh, boy. A whole two hours sleep.

I picked up the receiver on the second ring. Only a few people know the number at my house.

"'Lo?"

"Tony?!" Sue's voice was shrill and panicked. "Oh, thank God. I've got to see you! Right now! It's worse. Oh God, it's so much worse. Damn it!" I felt her anger like it was my own. All that was missing was the scent.

"Hey, hey," I said soothingly, now fully awake. "Slow down. What's the problem?"

"She's in a wheelchair, Tony. She's really gone over the top this time. There's a nurse and equipment and . . . Oh God! I just can't deal with this!"

I kicked off the covers and rolled to a sitting position. Her voice faded slightly and I knew that someone had tapped into our conversation. Probably on an extension.

"Listen carefully, Sue. Can you meet me at the place where you first saw me?" I was hoping she would take the hint to give as little information as possible.

She didn't even slow down. "Please come here. I really need to see you! Please, Tony."

I sighed. About half an hour later, I found myself driving the Mustang slowly down an older paved road. I'd at least taken the time for a shower, but I was feeling pissy. It probably wasn't the best day to meet her family. Oh, well.

I didn't recognize the address when she first gave it to me so I looked it up. 10522 Vivian Drive. It was way out in the country. I finally found the number on a brick gate post. I turned into the cutoff and found a gate. Luckily, Sue remembered that she had a security fence so I had the code. Out of habit, I glanced at the fence as I pulled up. It needed serious work. As it was, it was pretty useless for keeping people out.

I pulled up to the little box and opened my window. I entered four digits—4628. I shook my head again. A clear pattern that anyone with a lick of sense could guess.

A green light flashed and the wrought iron gates clicked open and swung haltingly inward. Hmm. Maybe a loose connection. Or they could just need oil.

Large trees blocked my view for more than a few feet as I entered the drive. Not good. When I could finally see the house I had to stop the car and stare. It was impressive enough for two stares.

The house stood slightly elevated on a hill. The graceful wrap-around front porch beckoned and the white paint gleamed in the sunlight. Jesus H. Christ! It was Tara! An exact replica of the Tara plantation from *Gone With the Wind*.

It's one of Linda's favorite movies. She loves sitting in front of that damn television with a box of tissues and a big bowl of ice cream. I can't imagine why—the battle scenes are almost laughable. I really don't get the attraction of watching something for the sole purpose of weeping uncontrollably.

I drove the Mustang around the circle drive and parked right in front. A Geo Metro painted English Racing Green was parked just in front of me. That had to be Sue's real car. It suited her.

Sue must have been waiting for me to arrive because the door opened just then and she ran out. She was crying, but from anger, not hurt or pain. Her fury caught me in the chest. It was hard to breathe past the flood. I was barely out of my car when she threw herself into my arms. I hugged her for a moment, nearly sneezing in the process from the scents that engulfed me, and then convinced her to walk with me outside. I didn't need anyone to overhear.

When we were a sufficient distance from the house and blocked by the trees, I turned to face her. "Okay, what's up?

She snuffled and wiped at her eyes with a bare arm. "It's happened again. This time it's her other hip."

I felt my brow wrinkle in amazement. "She threw herself off the balcony again?" Wow! Now that's just impressive.

"No, no. The doctor said it's because of stress. But she can't walk. What am I going to do with her, Tony? I can't take this anymore." She sounded about ready to scream. No doubt.

Uh, wait. Stress related hip failure? What a load of b.s.

"Who's in the house right now?" I crossed my arms and settled my stance, body centered and solid.

She took a deep, calming breath. When she spoke, it was a little steadier. "Mom and the nurse."

"Where'd the nurse come from?"

"Bekki. Apparently, it's okay for *Bekki* to hire a nurse." The burnt coffee bit at my nose. "Of course. *Bekki* can't afford to lose her job. *Bekki* has a family to help support; a *husband* to take care of. *I* have no reason to be running off and imposing on poor Bekki's family. I have nothing better to do and should have the *simple courtesy* to stay around."

She was trying hard not to believe the words but part of it was a lie. She *did* believe it.

I didn't comment on the discourse. "What doctor told you it was stress?"

She shrugged her shoulders, but her scent was a little confused. "Mom's doctor, of course. Where else would she get the wheelchair and the other stuff?"

Yes. Finally, the light was dawning.

"Supply houses deliver." I let her assimilate that information, open-mouthed. The emotions rode over each other until all that was left was scorched coffee.

Her eyes narrowed and her arms crossed over her chest. "That little BITCH!" she exclaimed ferociously. I like anger. It's a damn sight better than depression. Maybe it would make Sue take a leap to get out of this hell hole.

I looked in her eyes and saw the pain of all the disappointments and intentional cruelties that had been her life. Even angry, her eyes had a haunted look. But wrapped around it all was an innocence, pure and real. Sue still couldn't comprehend betrayal or pettiness. She wasn't jaded. Yet.

She deserved better than to get that way.

As much as I wanted to make the hurt go away, I wasn't ready to get in the middle of a family battle. Now that the immediate crisis was over I could work with her.

"Look, Sue, it won't do any good to confront her. She'll just deny it. Let's do something constructive and help you cool off a bit."

I led her back to my car and removed a metal clipboard. "I'm your security consultant as of now. There are some things you need to fix around here. I can't be here twenty-four/seven. It won't take long before people know we're an item."

My jaw clenched at the scent of the beginnings of fear. She'd made her choice, but the scene in the garage had shaken her a little more than she's like to let on. I tried not to notice.

"Let's just keep honest people honest and make the job a little harder for the rest, huh?"

Her eyes grew wide and slightly panicked.

"Look," I said quickly with cold fire in my voice. "Sometimes danger finds you. It sucks. But there's no reason to live in fear if we fix a few things." I reached out and touched her face with the back of my hand. "I'll keep you safe. I promised you that."

She stared into my eyes and believed the promise. I hoped I could live up to it. She nodded, determination growing through my touch. "What do we need to do?"

The first thing we did was change the passcode to the gate. Sue admitted that it had never been changed since she moved in. God knows how many people had the combination at this point. I picked a number that was uncommon. Random, without a pattern, is best. Then we walked around the perimeter of the brick wall surrounding the "plantation." The barbed wire was old and hung limply from its guides. We'd need to replace it. Next, I pointed out several trees towering overhead. Sue trailed along behind me as I made notes, nodding somewhat uselessly. I knew most of it wasn't sinking in, but the point was to get her mind off her mom.

"These will need to be trimmed. A person with a ladder could reach up, grab these branches and go right over the top of the wall."

We toured the grounds. It was obvious she was trying to make the place the showcase it had once been. The grass had been cut and aerated. Years of pine needles and leaves had been removed and new sod had been laid. She was proud of the work that she had done. I could smell it. She pointed out her room on the second floor. The window was surrounded by a cloud of multi-colored roses climbing on trellises. I'd have to take a close look at those from inside.

Next she showed me the swimming pool. She had been right about the geese. There were droppings everywhere. The large birds ignored Sue completely as we approached, but when I got closer, they milled nervously. I tried to speed up the process and barked like a dog. Except it didn't come out like I intended. I planned on it just being a funny moment. But the sound came from deep in my chest. Low and threatening and just like a wolf. Funny thing. The sound ended with a vicious snarl and I felt my lips pull back from my teeth. Sue looked at me a bit alarmed when the geese suddenly took to the air in a panic. Loud honking accompanied their flight and soon the ground was clear of unwanted visitors. A part of me wanted to go after them. Chase them down until the hunt was over. Fortunately, the moon was far enough past full that I could fight it down.

I must have looked as startled as Sue. Her voice was filled with amazement, "I felt that! How do you live every day feeling those things?"

She felt it? I tried to shrug it off. "I've gotten used to it. Fortunately, I don't like goose. Too greasy." Her eyes widened for a moment. Then I smiled. Once she realized that I was teasing her she laughed.

She hesitated when we stepped onto the wide front porch—no, more a veranda.

"What's up?" I asked.

"I'm just a little nervous. I've given you such a negative build-up of Mom that I'm afraid when you meet her you might not want to stay with me."

"I haven't exactly said I would yet, remember? But why wouldn't I?"

She struggled to find the words. "So many people believe her. I'm afraid that maybe I *am* the one who's nuts and you'll believe her instead of me. Or that you'll see her just like she is and won't want to stay with me with her around." She glanced up at me nervously and then lowered her eyes. She was embarrassed again.

I reached out to her, put a finger under her chin and raised her face. "I've spent a lifetime learning how to read people. It's a necessary skill in my trade." She opened her mouth to speak and I shushed her with a finger to her lips.

"I promise I won't judge you by what I think of her. Okay?"

She got an amazed look on her face. "Every time I think I've got you figured out, you surprise me. You have such strong opinions that it's hard for me to believe that you could sit by and keep quiet if you didn't like something."

That brought a dark smile to my face. "Well frankly, if I dislike her enough I'll probably try to scare her."

She looked alarmed. She grasped my arm frantically. "No, that won't work. If you scare her, she'll call the police. She's done it before. I don't want you to risk that."

I removed her clutching hand with a smile. "I know, Sue. It's okay. I was kidding. No scare tactics. It usually backfires. No, I'll kill her with kindness. It's one of my specialties."

She grimaced. "She'll see right through that."

I chuckled. "Doesn't matter. All she'll have are suspicions. I'll be sweet and thoughtful and very, *very* patronizing."

"And I'll do my best to keep a straight face." Sue gave me a weak smile and turned toward the door. I stopped her by touching her arm. Then I pulled her back and led her out to near the parked cars.

I made my face serious. I'd met people like Sue's mom before. "You should know that she's going to try to put a wedge between us. She'll make wild accusations. Without knowing a thing about me other than what's printed on my business card, she'll say that I'll put you in danger or that I'm just after your money. She'll tell you anything to scare you off from me. Some of it may even be true. Can you stand up to that kind of pressure? If you can't then it's better for us not to even start this. It'll only get worse if I move in."

"If?" Her voice was several notes higher as she said it. Her scent was a mixture of thick dew and tang.

I sighed. "I gotta tell you, Sue. I have a house and I like it. It might be better to just see each other on the side and not live in the same place. We'll have to see. Especially if you can't handle the pressure."

She listened and while I was speaking her jaw set. The hot metal determination nearly made me smile. She had decided and she would stick by it. "No. I want this. I'll do my best to handle it. If I can't, then we'll make other decisions."

I smiled at her. She would try but I wasn't sure she could do it. "Let's go in and greet the lion, then. But let me do the talking." She nodded.

"Let's start with me as the "security consultant," not your lover. We'll tour the house and I'll let you know what you need to have done. We won't mention the monitors out loud but I'll look them over as we go. Afterward, we'll go to my office to sign the paperwork."

"And where will we go instead?" she asked with a knowing smile.

I looked at her seriously and raised my brows. "To my office to sign the paperwork. So I can get started on repairs."

"Really? I mean . . . I thought . . ." I understood her confusion. I reached into my back pocket and withdrew my card case. I don't always carry it with me, but I'd grabbed it for today's visit. I opened it and handed her a white business card with black lettering and a swirl logo.

She took the card and read it out loud. "Specialty Services, Inc., Security Consulting, Anthony Giodone, President. You have a whole *corporation*?"

I chuckled. "Of course. I really do handle security systems. I rent out an executive suite downtown. Most of my clients are Family but a few are legit. It gives me something to do during working hours. It's also useful to have the run of the town after dark for my *other* job. Anything I install has a back door built in for my use."

"If you have an office, why did I meet you at that awful bar?" The sourness of her distaste drifted on the breeze.

"I'll tell Jocko you said that." The insult in my voice wasn't all faked. My face probably showed it.

She blushed and fidgeted. Embarrassment and shame replaced the distaste. She keeps forgetting these people are my friends.

"Hey, I'm kidding." But by the flat tone of my voice, she could tell I wasn't and flinched. "I meet clients at the bar to put them at a disadvantage. Keeps them nervous. It worked, didn't it?"

She nodded several times—vigorously.

"My office is in a high-rise downtown. I pay rent to the owner. He hired my company to install and maintain the security system in the building. So if you want me for *future services*, and we agree on terms, the transaction will be nice and clean."

Normally, I don't work for clients—because of that whole "known to associate" thing. But this one had a built-in cover. *Gee, Lieutenant. She was a rich client who paid her bills. Why would I want her dead?*

Her eyes grew a little wide right then. "Oh. About that." Her eyes shifted away from me.

My voice took on a sharp edge. "Getting cold feet?"

"Well, actually . . . I mean . . ." She looked up at me then and her expression grew warm. There was fear in her eyes along with something else. Something deeper. "I think I might be falling in love with you, Tony."

I recognized the smell. But I couldn't accept it for what my nose told me it was. She looked at me hoping for a reaction. She got one, but probably not the one she wanted.

I shook my head. "Please don't. It's not love you're feeling. It's lust. Or crisis bonding. It's intense but it doesn't stick. Doesn't last through day-to-day life. We can't possibly be in love yet. Not yet." The cold knot of fear that thought put in my stomach made me realize things may have already gone too far. Shit.

"Look." I put hands on her shoulders, deliberately keeping her at arm's length. "Even if there's something there, I'm keeping distance intentionally. I'd never be able to pull the trigger if I let it go too far."

Sadness filled her eyes and my voice softened a bit. "I decided when we first were together that if you wanted to get away from life bad enough to hire someone like me, it would be wrong to deny you. I'd be using you. Just like everyone else. Keeping you around because *I* wanted something. Do you see?"

She nodded. "But what if there comes a time when I decide I *want* to live?"

I felt a surge of hope and immediately crushed it like a bug. "Aren't we getting a little ahead of ourselves?" I deliberately injected a note of dark humor in my voice. "You haven't paid me and I haven't agreed to do the job."

She smiled shakily. I returned the smile, but my next words were serious. "Let's take it a little slower and see, okay? You may decide that you don't like me all that much."

She put one hand over mine on her shoulder. "I won't change my mind. Are you ready to go inside?"

I watched as she steeled herself. A buzzing began overhead and I glanced up to see that the old mercury vapor lamps dotting the yard were just coming on. My brow furrowed slightly as I looked at her. I lifted her chin with one hand and turned her head from side to side slowly in the flat white light. She gave me a puzzled look and I sensed her confusion.

"What are you doing?" she asked when I released her chin. I sighed and shook my head.

"We're not going to do this tonight, Sue. I'm going to go home now."

"What! I mean . . ."

"You've got dark circles under your eyes and your skin is sagging. Neither of us has gotten a good night's sleep for days." *I* hadn't slept soundly for almost a week. "If we go in there now and get started, it's going to be hours. I get grumpy when I'm sleep deprived, so I'm going to go home and you need to go to bed, too."

"But what about Mom? I can't go back in there alone, Tony. I just *can't*!"

"Sure you can. You just walk right in, ignore her, and go upstairs and go to bed."

"But she'll follow me, yelling. I'll never get a wink of sleep."

I smiled darkly. "Your mom's got hold of a double-edged sword this time, Sue. It cuts both ways. If she follows you to your room, she'll have to get out of that wheelchair, won't she? The nurse will back you up on it to your family. If she stays in the wheelchair, she's stuck downstairs, and you get to sleep. See?"

A shock of scent rose from her and her eyes looked startled in the growing circle of light. "But I don't know if Bekki paid the nurse to stay overnight."

"It's well past 5:00. If the nurse is still here, I'm pretty sure she intends to stay. She must have at least stayed last night, so she's already got a room in there somewhere."

"But I'll still hear Mom. The entryway echoes through the whole house."

"What? You don't have a stereo in your room?" I rolled my eyes. "Please." Then I fished in my front pocket and removed a small plastic packet containing orange pieces of foam. "But if it'll make you feel better, put in earplugs."

She looked at the plugs with delight and squished them through the plastic. She watched as they returned to their original shape and then did it again. I tore open the package and showed her how to compress and roll them and then insert them into her ears. I made her tap lightly until they expanded. One ear took a couple of tries to get it seated correctly. When she took them out and tucked them in her pocket, I continued.

"The plugs don't completely remove sound. They just dull it. You'll still be able to hear muffled loud sounds, but it won't be enough to keep you awake."

She reached forward suddenly and planted a whopping kiss on my lips. A hot wave of need flowed through me. My body was suddenly as hard and ready as the first time I touched her. I wanted more and I reached for her hungrily. But my brain fought the need. I balled my hands into fists before I could wrap her in my arms. No. I was *not* going to start again. I forced my hands to reach for her shoulders and I gently pushed her away.

"Get some sleep, Sue. I'll stop by first thing in the morning when we're both feeling better."

She backed up and nodded. She was feeling too many things for my nose to sort. I could relate.

Chapter 18

Where is he? He should be here by now.

I opened my eyes slowly and blinked several times. The words that I heard in my mind weren't a dream. I could feel tension and anxiety pushing at me, but distantly. I glanced at the clock and swore. It was already 9:00 in the morning! Damn! The last time I'd slept for twelve hours straight was—well, the last time I'd been *awake* for a week.

I started a pot of my favorite coffee. *French Market* blended with flavored fresh ground. Irish Creme works best. The scent of it brewing rode over the steam of the shower. I struggled to free my head of restlessness. I just knew it was Sue's frustration I was feeling. I didn't get why it was happening, but it feels the same as when I touch her and get her thoughts. Maybe I was spending too much time with her.

I booted the computer to check my e-mails and began to pick up the pots and pans scattered around the living room and bedroom. I'd been so exhausted last night that I was afraid that I'd miss the burglar alarm if someone broke in. So, I used a low-tech solution—I stacked three metal pans underneath each of the windows and turned out the lights. Anyone defeating the security system would make a bunch of noise. It's enough to wake the dead.

I was sipping an oversize mug of java and reveling in the scent. It never tastes very good after mint toothpaste, so I just enjoyed the scent for the time being as I sat down at my desk. The software informed me that it was downloading 32 messages. Well, there went my morning! Against my better judgment, I decided to check my voice mail. Let's see, with the Atlantic City job, the moon change, and the trip to

Vegas, I'd been gone for nine days. There were probably fifty messages waiting for me. I grabbed a pen and pad and started to work.

After I'd had to re-write a message to a customer for the third time because it sounded arrogant and condescending, I was sick of Sue's frustration pushing at me. I picked up the phone and dialed the number that I'd already memorized.

"Hello?" Sue's voice sounded like she felt in my head. All that was missing was the burnt metal scent of her frustration.

"Would you chill?" I snarled. "I've got to get some work done here. Go read a book or take a hot bath or something. I'll be by when I get business taken care of!"

I could feel her start in my head and then embarrassment washed through me. I hung up without waiting for her to reply into the receiver.

I'd probably been too harsh, but I had a life, damn it! I couldn't be there to hold her hand every second.

Once I listened to all the voice mails—I'd guessed high, there were only twenty-seven—I had a list of clients that I had to visit. But first, I needed to work off the rest of the tension in my shoulders.

I changed quickly into shorts, T-shirt and sneakers. Once again, I set the alarm, even though I wouldn't be gone for long. Atlantic City and Vegas still stuck in the back of my mind. Paranoia keeps me alive.

I checked my mailbox on the way out. No surprise that there was nothing in the box except a yellow card informing me that I would have to go to the Post Office to pick up my mail. It had sat too long.

"Mr. Giodone!" came a voice from across the street as I started to take the note back to the porch. "Tony?"

I turned to see Mary Stickey, my long-time neighbor. She doesn't like me much, but tolerates me because I'm quiet and I keep the lawn mowed. She was holding a box.

"Yes, Mary?" I asked tolerantly. The frustration I still felt made it hard to be civil. Mary always smells like Dr. Pepper. I'm not sure if that's her base scent, but she is always prying into everyone's business, so maybe it's antifreeze. It's not a trait I like in a person. Still, it keeps me on my guard, so she's useful.

"The UPS man was here yesterday. He's been by several times and asked if he could leave a package for you with me. Well, of course, I told him he could."

"Of course you did." The words came out a little sarcastic. Damn busybody. But I put on a smile when she started a bit and smelled disapproving. She handed the box over without another word. I glanced at the address and recognized it. Fortunately, the company doesn't advertise on shipping boxes, and it hadn't been tampered with, so she didn't know what was in the package. Mary also didn't know that she'd just made my day.

"Hey, great!" I said sunnily. "I've been waiting for this."

"It's so heavy," she said and the potent antifreeze scent of her curiosity overpowered the vinegar of her earlier disapproval. "And what a strange size."

The narrow box was about seventeen inches long. Yep. Just enough for packing material around it.

I didn't comment on her implied question. "Thanks, Mary." I turned and walked back to the house. From the corner of my eye, I saw her stamp her foot before grudgingly turning to go home.

On the porch, I noted what I had apparently missed in my exhausted state yesterday. Three gummed notes—all from UPS, telling me that they had tried to deliver a package on different days, and now it was waiting at their office. I guess after I didn't show up there, they tried one more time. I punched in my code to turn off the system and put the messages and box on the kitchen table next to the pad of clients to visit.

That done, I turned off the coffee pot, set the alarm a second time, and left once more for a run. I resisted the urge to open the box. I knew what was in it and I could play with my new toy later. First I would need to deal with business and Sue.

It was hours later when I finally got to her house. "What took you so long?" she asked.

I shook my head wearily. "You would not *believe* the day I've had. God, but people are idiots some times!" Even a long run and a couple of sets on the bench press in my gym hadn't prepared me. Usually a run will keep the wolf at bay and I can be professional and courteous. Today it had been a chore.

Sue's scent had started as embarrassed but frustrated. She'd kept her distance when I arrived and I could tell that part of her was annoyed with me for being late. She was also annoyed with herself for needing me to be there at all. But the air around was slowly turning to curious. I took off my wrap-around mirrored sunglasses as we walked into the shade. I joined her on an ornate, wrought-iron bench and tucked them in the pocket of my grey polo shirt.

"What happened? Was it that Sara woman again?"

I gave a little wave of my hand. "Yeah, her and others."

"Were you able to fix the sensors in her shop?" Sue was honestly curious. I could feel it and smell it. Okay, sure. I could let off a little steam.

"There's nothing wrong with the sensors, Sue. There never is at that store. It's always employee error or actual thefts. I had to give *yet another* demonstration on how to nullify the magnetic strips. The check-out clerks hadn't read the memo that said hardback novels are now carrying sensors in the center of the book, near the spine. They were just scanning the bar code but not running them over the demagnetizer. Every book that went out of the store beeped. But that was easy. At least I was in and out of the place in under thirty minutes."

And I'd decided that Humphries' Department Store was about to get a whopping increase in their annual maintenance charge. I figured that if I tripled their fee, maybe they would move their business, or at least hire someone with a lick of sense to manage. I had made more than twenty service calls in a single quarter. That's just ridiculous.

"You figured it out and gave a demonstration that quickly?" The clove scent of her pride blended with surprise.

"It didn't take a brain surgeon. All I had to do was watch

the clerks for a few minutes. I *wrote* the memo. It was obvious that they hadn't read it."

"You must have had a lot of calls to handle after being away for so long." She was trying to give me the benefit of the doubt.

I shrugged and shook my head. "Not too many, really. Most of the calls were billing questions. Bookkeepers always complain about my bills until I show them an itemization. I just had a lot of things to do."

I didn't want to make excuses by blaming my clients. I wanted to prove that I could continue on with my regular life, despite her existence. But whether or not I wanted to admit it, I had to struggle constantly all day not to come over and be in her arms. I really hated how tough it had been.

"Do you bill every time you go somewhere?"

I chuckled. "Only when they're idiots. Fortunately for my pocketbook, that's pretty often. The annual fee covers quarterly check-ups on the equipment and routine maintenance. If it's employee error, it gets billed."

I could feel that she didn't understand. It'd be easier to illustrate. "Take this doctor's office I went to. Just after I left to go to the east coast—before I met you—the last person out of the office forgot to lock the front door, but set the alarm. The wind kicked up, opened the door and the alarm went off." I glanced at her and saw that I had her full attention, so I continued. "The security monitoring company called the police. They checked it out and found nothing wrong."

I leaned back then and stretched my legs. I arched over the back of the bench and heard a couple of satisfying pops as my spine slid back into place.

"But why would they call *you*?" she asked.

"You've got me. The monitoring company turned off the siren by remote after the false alarm. On most systems, all the lights blink after a reset until you enter a three or four digit code. It's all explained on a sheet that I give customers when I install the system. I even wrote down the name and number of the monitoring company supervisor. There's a copy for each person with a key to the building. But did they even glance at the instructions?"

"No?"

I shook my head with a patronizing look. "No, they didn't even try. So, I'm gone for, like, nine days. This whole time, the system has been down. It's just merrily blinking away on the wall. They're just damn lucky that nobody walked in and cleaned out the place."

I shook my head as I remembered the rage of the two doctors who owned the building when they'd found out. Of course, they're *never* the last to leave, so they didn't know about the alarm until I presented my invoice. Several of the front desk girls had been terrified they'd be fired. The scent of their fear had made me ravenous enough to stop and pig out on a triple decker burger on the way to the next call.

"And, as always, there are the employees who forget their codes and can't get in the building, or can't remember their codes so they write them down on paper and lose them. Then I have to pull out the laptop and assign a new passcode in the master computer. It was all typical stuff. It was just annoying and tiring."

I saw Sue flinch at one point during my tirade and it reminded me.

"By the way, what was the emergency this morning? You seem fine now, but you were really antsy earlier."

She looked at me and the dry dusty heat that spoke of embarrassment and shame burst from her. "I guess I'm one of your idiots. I forgot the code for the gate and nobody could get in or out of the estate today."

I stared at her for a moment, open-mouthed. I shut my jaw and tried to think of something to say that wouldn't be interpreted as an insult. "But you wrote it down. You asked for a sheet of paper, and then tucked it in your pocket. It can't have gone far."

"I did?" Her look of alarm was blending with the anger. She thought for a moment. "You're right! I did." Burning coffee and dust seeped off her, slowly intensifying until it filled the air. "Then I must have lost it. I can't believe that I was that stupid!"

I reached out and put a comforting hand on her arm. I moved it up until it rested on her neck and then rubbed the muscles gently.

"Hey, don't be too hard on yourself, Sue. You were exhausted. It's why we both went to bed last night. It's no big deal. Really. What did you do all day?"

Her mood began to lighten as I rubbed and she relaxed into the massage. "Actually, it was a pretty good day. I got the whole upstairs cleaned! Then I read a book and relaxed in a long bubble bath for the first time in months."

I forgot to rub for a moment. "You don't have a house-keeper? You clean this place by yourself?" She'd already explained why baths were impossible. Every time she would try, her mother kept interrupting, asking for stuff and being generally annoying.

This time, I earned the patronizing look. "No, of course not. I have a housekeeper that comes in once a week—today. But she can barely keep up with the kids. Fortunately, *none* of them could get here today."

"Kids?" I'd never thought to ask, but that could be an issue in a long-term relationship. I don't *dislike* them, precisely.

She caught the tone of my voice and shook her head. "No, not mine. Bekki's. And frankly, after dealing with them for the past two months, I may *never* have kids."

"So you babysit every day?" That would explain why she'd gotten beat down enough to want to kill herself.

She nodded angrily. "You might as well say that. Actually it was *Mom* who agreed to watch the kids for the summer. It just ends up being me because Mom never does the things that need to be done."

"Such as?"

"Mike has T-Ball, and Cindy has swimming lessons at the Y."

"But your mom doesn't drive. Why would she agree to take them? And why would *Bekki* set it up to fail?"

"I told you. I'm supposed to be attached at the hip. What

Mom agrees to, I'm part of. It's the way it is. I'm usually happy to take them somewhere, though, because otherwise they destroy the house. They play tag and knock something over, or leave the kitchen a disaster because they "made cookies" when I went to the store. Last week, Mike dropped a crystal punch bowl from the top of the stairs because he wanted to see whether it would explode. Big surprise—it did. Mom never makes them clean up. That's *my* job."

I suppressed a smile when Sue mentioned the punch bowl. I did a similar thing when I was a kid. Of course, I *did* have to clean it up and got grounded for a week to boot. "Well, the timing's good for us to do this today, if the kids aren't here. Remember what we talked about, though— "security consultant", right?"

She looked at me and winced. Then she smiled bravely. Tangerines filled the air. She leaned over and gave me a hug. I returned it with interest. "I'm glad you're here," she said.

Chapter 19

A moment later, we walked through the massive oak doors and I was greeted by my first sight of Sue's mother. I had to admit that she was truly pathetic looking. I almost laughed but that probably wouldn't set the right tone. Sue glanced at me but couldn't read my expression. Blank is one of my best expressions—I've had lots of practice.

Myra Quentin sat in a wheelchair with a nurse standing primly at her back. Her face looked pained and her eyes were dark with a sunken appearance. She hunched slightly in the chair and rested heavily on one armrest. She made herself as small as possible by scooting in the seat. Her legs shook visibly from the strain.

The problem was, she smelled of deceit. Lies upon lies until the black pepper smell made my nose burn. She also smelled like that buzzard daughter of hers. Not Sue. The blonde witch. That made me immediately more wary than I might otherwise have been. Well, that and the sharp smell of vodka that hit me like a wind. Odd that Sue hadn't mentioned mom was a drunk.

Myra's eyes were bright with suspicion and anger. That's not a real common trait in someone truly sick or injured. Pain dulls the eyes. If she had an injured hip she would favor it and keep weight off it. Sue told me it was her left hip that had been replaced. She should be leaning on the left hip, instead of the right, supposedly injured one.

When I looked closely, I could see that the pale face and sunken eyes were make-up. The dark circles from truly sunken eyes are actually blue from irritated blood vessels

under the skin. Her "sunken" eyes were created by brown
eyeliner. I could smell the waxy cosmetic. The dark wasn't
uniform, meaning it had been applied somewhat hurriedly.
Her nose was slightly more pale than the rest. Tsk. A bit too
much facial powder. She probably pays better attention to
detail when she's sober.

I glanced at Sue to see if she noticed. I could feel in my
head her embarrassment and frustration at her mother's
transparent ploy. What I couldn't figure out is why Sue had
never called her on it. Part of me wanted to reach out and
rub a finger through the liner and say, "Oops. Missed a
spot." But again, not the right tone.

I could tell Sue's mother had once been a pretty woman.
Now she was unattractive. It was intentional, which made
it worse.

I decided to try a soft approach. I squatted down in front
of the chair. I wanted to be eye to eye with her to watch her
reaction. The smell of vodka nearly knocked me over. I had
to breathe through my mouth to stay in character.

"Mrs. Quentin," I said loud and slow, "my name is Tony
Giodone. How are you today?"

Her eyes flashed with anger and her voice was filled with
venom. I pretended not to notice. "I'm in pain, not deaf. Idiot!"
Hmm. I'd have thought she would try nice first. Try to swing
me over to her side. Okay, Giodone. Time to pour on the charm.

Keeping in character, I raised my eyebrows and appeared
apologetic. I lowered my voice to conciliatory. "I'm very
sorry, Mrs. Quentin. Sue mentioned that you hurt your hip.
Can you stand at all?"

Her eyes lightened and her head rose slightly. The sweet,
cloying, black peppery scent of deceit and dark glee overpowered the alcohol for a moment.

Her sigh was heavy and faked. "No." She was pleased
that she was apparently fooling me. She smelled more like
Leo than I'd care to think.

"It's just the stress of everything lately. I do wish that I
wasn't such a *burden* on dear Suzi." I glanced at Sue, who

smelled hurt and angry again. "I'm sure that an old, crippled woman cramps her style." The words ended with a knife edge.

My response was saccharine sweet. "Well, that's about to change, Mrs. Quentin. May I call you Myra? I'll be around more to help Sue take care of you."

I smelled Sue's surge of hope and I flinched internally. Jeez! Why did I say that? The logical part of me knew I needed to keep my distance but I just couldn't seem to stop myself. I managed to keep the pleasant, professional look despite being startled.

I saw Myra's eyes light up with distrust and a healthy edge of foreboding. Still, she tried for the soft sell. "I prefer Mrs. Quentin, thank you. I'm afraid I don't understand, Mr.—Giodone, is it? Why would you be around more?"

I glanced at Sue as though in surprise. It wasn't all faked. She kept a straight calm face. Attagirl! I looked back at her mother and said, "Didn't Sue tell you? I'll be moving in to the basement." My voice dropped at the end. It held a note of finality that disturbed me a little. Meeting Myra decided it. I didn't like the smell of her. She smelled like a threat to my mate.

That stopped me cold. Mate? It's not a word that I've *ever* used to describe a girlfriend, but I didn't have time to think about it now. Not with Myra right in front of me.

My voice was cold but calm as I continued. The threat needed to be *very* visible.

"I've been hired to handle the security for the estate and be a bodyguard. You won't ever take another fall like you did." I smiled and it was probably the same smile the snake gave Eve. "I'll make sure that you're taken care of in the *exact* way you need to be."

I was hit by a blast of scorched coffee scent. Honest shock and anger shattered the act. She could sense I was on to her so she changed her tactics. She didn't bother to be subtle.

"We don't need any help here! So you won't be moving in. Get out!"

"Mother!" exclaimed Sue. "You said you didn't want the nurse, and what about that horrible man who called? We need to have someone around. It's my house and I've made the decision. Tony stays."

I was getting a headache. The burnt metal of Sue's determination and frustration overpowered the carmelized coffee from her mother.

Myra's eyes narrowed for a second before they returned to schooled innocence. The coffee scent did go away. "But, Suzi dear, that will be so expensive."

Sue's jaw thrust forward and her voice was steady. "I've got the money, Mom. Remember? Aren't you the one who told me I should reimburse Bekki for the nurse since it was *my fault* that she had to be hired. You said that I've been frivolously wasting my money and I should be spending it on something useful. Well, this is useful. And you won't take it away from me!"

Ooh, bad move. We probably should have discussed the script a little more. I could already hear the reply. A new wave of anger exploded into my nose, cranking my headache up another notch and tickling my nose enough that I had to fight not to sneeze.

Myra pointed a shaking finger at Sue. "Don't you dare use that tone with me, Suzi Lynette Quentin! I don't want some strange man living in my basement. We don't know anything about him. He could be an axe murderer for all you know!"

Yup, that was the next line.

Sue turned to me with an expression of stubbornness. "Are you an axe murderer?" Her voice quavered with anger.

I thought for a moment and then smiled darkly. "Nope. Never used an axe before. I could try it if you like."

Myra's eyebrows shot up and her hand went to her mouth in shock and disapproval.

"*Tony*!" Sue spoke through clenched teeth. There was a brief blast of annoyance. I guess I wasn't helping.

I fought not to grin. "Sorry. Mrs. Quentin, I've been hired to *protect* you. I've been in this line of work for years. I'll do my best not to intrude on your life. You'll hardly know I'm here. But I will be here. For your benefit and for Sue's." There was a trace of warmth in my voice. It was intentional.

"Bedded her already, have you?" Myra turned and glared at Sue. "You've always been weak. Your father hated that about you." I didn't react but Sue jumped like she was struck. Hot wetness filled the air and tightened my throat.

"I tried to raise you to take some pride in yourself." She shook her head in disgust. "But look how you've let yourself go. It's disgraceful." Myra reached out slapped Sue's thigh with stinging force. She winced as a red handprint blossomed on her skin. "Look at that flab. No wonder you have to whore yourself. You know he's only after your money. What *decent* man would want you?"

My eyes narrowed and I struggled to hold my temper in check. "What you believe," I said coldly, "doesn't concern me. But understand that the decision has been made. Whether or not you approve."

Myra glared at me. Her arms tensed on the chair and I thought that she was going to rise out of the chair and strike me. God, I could hope! I wouldn't hold myself responsible if she did. But no. She turned her fury to Sue who visibly flinched. I stepped closer. I didn't give a shit who she was. No way was she going to attack my lady.

"You are going to regret this, Suzi. Mark my words. This decision will cause you no end of grief." From the look on her face, I could tell who would be at the giving end of that grief. I turned to face my new adversary. I let my eyes grow cold and deadly. White anger flared between us.

"I hope that we can work together, Mrs. Quentin. Sue needs both of us to keep her healthy and happy. I'd rather work with you than against you to achieve that goal." That at least was the truth.

"Her name is *Suzi*," Myra said sarcastically. She addressed Sue: "I'm sorry that you don't like your given name enough to use it. It was your father's favorite. But I guess that doesn't matter to you, you stupid ungrateful slut."

Sue was near tears. We needed to end this confrontation.

I looked down at the middle-aged actress in the chair. My words were steel. "I'll be moving in by week's end."

I moved a fraction of an inch closer, invading the hell out of her personal space. She leaned back in the chair in response. Good. The blast of alcohol scent was nauseating. "Understand that *Sue* hired me. I will report to her and her alone. About *any* threat to her." With that promise I stood and turned toward Sue. Myra's anger and indignation beat at my back. I didn't need to smell it.

"Are you implying that I am a threat to my own daughter?" Myra asked loudly. Her offense was genuine but there was guilt there, as well. "Well, I don't need to sit here and be insulted!"

I didn't give her the satisfaction of looking at her. "No. You certainly don't. You're welcome to leave any time you wish." Sue got an alarmed look on her face but I shook my head the smallest bit. She bit her lip and kept silent.

"Suzi, aren't you going to say anything." The tone was an order not a question.

Sue swallowed hard and closed her eyes. "Only that I think it's time I showed Tony where he'll be staying." I blew a kiss at her as a congratulations. She let out a slow tense breath that Myra couldn't see through my body.

"I *see*," said Myra. She glared daggers at my back. I could smell the roasting jalapeños of her hate over the stench of alcohol. "Well, I wouldn't get too comfortable. If you manage to move in at all you won't be staying long!"

I could afford to ignore her so I did. I took Sue's arm and led her away. I glanced at the nurse as we left. Her eyes rolled and she let out a disgusted breath. Personally, I wouldn't stoop to earning a living by catering to whining hypochondriacs. But to each their own.

Sue's steps were shaky at first but she gained confidence the further away we walked from her Mother.

We toured the upstairs and Sue pointed out the location of the hidden monitors. No good. The coverage was too sketchy. Luckily, I have a friend in the business.

Entering Sue's room was an experience. The smell of flowers was overpowering; the pollen in the air thick enough to walk on. Twin trellises overflowed with climbing roses just outside the open windows. Pink on one side, yellow on the other. Only a screen kept out the dozen bees flitting back and forth.

The trellises had to go.

Sue scowled when I told her that. "No! Those trellises are the only reason I took this room. I love them right next to my window!"

I was surprised at the strength of her response. I glanced at the positioning again. "Well, I guess we can trim the trellis below the window."

"Absolutely not." Her arms crossed over her chest and her stance was final. The hot metal of her determination bit at my nose. I could see she wasn't going to budge on this one.

"Okay," I amended, opening the screen and looking outside to get a feel for the construction, "How about we move it off to the side where it can't be used as a ladder?" I brought my head back inside before the bees could follow. "Or we can install windows that can't be entered. Those are the only choices that won't get you killed."

"The roses are wonderful in the summer." She was lost in thought. "They're the best part about the house. I'd rather fix the windows."

"It'll cost you. But . . . if it's that important to you." She beamed a smile at me. It made me sigh again. I was turning into a softy for that smile. Bad plan.

However, her mood made it a good time to bring up a sore subject. I closed the door and heard it latch. Arms over my chest and I centered my stance. I kept my voice low and locked eyes with Sue. "How long has your Mom been an alcoholic?"

Her expression was dumbfounded. "What are you talking about? Mom doesn't drink! Why would you think that?"

A harsh laugh exploded from me before I could stop it. She continued to look confused. Wow! That level of denial was more than *I* would be able to fix, but I had to at least try.

"Remember I can smell things other people don't, Sue. The woman *reeks* of vodka."

The wheels started spinning in her head and she paced the room for a moment. I could hear her thoughts as she moved around the room. It can't be possible. He must be wrong. But Grace at work was and you didn't notice that until she went into treatment. Oh, my God! What if he's right?

She didn't comment one way or the other, but when we walked back into the hallway, she was shaking. She tried to talk normally, but it was a lie.

She showed me the basement next.

It really was a full basement—nearly the size of my whole house. It was decorated in dark walnut paneling and burgundy carpets. The paneling could stay but the carpet had to go. It was too somber with both. I said as much to Sue.

"Pick any color you want. Buy new furniture if you don't like this. But please stay." Sue was almost frantic, thinking I might change my mind after meeting her mom. Especially after learning about the vodka. I could smell it, feel it inside me.

I looked from the full kitchen to the huge bathroom that dwarfed mine. A regulation pool table sat in the den, balls racked for the next game. A pinball machine rested against the wall. Sue would be just upstairs. Always. She could come downstairs or I could go up.

"I'll probably regret this . . . "

Sue grinned broadly and threw herself into my arms with an exclamation of joy. Citrus and baking and spices galore.

I hugged her in return. "Remember what you said, though. Come and go as I please. Right?"

There was a flash of fear and jealousy that didn't bode well. I decided to keep the feeling warm so I steered her toward the bedroom with the king size bed. She tried to pull back.

"I can't!" Her loud whisper echoed the frantic pounding of her heart. "Mom's upstairs!"

"We're not fourteen." My smile was both gentle and

amused. "We're allowed." I pushed her backwards and she ended up lying down on the bed after a gentle bounce.

"Besides, I take my job as bodyguard very seriously. If I see the slightest hint of danger," I said, as I fell on top of her, "I'll throw my body on you."

She giggled. I kissed her.

"What's the danger?" Her voice was thick with amusement and the beginnings of desire. I tried to focus on her words, but my body wanted to control. I pointed to the ground. Her eyes followed my finger to a small black cricket making short hops across the floor. "It could be poisonous." I ruined the serious words by grinning. She laughed.

The doorbell rang and it echoed through speakers in the downstairs living room. Good engineering. I approve.

"Mom will get it." She kissed me deeply.

The realization hit me and I pulled upward sharply. I scrambled off the bed and headed toward the stairs.

"What's wrong?"

"We changed the code at the gate. Who could have gotten to the door?"

Her hand flew to her mouth. "Oh, God! Mom!" The musk of her desire was suddenly replaced by sourness.

She moved quickly enough that she beat me to the stairs. I grabbed her arm roughly and pulled her back behind me.

The Sig came out from where it hid in a holster underneath the polo shirt. In one quick motion, I jacked a cartridge into the chamber. I heard voices as I entered the main floor. The nurse was unconscious on the floor. An old acquaintance, Vinny Coblentz, stood over Myra's wheelchair. Vinny is Family on his mom's side. His dad doesn't really approve of his career choice.

One beefy hand rested on each arm of the chair. His Baretta 9mm was visible in a shoulder rig under his sport coat.

"We can make this easy or hard, old lady." He smelled like wet clay. I'm not real sure what emotion that is. Maybe it's just him.

Myra Quentin was sputtering angrily. "Why, you . . . you bastard!" Vinny smiled. He always did like that term. He works hard to live down to it. "You can't just barge in here and threaten me. I'll call the police!"

He shook her wheelchair roughly and she shrieked. I glanced down as an amber pill bottle dropped to the floor. My eyes focused in on the tiny print. Interesting! Generic oxycodone, commonly known as Percocet®. Well, well. Not just a drunk.

Vinny laughed just then. He knew the old lady wasn't a threat, so he was toying with her.

Maybe she's not. *But I am.*

Sue tried to push past me but I held her back firmly and used a sharp look to command her to stay put. Her expression was frantic, her scent ammonia with panic, but she did as I asked. She moved to where she could see the scene and still remain protected by the thick walls.

I pointed the Sig at him at hip level as I stepped out from the stairwell. "Back off, Vinny," I said.

He looked up and reached for his piece at the same time. "Don't even think it!" I brought the gun up into a two-handed grip with preternatural speed and stared down the barrel at him.

His hands froze. He raised them away from his body and then backed away from the wheelchair. A greasy lock of sandy-colored hair fell across his eyes. His voice was condescending. "Well, well, Tony the Nose. Haven't seen you in a long time."

"Likewise." I walked toward him. I stretched forward while holding the gun steady and took his Baretta from the holster. He didn't try to stop me.

"This ain't your turf," he growled after I stuck his gun in my belt. Myra was actually too surprised to speak. Sue had entered the room and stood by her mother's side, watchful.

"It is now. These ladies are under *my* protection."

"Thought that wasn't your thing." His eyes narrowed slightly and he smelled suspicious.

"I've been hired as their bodyguard." The truth is always simpler than a lie.

He lowered his arms slowly, watching my body language as he did. In a moment his grey eyes cleared. "Bodyguard, huh?" He accepted the statement with a nod. Then, as is the proper way, he began to address me as the protector, the head of the family.

"The old lady made a deal with me, Tony. She owes me money. She's been avoiding my calls. I feel insulted." He put his hand over his heart to show his sincerity. He actually *did* smell offended. "I gotta collect. You know that. It's the only way to make amends."

I shook my head. "She hasn't got any money, Vinny. She promised you money that ain't hers to give."

"I don't care where the money comes from. Promises have been made. I offered her services. She accepted. If she's hired you now, fine. I'm willing to negotiate." The statement was flat but he kept his eyes locked on mine. I had the upper hand. He had no choice but to negotiate, but he would be stubborn. Trouble was, I agreed with him. That wasn't to Sue's benefit. Damn it.

I motioned at him with my gun. "Let's discuss this outside." I wanted to know how he got into the estate. Vinny wasn't one to climb trees. Also, I wanted him away from the ladies in case the "negotiations" got ugly.

He walked toward the door. I didn't like the way he was moving. His scent changed. Like he was getting ready to pounce. I slapped him on the back of the head with the Sig. "Don't try it, Vinny. Blood's tough to get out of hardwood." He stopped, nodded without turning and opened the front door.

I followed him out and we walked toward the gate. There were no additional cars in the drive. "How'd you get in, Vinny? You're not a climber."

He shrugged. "It's an old system. Cut the electric feed and the gates pop right open."

That was annoying. "You don't have to cut the power to the whole estate?"

He stopped walking, turned and looked at me. "Why should I tell you? What's in it for me?"

We were out of sight of the main house. I removed his 9mm from my waistband and popped the clip with my thumb so that it dropped on the ground. I handed him back the unloaded gun butt first. He looked surprised but took the gun.

"Open the chamber," I held the Sig nice and steady in a one handed grip against my body.

He jacked back the slide and a single bullet jumped into the air and landed near the clip on the ground.

"Happy?" he asked sarcastically.

"Don't bitch. I didn't have to give it back."

He followed the logic. "Yeah, okay. So, anyway, what's your piece of this? You're a bodyguard like I'm Santa Claus."

I thought about lying, but questions were going to be asked anyway. It's a surprisingly small Family despite the number of people. I shrugged. "The daughter's my new lady. She hired me to bodyguard her and the mother. It'll even be on paper."

"Shit. Well, that sucks! I'm going to have to go through you to get the money I'm owed?"

I shook my head. "There won't be any money, Vinny. Not for protection. How much the old bat promise you a month?"

"Ten grand," he said sullenly.

I whistled. "Protection's gone up a little since I was in the biz."

He pursed his lips and shrugged one shoulder. "I'd have done a good job. Kept all the other vultures away."

"No vultures will get past me, either. It's time to leave, Vinny." I reholstered my Sig. I could handle him without it. I walked him to the gate and could smell that he was annoyed. He turned and faced me and I thought he might take a dive for me.

Violent anger suddenly flashed through my body, charging my muscles with adrenaline. It wasn't mine. Somehow I knew that but it affected me the same way. I fixed Vinny with a look and saw his eyes go wide. I could see the glow in my eyes reflected in his. Well, that's a first this far from the moon. I'd have to work on that. I forced myself to calm. The wolf inside me settled down. Like it was a separate thing. A dog on a leash.

"Yeah sure, Tony. Whatever you say." Ammonia replaced the burnt coffee. I .*wanted* him to run, hoped he would run so I could chase. He left carefully. Slowly. Damn.

I waited at the gate until he drove off. My muscles were trembling with energy. My eyes twitched. I'd never had this strong a response so far from the moon. Deep down I knew it was because of Sue. The pleasure, the bonding—it was all making the other qualities that I'd been repressing come to the front. The wolf inside waited with confident anticipation. I was being led by my instincts toward an end I couldn't see or understand. I didn't like that I couldn't look around the next bend.

With Vinny taken care of for the moment, I went to check the fence. I saw what he meant. There was a separate feed to the fence, direct from the pole. There was no need for him to cut the house. I walked back up the drive, musing on how to secure the electricity. I caught the tail end of a discussion that appeared to have been going since I went outside. It was mostly one sided. Myra was raging at Sue, trying to drive in that wedge. It was Sue's anger I'd felt. I listened outside the door for a few minutes.

"For God's sake, Suzi!" I heard Myra shrill. "He knew the man's *name*."

Oh, please! So did she.

Sue's voice was conciliatory, despite her anger. She was trying to appease her mom. That wouldn't be my choice. I'd scream right back at her.

"That only proves that he's talked to him, Mother. You knew his name too." There was a pause. "Besides, what good is a bodyguard who doesn't know which people are a threat?"

"They had *guns*, Suzi! Is that the kind of people that you want in this house? What about Bekki's children?"

That was Myra's problem, not Sue's. And it was the old bat's own fault for agreeing to Vinny's terms. It was lucky for her that Vinny respects me or he would have hurt them.

I almost felt it as Sue released an exasperated breath. I was taken aback when the words from her mouth nearly mirrored mine. Maybe the connection was working both ways.

There was anger in her voice. "You started this, Mom. Vinny came here because *you* made promises. You had *no right* to commit to things that involve me. And as for guns, you should be *happy* that Tony has a gun. What would we have done if that man came here and Tony *wasn't* here or didn't have a gun?" Sue's voice got louder, harsher. "Do you want to spend the rest of your life in a *real* wheelchair? He could have beat us, raped us, or even killed us!"

Silence stretched long seconds. I could hear the bitterness in Myra's voice along with surprise that Sue was talking back to her. "A *real* wheelchair. Just what are you implying?"

I opened the door just then and they both turned toward the movement. The nurse was no longer on the floor. I didn't know where she was. "Nothing, Mom. Just nothing, okay?"

She walked toward me and was going to put her arms around me but I gave a slight shake of my head. She stopped in front of me and smelled strongly of disappointment. Her breathing was fast. I could see the pulse in her neck beating furiously. These confrontations weren't doing anything good for her blood pressure.

"All taken care of," I said.

"Did you call the police?" asked Myra. "Has he been arrested?"

"No. He was merely trying to collect something he had been promised. I convinced him that it wasn't a good idea. He left. I'll call a friend I know to fix the fence. By the time I get back, the gate and the walls will be secure."

A blast of fear roiled into my nose. Both Myra and Sue looked nervous. "You're going somewhere?" There was an edge to Sue's voice I was coming to recognize. A combination of fear and jealousy.

You're *leaving?*" exclaimed Myra. "What kind of bodyguard are you?" From the expression on Sue's face she agreed with her mother on that point. Uh, oh.

I took a deep breath. "Look, Sue. We need to go to my office, fill out the paperwork, and plan a schedule that works for both of us."

Sue hesitantly agreed. The nurse came out then. She was sporting a black eye that touched the edge of her greying blonde hair. Vinny must have decked her when he first arrived. She had her purse on her arm and was ready to leave. It was hard to tell with all of the other emotions floating in the room but I think she was afraid and angry.

I sighed. Sue wouldn't leave her Mother unless someone stayed. One look at the nurse convinced me that she had quit whether or not she had actually said the words.

I pulled the nurse to the next room so we could talk privately. I took my wallet from my pocket and peeled off three hundreds. Then I wrote a phone number on one of my business cards. I handed them to the nurse as a single package and said, "Can you stay for a few hours more? I'd really appreciate it. We need to sign some papers just a few minutes from here. The number is my cell phone. Call it immediately if there are any problems. I'll can get here before the police. Deal?"

She glanced at the door. Her voice was a hiss. "I will *not* be responsible for that woman! She specifically requested a nurse practitioner so I could load her up with Meperidine. Her arms are so full of scar tissue that the injection had to go in her hip! She also pops Percocets like candy and washes them down with vodka. I will *not* participate in that abuse!"

I raised my brows. I couldn't disbelieve the nurse. No wonder Sue was messed up. I've seen others riding on that particular roller coaster. The nurse smelled angry and afraid. I smiled hopefully and peeled off two more hundreds. Her eyes followed the movement and greed added to her scent. I added a little flattery for good measure. "I really don't trust anyone else at this point . . ."

A sigh told me I had won. She held up a pair of fingers. "Two hours. No more. But if just one thing goes wrong, I will call 911 and wash my hands of her." She folded the bills neatly and put them in her purse. Then she turned and went back where she came from.

I decided that the money would come out of Vinny's pocket or his hide. The nurse wasn't even part of this. I just hoped she was the same one that treated him after I was done with him. It'd serve him right to get patched up with no pain killers.

Chapter 20

I went over the details of the bodyguard agreement as we drove to my office. It would cover all contingencies but have a specific exclusion for suicide. That's standard. You can protect a person from the world but not from themselves. So her death would appear to be a suicide. She nodded nervously. Worry and fear surrounded her like a cloud.

"How much?" she asked when I had finished the conditions.

I sighed. It had been tough to imagine watching her die. I could do it—I'd seen others I cared for go away—but I didn't like it much.

"A million." I didn't watch her face as I said it. I kept them squarely on the road. The resulting silence in the car seemed endless.

I finally glanced at her but it wasn't long enough to read her eyes. When I looked back again, tears were streaming down her face. I couldn't tell whether she was happy, sad or angry. The smells were all mixed. So I waited to hear it from her own lips.

"Deal." She started to cry into her hands. Great. I still didn't know what she was feeling. I guess I shouldn't be surprised at the tears. She's an emotional wreck right now. She could use someone to talk to who wasn't so *involved*.

Ah. I knew just the person.

I placed another call using the speaker phone attached to the cell. I really hate people who drive with a phone glued to their ear. A woman answered, "Good afternoon, Dr. Corbin's office."

"Hey, Karen!" I said. "Is John-Boy in?"

A deep-throated chuckle escaped her, but then she must

have heard Sue crying in the background. Her voice grew more serious, concerned. "Can I tell him who's calling?"

"Yeah. Father Guido Sarducci." I tried to ignore Sue sobbing beside me. She was exploding with anger and gratitude and pain. I started sneezing and nearly ran off the road. Damn, what a cocktail. I didn't even know if it had anything to do with me. I acknowledged her tears by handing her a tissue from a box tucked under my seat. She accepted it with a glance in my direction and I heard her blow her nose. I turned on the first road east toward the 'burbs.

"This is Dr. Corbin," said a pleasant tenor. "Who is this?"

"Trouble. With a capital T. How you doin', John-Boy?"

There was a sigh deep enough that it came over the speaker. "I really hate it when you call me that, Tony."

"Hey." I shrugged automatically even though I knew he couldn't see me. "You started it."

"We were kids! *I* grew up."

We could continue bantering all day but I had other issues. "Yeah, well . . . anyway, I need an appointment for a new patient."

Dr. John Corbin is one of the top psychiatrists in the city. He's also a childhood friend. I trusted him to help Sue get through some of her problems. I hadn't been lying. I wasn't a therapist or a social worker. John is. Sue needed someone to help her work through stuff—with her mom *and* with me. If she could heal some of her pain maybe there wouldn't have to be a final act to the play.

I really wanted to believe that.

"Finally decided to get your head examined after all these years, huh? About time." John knows full well what I do for a living. He's Family too.

"My head is just fine," I replied. "I'm perfectly well adjusted."

There was a pause. His voice grew deadly serious. "I wish I could believe that, Tony."

I didn't respond to that comment. Well-adjusted is a state of mind. Anyone—mother, hooker, teacher, accountant, killer—can be comfortable in their roles. I am.

"This is for a friend. She needs someone to talk to."

"Fine." A small sound that might have been a tired laugh came from the speaker. There was a pause and shuffling of papers. "I can fit her in next month, around the 20th."

"I'm about one minute from your office, John-Boy." Only a trace of humor remained.

"Tony! Jeez, buddy. I was about to walk out for the day."

I pulled into the parking lot and drove to the opposite end. "And I'm about to walk in." Sue watched me with amazement. "Let's see, the black Mercedes is yours?"

"Yeah . . ." he responded slowly. "Why?"

It was the only car at the north end of the parking lot. I parked cross-ways behind it. "I just blocked you in. Now you have time to see us." Sue laughed but the tears were still near the surface, hot and salty.

There was another long-suffering sigh. I have that effect on him. "I take it my patient is in the car with you?"

"Suzi Lynette Quentin. Have Karen make a file."

"Whoa, whoa. I know that name. Wasn't she on the front page last year? The Lotto winner?"

"The same. See, I even bring clients who can afford you. Am I a pal or what?"

He was laughing when I hung up. Sue got out of the car. When she looked at me, her face was etched with sorrow. I could feel her betrayal and hurt. "Even you think I'm crazy?"

I smiled at her and thought warm fuzzies that I hoped would reach her. "You're not crazy. You've just some stuff in your head that I can't help you with. I want you to make an informed choice on whether or not you want to end it. John will help you make that choice." She smelled surprised. Nothing more.

We walked into the building and checked in with the guard. I flashed my carry license and showed him my piece. He didn't ask to keep it but he did write down my name and permit number.

"Why do you call him John-Boy if he doesn't like it?" she asked as we entered the elevator.

I smiled at her. "His name is John Walton Corbin. The middle name is his mother's maiden name. Keeps the family heritage going, you know? So, John Walton? John-Boy Walton?" I smiled hopefully.

She got the joke but it wasn't as funny to her as it still is to me. I shrugged. "What can I say? It was a hot show when we were kids. Besides, he started it."

"You said that. How did he start it?" A little humor was finally reaching her voice as we stopped at the seventh floor.

It was nice to know that she listened well. "You heard what Vinny called me when I got the drop on him?"

She got an embarrassed look. "Actually, no. I was a little preoccupied."

"Tony the Nose. I've been saddled with that moniker for nearly thirty years."

She stared at me briefly and then laughed. "Tony the *Nose*?" Dr. Corbin gave you that name?"

I shrugged but grinned. "Hey, I had a big nose as a kid. I grew into it but nicknames stick."

"Tony the Nose . . ." she repeated and tried, without success, to fight back a grin. She smelled nervous but it was blending with amusement. Good. Nervous is better than hurt.

We reached John's office. The door had been propped open. I pushed it open carefully, shielding Sue with my body. She'd agreed to the fee. I might as well earn it.

John Walton Corbin, M.D., Ph.D., was sitting at the receptionist desk playing solitaire on the computer. The sugary smell of semi-sweet chocolate wafted to me. It's not an emotion. John just smells like chocolate.

"I think holding a doctor hostage is a felony in some states," he remarked as a greeting. His eyes were twinkling when he said it.

"I'll remember that."

He closed down the computer. "I told Laura that you were buying next time since you canceled our dinner reservations."

I snorted. "I have to buy every time. You're so damn cheap!"

He grinned and then turned to greet Sue. "Hello, Sue. I'm

Dr. Corbin. It's a pleasure to meet any friend of Tony's. His friends are some of my best customers. He's not insane but I've suspected for years that he's a carrier."

Sue smiled broadly and citrus blended with the chocolate. Nice. "Well, he's not dull." She glanced at me and I smiled. John's always been good at putting people at ease.

John led Sue into his office and I cooled my heels in the waiting room. I was glad that he introduced himself as "Dr. Corbin". I wanted to keep their relationship professional. I know I shouldn't be jealous, but damned if I didn't feel a twinge.

Now, I expected to hear their conversation. It's normal, considering my ears. It's why I stayed. I like to know things. But the other, that was just weird.

I didn't expect to experience her every emotion. All of the emotions that I know and a few I didn't blasted at me for over an hour. Not just smells, actual feelings. I fought through tears, laughter, lows, highs. I didn't know what to think when she told him about me.

She wasn't going to at first. But then he interrupted her as she stumbled along trying *not* to use the word, "Assassin."

I could hear the smile in his voice as he replied. "It's okay, Sue. I know that Tony kills people for a living."

Her voice was small, a tiny squeak of noise. "Oh."

Then she started to open up. She didn't tell him about the wolf part. It hadn't even occurred to me when we arrived, but it should have, damn it. I'll have to mention that subject is taboo. I'm not sure if John would believe her or not. He might, and that could be a problem.

But she *had* felt betrayed when I actually named a price to do the job. I sensed it, smelled it. Had she expected me to refuse the job? Wouldn't that have gotten the same reaction? I wish I knew what she wanted from me.

John considered what she said for a few moments and the silence stretched. Finally, he asked in a soft voice. "Do you understand why he did that, Sue?"

Her admission followed snuffling and blowing her nose. "No."

I had to agree. I *thought* I'd just picked a number out of the air. A high one, admittedly, but random.

"I know Tony's normal price for a job, Sue. The fact that it's so unusually high means two things: One—he cares for you a great deal. He doesn't want to see you dead, but he's a businessman. You asked for his services. He'll do it—make no mistake. But he set the price high enough to try to force *you* to refuse."

Sue's emotions soared. I could hear her heart skip a beat. Or maybe it was mine. Damn. I hate it when he's got me pegged.

"And two—he needs enough money to disappear somewhere for a good long time afterward. Somewhere where he can drown himself in a bottle, or at the tables, or be around so many people that he doesn't have time to think. He knows what he needs to get past losing you. He's smart, Sue. He understands psychology at an almost savant level." He added with a note of chagrin. "He certainly got better grades in college."

"He has a *degree*?" She sounded surprised. I was a little offended. She just doesn't get that this is a career choice, not merely the only thing I'm capable of doing.

"Yes, indeed—in business, with a psychology minor. It should have been his major, as talented as he was. I just kept going into grad school. He went . . . well, in a different direction. Still, I wouldn't suggest trying any manipulation on him. Ever. Be straight with him and he'll be straight with you. Provided he isn't lying to you, which he *also* does better than anyone I know."

No. Lying's reserved for business. Personal life gets too complicated. I'll keep my mouth shut, but I won't lie. John should know that, but I suppose this is a rare exception. I normally don't mix the two.

When the door opened finally, John motioned for me to step in. Sue passed me on the way. She watched the floor intently. She knew I had been a part of the session. She smelled guilty and a little afraid. I touched her shoulder as I walked by and she jumped a foot. She looked at me with startled eyes. I kept my hand on her arm and winked. A shy smile appeared but the guilt didn't go away.

John closed the door behind me. I sat down in a guest chair and noted his wall of fame. He has some very impressive pedigrees: Past-president of the National Psychiatric Council, Johns Hopkins, Notre Dame. All real; each one earned. I like having intelligent friends. Keeps my mind sharp.

He sat and stared silently at me for some time. I ogled him back. I crossed one leg over the other knee and leaned back in the chair. If we were going to have a stare-down, I might as well be comfortable. He smelled puzzled and a little annoyed.

"I'm not sure why you brought Sue to see me," he said. "I originally thought that you were looking for a trumped-up diagnosis . . ."

I gave a little sniff. "I wouldn't ask you to lie, John. I never have. And I don't think you're going to have to fake anything. What did you find?"

He tapped his fingers on the desk and took a deep breath. Then he leaned back in his high-back chair and laced his fingers behind his head. The springs creaked, sounding loud in the room. He stopped just inches before the balance would have pulled him over backwards. He took a second deep breath and let it out slow.

"You know I can't tell you that, Tony. However, I can say that she is very likely clinically depressed."

"No shit. I could tell you that."

"In short," he concluded seriously. "She's bordering on suicidal."

Oh, way beyond *bordering*. "I know." I nodded again to confirm it.

He dropped back to a sitting position abruptly, palms landing flat on the smooth wood with a sharp sound. His scent was mildew and burned coffee. Mildew must be amazed: Hey, I learned a new one!

Annoyance edged his voice. "Then why haven't you brought her in before now?"

I laughed and he frowned. "I just met the woman, John. This is the first chance I've had."

His anger reminded me that I needed to let him in on why I'd brought her in. I didn't want him to get the wrong impression, and assume I wanted her to be *treated*.

"The goal here isn't like your regular ones, John. She probably didn't mention how very suicidal she is." Although I knew she had. My voice flattened with edges of warning tones. John and I have a few philosophical differences. "Understand that she gets to die if she wants to, John. That's her choice. Your only job is to find out if she really *wants* to. I don't want her to spend years struggling from appointment to appointment with little hope of ever being happy. If she's ready, I'll do my job."

After a moment of internal sorting where his scent changed to thoughtful, he asked, "So what is she to you then, Tony? Why are you trying to help her, instead of just hunt her?"

"That's my business." My smile disappeared. He was fishing for confirmation on his guess to Sue. No dice. My words had a tone of finality. But he would have none of it.

"I've known you for years, Tony. I've seen that look before. You only think that your face is blank. But I can read you like a book."

I settled in. "Give me your best shot."

"You're in love with her." His face was serene.

"No, I'm not!" My temper flared.

He shook his head with amusement. "You always did fall for people with problems."

"Hey! Not always. What about Linda? She's normal."

"Linda?" He guffawed. "You think Carmine's wife is *normal*?" He rolled his eyes. "Wow!"

His face showed that he was feeling in control. He was wrong. I changed the subject. I didn't admit or deny his earlier statement. "Did she mention her mom's a junkie?" I knew she hadn't so John's raised brows didn't phase me.

He picked up his pen and cocked his head. "How would you know?"

I shrugged. "The nurse told me. Prescription painkillers, mostly—pops Percocets like candy". I raised my hands to add in the quotation marks. "Plus, she has track marks all over her arms." I raised one finger as I remembered, "Also, she's a heavy drinker. I smelled it on her breath."

He added the words "enabler" and "co-dependent" to the list on his pad.

When he was done I leaned back once more. I fixed him with a stare to bring him back to the subject. "So, can you make her happy? Or do I need to start making plans?"

He hedged just like a doctor. He grimaced so slightly that most people wouldn't have noticed. He leaned forward and rested his forearms on the desk, hands clasped in front of him. The body language and the scent said sincere and concerned.

"You know better than anyone that nobody is happy 24/7, Tony. We all have our doubts, our fears, our bouts of depression. I *do* think that I can help her make an informed decision. I think I can help her want to live."

See, there's that philosophical difference again. The concept that dying isn't an *informed* decision. Still, John's good. If I keep him on track, he'll end up doing the job I want.

I pointed a finger at him. "Without drugs." I'd met too many people that ended up more screwed up after they started taking medication. Then it really wouldn't be an informed decision.

"I won't prescribe them." His hands raised in a placating gesture. "I deal with behavioral problems. Sue is missing tools that most people are born with. She calls it backbone."

He waggled his hands. "As a tag, it'll do. She needs reassurance that she has value. She thinks she's worthless, ugly, unlovable. For a while, constant encouragement couldn't hurt. Congratulate her when she does something firm where her family is concerned."

He wasn't telling me anything I didn't already know. I wouldn't have even bothered to sit down with him except I didn't want him to know that I'd heard the whole session.

"Oh, I think I'll get plenty of opportunity for that after I move in. I'll be all alone with her and her mother."

"Move in?" I could tell from his scent that he had found a bone to chew on. That's right. Sue hadn't mentioned it. Interesting. He sat with his mouth open just an inch, the question trembling on his lips. Then he dropped it. He blinked but his face gave nothing away. His scent did, though. He'd just realized that Sue wasn't being completely open. It was a pretty big thing to leave out of the session. His words were quiet and calm.

"Well, that will help. Really, though, she needs to be somewhere far from her immediate family. I suggested that but she didn't feel capable. With you there, she can learn how to deal with her mother and family one issue at a time with space enough not to feel trapped. If you can keep even a little professional distance and not get sucked into the mess, I know we can set the right wheels in motion."

Right is relative. My final diagnosis might end up being different than John's. If the tricks of the trade don't show a turn-around in her death wish in a reasonable time, I'd make my plans without telling him. Still, I nodded.

We talked for a bit longer, catching up on mutual friends. When we finished, I joined Sue in the waiting room. She spoke cheerily but it was a lie. "Am I a total fruitcake? You were in there a long time."

I smiled. "John didn't tell me anything I didn't already know. He says you need a buffer between you and your family. He also says that he wants to keep meeting with you. Would that be okay?"

She looked from me to John, then nodded shyly and a little embarrassed. "I enjoyed talking with you, Dr. Corbin. I'd like to meet with you again."

"I enjoyed it as well, Sue." His smile was warm and genuine. "Why don't we meet tomorrow, around the same time."

"Will Laura get pissy?" I asked

He shook his head. Just chocolate, no black pepper. "Nah. She's got some monthly meeting to attend. I was on my own anyway. I think this is important." He looked at Sue very pointedly. "I think *you're* important." She smiled but dropped her eyes. I guess I need to work with her on how to take a compliment.

We drove to my office next and signed the security consultant and bodyguard agreements. We agreed that a lease for my space in the basement would be a good idea. Sue read each document entirely and then initialed each page before she finally signed them. She even corrected a typo in the form.

"Do you really have to leave town?" she asked nervously after all the paperwork was signed. I gave a copy to her and kept one for my file. "What about the gate? And Vinny?"

"Yeah, I've got to go. They're expecting me. I wouldn't worry about Vinny. He won't come back for awhile. But if it'll make you feel better I can leave my car at your place. I'll take a cab. Vinny knows my car. But I don't think he'll risk his life for such a small amount of money."

I didn't want to alarm Sue, but I *was* a little worried. I called Gary right then and there and explained the problem. He agreed to fix the fence as an emergency call that day.

Chapter 21

Sue sat on the bed at my house. We drove there after the office so I could pack. The poker game sometimes lasts more than a day so I usually take spare clothes.

"Can I go with you?"

I shook my head and stuck a couple of shirts and a few pairs of underwear in a bag. "No ladies. No exceptions."

Sue hugged her knees to her chest. She looked miserable. Sad and embarrassed about Myra; about everything. "I'm sorry," she said, for the tenth time.

I sat down next to her on the bed. "Look, this doesn't have anything to do with you. This is something that I do every month. I'm not running out. But I told you—I won't change my life."

She smiled but it was sad. I hated seeing her sad when I was going somewhere to have fun. An idea occurred to me.

"Say, tell you what!" I sat down next to her and slipped my arms around her shoulders. "All of the wives and ladies of us guys will get together tonight while we're playing. Why don't I see if you can go along with them? I've heard they have a great time. They use a limo and everything!"

Her eyes lit up with equal amounts of excitement and fear. "Do you think they might? I don't know any of them."

"Hey, they're great gals. Lots of fun! I'm sure they won't mind."

I picked up my cell phone and dialed a number. Carmine answered and I explained my brilliant thought. He put Linda on the line. A few minutes later, it was all set up; Linda was real curious to meet anyone who had caught me, and she'd come to pick Sue up on the way to get the other women.

Linda suggested that Sue dress up, since they were going "clubbing." My brows raised. I've been clubbing with Linda before. It's an event. I chuckled and hung up.

I suggested that Sue not tell Myra that she was going out. We both knew the old bat would try to spoil it. Sue flat refused.

"No. I should be able to go out once in awhile. I should be able to have friends. Plus, I can't exactly *sneak* out with a limo sitting in the drive. I'll just have to ignore Mom's reaction. I hope it won't embarrass Linda too much, though."

I nodded, but added. "Don't worry. Linda will make sure you get out the door. She can handle Myra without even sweating."

I drove her home. When I kissed her goodbye, it took longer than I planned. I was hot and bothered by the time I left, and she was pleased and proprietary about that reaction.

Chapter 22

I arrived at Carmine's with a few minutes to spare. I stopped by the bank first. Then I remembered I had forgotten the briefcase from Vegas and had to go back to the house. I knew the case wouldn't make it past the guards, so I put it in the trunk after sliding the papers into an envelope using my gloves to keep any prints intact. The guards met me at the door. I handed them my Sig and the Colt derringer back-up. I pulled a wad of money from my pocket and turned that over, as well. The game is cash only. No checks. No house credit.

They still patted me down and ran a metal detector wand over me. Hey, it's a lot of money. I can put up with certain indignities. They got to look in the envelope without touching, but didn't get to read the contents. When I was cleared, I was given a tray of chips. They're normal plastic chips like you buy at the discount stores but they're assigned much higher values than dimes, nickels, and quarters. More like fives, tens and hundreds.

Carmine has a great house. It's a rambling ranch-style with a separate enclosed poker room where we can lock ourselves away from the world. If you can think of a debauched activity, you can find it at Carmine's. Drinking, smoking, gambling; as much and as often as you want. No sex or drugs, though. At least, not on poker night. The poker games are guys only and drugs are out.

Five of us play each month. Me, Carmine Leone, Joey "The Snake" Karasiuk, Ira Hillyard, and last but not least, Louis—pronounced "Louie"—Perricone. The five of us grew up together in the Family.

The drill is that you arrive, pay the guards the buy-in of

ten thousand, plus a grand each for their fee. It's the same guards every time, so no surprises. The fee from each of us keeps them neutral. They clear you, hand you a rack of chips, and keep your weapons. We play until there is one winner, and the winner always takes home the fifty thousand. It either pays the rent or lays you low. On a good month the game lasts a couple of days

Carmine was at the bar fixing a drink when I was ushered in the room. Carmine smells like whiskey, cigar tobacco, and recent sex. Carmine always smells like recent sex. Today he smelled specifically like Linda.

It took awhile for me to find something that smells like Linda. When I did, I had to laugh. She smells like a *sarracenia rubra*. I didn't take much botany, but when I smelled one in a little flower shop back east, I looked it up. The common name is the Sweet Trumpet Pitcher. It's carnivorous, like a venus fly trap, but the flowers smell like roses. That's her, all right. Sweet but deadly.

"Hey, Tony! Glad you could make it!" His hearty words were tinged with curiosity. He motioned to the bulky envelope I carried.

I lowered my chin to acknowledge his unspoken question.

"Wouldn't miss it. Do you have a second? We need to talk."

He nodded and motioned with his head for me to follow him to the back. On the way past, I said my hellos to Ira, who's an accountant, and Louis, who handles protection gigs like Vinny. Ira smells like fresh cut lemon grass with overtones of cherry cough drops. Louis reminds me of the desert. Sort of dry and sandy.

Carmine closed the door behind me as I entered a small conference room off the back of the bar. He sat down at the table and motioned me into a chair.

"What's up?" His face was serious. I could smell his anger. I had invaded a "play" night with work.

I told him about the whole Vegas trip as quickly as I could. He kept his eyes on me and listened with his whole body. He didn't interrupt me once; he just waited until I finished.

I handed him the envelope. I watched his face and scent flow from concerned to angry to outright fury.

"Any ideas who's been telling tales?"

I was sitting back in my chair with my arms crossed over my chest while he looked over the papers. I shook my head. "Not one. I'm just the bearer of bad tidings, I'm afraid. They wanted you to think it was *me*."

His scent muddied—too many things to sort.

"I'll take care of this," he said flatly. "I hate to say it, but I'm glad you brought this with you. Nothing can be done today, but I'll start the wheels in motion. You just keep doing what you're doing—and watch your back," he added.

"Always do. Let me know when you find out anything. I want a piece of it." My voice was flat and cold. I don't like being set up.

He nodded his head once. "Let's go play some poker. It'll help me think."

Joey the Snake arrived just as we sat down at the table. Joey probably has a scent, but he always smells like Vick's Vapo-Rub. I don't know why he uses it so much, but the eucalyptus overpowers everything else.

Carmine was the host so he dealt first. After that the deal goes around the table, clockwise. We were six deals in when the phone rang. Carmine turned to watch one of the guards answer it. It didn't slow down the conversation for the rest of us. We were discussing the state of affairs in the Middle East. No business talk; sports or current events only.

"Tony?" Marvin was holding the receiver out to me. "Phone call. It's Linda."

Carmine looked at me sharply. It's amazing—and flattering—that after all these years he's still jealous of me. He crossed the room, took the phone and the guard backed off.

"What's up, baby?" I didn't watch him. I went back to my hand. I had four out of five for a straight flush. The odds of drawing into it were hopeless but what's life without risk? I put one card on the table. It wouldn't be dealt until Carmine returned.

"Hell no!" Carmine growled. "No way."

I could hear Linda's voice over the receiver. If I focused I could listen. Linda has a real penetrating voice. Not shrill or sharp, but it carries. If you want to save your eardrums when you're talking to her, hold the receiver away a few inches. In fact, Linda's whole personality carries. Her essence. You can walk into a room and you just know that she's there or has been there.

Linda is lovely. That's not a word that you can use to describe most people but she is. She's not beautiful, or hot, she's lovely. She looks delicate and fragile, but she's as tough as nails.

She's probably about 5'6" with straight, blonde hair. Her piercing eyes are ice blue. Her body will stop traffic but only because she works at it. She knows her assets and her faults and plays them right. Linda's bubbly and outrageous and intelligent. If she hadn't been so damn avaricious, we probably would have stayed together. Still, you can't help but like her. I figured that she and Sue would hit it off.

The table conversation had moved on to sports. The Broncos were having an undefeated season but the puppy quarterback was hurt. The discussion was whether he would play the next game. Since Carmine was the dealer, we couldn't play without him. The bet was six hundred to him. Joey folded when I only wanted one card. Ira was hanging in there. He doesn't bluff, so I was in for some stiff competition.

Carmine came over, the portable phone to his ear. He said, "Yeah, hang on," and handed the phone to me. "Your lady needs a sitter."

I nearly spit out a sip of beer. "Oh, shit. Don't *even* tell me!" I took the phone. "What's up, Lin?"

I could hear loud voices in the background. Someone was arguing. "Hang on, Tony, let me get outside." I could hear her staccato steps on the polished hardwood. A door opened, then closed and then there was blessed silence.

"Tony, baby, you there?" She calls everyone baby, and everyone hates it.

"I got here about half an hour ago. Ohmagawd! Did you see this place! It's *Tara*! I didn't know this place even existed. I really like Sue, Tony. She suits you." There was static and she faded out for a second.

"You're breaking up, Linda," I said. Carmine dealt me a card. It wasn't what I needed so I folded. Then I told Joey to deal me out of the next hand and backed up my chair so the others could play.

"I've got a situation."

I moved to the other end of the room and sat on a bar stool. The static cleared on the phone and I heard Linda's voice again. "Can you hear me now?"

"Yeah. Go ahead."

There was silence for a moment. "Eeww, there's goose poop all over the ground! I just got it on my new shoes. Just a second." I heard movement again.

"Come on, Linda," Frustration edged my voice, "Pick a spot." I spoke loud since the phone wasn't by her ear.

I repeated the words several times. Finally there was a response. "Okay. I got in the limo. Anyway, here's the deal. I get here and Sue is dressed, but not good enough, you know? All she's got is really dowdy office stuff."

I twirled my hand, hoping she would speed up. The one thing you can't get Linda to do is go faster than she wants to. And it's questionable whether you want her to. Once she gets going it's like a runaway freight train.

"But she's got the greatest hair, Tony! You ought to see it up like I did it!"

"Linda . . ." I said pleadingly. "The game?"

She remembered where I was. "Oh yeah, sorry. Anyway, I told her that the clothes just had to go! I had to dig through her whole closet and then chop up a silk shirt with sissors. But we found her something to wear. You ought to see her, Tony. She's hot! She'll make the guys go crazy at the clubs."

My eyes narrowed and my voice grew flat. I've seen Linda's version of 'hot'. "I'm not sure I like the sound of that."

She blew out an annoyed breath. "Oh please! We're going to Carmine's clubs. We don't have a *hope* of getting hit on."

I had to agree with her. Carmine is the jealous sort. Everyone knows it. Nobody would want that kind of trouble.

"So what's the problem?"

"Oh yeah! Anyway, we're all set to go and jeez—that mother of hers. She's like the bitch from hell!"

I let out an exasperated breath. I was wrong. Linda's a runaway freight train with multiple spurs. "No shit. But can we move this along a little, Linda? I've got to get back."

I could imagine her placating hand movements. "Okay. So anyway, we were just about to leave when the front door opens and in comes this little yuppie family. Dad, Mom, and two rugrats." She paused and then sighed. "Actually, that was mean. The kids are cute. It's the parents who are jerks. The mom is Sue's sister."

Yep. I knew it.

"They started in on Sue, saying that *Mommy dearest* had promised that Sue would watch the kids 'cause of how Sis was *inconvenienced* last week, whatever that means."

I rolled my eyes. "Sue and I went to Vegas together— without *permission*."

There was a pause before her incredulous voice. "You're *joking*. I hope."

"'Fraid not."

There was a slow exhale of air. "Oookay, then. So we've established that Mom and Sis have it in for Sue. Problem is, Sue's trying to cancel. She says she feels guilty."

I shrugged. "No surprise. She's seeing John Corbin for that very thing."

I could hear a smile in Linda's voice. "John-Boy? No kidding! I haven't seen him for ages. How is he?"

I glanced at the poker table longingly. Another hand was starting without me. "Stick to the subject, Linda. I want Sue to go out tonight. Any ideas?"

"Well, I actually did have an idea but Carmine shot it down. If you can get him to bend we'll be home free."

Carmine glanced at me just then like he knew what Linda was saying. "Go ahead."

"Mike and Jerry are our bodyguards tonight. You know how Mike adores kids. Got four and a bun in the oven. He hates clubbing but Carmine insists on sticking him with it 'cause he's big and mean looking. We're not going to *do* anything tonight, Tony. We'll stick to Carmine's clubs. Word of honor." I could see her in my head, holding up her hand like in a Girl Scout salute.

"So . . . what? You're suggesting that *Mike* watch the kids? Why not tell the parents to get screwed and just leave with Sue?"

"Easier said than done. We're in the limo. It's Carmine's new baby—this year's model. We're blocked in by the other car. We'll have to satisfy them or ram the car out of the way. Carmine wouldn't like that." I had to agree with that. God knows how much insurance costs on one of those beasts.

"I asked him, Tony. Mike, I mean. He'd rather stay here with the rugrats than go with us. Carmine said he won't pay for Mike's time to babysit. I suggested it to Sue and she said she would pay. Thing is, I don't think she should be responsible for it. I mean, it's not like she said she would and *forgot*. Someone else promised her time. That just isn't right. The kids already adore Mike. You know how kids are around him. He's playing some board game with them in the next room while we're working this out. So what do you say? Carmine will okay it if you pay. I still think the parents should pay. I'll try to push for that on this end. But Carmine will want *your* word."

I thought about it for a moment, and as soon as I thought of Sue I could feel her. Angry and hurt. She wanted so badly to go have fun. She liked Linda. But she felt guilty even though she knew she had no reason. That decided it. I held the phone away from my ear without covering the speaker.

"Yo! Carmine." He turned to my voice. I could see his hand. Unless someone could beat a full house, Queen high, he had the pot. It made me glad I wasn't sitting in this hand. It was a pretty big pile, with mostly blue chips.

He raised his chin slightly in acknowledgment.

"I'll pony up for Mike if you'll okay Linda's idea. What do you say? My lady needs a night out. Her family are assholes."

He snorted lightly. "From what Linda says, they beat out Joey's family." He let out a slow thoughtful breath as I walked closer to the table.

Joey responded to that statement with raised eyebrows. "Gawd, I hope not! I feel for your goil if they do."

His people are serious jerks. Talk about dysfunctional. Unfortunately, I had to agree with Linda.

"C'mon, Carmine, what say? You know that Mike would rather be with kids. I'll pay his fee."

He tapped his finger on the table. "It's not just that, Tony. I'm just not sure that I want the girls going out with just *Jerry* watching them."

I knew that he'd been having trouble with Jerry for a while now. Had it gotten worse? Was I sending Sue into danger?

I could hear the edge in my voice. "Yeah? What's up?"

He moved his head in tiny little shakes. He was trying to fight off a bad feeling. He smelled a little angry and worried. He set his cards on the table face down while he thought.

"He's been real pissy lately. He asked for a promotion and I turned him down."

"What did he want a promotion to?" Carmine doesn't usually hold a guy back if he wants to move up in the world.

He looked at me pointedly. "To *your* job." Well, I'll be damned. I didn't know he was interested in my line of work.

"I told him I was satisfied with your work for me and we didn't need two in this region. Not anymore. The work's just not there. He knows that he can't freelance without my support but he's not happy." He shrugged. "But, I guess it's not the end of the world. He'd never hurt the girls. He knows what I'd do."

He thought for a moment while I held the phone at my side. I could hear Linda trying to get my attention. I pressed the mouthpiece more firmly against my thigh, muffling the words.

"Mike got a raise last year. Think you're up to it?"

He named a figure and I let out a slow whistle. "Guess I'll have to win tonight."

"So you'll pay? Up front?"

I reached into my stack of chips and sadly removed most of my blue chips from the pile and dropped them into his stack.

"Agreed?" He grimaced for a second but nodded reluctantly. I started to put the phone back to my ear. I stopped when he suddenly snapped his fingers. He raised an index finger in the air and shook it slightly.

"Wait. Have them stop at Carlin's first. They can pick up Jake to take along. Yeah. That'll work." He smiled the smallest bit, then went back to his hand without a word. His scent calmed immediately. He was no longer worried. That relieved my own unease.

"You catch all that, Lin?" I asked.

"Thanks, Tony! I'll make sure that Sue has a real good time tonight." She paused and then added, "Did you know they call her *Suzi*? Makes her sound like a Barbie doll. Blech!"

"Well, it *is* her name."

"So? Damn it, when you know that someone doesn't like the name and she said so right in front of them, you ought to call them what they want. Hell, she could want to be called Carmen Miranda and they should respect that, you know?"

I couldn't disagree.

"And her mom! God, that woman's attitude sets my teeth on edge, you know? She started complaining about how she was so *helpless* 'cause she's in that chair." Linda's voice was bitter and sarcastic.

I spit the words angrily. "She's faking!"

"Hey, doesn't matter! *My* mom's in a wheelchair too! She does just fine."

Shit. That's right. I'd forgotten that. Once upon a time, I thought Lissell was going to be my mother-in-law. She's great; got a real zest for life. Linda inherited that from her.

"You remember. It was such a stupid thing," said Linda with equal parts of anger and sadness. "She got drunk and fell down a flight of stairs. Broke up her back real bad. She's paralyzed below the waist. Won't ever walk again." The words ended flat but I knew Linda. She was near tears thinking about it.

"How's she doing, anyway?"

Her voice firmed up. In my mind, I could see her chin raise high defiantly. "Mom didn't take it lying down. Shit happens. Carmine bought her one of those motorized wheelchairs. You know, the ones with the buttons to move around? She buzzes around her place like a madwoman. It's solar powered and everything. Mom insists on living by herself. She even does her own shopping with a little cart that she drags behind. Last month, she went to Hawaii with her cronies. They fixed the wheelchair so the back laid down."

She hooted with laughter for a moment. "She did the limbo! *and* won the contest! Got a trophy and everything." She snickered. "Although I think they probably *let* her win."

I laughed. That sounded like Lissell. "Glad she's doing well."

"So I don't have any sympathy for someone that doesn't even *try*."

"Did you say that?" My grin was a mile wide.

"Damn straight I did! Didn't win me any friends. Except maybe Sue. Oh! I forgot to tell you. Mom asked me if Carmine might buy her one of those special wheelchairs with the tilted-in wheels. She wants to enter races! Can you believe it? She lost all of the fat on her upper arms when she had a regular chair and doesn't want to go soft." Her voice was proud, happy.

I laughed.

"Hey, I've got to get back before they bum Sue out for the whole night. Catch you later! Give Carmine a big smooch from me! He's great!"

"How about I let you—" But she hung up.

I clicked off the phone and handed it back to the guard.

"Everything kosher?" asked Ira when I returned to my seat. There was a new pot and a big stack of chips in front of Joey. Well, I'll be damned! He beat Carmine's hand.

I nodded. "Yeah." I turned to Carmine. "Linda said to give you a big smooch. Want it on the lips?"

He looked at me and I made kissing motions. His broad face split in a smile and he reached for his belt. "Yeah, baby. I'll show you what I want you to kiss. Pucker up."

Chapter 23

It was about 4:00 in the morning when Mike and Jerry were admitted to the poker game. Verbal reports won't do for Carmine when it comes to the girls. People can be bought or tortured. Carmine wants to see their faces. He's really good at spotting lies. He was better than me before I got my new nose.

Ira lost his money early and was snoring away on the couch in the corner. Louis had just lost his last chip and was sulking at the bar. If I didn't win the next hand, I was out too. Joey and Carmine were about even so it looked to be a long game in front of us.

See, once a person is out he can't just leave. We have certain rules. Fifty grand is a chunk of change and it's all cash. So all the games are on weeknights. That way there's a bank open the next day.

Then, to prevent any "accidents" as the winner is leaving, one of the guards escorts the winner directly to his bank. The rest of the players are stuck in the house with the other guard until the winner makes his deposit. Anything happens to the winner or the guard, the rest of us are held until we determine who's responsible. Then that person is eliminated from the game. Permanently. It's how Louis got his seat and Marvin his job.

Louis's predecessor had a turn of bad luck. He decided he needed the money. He should have asked for a loan. His problems were taken care of the hard way. Pity. Harry was a nice guy, but he let his problems get in the way of his ethics.

When Mike and Jerry came in, Joey took a bathroom break so Carmine could talk to them. Mike stepped over to the table while Jerry grabbed a beer from the fridge. Mike smells like good quality Italian spice—probably from Marie's cooking, like fresh basil and garlic.

"Everything okay?" Carmine asked.

"Yeah. The girls are all home safe."

"You get paid?" I asked Mike. "Or does Carmine owe you?"

"Nah." He gestured casually. "They paid. I cut 'em a break. They were nice kids."

"How much did you charge?" Carmine's voice had an edge to it. I wasn't sure what it was. Sort of a mix of stuff.

He shrugged. "Five hundred. Like I said, Cindy and Mike were real well behaved. Good kids. They just need a firm hand. Shame they're saddled with those parents. Little Mike—that's what I called him, has a real interest in shooting. Parents won't let him." He shook his head. "Shame to waste potential talent."

I chuckled under my breath when I thought about it. Bekki and hubby probably didn't plan on a five hundred dollar sitter bill.

"You charged them five hundred? What the hell am I paying you twenty-five hundred for?"

I replied before Mike could. I knew that he wouldn't speak his mind to the boss. He'd come up with something that would satisfy Carmine, but it wouldn't be the truth.

"You got him doing something he doesn't like doing, Carmine. You know as well as I do that costs more."

Carmine looked steadily at Mike. He smelled suspicious and a little angry. "You don't like going with the girls?"

Mike shrugged again. No big deal. "I can take it or leave it. I do what you tell me to do."

"Do you like it?" he asked slower, and a little dangerous.

Mike never lies to Carmine. Nobody does. "Truthfully? I'd rather be home with Marie and the kids. But the girls only get together once a month. I'll do it. No sweat." Carmine nodded, satisfied.

Mike turned to me. He smelled warm. "That's a real nice lady you've got, Tony. She's a keeper. Settling down material."

Carmine interrupted. "You and Tony can talk when you've finished reporting." Carmine doesn't take a back seat to anybody.

Then he turned to Jerry. Carmine's scent was suddenly different than when he talked to Mike. More aggressive, more heavily musky.

"Where did the girls go?" Carmine asked.

Jerry sat his tall frame in the chair that Ira vacated. Even sitting, he's a head above everyone else at the table. Jerry and Mike are both big guys but Mike has more upper body build. Jerry is slender but it's deceiving. He's actually the meaner of the two. Jerry brought a closed fist to his mouth and coughed. It's a nasty hack, from years of smoking.

Jerry smells like infection. Something's really wrong with him but he refuses to go get it checked out. It's a pervasive, thick smell. It's not the scent of death, like Leo, but close.

When Jerry got control of the cough, he replied, "We went to the usual places. Carlin's first for dinner. Then the Blue Velvet Room and finally Margarita's for dancing."

Carmine got a look on his face that I couldn't place. He smelled like anticipation; lust. "Anything *interesting* happen?"

Jerry leered, showing uneven yellow teeth. "Yeah. Linda hit on the new stripper."

Carmine's face lit up with a smile filled to brimming with triumph and lust. He smelled heavily of fresh sex. "Which one?"

"The little redhead at the Blue Velvet."

Carmine closed a fist and brought it down once sharply in front of his chest, victorious. "Yeah! I was hoping she'd see that one. I've been looking forward to doing that pretty little number ever since I hired her."

I shook my head with a smile. Carmine and Linda are quite a pair. They've agreed that it's not cheating if they're both doing the same person.

"She respond to Linda?"

Jerry smiled and it was a touch sinister. Made me look twice. Now he really did smell like Leo. Not good.

"What do *you* think?"

While Carmine was savoring his victory, I took the chance to ask, "How did Sue get along with the other girls?"

Jerry turned my direction. Jalapeños dusted my nose. No big surprise, I guess. But his words were polite. Good thing.

"She was real shy at first but Linda drew her out. By the end of the night, they were both wild. The only downer of the group was Carol."

Louis heard Carol's name and turned from his drink. "What did you say about Carol?"

"Just that she's out of sorts," said Jerry. "Real bitter right now. I think it had something to do with that kid she was seeing. She said you offed him. She was warning Sue to stay away from Tony, 'cause Sue would end up *property*, just like she was."

"Fuck!" Louis exploded with a level of anger and hurt that surprised me. He slammed his drink onto the bar hard enough that most of it spilled out over his hand. "She starts screwing around with some punk kid and just because he disappears, she assumes I did it? It never occurred to her that he might have just walked out on her?" Louis smelled betrayed; wounded.

"You tell her that you didn't help him disappear?" I asked.

"I never even confronted her with the affair! I figured it was a passing thing. Thought it might spice her up a little bit to hang around with a kid. She's been feeling old lately."

There was a sadness with that last. He stared off into space for a moment. I knew he was remembering better days. They've been together for almost six years. A record for Louis.

I almost didn't want to interrupt his meditation. "You might mention that you didn't do it. Maybe even help find him to prove it. She'd think better of you. It'd make points. Just don't rough him up when you find him. Tell her that you hope that she'll stay with you. That you want her to."

Damn! I sounded like John-Boy again. Every month it's the same. Maybe John needs to sit in on the next game and give me a break.

"Yeahhh," he said slowly, thinking. Hope rose from him

like a balloon. It lifted the edges of his lips into a smile. "I'll find the kid, give him back to her as a present. I'll be the good guy for a change. Yeah. I like that." The air became thick with citrus.

He pulled a cell phone from his pocket but J.R. tapped his shoulder before he could dial. J.R. held out his hand for the phone without a single word. Louis sighed with annoyance and embarrassment, flipped it closed and handed it to him. "Forgot. No calls out." He turned to Carmine. "Sorry."

Carmine shrugged like he hadn't even noticed. But I knew how intently he had been watching Louis out of the corner of his eye. "It's a joint rule, not a house rule. Nobody else cares, I don't."

I shrugged. "I don't care. You, Joey?"

Joey was just sitting down again. His scent was determined but not quite hostile. His face was blank. "We've got rules for a reason. I had to give up *my* phone. No calls. You'll be home in a few hours. Deal with it then."

I stood and walked to the bar to get another drink. Louis was still behind the bar so he passed me a beer in a green bottle. I like some of the imports. Others taste like boot polish.

Jerry sidled over to me. His smell preceded him and I had to turn my nose away. It's like standing next to someone who hasn't bathed for a year or so. "I hear that you've been referring out some of your jobs lately."

I glanced at him suspiciously. Where had he learned that? "Yeah. So?"

He was trying way too hard to appear nonchalant. It didn't wash. "So I'm available if you ever need a back-up. I'm sort of trying to break into the business. If you're thinking of easing up on your schedule . . . " He didn't finish the thought. He shrugged. "I could use a referral from you. It would carry weight."

"I'm not retiring, Jerry." I stood and walked around the end of the bar. I needed to find something to take the near-death smell out of my nose. Something strong. Peppers, maybe. Or garlic. Salsa! Yeah, that would work. I leaned under the bar, searching for an unopened bottle.

"How do you know that I've been turning down jobs?" I asked without looking up.

He didn't answer right away but his smell changed. He was thinking that I had stepped away because I was afraid of him. It raised my hackles. Okay, bad term, but it did. I looked at him sharply and abandoned my search for picante sauce to come around the bar and stand up close and personal. If he wanted a challenge, I was up for it.

Carmine was suddenly next to Jerry as well. Like me, he was standing a little too close. Jerry's eyes darted quickly between us and I could hear his heart beat faster. The blood in his veins was close to the surface and he smelled of fear and anger. Good. My senses now alert, I could hear a slight rattle each time Jerry breathed. He would be slow; an easy kill. A part of me wondered whether his blood would taste bitter. Would it be a taste I would enjoy? A little shiver raised the hairs on my skin. I let the thought rise to my eyes. I let him see exactly who he was dealing with.

"What the *fuck* do you think you're doing, Jerry?" Carmine asked forcefully before I could get a word out.

"Just chatting with Tony here." He tried to focus on Carmine but couldn't take his eyes off me. I knew my eyes were still human. No tell-tale glow. But they were the eyes of a hunter. In either form I was one.

He didn't immediately give Carmine his undivided attention. It was not appreciated. Carmine reached up and grabbed his chin. He twisted Jerry's face sharply until their eyes met. His voice was soft but had the weight of lead. "I said no, didn't I? Didn't I tell you that I don't want you doin' jobs? What, you deaf or something?"

Jerry swivelled on his chair to face Carmine. Satisfied, Carmine let go of his chin but not before he nearly took off a chunk of skin. Carmine was *really* in no mood tonight to have people go against his orders. Jerry had to look down to meet Carmine's angry gaze. Carmine isn't real tall, but that doesn't matter when you're the boss.

Jerry didn't look happy. He was much more hostile than he could afford to be. It made me wonder what he was hid-ing. "You said that as long as Tony was in the biz, I wasn't needed. If he's stepping down, I want a shot at it."

Something about the way he said that . . . "Did I say I was stepping down?" I moved a fraction of an inch closer. My voice was cold and heated at the same time. "When I'm feeling old enough to retire I'll let you know. And you better *hope* I never hear you were thinking of speeding along the process."

Carmine's face took on a wary look when I suggested advancement by assassination and his glare could bore holes. Jerry's eyes darted back and forth between us and his tongue flicked out nervously. "I didn't say nothing like that. I'm just asking for a chance to show my stuff."

Carmine poked a finger into Jerry's big chest, nearly pushing him backwards off the chair. You forget how strong Carmine is until he needs to prove it. "You'll show the stuff *I* want you to show, Jerry! Got it? I don't want you going behind my back talking to Tony or anybody else. You go through me and me alone. *I'll* decide when I think you're ready to try something different. *Capisce?*"

Jerry nodded, eyes flashing. But he didn't talk back.

"You and Mike head home. We'll discuss this tomorrow. Carlin's, nine sharp."

"Sure, Carmine, whatever you say." The words were cautious, not angry or sarcastic. Good plan. Carmine's got a short fuse. Mike had wisely stayed out of the fray and quietly followed Jerry out the door.

I sat back down and Carmine followed. He visibly smoothed himself out like a bird settling ruffled feathers. The table was empty of chips, so Joey must have won the last hand. Carmine picked up the deck and began to shuffle. Joey had taken in the whole scene without a word. Carmine responded to Joey's earlier comment about the turning off the cell phones as though he had never been interrupted.

"A few hours, my ass. You'll be cooling your heels until I get back from the bank, my friend."

Joey snorted and picked up the cards as Carmine dealt. When he had finished the deal, I remembered something. I held out my hand toward Carmine. "By the way, I think I have a refund coming?"

"Yeah, yeah." He dropped a stack of blue chips into my hand. I asked for smaller chips instead. It might keep me in the game long enough to win a hand.

Chapter 24

I got back home around noon the following day. Joey won the game. First time in months.

I went directly to bed. I called Sue, telling her to stop over if she wanted to. I must have been totally zonked because I didn't even hear when she unlocked the door with the key I had given her. Fortunately, she remembered the alarm code. I'm not positive giving her a key and the code were good things, but I did it.

I woke to warm hands rubbing my back. I was annoyed that I hadn't heard her but sighed contentedly anyway. I could smell her perfume, but underneath the artificial mask was her own scent. Sweet and musky. It made me feel warm inside. I glanced sideways and watched her hand squeezing the knots out of my muscles.

A part of me really resents that I'm getting this attached to her. But it isn't her fault. It's my problem. I need to pull back from her. I know it, but I don't want to. I also know that John was right. It's going to hurt to pull the trigger; hurt to see those hands lying lifeless on the ground. I'll dream about it. I know that, too. Maybe I'll end up needing to pull the trigger again to stop the dreams.

I fought my way back through the dark images to the feeling and scent of her very alive body. "Did you have fun?" I asked sleepily and then yawned.

I could hear a smile in Sue's voice. "I had a wonderful time! Thank you so much for setting it up. Linda and Ellen are great. Carol's a little odd, though." There was a tenseness in her voice that made me roll over to see her face.

I stared into her startled eyes and shook my head. "I heard about that. He didn't do it."

Her breathing increased. "Carol swears that he did. Just up and killed him. She feels trapped and scared for her life." Sue actually seemed afraid for her.

I frowned a bit. "Carol talks too much. But Louis is nuts for her. Always has been. He wouldn't do that to her. Jerry told him what Carol said at the club. He's going to try to find the kid and hook him back up with Carol if that's what she wants."

Astonishment passed over her face and wafted into my nose. She dropped her jaw. "He'd do that? She made him sound like such an ogre."

"Don't get me wrong," I replied seriously. "Louis *is* an ogre. If he didn't love Carol he *would* have offed the kid. It's not like it's beneath him."

"Oh." Her voice was small and quiet. Then she looked at me with a trace of annoyance and punched me lightly on the chest. "*You* didn't tell me that you and Linda used to date!"

That took me by surprise. I guess it never occurred to me. But now that I thought about it, it probably should have. "You know, it didn't even cross my mind. Is it a big deal?"

"It was so strange. When she first arrived, she looked around the house and was just in awe. She had to look in every room. She kept muttering under her breath, "It's Tara. Oh my gawd! It's Tara!" Then she said to me, 'Wow, Tony's doing well by you!'"

I laughed. It hadn't occurred to me that Linda would think I bought the house for Sue. I *did* expect the house to be a hit with her.

"I tried to explain that it was my house and she just nodded her head in that certain way. You know, the one that says, '*Sure* it is'. Then she said that you must really like me because you haven't spent this much for anyone *since her*."

I winced. Again, the truth was best. "Okay, I get the point. Linda and I were an item for a couple of years. But we broke up." I shrugged like it was no big deal. Truthfully, though, it had been a hard decision. One I regretted for months.

"We had different values. She wanted money and power

and I wanted someone to kick back with. They were mutually exclusive goals. She and Carmine hooked up. They're better suited."

"She's so pretty and fun. Do you ever regret not staying with her?"

I gave her a warm smile. Still self-conscious. "Feeling like a sparrow in a flock of peacocks?"

She nodded. "All of them are just gorgeous." I had no doubt she felt envious. I could smell the odor—it's pepper, but closer to cayenne flakes and seeds, like the ones you sprinkle on pizza.

I reached up and touched her face. She leaned into my hand. "They're trophies and they know it, love." I pulled her against my chest and spoke into her hair.

"If I wanted a trophy, I'd be with one of them. I want brains—and personality. Looks only last so long. One of these days Carmine, Louis, and Ira are going to want to trade in last year's model." Sad but true.

I tightened my arms around her in a hug. The scent of her this close stirred something inside of me. Something that made me think of home, safety—eternity. I fought it down with effort. I *like* to be alone. Unfortunately, the more I tried to convince myself that I wanted to remain alone, the more I smelled my own lie.

"What do *you* want?" she asked in something close to a whisper.

I thought about Mike's words—a keeper. Did I want one? I just didn't know. I kissed her hair. "You."

It slipped out, just like the 'love'. Warm sugar and cinnamon wafted through the summer forest. I breathed it in deep and had to shake myself to come back to my senses. I changed the subject back to the evening. "Other than Carol, did you have fun?"

She smiled and I could smell her happiness. "Linda is so wonderful! We spent the whole night talking. We probably bored the other girls. We have so much in common! I feel like I've known her my entire life after just a couple of hours."

Then she moved her head a little, amending with a bit of chagrin, "Actually, more than a couple of hours. We dropped off Ellen and Carol around 1 a.m. and sat in the back of the limo drinking wine and talking until almost 3." She started laughing suddenly and her chest bounced on mine.

"It was so funny! When we went to a club called the Blue Velvet Room, Linda was pretending to hit on female strippers! I swear I've never laughed so hard!"

She couldn't see my face. I bit back a laugh. I didn't quite know how to tell her. I wasn't sure she could wrap her white-bread middle class values around Linda.

I raised my hand to scratch an imaginary itch on my upper lip. It hid the smile. I don't think I hid the twinkle of amusement. "Um, she wasn't pretending."

Sue raised her head and looked at me curiously. All she could see was my hand scratching. "What do you mean?"

I removed my hand and the smile peeked out. "Linda swings both ways."

Sue continued to look confused, shaking her head to indicate that she didn't understand. I tried again. "Linda is bisexual. You understand that term, right?"

Her face was a case study in amazement. Her jaw dropped. "She *has sex* with *women*?"

"As well as men." I waggled my hand. "Actually only one man—Carmine."

Her voice was incredulous. "And he doesn't mind?"

I shrugged. "Not a bit. He likes to watch." I watched her take in that bit of information. Her eyes stayed wide long enough that I had to ask, "Are you okay? You look a little weird."

"Well . . . it's just that Linda was in the room when I was changing. And she was so attentive to everything I had to say in the limo! I mean . . ." she stammered.

I understood immediately but her assumption wasn't correct. "Did Linda *hit* on you?"

She cocked her head a tiny bit. "Well, no."

"Then don't presume she's interested in you." She couldn't quite seem to get past shocked. A small laugh escaped me.

Probably rude but I couldn't help it. "Haven't you ever had any gay friends?"

"Yeah, in college. But only guys. I've never had any female friends that were—well, like Linda."

I hoped that she realized that I wasn't laughing at her but I couldn't keep the grin off my face. "Sue, do you leap into the lap of every man that walks in the room?"

"God, no!"

I looked at her pointedly. "And Linda doesn't leap into the lap of every woman that walks in the room."

She still seemed nervous so I turned off the smile and looked at her with as much seriousness as I could muster. "Look, Linda knows that you're with me. That means that she knows you're straight. She also knows I don't share so she would never approach you. Would you think less of her if she only dated Hispanic men? Or black men?"

She shook her head.

"Of course you wouldn't." I shrugged. "So what if she likes both men and women? Big deal. You can still be friends with her. She won't try to seduce you. Unless you want her to . . ." I added cautiously. I didn't really know all that much about Sue's tastes. I shouldn't automatically assume.

Her face immediately panicked. "No! No, that's not my thing." All of a sudden, though, she looked pensive and then blushed. She smelled of something just short of desire laced heavily with embarrassment.

"Thinking about it?" I asked slyly.

She shook her head. "Not really. I'm just not sure whether to be grateful or insulted that she wasn't interested in me."

I laughed loud enough that she finally broke into a smile. I hugged her against me tight. We laughed and rolled in a contented glow. I wanted to stay like that forever, just being happy; being together. Trouble was, I knew someday the other boot would drop.

Chapter 25

A couple of days passed. Things were going well with Sue. I was gradually spending more time with her, getting to know her. We went out to dinner last night with Carmine and Linda. Carlin's has the best Italian in town. Big surprise. We all ate more than we should have and then stayed up late playing poker back at my place. You'd think I would have had enough of the game, but nah, I love playing. My favorite is Texas Hold'em.

I find that I'm not sleeping at Sue's house much. I had tried. I'd spent a few nights there, locked away in the downstairs. But Sue could never get comfortable enough to do more than snuggle. She was too antsy for sex and couldn't sleep. That doesn't work for me. It left me frustrated beyond belief. I've put a couple of changes of clothes there, and some toiletries, but nothing permanent. I don't trust Myra enough to store my guns there. And where I go, my guns go. I know it bothers Sue, but there's no helping it.

Speaking of guns—I had finally assembled my new toy. The Thompson Center Arms Encore pistol was gleaming softly in the fluorescent over my reloading bench. I'd just finished wiping it down with the last coat of oil. The package Mary had given me contained the final custom piece. It was a 15" stainless steel barrel, chambered in 6mm PPC, with a black chromium oxide finish. You can't buy a black chrome stainless steel barrel off the shelf. After all, who'd want to blue a stainless finish? Me. I like the weather resistance of the stainless, but they're way too visible at night.

I'd debated long and hard about the scope, but finally

settled on a Burris Black Diamond Titanium 4X-16X-50mm ballistic. It's a little big for a pistol, but Encores are adaptable. They're intended to be either pistols *or* rifles. The frame holds the scope and it can be fitted with any number of barrel calibers and lengths. I was still doubting Burris' claim of a true "scratch-*proof*" lens, not just scratch resistant. Supposedly, you don't even have to use a clean, dry cloth on it. If it's true, it will be hugely useful in the field. And I like Burris scopes. People will say that there are better foreign optics available. Maybe. But any guy who would quit his job as a top designer and start his own company just because his old firm was cutting corners earns my respect.

I was looking forward to taking it to the range to sight it in, but not today. I'd gotten an interesting message on my cell phone while I was in the shower. It was the second odd call in the same number of days. The first one had been from Leo. I'm not sure how he got my number. I wasn't surprised at the call when his spy failed to retrieve the papers. The day after the poker game, I'd remembered about the briefcase in the back of my car and went to retrieve it. The trunk had been popped and the case forced open. It could only have been one of Carmine's people—or, more precisely, one of Leo's people.

Leo's snarl came over the tape. "I want my property back, Giodone. You give it up or things will start getting messy."

Things were *already* messy. I was pissed that I had to take the Mustang in to get the trunk latch fixed. I told Carmine about the call over dinner. He cut off any speculation by Linda with one sharp word—"Enough!"—and then went back to eating dinner. Conversation was a bit tense after that, but I managed to lighten the mood after a few minutes.

I called Leo back when we got home and left a voice mail of my own. "Screw you."

Today's message *was* a surprise. I'd recognized the voice, but only because I'd spent some time following him. He apparently knew it, which bothered me a little. The little shit really *is* good.

"We need to meet," Scotty had said. "I have some information you'll want. Southside Mall, in front of the pretzel stand. 12:00."

I didn't really trust the kid, but he'd never called me before. He piqued my curiosity. But I wasn't going to meet him in public. He'll understand if it's not a set-up.

I dropped by a store on the way. I got to the mall early and wandered around some, stopping in the gift shop to pick up a card and some candy for Sue. Holding a bag made me look more inconspicuous. I couldn't spot any plain-clothes cops, and none of the mall guards even glanced my way. No surprise. Today I was a blonde with a mustache wearing a ball cap.

When Scotty arrived, I followed behind him at a distance. He was nervous—that much was obvious. I wasn't close enough to smell his emotions, but his body language was definitely edgy.

I got lucky. He stopped to tie the lace on his running shoe, raising his foot onto a bench. I had been wondering how to work my plan. He stood in line at the pretzel stand, ordered a hot salted one, and then drenched it with mustard after he sat down.

I walked right up to him and tapped his shoulder. He jumped a foot.

"Hey, kid. You left your cell phone back there." I placed the prepaid cell phone that I'd bought across town face down on the table. I could suddenly smell him—the painfully raw fear blended with cloves when he recognized my voice. The shock of surprise was enough to tell me that he was nervous not because of any set-up, but because he was scared to meet me in person. He was just that impressed with me. Okay, that was a little flattering.

I didn't wait for a reply. I just walked away as he stared at the phone in shock. In the reflection of one of the store windows as I walked away, I saw him pick it up and turn it over. He saw the yellow sticky with three words printed. "Go. Five minutes."

I exited the mall. He's a bright boy. I figured he would

understand. We're both in the same field. We can't afford to meet.

I went to the Camaro I'd borrowed from Carmine and sat down to wait. When the sweep hand reached the last second of the five minute mark, I hit the speed dial that would ring his phone.

His voice was cautious when he answered. "Hello?"

"What's so important that we have to talk, Scotty?" I could hear a roaring sound in the background that grew and faded at intervals. I listened closely for a minute. Ah. He was at the skateboard park. Good choice. He should be able to spot any undercovers without sweat.

I pulled out of my parking space and headed onto the freeway. "Man, that was sweet, Mr. Giodone!" he exclaimed. "I didn't even recognize you at first! And I like the cell phone idea."

"Glad you approve. When we're done, destroy the phone. I'll do the same." I said flatly, but it pleased me that he didn't call me "Tony." He hadn't earned the right yet. "What's the scoop?"

He went business on me. That's Scotty—he can turn it on or off like a switch. "There's some new talent in town. Word is that your boss is under contract."

That got my attention. How the hell would *Scotty* hear about a new assassin in town who was after Carmine?

My silence must have been interpreted as disbelief, because he continued. "I've got a friend who works the streets. This new guy likes them young—and she looks it, so he's been spending some time with her. I spend time with her, too. The guy talks in his sleep and she listened in."

"Why would *she* care if something happens to Carmine? And why would *you*?"

"She doesn't care. She told me because she knows what I do and he was competition to me. I guess she's sort of sweet on me."

He tried to pass that off as an explanation. No good. "What's in it for *you*?"

There was silence for a moment. I could hear him

breathing. I wished I could smell him. His voice lowered to a whisper. "I got made the other day. The mark took off running because he got nervous. Kids aren't supposed to make people nervous." He sounded annoyed, and a little scared of the truth.

He isn't a kid anymore. Teenagers absolutely make people nervous. Scotty was entering a new phase of his life.

"So, anyway," he continued, "I'm hoping that if the info is useful, you'll teach me stuff. New methods."

Ah. He wanted to learn about guns. He was going to have to stop doing close-in work.

"And?" I pressed.

"And . . ." he grudgingly admitted. "If Leone is dead, he can't put me to work. He's the only game left in town, other than the crappy whiners who really don't want it done *right*."

Good. The kid's got some pride in his work. He's right. Most people don't want to let an assassin do his job. They want *input*. That leads to mistakes.

"Let's say I believe you," I said, as I turned randomly onto a residential street. "Can your friend ID the guy for us?"

"Um, I took a few liberties," he said nervously. "I was going to just . . . well, but no go. I can't do the guy. He's too good. He made me in a heartbeat. I just barely got out. But I've got him *set up* to do. Sally's already got a date with him for tomorrow. He'd wanted it earlier, but she stalled. He's coming to her place, or what he *thinks* is her place. There's a parking garage across the street that closes at 10:00. Her appointment is at midnight." He paused and when I didn't respond, he hurried on. "It'll check out. I promise. Put in a good word for me. I know you can find me if you're willing to show me a thing or two. Thanks."

He hung up. I thought about calling him back, but if he'd followed instructions, his phone was already dead. I pulled off the battery from the unit in my hand—it would work on my regular cell. Then I closed my fist around the phone. I felt the plastic begin to give as I applied pressure. I squeezed harder. A moment later, it shattered in my grip. So much for that hundred bucks. These new muscles are occasionally damned useful. I dropped the shards of plastic in the trash bag hanging from the gear shift. I'd dump them at a couple of different car washes around town. I swung the car around at the intersection. Carmine's house was my next stop.

I wasn't there long. He wouldn't believe the tip without talking to Scotty, "up close and personal." I couldn't blame him. There hadn't been a peep on the street about Carmine. We'd checked. So now I was driving a black sedan with Mike in the passenger seat next to me and Carmine in the back.

Normally, Nico would be in the car beside me instead of Mike, but Nico was . . . unavailable. His current residence was at the bottom of a lake. Carmine's boys had lifted some nice prints off one of the papers in the briefcase. Nico shouldn't have had any access to the document to have a print on it. After some prompting, he'd admitted to searching my car.

Carmine still wasn't satisfied that he had plugged all the leaks. He was taking the whole thing very personally, and very seriously. We were in the bulletproof rig today and he was packing in a couple of places.

I had to admit, I was surprised about Nico. I would have bet my favorite body part that Jerry was the leak. But Carmine swears that he's had no opportunity. I guess I have to believe him. But if I were Carmine, I'd be watching my back with that guy.

We'd been following Scotty for a couple of blocks, looking for an opening. I saw him start to cross the street to reach an arcade when I made my move. He looked both ways and darted into the street between two parked cars. I stomped on the gas and felt the car leap forward. Then I screeched to a halt in the middle of the road right in front of him. Carmine opened the door of the sedan on the fly, just barely missing his leg. I turned in my seat and lowered my sunglasses so he could see my face.

"Get in, kid."

Scotty's face was surprised, but he did what he was told. He slammed the door behind him and we took off again. I could hear Scotty's heart beating like a triphammer. He was good, but he knew he was out of his league. I'm sure he recognized Carmine. He's been in the papers a lot—mostly in the society column. Carlin's is a favorite of the "in" crowd.

The air was suddenly awash with hot and sour soup. It made my jaw clench and I felt a trickle of spittle at the edge of my mouth. I wiped it away before anyone noticed. Damn it. I should have eaten before I went to Carmine's. My stomach was going to start growling any second.

I kept my attention on my driving while Carmine talked to Scotty. Mike and I both pretended we were deaf.

"So you're Scotty," he said. Carmine's voice gave nothing away.

"Yeah . . . I mean—uh, yes sir, Mr. Leone." Good boy. Make some points.

"Tell me what you told Tony. I want some more detail."

Scotty cleared his throat. "Okay. Well, I've got this friend named Sally, and she . . ."

Carmine interrupted. "Define *friend*."

I could see him shrug in the rearview mirror. "We hang out. Sometimes we have sex."

Mike shook his head and sighed. The kid's pretty young, but he wouldn't be the first.

I asked a question from the front seat. "I thought girls made you nervous. And how do you see her when you still live with your folks?" I'd told Carmine I would only butt in if it was something important. His relationship with the girl could be.

"Well, I mean, Sally's not a *girl*. She's a hooker. And I don't live with my folks anymore. I got bored and took off. I live with another guy." He shrugged. "He doesn't care what I do as long as I pay him rent."

Carmine was the one to ask the next question. His voice was sharp and intended to frighten. "What is this "Sally", some sort of drag queen?"

"No, no. Nothing like that," replied Scotty, who was starting to smell confused. "I mean that she's not a girl you *date*. She's just a hooker."

Ah. Mike gave me a knowing look. It's a common attitude. They've even got a name for it: the *Madonna complex*. Either a girl is a *good girl* that you date and marry, or she's a *whore* and not even seen as a person. That attitude wouldn't win any points with Carmine. He's very equal opportunity. Of course, he has little choice with Linda around.

"So tell me what Sally told you." Carmine's voice wasn't warm and fluffy, but he kept on point.

"Just that there was this guy that picked her up. She got him off and he fell asleep. He started mumbling your name and some other stuff. She really didn't know what to think. The next day he picked her up again."

Carmine was listening intently. He was leaning against the locked door, watching the kid's face. I was doing the same in the mirror when I could spare a second.

"So anyway, the next time he fell asleep, she checked out the room. She found a case and opened it. I guess there was a gun inside that breaks down and fits into foam. She put two and two together. She told me because she thought he might be competition. She doesn't like the guy much and wants to help get rid of him. She said she can set him up. Get him wherever in the room you want him. The apartment belongs to a friend of hers. You'll have to pay for anything you break, though."

Carmine sat silently for a long moment, just watching the kid. He was sorting. Without taking his eyes off Scotty, he said, "Tony? Mike?" I knew he was asking our opinion.

On the way to Carmine's, I'd driven by the only apartment building in town that's across the street from a parking garage. Each unit had a balcony overlooking the street that is accessed by a sliding glass door. It wasn't a *bad* set-up, but it was obvious that Scotty didn't understand how to plan a job using a firearm. The garage was too close to get away after a gunshot sounded. The complex has a full-time security guard. He would recognize the sound and either investigate or call the police.

But I did like the idea of using *a* garage. Fortunately, there was another parking structure about a block and a half away with a clear line of sight to that side of the building. The Thompson with the 50mm scope would work fine so long as I loaded the shells a little hot and she could get that glass door open. The Thompson is a single shot, not a semi-auto. I could use one shot to take out the window, but couldn't reload before he took cover.

"The girl will need to get him out on the balcony," I said flatly, implying to Scotty that I already knew where the job would take place. "Or at least get the sliding door open. I'll only have one shot. The mark will be paranoid—especially since *you* already made one try for him. He won't want to be in the open like that. I sure as hell wouldn't if I was on a job."

I conceded a point. "Of course, if the girl flubs it and he kills her, I can probably still pop him when he comes out on Vine Street. It's the only exit he can use. The back one has a dead bolt. Killing her would be an impulse. He wouldn't have time to get a key."

Scotty started when I said all that, because he knew that he hadn't said anything about the location. Once again, the cloves and fear returned, blended with amazement.

"Yeah, he might be paranoid like you, Tony," said Mike, "But *you* wouldn't visit a hooker during a job and let her see your piece." said Mike. "The guy sounds pretty dim. It should be an easy hit. I say we believe the kid."

Good point. I took a deep breath, trying to sort out which scents belonged to Scotty. He smelled mostly like mustard—probably his underlying scent, but there was no deceit. I'd say he was possibly being used by the girl, but he hadn't smelled particularly warm or concerned when he talked about her, or when I suggested she might die. And he already tried to take the guy out. No, if Scotty said the guy was a pro, he probably was. He seems to know his limitations.

Carmine watched me in the mirror and then turned his attention back to Scotty when I gave a brief nod. I was nearly back to the spot where we'd picked him up. I stopped the car just a little up the street.

"I'll be in touch, kid," said Carmine as Scotty left the car. It was the closest Scotty would ever get to a "thank you." If it played out, I'd check with Carmine about some apprenticing.

When I left Carmine's after the meeting, he said that he would do some checking and get back to me, one way or the other. It would be at least hours, maybe even days. I might as well take the card and the now melted candy over to Sue.

Chapter 26

"Tony! Wait!"

Sue's plaintive call was cut off sharply as the door slammed shut behind me. I stalked to my car. I was more furious than I'd been before in my life. The sun was just setting, creating long shadows as I walked. As I reached the car, the pole lights around the circle drive blinked on and chased my shadow away.

The other boot I had worried about had dropped, all right. Right on my frigging head.

I got the car keys out of my pocket and promptly dropped them. I just barely stopped myself from kicking the car door. I'd be really pissed if I had to take the Mustang to a body shop because I couldn't control my temper.

One tall oak door opened as I reached down to pick up the key ring. Sue raced out, leaving the door open. "Tony, please! Don't go. I'm sorry. It'll never happen again."

I looked up at her, furiously. "Damn straight it won't!"

I could hear Myra's shrill voice through the open door. "Just let him go, Suzi. He *must* have something to hide if he got so angry over an honest mistake."

I glared at the voice behind the triangle of yellow light and bit back a smart-ass reply with gritted teeth. She wasn't worth the effort. I should have trusted my first instinct and dusted her when I met her.

Sue was in tears as she ran around the car. I stepped back. I didn't want her to touch me right now. I was entitled to my anger and I would be damned if I would let it roll away in that silvery glow.

She stopped when I backed up, not coming any closer.

Her chin was quavering and salty tears rolled down her cheeks. I felt her embarrassment and pain. Fear and sorrow tightened my chest and all I wanted to do was wrap her in my arms. No, damn it! I'd been careless enough.

"I'm so sorry," she whispered.

"Not your fault." It wasn't. But it didn't calm me down any. I unlocked the car door and she let me.

Her voice remained soft and guarded. She didn't want to be overheard. "Where are you going?"

"Out."

"Are you coming back?" Her fear hit me full in the nose. She didn't include the word, "ever" but it was implied.

"Probably not tonight."

She nodded, miserable. The fear was a little less but only a little. "Can I come with you?"

"I'm not real good company right now, Sue. I need some time alone." The tension was still in my voice. Big surprise. "If you don't want to stay here with *her*, go to a motel, order some room service and veg out in front of the television. Or go out somewhere."

Her arms were wrapped around her body, hugging tight against the world. Her head dropped and glittering tears fell to the pavement. "I don't know anyone to go out *with*. And I don't want to stay in a motel. I don't like motel rooms when I'm alone."

I stopped as some of my anger was defeated in her pain. I leaned against the car, hands resting on the open window jamb. I bowed my head and took a deep breath. "Why don't you call John? I'm sure he wouldn't mind."

She shook her head. "It's almost seven. He's probably already left."

I opened the car door, leaned inside and grabbed a pen and paper. I wrote a number and handed the sheet to her, being careful not to touch her skin. "This is his home number. Call him." When she wouldn't meet my gaze, I touched her shoulder. I fought off the familiar pulling in my groin. She looked up suddenly and gasped at the contact. "Call him, Sue. Please."

She took strength from me gratefully and nodded. It was shaky but she nodded.

I drove off with a roar, leaving her standing alone and forlorn in a circle of light.

I went to Nick's. I needed somewhere where I felt at home. The band was up and running as I stalked in the place. The joint was packed. A gust of wind caught the door and slammed it shut behind me, rattling the windows.

"Hey, easy on the building," Jocko exclaimed as I grabbed the only available stool and pulled up to the bar, "It's not paid for yet."

Not funny. I glared at him. One look at my face made him utter a low wistle. He grabbed a shot glass with one hand and an unopened bottle of Maker's Mark with the other. He broke the thick red wax seal and poured the caramel-colored liquor into the shot glass, stopping just short of spilling.

Without a word I grabbed the glass and carefully lifted the whiskey to my lips. I threw it down my throat but forgot to inhale first. The liquid seared and nearly went down the wrong pipe. I refused to cough. A shudder passed through me, and I closed my eyes and took a deep breath. Warmth spread through my chest as it flowed toward my stomach. When I opened my eyes again, the glass was full. A small smile played at the corner of my mouth and I gladly downed the second shot. I couldn't get drunk anymore, but the effort made me feel better.

After a third shot, Jocko finally said, "What's got you so lathered up?"

I snorted and pushed the glass toward him a fourth time. He tilted his head and shook it a little with a sigh. He smelled nervous. A bartender really doesn't like to get an angry guy drunk. But he poured.

My voice reflected my irritation. "I got a visit from Bob Sommers today." I sipped the whiskey this time to make him feel better.

"That homicide dick from the Fourth? Shit. He's so Ivory Soap that he squeaks."

I was sipping when he said that and I laughed abruptly,

spraying whiskey on the marble bar. It wasn't all that funny but it just occurred to me that Sommers really *does* smell like Ivory Soap. I hadn't realized it until that moment.

Detective Robert Sommers is tall with greying blonde hair. Blonde hair doesn't grey well. It makes him look jaundiced. He has a perpetually rumpled look that always reminds me of Columbo. They'd have been pals.

Jocko wiped up the spray of whiskey from his prized bar top. When I didn't elaborate further, "And . . .?"

I noticed that the person at the next stool was unusually interested in our conversation. He didn't look at us but he stared too studiously ahead and smelled anticipatory. I motioned with my eyes alone to Jocko that we were being overheard. He caught the look and without a word looked up and glanced around the bar.

He raised a huge arm and caught the eye of one of the waitresses. She moved through the crowd toward him. When she reached the bar she waited.

"Watch the bar, Marni, I've got business."

She nodded her head and moved behind the bar, sparing me a smile. I returned it with a nod.

We wound through the crowd. The smells and sounds were nearly overpowering. Not as bad as the casino but it didn't help my frayed nerves any. When we got to the edge of the dance floor, I almost laughed. Wall to wall people and my booth in the corner sat eerily empty.

We sat and I noticed for the first time that he had brought the bottle and two glasses. I must be really messed up.

He poured some whiskey in my glass and then in his own. He took a sip, but you could hardly tell the difference after. I knew Jocko. He could nurse a shotglass all night and nobody would know it was his first.

We sipped, me silently, him with a quiet slurp. He set the glass on the table in front of him and rested forearms on the chipped and scarred wood. He smelled patient. There is no hurry to Jocko, no rushing. He's the perfect bartender. Wait long enough and you'll find out everything.

"Like I said, Bobby-boy dropped in." He nodded. He

glanced at the crowd as I took another sip, watching for any signs of trouble. I didn't begrudge him. He's the boss. His eyes darted from group to group, picking out voices a little too loud, movements a little too sloppy. He lighted specifically on one group of boys just out of their teens. As we watched, one of the kids lifted a mixed drink from a neighboring table when the people left and started to sip it. Jocko stood. "Hold that thought."

He never took his eyes off the table as he wove through the throng like smoke. Quite a trick for someone his size. He reached the table and descended on them like a storm. Angry energy crackled around him, almost enough to see. He plucked the drink out of the kid's hand and spoke quietly enough for only that table and my wolf ears. "Out."

One of the boys started to argue. Jocko simply crossed his arms over his massive chest. Muscles strained and rippled under the short sleeved white T-shirt, the product of years of training.

No argument would be sufficient. He could lose the business, lose everything. He has no humor for that. The kids swallowed their pride before they started swallowing their teeth. The kid with the drink didn't even look at him. He just picked up his stuff and tried to slip out while his friends were blustering. Jocko reached out a beefy hand and tapped his shoulder. He froze and turned nervous eyes to Jocko.

Jocko studied his face for a moment. I knew he was committing every feature—the color of his eyes and the slope of his nose to permanent memory. "You're 86ed."

The boy opened his mouth but Jocko just turned away and walked back to my table. Trusted that they would leave as instructed. They did.

The people descended on the suddenly empty table like vultures. Hands reached for chairs almost before the bodies were completely out.

By the time Jocko returned to the table there was a new party in the same spot as though the previous group never existed.

"Sommers bothering you again?" he asked me like we were never interrupted.

I took another slug of whiskey. "He was investigating a grand theft."

Jocko leaned forward, eyes intent on me, his whole energy engrossed. "You don't steal and that's not his turf."

He's right. I don't steal. My next words were bitter. The anger returned full force. "Apparently, *anything* is his turf if it involves me."

"What happened?" Antifreeze seeped from his pores.

"Myra," I replied with biting intensity, as though the word was enough. It wasn't.

"Myra?" He paused. All of a sudden he thought he understood. I knew it from his smell. A new lady. A new problem. Partially right.

"Sue's mother." Then I realized that he doesn't even know about Sue. It felt like we'd been together years, but it had only been a little over a week. "The brunette I was in here with last."

Jocko nodded knowingly. Cloves drifted to my nose. Right again.

I told him the whole sordid story. How I got to Sue's house earlier to find Sommers' car. I didn't tell him about the panic that pounded my heart when I saw he and Myra in earnest conversation inside. If he had a search warrant, I was screwed. I'd slept down there at least two nights. He's never had any way to get my fingerprints or DNA before, and I wanted to keep it that way. Shit.

But he didn't have a warrant. He had merely intercepted a phone call. Myra was missing a brooch—a Tiffany's special. Compliments of Sue and the millions of gamblers in the state. Cost more money than my car, which made it grand theft. He heard my name mentioned when the call went out and dropped by himself. He'd sell a good chunk of his soul to get some samples.

Sommers isn't stupid, though. When I'd gotten there, he stepped back from the whole deal a bit. I could tell he was suspicious. Myra seemed to know too much about the crime.

"Do you mind if I have a look around down there?" he had asked Myra.

"I mind," I replied hotly. "There isn't any way that I could have gotten upstairs to get any brooch, Lieutenant. I come through a separate entrance in the back. I don't even have a key for the stairwell door." I'd made certain of that.

He turned to Myra. "Is that true, Mrs. Quentin?"

"Absolutely not! He comes and goes in this house as he damned well pleases, Detective. Don't believe him! I know he took my pin."

Sue spoke up, to my surprise—and certainly to Myra's. "It is true, Lieutenant. And I would appreciate it if you would address your questions to *me*. I'm the owner of this house and I'm the one who wrote the lease with Mr. Giodone."

Wow! I was surprised, but pleased, at the force of her words. One word had perked up Sommers' ears. His scent was suddenly a blend of odors. His face looked suspicious and frustrated. "Lease? I wasn't aware that the basement was a separate dwelling." That one word changed the whole complexion of the investigation.

I shrugged. "It didn't used to be before I hired on with Ms. Quentin to help her install some new security components. You can see the state of the fence outside, Lieutenant. She wanted the work done quickly and I've stayed a few nights to write up plans."

I thanked my lucky stars that Sue and I *had* written up a lease when we did the bodyguard agreement. Without permission from me, Sommers wouldn't touch the case. He once told me that if he ever caught me he wanted it so clean you could eat off it. He was ready to leave. Hat in hand.

But then I had a brilliant thought. I remembered the monitors. When my buddy Gary had come in to repair the fence, Sue had him change the tapes in the monitors. Just yesterday, I'd set up a machine in a back room to review the tapes. There had been nothing of interest, but that was before Myra called the cops. Every camera doesn't overlap perfectly, but there *is* one hidden right over the stairwell doorway.

Myra probably had never noticed it.

"Lieutenant, I think you might want to see something." I had led Bob to the room and shut the door behind him. Then I rewound the tapes for the day.

"What did they show?" Jocko asked. He was smiling wickedly as I related the story to him. Sweet thick antifreeze hung in the air and his eyes glittered with unconcealed glee.

The lights blacked out just then and my heart rose to my throat. The strobes began to flash, the glittering ball smoothly turned and the music slowed. The male lead's voice lowered to a seductive whisper, the stuff of frantic hearts and satin sheets.

I returned my gaze to Jocko and saw him in snatches and flashes through the darkness. Multi-colored light played across his face. The drumbeat was in time to the strobe. I felt each beat in my chest. I closed my eyes to block out the input. Everything became surreal. I started to speak, to answer his question. Then I was free-falling. I was weightless; breathless.

The channel changed. My voice was a thready alto and I was telling the same story all over again. As I opened my eyes I was staring at a ceiling. The colors were warm, the air smelled of cinnamon.

I heard John-Boy's voice. "How did it make you feel when your mother set up Tony?"

I knew the answer before the sound reached air but it wasn't my voice. They weren't my thoughts. "Horrible. Terrible. I was embarrassed, angry, guilty. You name it. She had no right!"

"Could she be worried about you? Worried that you've made a mistake by getting involved with him?" Always playing devil's advocate, huh, John?

Hell, no! But that wasn't what I said, what We said. "Maybe. I like to believe that sometimes she cares. But probably it's because she doesn't like Tony. He stands up to her. She can't bear that. She always has to be the strongest. Has to be the *only*. I spend time with him. That's not allowed. If I spend time with him, it's being taken away from her. They can't co-exist."

"So, what else did they show?" The warm tones and cinnamon were still there but John had Jocko's voice, a
scratchy baritone. I felt an awareness. A knowledge of who
and what we were. Then blackness again.

I was back in the bar. The lights were up, the song long
over. Had I been speaking? I couldn't remember.

"What?" I asked hazily.

"The tapes, Tony. You said you rewound the tapes and
showed them to Sommers. The tape showed Myra walking.
You said it like it was a big deal. Then you just blanked out
on me. You was there but you wasn't. Ya know?"

I tried to focus on him. Really. I wanted to tell him what
was happening to me. I wanted to tell someone. Anyone.

No. Stick to the subject. Angry was better than confused
right now. The tapes. Yeah.

The tapes showed Myra getting out of her chair. No surprise to me, but it was to Sommers. He was angry. I could
see it, smell it. There was Myra, in living black and white,
unlocking the door to the downstairs with a key. I wondered
where the hell she got it. I heard a sound from Sommers that
was amazingly like a growl as we rewound a second tape
near the wet bar downstairs. It showed Myra's right side as
she snuck into my bedroom and stashed the pin under my
mattress. Oh, real smooth.

He gritted his teeth and I heard a slight grinding as he
spoke. He grudgingly asked me whether I wanted to press
charges. I could. Breaking and entering, false accusations.
Sommers hated asking, hated that I was the good guy for a
change. But he's right wing law and order. It's his job.

I declined gracefully, but I thoroughly enjoyed watching
him dress Myra down on his way out. Threatened to prose-
cute her for false reporting. That's a crime too. The best part
was, he'd never again believe her. That made me a little less
pissed about the whole thing. Only a little.

"Damn!" Jocko let out a slow breath and finished his
whiskey with a fast swallow. "You sure you want to get
involved with that one?" He shook his head. "It's not starting out real well."

"Myra's been at my throat ever since I moved some stuff in." I tipped over the shot glass on the table and busied myself rolling it in circles. "I swear to God, if she ever pulls . . ."

"Whoa, whoa!" interrupted Jocko quickly, "Back up. Since you *moved in?*"

I tried to dismiss it quickly. "Moved *some stuff* in. I've still got my place. I just keep a few things over there."

"Even so . . ." He suddenly smelled a little worried and slightly happy. "You never even left a toothbrush at Linda's and you *proposed* to her."

I didn't know how to explain it. It's not like I had a choice. It sort of happened without much input from me. I can't just make the feelings go away. The need to be with Sue. A part of me doesn't *want* it to go away. I feel things I've never felt before and it's incredible! But it's scary and annoying and frustrating too. That much I told Jocko. He nodded sagely like he'd been there before.

Then it happened again. Free-falling; frozen in place. Again I was in two places at once. I could see Jocko. See the bar, feel the table under my hand—but I was somewhere else too. I felt happy. Heard a second heartbeat that wasn't my own. There were hands on my shoulders rubbing gently and it was nice. I saw light and polished wood superimposed over the bar. I heard a loud crash, like wood breaking but hard and fast. There was female laughter. I smelled Linda's signature perfume.

I looked around me. She wasn't anywhere close that I could see. Wherever Sue was, I was with her again. I felt her surprise when she felt me with her and the shock broke the connection. I was myself again. It was like a brick wall was suddenly constructed in my head, shutting out the sensations. The wall smelled like fur.

"You okay?" I heard Jocko ask as though in a dream. "You disappeared again."

I sounded as shaky as I felt. "Yeah. I'm fine."

I stayed at Nick's all night. Jocko let me stay in my booth even after he closed up. He did take the bottle away from me. It's the law.

I got back to Sue's place around dawn. She was still up.

When I walked in the door I could smell her. Soft and musky, worried and remorseful. She had fun but would rather have been with me. I wanted to hold her, touch her. But I knew that if I laid a single finger on her, all would be forgiven. I couldn't seem to help it. I didn't have to like it, though.

We went downstairs so we could have some privacy.

"Did you have fun?" I asked casually as I stripped off my shoes, emptied my pockets and checked my piece.

"You know I did." She gave an amused sniff that was not quite a chuckle. "You were there for part of it."

I couldn't acknowledge that. It was too weird. *Way* too weird. I kept moving, kept the hell away from her. "Where were you?"

"I saw John but you know that. He didn't think I should drive. So I called Linda. I couldn't think of anyone else. She came and got me. We bowled."

"Bowled?" It would explain the images. Bright lights, pins falling.

"They've got a bowling alley in their basement." Bright citrus blended with some other emotions that I don't know yet. "I like Carmine. He reminds me of you."

He should. We grew up together.

Sue smiled happily. "He's decided that Linda and I were twins separated at birth."

"How so?" I sat down on the couch and patted the seat next to me. She sat down with a little bounce.

Her smile remained. She turned in her seat and moved one bent leg onto the cushion. She put her left hand on the back of the couch, not quite touching me. "We are so much alike! We have the same views on politics. We like the same movies, the same foods." She smelled sad suddenly yet still happy. Wet tangerines. Weird.

"It's how I always thought having a sister would be. But how can I be so close to someone that I barely know? It was like . . . okay, she told a story about when she was a kid. Her older brother stole a candy bar and then blamed her. That happened to me all the time. But I knew what she would say next. I knew how her parents punished her, as though I remembered hearing the story before. But I just met her! Is that strange?"

It's strange all right. *Scary* to be more accurate. I knew that story. Sue was picking up on my memories. Feeling the warm fuzzies I still have for Linda.

I shook my head, trying to break that image and at the same time remembering something else. "Who else was there? There was someone else."

"Oh!" She blushed. "Barbara was there too."

"Barbara?"

The blush remained. "She's the woman from the Blue Velvet Room. The one that Linda was . . . well, *interested in*." I smiled knowingly. I reached up and touched her arm to ease her embarrassment. I ran fingers along her skin. I couldn't help but admit that I enjoyed the electricity as it played over my hand.

She tipped her head like a bird. "That was strange too. Their relationship doesn't seem to bother me anymore. Once I saw them together . . . it's like they're a couple and so are she and Carmine. We talked about how odd I felt at first. Linda was real open and honest about why she's the way she is. She made it seem so absolutely *normal*. We talked about everything and nothing. Carmine took Barbara home about one and then went to close one of the clubs. Linda and I stayed up all night and told dirty jokes and laughed about stupid crooks, the television and people we both know. God! Just everything. I just got home a few minutes ago myself."

So, not waiting up after all. She stopped suddenly and looked at me as though she just remembered something. "Oh! That reminds me. Barbara says hi."

I shook my head. "I don't know anyone named Barbara."

"She knew a lot about you. It was definitely you." She tried another approach. "About 5'2", long, reddish-gold hair? Has a body that would stop traffic?"

She saw my confusion and tried to think of something that would get a response. "She has the most incredible eyes. They're almost golden, with a darker ring around the pupil. It's a real startling effect."

Golden eyes. Wolf eyes. That did it. My voice was awestruck and horrified. "B*abs*! Linda and *Babs*?" I couldn't even fathom Linda sleeping with my mentor/attacker.

Sue seemed startled at my reaction. "Is there something wrong? You suddenly smell scared."

Linda and Babs. Wow . . . Carmine would have his hands full with those two. It sunk into my brain slowly, from a distance. I apparently wasn't hitting on all cylinders. "What did you say?"

"I asked if there was something wrong," she repeated, confused. "You look nervous."

I shook my head, quick and tense, standing up and backing away. "No. That's not what you said. You said I *smell scared*."

She shrugged and stood as well. "I might have, I guess. It's the same thing."

I felt my heartbeat increase and there was a whole flock of butterflies or maybe bats in my stomach. She was smelling emotions like I could. It wasn't a big deal to her. That was worse. Yeah, definitely bats. Clawing and churning and making me nauseated. Scared didn't cover it. The connection between us was getting tighter. The circle growing smaller. Ever closer. Like a noose. If she was getting my wolf traits and I was seeing things through her eyes, where would it end?

"Are you all right?" Sue seemed truly concerned. She moved closer to me and I backed away almost unconsciously. I could smell her. Smell her worry; concern; affection. Sweet musk. Trees and dew and moss. As she stepped closer I could smell the thick sweet beginnings of her desire. She stopped suddenly and her nostrils flared. Like she caught my scent too.

Now closer still. I could see the desire and hunger flare out from her eyes. They grew darker and more electric. I stopped abruptly as my back hit the wall. Why should I be afraid of this? Why was I terrified that she would touch me?

As soon as the questions appeared in my mind, I knew the answer. The feeling that I get when I'm with Sue, even without sex, is like an addiction. There's a high when she's there and a dark and bottomless low when she's not. Like any addiction, it's out of control. Out of my hands. I *need to* be with her.

Sex is one thing. I know people who are addicted to sex. It's the physical sensation, the carnal need. That's the addiction. Not the person. This addiction was to *Sue*, not what we did in bed.

I realized that if she were in danger I would kill for her. I *had* killed for her. I would drop everything in my life to be with her. With a shudder I realized that I'd die for her. I would willingly lose my entire personality. Thirty-seven years of individuality . . . gone.

She took one more pace. We were almost touching. I was shaking but couldn't seem to tell her no. I couldn't convince my muscles to move away. She touched my cheek with her hand and it felt so incredibly good. I closed my eyes and savored the tingling contact.

She moved that last fraction of an inch and I let her. I kept my eyes closed and breathed in the scent of her. I balled my hands into fists to keep from reaching out to pull her against me. I desperately wanted to wallow in her scent, in her body. But I couldn't stop her from touching me. God help me. She ran hands down my cheeks, down my neck and ended up by resting them on my shoulders. She leaned forward and pressed her body the full length of mine. My hands were shaking now. They wanted to do something that I refused to let them do. I could feel my teeth clenched tight together. All of the muscles in my body were rigid, fighting the need. I could beat this. I would have control of my own life!

Her words were a whisper, hurt, confused. "You don't want me . . . Why?"

She moved back from me. I could feel the electricity between us lengthen and stretch like a rubber band. It danced along my body and made me open my eyes to look at her. She stood in the middle of the living room, her eyes were wounded. She wouldn't meet my gaze. But even through all of that she smelled like warmth and desire. She smelled like something that belonged to me. Just me. Like a favorite sweatshirt or a child's blanket.

I spoke softly but it was loud to my ears. Being around her seemed to bring out the wolf qualities more strongly. "I'm losing myself, Sue. Getting lost inside of you." I walked toward her even though I knew it was a bad idea. The current strengthened; sweet tingles. I stopped.

"Any more I don't know whether I'm feeling my own emotions or yours. I don't want to lose my identity; my sense of self."

She looked at me then. Then she nodded. "I know. Like running with you when you were a wolf or seeing the bar when I was at Linda's."

She saw the bar? I didn't realize it went both ways!

"But I'm not as afraid of it as you are." She moved a little closer to me. "It's not bad. It's just different. I sort of like some of the stuff, like the running. And the sex! You can't deny that it's incredible." She smiled and it made my stomach pull.

I was actually trembling. "No, I can't deny it. But don't you see? That's the problem. It's *too* good."

She slipped her arms around my waist. She smiled at me. "For the first time, Tony, I think that there might be a reason to live. It's because of you—because of whatever is happening to us. Maybe if I try real hard, I can have a life. Who knows? I might even stand up to Bekki and Mitzi."

My body didn't listen to my brain. It did nothing to protect itself. My arms reached for her and pulled her against me. I swallowed hard. She slid her hands underneath my shirt. The tingles made me shudder. It could be so good. But the thoughts of danger kept rising from the depths of my mind like creatures from a Lovecraft novel. She had already been used against me once. My enemies were becoming her enemies, and I couldn't be with her twenty-four hours a day.

The bottomless emerald of her eyes sucked me inside them once more. The pleasure raced across my mind, smothering the doubts. All I could think about was her body against mine; her skin touching me; her lips; her scent, and I was lost again. Drowning in her, basking in the warmth of the electric tide that crashed over me. I kissed her slowly, deeply. Like I would crawl inside her body.

When it ended, she took my hand and led *me* into the bedroom. I gave in. Damn! what a wimp I am. I didn't stop her when she opened my shirt one button at a time. She planted gentle kisses on my skin in a downward path. She was kneeling in front of me when she pulled down my pants to expose a part of me so dense with blood it was almost painful.

She took me in completely and it was at once both velvet soft and cutting sharp. My head fell back of its own accord and my eyes closed. I was beyond breathless. It was even more intense than I had imagined. Her teeth scraped me lightly and it was my turn to cry out; pleasure and pain. She only took a taste; a slow, lingering sample that ended with a quick pull that weakened my knees and shut out coherent thought. She stood and pushed me back on the bed. If I bounced, I don't remember.

I watched her with animal hunger as she slipped off the silken panties she wore. When she sheathed me and straddled me I couldn't think. I just let it happen and enjoyed the rush.

She moved over me and instinct took over. I ran my hands along the curves of her body, kneaded her breasts as she rocked over me. I grabbed her forearms and pushed her backwards to change the angle while she moved. She cried out as her back arched. It pleased me. When she finished trembling from the climax, she leaned over me and kissed my neck. She murmured in my ear. "I love you, Tony."

It touched something in the deepest center of the wolf inside. Sparked something that reached out to her. When it pulled, she went. She followed the lure through a door that I didn't know was there. I rolled her over, still in her. Her legs wrapped around me and we moved together like we were one body. I could see the edge. I could have it all if only I'd let go. I just had to let it happen.

I kissed her neck then bit her softly. I gripped her skin and ran frantic hands over her body. Her clothing defeated my need to touch all of her. I needed more, even more than the first time I was with her. She clung to me, bit me with abandon. She moved against me with a fury and passion that made my last shred of willpower break.

My arms tightened around her until I finally had to let go and clutch the bed for fear of hurting her. Every thrust built power. It flowed between us and grew to white hot intensity.

The orgasm caught me unaware. It centered nowhere and everywhere. Every nerve, every muscle achieved the absolute height of ecstasy. It was unlike anything in my experience. Sort of like living your life with only the moon; and suddenly seeing the sun for the first time. No other woman would ever be enough. No other sensation could fulfill.

I wanted to say so much but I didn't have the words. It wasn't love. It was more and less. I couldn't think of anything to say to her words except, "I know, baby. I know." And I did know. I could smell it, feel it like a pulse against my brain. I felt another barrier break inside me. A little one but still . . .

Tighter and tighter squeezes the noose.

Chapter 27

I was sitting on the floor in Humphries' two days later, tearing apart the security sensors for regular maintenance when my phone rang. I was going to let the voice mail pick up, but when I glanced at the display, I answered it.

"Tony here."

Carmine's voice hissed over the line. "It's on. Find the kid. He's got the details. Your usual fee." He must have finished the arrangements. I sighed. Tonight wasn't the best night. I'd paid a bunch of money for tickets for a traveling Broadway show. They were second row center, and Sue had been ecstatic. But there was no way I could attend the play and still make the hit and this job was more important.

"This one's on the house," I said with a dark smile. I'd been thinking about the new hitter in town. The only ones who could have sent him were Vito or Leo—probably Leo. It was his style.

Carmine and I had been very busy boys for the past forty-eight hours. I hadn't seen much of Sue, but that was okay. She's been spending a couple of hours a day with John in therapy. Linda and Babs have been keeping her busy in the evening playing pool and bowling. Anything to keep her away from her family. I'd have to thank Linda for that. Of course, it helped that she'd met them.

I could feel in my head that both John and Linda were helping. It made my life easier. I could continue on with the plan without worrying about Sue. She was in safe company.

Carmine's been real low-key about the whole operation. He's been having Marvin pose as Nico when calls come in. Nico's contact has been getting fed bad info. In the meantime,

Carmine has been changing schedules and locations of materials like mad, so that the paperwork is no longer valid.

I hung up with Carmine and immediately dialed in the number to the theater box office. There was one more showing the following night. I was able to switch the tickets, but not for the same seats. Oh, well. Sue would just have to understand that I had to work. I couldn't tell her what sort of job I had to do. I'd already changed some things in the past couple of days so I could work on systems after business hours.

One of the systems had been at Carmine's house. We rerouted a bunch of his security sensors and feeds so that if you cut the wiring, the lights on the panel will go out, but a silent alarm trips in Carmine's war room in the basement. That's where he's been spending most of his time. Linda hasn't said anything, but she goes around armed for bear. I can't tell her that there's no need. The wolf bitch living with them can protect her just fine.

Babs tried to talk to me again when I was working on the alarms, but I wouldn't listen to her. I just kept asking Carmine to remove her so I could work. Fortunately, he complied. I know I'll have to deal with her eventually, especially if they were going to stay a trio—and it looks like they are. It's not just lust I've been smelling.

I'd be happier if I never had to see Babs's face again. Every time I do, the nightmares come back.

It's as much a memory as a dream. I'm lying on my stomach, wearing black. I'd been studying the redhead for a week, watching her every move. I knew she would be walking this path, at this time. When she reaches the top of the rise, I raise my weapon.

She stops halfway down the other side of the small hill. I see her head raise. Her nose points into the air and she turns in a circle in the light of the moon. She gazes directly at me, as though she can see me through the dense trees.

I pull the trigger.

It's impossible, but she moves out of the way. I couldn't possibly have missed from that range. There's a blur of motion and she's suddenly next to me.

"You have no idea what you're dealing with!" I was too surprised to ask what the hell that meant.

She reaches up in a blur of speed. I feel her fingernails grip my throat and dig in. She lifts me into the air like a toy doll as blood pours over her upraised arm.

I clutch at her hand but her fingers are like iron bars. I kick out with my legs, but it's useless. With a sudden movement, she flings me to the ground and my throat tears away in her fist. The pain was immediate and intense. White waves of light shoot through my brain. My scream was cut short when the equipment necessary to make sound falls where she threw it to the ground beside me. The only sound I can make is a gurgle that I've heard before. I try to use my hands to stem the flow of blood, but found that the hole was too big. I was going to die.

"Don't worry," she says coldly as I lay bleeding to death on the ground, wiping her hands on my shirt to clean them. "It will only hurt for a few minutes. It's more than you deserve, assassin. I should tear you apart and feast on your bones for hunting me."

My life flashes before my eyes. No regrets. I've always known I'd come to a violent end. Someone out there would be faster or meaner. I was just surprised at how much it hurt. I'd always expected a bullet in the brain.

Mercifully I blacked out, expecting to die.

I hadn't died. I'd woken up screaming the next morning—and every morning after for nearly a year. This morning, I felt Sue in the back of my mind, trying to grasp what had happened. She felt nauseous from the images and I knew when she threw up on the floor beside her bed.

God, I hate Babs. Someday I'll see that bitch dead, but not while she's with Carmine. Whether I like it or not, he feels something for her.

I put the sensors back together quickly and tested them to make sure they functioned. Then I cleaned up my tools and headed home to prepare. Carmine has given no indication to anyone that he even knows the briefcase exists. It's intentional. When I kill the hitter, the body will get misplaced in the morgue. Then we'll wait for Leo's, or Vito's, boys to come into town to investigate.

We hoped that by not letting on, the person behind it might make another grab for the case. The hit on Carmine was the start. I figured that someone would probably show up on my doorstep next. I was taking extra precautions with security at home and in my car, but not letting on that I was expecting anything. The only ones in Carmine's organization who know the whole scoop are me, Mike and Marvin. Even the regular guys were out of the loop for this deal until Carmine is certain of their loyalty.

I glanced at my new watch, a Timex SeAL model with an Indiglo face. I cancelled the rest of my maintenance calls for the day and spent the remainder of the time preparing myself. I met with Scotty and he gave me the details. Sally had stalled again and set the meeting for tonight. The girl would try to get him to bend her over the bed so that he was in position. She wasn't sure it would work. Neither was I.

The next time I'd glanced at the lighted dial, it read 12:01 a.m. I released the button, and the darkness closed around me again, cool and silent. I leaned against the concrete wall, feeling a mild chill seep through my coat. I always wear a coat on jobs.

The night was warm, but the dimly lit garage held an air of the approaching fall. The window that I watched remained dark. The girl had assured me that he would come to the room before 12:00.

I waited.

And watched.

A distant rumble warned of an approaching car, even before I saw headlights scan the wall. Damn it! The place was supposed to be deserted. The car turned the corner to the next level. My level. I stepped behind a massive pillar. The floor moved under me as the car neared, then passed me without notice. I observed with mild interest as the car parked, and the engine shut off.

The door of the car opened, and a high heeled pump attached to a nylon-clad leg appeared. The woman stood.

She reached into the car and removed her shoulder bag. She was attractive in an elegant way. Her vivid blue business skirt and patterned shirt set off her dark hair. She was intent on her own business, not even caring to look around her. Stupid. If I were a rapist, I could take her now. She started to walk toward the elevators, across the darkened garage, her heels clicking on the concrete floor. She stopped briefly to point the remote lock toward the car. I heard the familiar 'beep, beep, boop' as the door locks latched.

Isn't that the way with people? Protect the car, but ignore their own safety. The car can be replaced. Oh, well.

She took no notice of me. No surprise. I'm never noticed unless I want to be.

A flash of light caught my attention, and I turned away from the woman. Back toward the apartment. I reached under my leather duster and carefully drew my weapon. The drapes in the room were open slightly and the door had been blocked open by inserting a screw into the guide. The mark wouldn't be able to close them. The man came to the sliding door and fought it for a few minutes before giving up.

He looked out into the darkness, right toward me. I knew he couldn't see me over a block away. I could see him without much strain of my supernatural eyes, although not clearly enough to use the gun without a scope.

I recognized his face from the packet that I had taken from Scotty. It was a shame that I had insisted on using the Thompson tonight. With a semi-auto, I could take him right now.

Through the open curtain, I saw the girl, Sally, enter the room. She *was* young, not more than seventeen, although she looked fifteen. She was wearing a halter and shorts, and had her long blonde hair tied in pigtails. She had a fringe of bangs, and wide blue eyes.

They wasted no time. The mark walked past her and locked the door. She was waiting for him when he turned, and stepped into his embrace. Their clothing disappeared in moments, and I watched as he lifted her onto the bed and they began to have sex. Not make love. There was no feeling, no emotion. The parted drape gave me a clear view of their act, and I raised my gun in front of me.

Sally ran her hands through his hair and whispered to him. She smiled brightly—convincingly. He pulled out of her and she scrambled off the bed. She bent over the mattress and I saw him stand up behind her. It was now or never.

It was then that I realized that Sue was with me, feeling what I felt—the weight of the gun through tight leather gloves, the cool air blowing strands of hair back from my forehead. She knew what I was doing, and she was appalled.

That made me angry. She had no right. I had no time to feel her emotions as I stared through the scope at the target. I cut the tie to her abruptly, using my mind. It was the first time I'd ever been able to do so.

When the mark raised his head the next time, I pulled the trigger. He was thrown forward by the impact and landed heavily on the bed with Sally pinned beneath him. She scrambled from under his dead weight, covered with blood. She backed away from the body with a scream that cut the night. Panic filling her face. She hadn't understood the reality of what she'd agreed to—what she started. She grabbed her clothes and ran from the room. I watched for a few seconds more to make sure that the mark didn't breathe or move.

I turned back to the darkness of the garage. It was time for me to leave now—before anyone could decide what to do. I placed the Thompson back in its shoulder holster, and buttoned my coat. It had been a trick to find a holster to fit. Usually, I keep my weapon in a secret compartment in my tool kit. I have two identical repair kits, down to the nicks and dents, with one difference. The black electrical tape that winds around the handle in a seemingly haphazard fashion—isn't. My *day* case is wound clockwise, while my *night* case is counter-clockwise. I can tell the difference by touch. Unfortunately, the scope on the Thompson wouldn't fit in the case. I'd had to search all over town for a holster to fit it. It weighs about the same as a hunting rifle under my arm and has an extra strap around my waist to keep it at a decent drawing angle. Another reason for the coat.

I picked up the grappling hook and rope that waited on the floor beside me, and strode toward the center of the garage. I was parked on the first floor, but a man walking down the stairs or leaving the elevator might be noticed even this far away.

I had taken care to file off the barbs from each of the five hooks. I gently placed two of the hooks over the railing that guarded the opening in the center of the garage. The core was open from the first floor all the way up to the fifth, where I was. The rope had been painted grey to match the concrete. I flipped the rope over the railing and watched it spiral down. When it stopped swinging, I climbed carefully over the railing.

That's when I heard a woman's muffled scream. I had no time for curiosity, but I silently climbed back over and moved toward the sound.

The woman in blue was pressed against the wall. A fat white man with long black hair, and clad in a dirty T-shirt, was fondling her with one hand. The other hand was tight over her mouth. Apparently, I had not been the only predator in the garage this night. The woman was no concern of mine, and she had been careless. I turned back to my own business.

Then I started to think. I hate it when I do that. Sue was becoming a bad influence, even when she's not in my head.

Did the woman deserve to suffer this man's touch, his penetration? What she had endured so far would teach her to be more careful.

I sighed and reached under my coat again. I was close enough that I didn't even need the sight. In fact, it wouldn't work at this distance. I opened the action to remove the spent shell and insert another from my pocket. The shell wasn't supposed to, but it popped out of the action and flew through the air. It landed in the darkness, and I could hear it roll down the concrete ramp. I followed it as quickly as I could without being noticed. The pair at the elevator didn't hear the tiny metallic sound or my movements. I caught sight of it again, just as it was rolling into a sealed drain. Damn it! I'd have to leave it.

Now I was angry, which made it simpler. I inserted another bullet and slowly worked the barrel up the man's back, to his neck, and then to his head. He didn't notice. His breathing was heavy, and he moaned as he pressed his body against her. The sound was louder than the woman's smothered protests.

Her eyes were closed. She had stopped struggling, becoming passive. She was no match for the big man's strength, and so had given in to the inevitable.

But she didn't want to see what her attacker was doing, so she didn't see me.

I felt a certain satisfaction as the bullet erupted from the muzzle.

The man dropped to the ground wordlessly. His stringy hair covered the entry hole nicely. The woman stood there startled for a moment, and then screamed. The sound bounced off the low ceiling and filled the garage.

She gathered her ripped and ruined blouse around her and ran toward the elevator, and safety. She was missing one of her pumps. It didn't occur to her to take the other one off, so she limped toward the protection of humanity. I really need to get out of here fast now. Damn it to hell! I should have left her to her fate.

I hurried back to my task, since the attempted rape would bring the curious quicker than the murder down the block. I slid down the rope faster than normal, the rough nylon stinging my hands even through the black leather gloves. My suede duster billowed around me like a cape as I descended.

When I reached the bottom, I made a sudden movement of the rope, and the hook detached from the railing, falling into my arms. Just the way it's supposed to work. I practice. A lot.

I quickly, but not hurriedly, walked toward the rental car. I opened the trunk and put the hook inside, underneath the spare tire. I took off my gloves and my coat and put them in the back seat under a blanket, along with my holster. I was wearing a business shirt underneath, complete with a tie. I got in the car and drove out of the garage, making sure I fed the proper amount into the machine at the gate before I left.

My work here was done.

The next night when I called to tell Sue to get ready, she abruptly cancelled. She said Myra was sick. I hadn't been able to feel her in my head all day. It was sort of pleasant, but unnerved me a little. When I figured out that we weren't going anywhere and all that money was wasted, I was royally pissed.

I decided I might as well take care of my equipment. I always clean my piece after I use it. Then I clean all the others—in case I forgot one last time. It's relaxing. I heard her unlock the front door, and I breathed in the scent of her summer forest. It was made bitter by the boiling coffee that surrounded her like a cloud.

Something inside of her was enraged that I *needed* to clean the Thompson.

"You did it, didn't you!?" She slammed the door behind her. She was trying to make me jump. It didn't work.

I shrugged noncommittally. "Did what?" Pieces of the Thompson lay on newspaper on the coffee table. I had removed the barrel and it was soaking in cleaner. I was preparing to run the rod through. The frame had already been oiled. The Taurus and Sig waited their turns on the floor.

"*Killed that man,*" she whispered tersely.

"Yeah. It's what I do. Your point?"

She didn't reply. She just stood there, ammonia horrified, burnt coffee angry and thick, wet betrayal. She must not have known whether or not I completed the job.

"You don't feel anything, do you? Some person is dead—lying in a gutter and you just don't give a shit!" She was more angry than I had ever seen her. Getting my temper too. A small part of me was pleased.

"He wasn't in a gutter. He was on a bed. And I really don't

want to discuss this, Sue." I pushed cleaner through the barrel with a wire scrubber.

"Afraid someone will *overhear?* Feeling a little guilty?" Her words were sarcastic, biting.

"No." I stopped my cleaning to look at her. "The place is soundproof. If you want to blast the place, knock yourself out. But it's none of your business. It's my job; my life. I explained that."

I returned to the gun. Over and over, I scrubbed the cleaner through the barrel. Like I could clean away the sour smell of her disapproval if I just kept working.

I decided to take the bull by the horns but I kept my cool. "What's the *real* reason you cancelled? I know damn well it's not your mom." I didn't look at her. I already knew the answer but I wanted to hear it from her lips.

"Fine." She walked toward me and stood over me with hands on hips, "You want to know? I could *never* enjoy watching a play knowing that someone had lost their life."

That's what I was afraid of. She could have left her mom for the evening, but she wouldn't sit with a killer.

Goddamn it! No! No matter what bound us, it was none of her business. I'd just have to find a way to keep her out of my head during jobs—control her involvement.

I stopped cleaning and carefully placed the Thompson, cleaning rod still in the barrel, on the newspapers. The pungent smell of the chemicals gave me a headache, which was annoying. It didn't improve my mood. I stared at her and she stared back. My eyes were as angry as hers. She looked away first.

"No! Don't look away," I said harshly. "Look at me!" I paused and repeated softly but still with force, "Look at me, Sue." She did. Her gaze was both angry and pained.

"I am an *assassin*. I kill for a living." She looked away again.

"*Look at me!*" Her head snapped back. "Don't start this holier than thou shit, Sue! You sought me out because of my profession. Wanted to hire me to *end your life*. This is no surprise. No big secret that I've kept from you." I stood and walked toward her. She stood her ground without flinching. I wouldn't hurt her. I *couldn't* hurt her. The tricky part was, she knew it. It made me wonder whether I'd be able to do the job.

"When I met you I had three jobs to do. Three jobs that I had already accepted, had already been paid for. This one was a surprise. But I told you about the others." I put a hand on her shoulder. Even angry, the tingles were still there. Her gaze was on the floor. She wouldn't meet my eyes.

"Since I agreed to be your bodyguard I've had nine calls on my pager. Nine prospective jobs." I let the words sink in. "I *turned all of them down*." Surprise showed on her face as she glanced into my eyes.

"A bodyguard," I said, "Is a lifestyle. I guard your body. Only yours. Nobody gets near you. Nobody hurts you. I will kill for you. I will take a bullet for you."

There was tense silence for a moment. "But what about the others? You said three jobs. What about the people who are going to die—who you're going to *kill*? How can I live with that?"

I shrugged. "I don't know how you're going to make peace with yourself, Sue. All I know is that I have. Three people were scheduled to die. If not by my hand, then by someone else's. But understand that they *will die*."

I put my hands on her waist. She let me, but only just. "If it will make you feel any better, this guy was a killer. He was sent here to assassinate Carmine. Linda probably would have been eliminated, too. As for the rest, they've done enough crimes to get them life in prison. One would probably get the chair. None of them are disgruntled spouses or ex-lovers. These jobs are just business. But understand that even if they weren't, I've made commitments and I *will* fulfill them."

She had smelled startled when I revealed the nature of my job last night. I could feel her anger and hurt disappear in a flurry of worry about Linda and Carmine.

I tilted her chin with one hand, lifting her eyes to mine. I spoke softly, but with conviction. "I don't want to lose you over this, Sue, but my promises are important to me. Can you understand that?"

She nodded but didn't speak. She was near tears. I couldn't help that. I pulled her into my arms. Eventually, she held me back. We stayed like that for some time, while she tried to sort things out in her mind. By the time she went home, she was better. Still tense and skittish, but better.

I knew this was going to be a sticking point. A make or break. One of us would have to bend.

It wouldn't be me.

Chapter 28

The moon was nearing. I could feel it like a shadowy presence just behind the sun. From now until it's full, when I look into the vivid blue sky, I'll feel the pull. Soon, said the wolf. Soon we'll be free.

Sue had been spending more time in appointments with John since the hit the other night. She was keeping herself consciously closed off. It annoyed me that I was sorry she didn't want to be inside my head, while at the same time I didn't want to be in hers. She seemed to be more proficient at cutting the ties than I was. Maybe it's because she accepts it as real, and can therefore deal with it better.

I felt it when she left this morning. I slept in for a change, and after a slow and leisurely shower, I decided to have lunch at Nick's. John-Boy's office is on the way. As I was driving past, I got caught at the light. I noticed Sue's little green car in the parking lot. No surprise.

But as I thought about her it happened. Not like last time. This was different. I started hearing her voice as though on the radio.

I was just sitting there in traffic when suddenly the conversation was clear as a bell. It was odd because John's office is soundproof—and I was seven stories down, on the street.

I should have just driven on but I didn't. I turned into the parking lot and found a space. Then I sat there and listened. I put the newspaper that I had planned to read at lunch on the steering wheel so it looked a little more normal.

"Thanks again for seeing me, Doctor Corbin. Really. I'm sorry I'm so much trouble."

"You've said that five times now. You don't need to keep apologizing. Go ahead with what you were saying."

"I just keep going back to the fight we had. I can't seem to get past it. I don't understand why I was so angry with him. He was absolutely right. I know what he is."

John said nothing. He knows his biz.

Sue paused. "Before I met Tony my life was so . . . sensible. But I hated everything about it. I wanted to die. Now, I've met gangsters and their wives, strippers, killers, and detectives. Those kind of people are normal for Tony. But it's all new to me."

I got sucked inside again. I heard the smile in her voice. "I've never met anyone as wonderful as Linda. I never imagined that there could be people as twisted as Leo." I felt a wave of fear race through her. I couldn't quite smell it.

"I've been places and done things most people only read about." She stopped for a moment, lost in thought.

"Mom set up Tony, but what if it had been real? What if Mom had found evidence on something he's *actually done*? I know what Tony does. He would go to jail and that scares me. But a part of me believes that he should be in jail."

Well, this was interesting! I turned a page of the paper by instinct. Nobody reads a paper without moving pages.

"But *another* part of me agrees with him. The people would die anyway. People die every day. Why should I feel sorry for them? I really don't want Tony to change. At least I don't think I do."

She paused. "No. I don't. What he does makes him what he is. He's smart and funny and affectionate. But he can also be cold and ruthless. He's got this sense of . . . completeness." Her words were soft and warm. "I don't understand it, but I think I like who he is more than I like myself."

Then she stopped. Her voice sounded odd. "He told me once that I'm not really in love with him. That it's just the excitement, the constant intensity."

A part of me never really believed that.

"Is it?" asked John.

She must have shaken her head. I felt soft hair brush my

neck. This is too weird. "No. He's wrong. I'm drawn to him. He's a part of me that I didn't know was missing. Does that make any sense?"

There was a moment of silence. "Sue, what you're feeling is very common. Not that Tony is common, mind you. Tony marches to music that only he hears. But your confusion between your duty to yourself and your role as a human is absolutely normal. Should you stop death or pain when you can?" I knew John. He would be shrugging about now. We'd had this discussion before.

"It's a question I've asked myself more than once. Where a person draws the line on their involvement with the rest of the world is something that each of us deals with. Some people choose to be activists. They make their role as a human more important than themselves. Other people travel the opposite direction. They let the world handle itself and concentrate only on their own lives. Neither is wrong."

Another pause. "In other circumstances I would advise someone like you not to get involved with someone like Tony . . . "

Gee, thanks, John. I love you too.

"But we *are* talking about Tony. I understand Tony. He has value. I grew up in the same world he did. He's ruthless, but he has morals. He wouldn't kill a child, for example. He has the ability to love. Most killers don't. I won't say that he *can be saved* because he doesn't need saving. If I thought that, or thought that locking him away would help him, I would have done it myself years ago. You need to decide whether or not you can let go of what you consider to be your role in the world and love Tony."

"I can't have it both ways, can I?"

John laughed. "Not without becoming a split personality. What Tony does for a living isn't 'right' as mankind defines it in religious writings. That's where you seem to be having the conflict. But it also isn't evil if you look at intent."

I felt it again when Sue nodded. "He doesn't *wish* death on others. He said that once."

"Correct. What he does has always existed. Tony wasn't

kidding when he said that if he didn't do it someone else would. I know several that would like to take his job right now."

"Will he ever stop? What would he be like if he did?"

"When he gets tired of the running, and the smoke and mirrors he deals with every day, he'll stop. Tony doesn't run on adrenaline like some do. It's a job to him. Someday he'll quit. His Dad did just fine when he retired. I understand he's an upstanding citizen down in Florida." I heard Sue chuckle.

"A lot of 'upstanding citizens' throughout history were scoundrels early in their life. Can you wait Tony out? Or if he never changes, is he worth it?" There was another pause.

"I have to decide that, don't I?"

"Yes, and you *can* decide it. You're capable of it. Don't think about your mother or what she wants. Don't think about your sisters or their children. Don't even think about Tony. Think about Sue. What is best for *you*?"

"I'll think about it. I either have to accept him and love him, or . . ."

"Or not. But even without him, *you* have value. You don't need to die, Sue. You only need to find your place." I felt her accept that, believe it. It pleased me.

"But what if my place makes *me* a different person? What if Tony only stays with me because I'm like I am now? Will he leave me if my place is somewhere different?"

Hmm. Good one. I had to think about that for a minute. Do I only want her as she is now? Or am I trying to raise her to become a vision of I want her to be? I think it's both. Why would I be helping her get her head on straight if I wanted her to stay the way she is now? And if her place is somewhere else, then so be it. I'd already steeled my emotions to lose her anyway.

"I wish I could answer that, Sue. I don't know what's in Tony's head right now. But I can tell you how he's responded to similar situations in the past. He appreciates— even demands growth in himself and in others. He challenges his mind daily. Reads constantly. He's annoyed by stupidity and laziness. He wouldn't even put up with you unless you were bright. I think the more you grow the more supportive he'll be."

His voice changed slightly and I could imagine him shrugging. "I could be wrong, of course. I have been before."

Then he changed the subject. "But what about your meeting with your sister today? Why are you seeing her? I thought after the fight you had . . ."

I folded up the paper and started the car. They'd be going on for a few minutes. I'd heard what I wanted to. She was slowly healing. But I wished I hadn't gotten a knot in my gut when John suggested "without him." Shit.

I flipped on the turn signal and entered traffic. As I drove away I expected that the conversation would fade. It didn't. I couldn't seem to shake the voices. It was like they were in the car with me or talking on the radio. It was sensory input, not mental.

"You remember the fight?" Sue sounded surprised.

There was a distinctly male chuckle. "I have a good memory, Sue. Yes, I remember the fight. It was about riding lessons."

"I still can't believe her *nerve*! Where does Bekki get off thinking that just because I have money I should support her family for the rest of my life? It's *my* money. *I* bought the ticket. Bekki called the Lotto a waste of money. A tax on the stupid. Now suddenly she deserves to share in my fortune?" Spite and bitterness rushed through my head.

I chuckled. I could almost see her gesturing with her hands. She and Linda have that in common.

"I set up the trust, tried to be nice about it. Now that they've become *nouveau riche*—because of me—they suddenly 'can't live on' what the trust gives them. Bekki and Robert are set for life and *I'm* supposed to pay for riding lessons for Cindy and Mike? Because their new friends at the country club are laughing at them and they 'just can't afford the extra expense'? I don't understand that. How could she have the gall to even ask? Why do they feel entitled to things that I have? I just don't understand!"

"It's not unusual, Sue. I know you're having a hard time

grasping it but it's a common way of thought. You have more money than you need. You should share happily because they're your family."

There was a exasperated release of breath from Sue.

"I can only explain them, Sue. I can't change them. So why do you want to talk to her again? Why are you setting yourself up for more pain?"

"I did something before I came here. I want to tell her in person." There was determination in Sue's voice and just a hint of fear.

When I opened the car door and stepped onto the sidewalk, the voices suddenly disappeared. It was as though the car was some sort of antenna and when I moved away from it the reception dissolved. I was suddenly by myself again. Why did it bother me that I missed it?

I almost walked back to the car to see if it would start again but I didn't. As curious as I might be about what Sue had done, if she wanted me to know she'd tell me.

I walked in the tavern and sat down on a stool at the bar. I heard a cheep on my hip and realized that my pager had been going off for some time and I hadn't heard it. I unclipped it from my belt and read the display. Three new calls. I didn't understand this sudden increase in business. I used to go for days without a single page. Now it felt like I was getting one every hour.

I spent the next ninety minutes on the pay phone in the hallway. That's twelve jobs I've refused. I think it's a new record. I sent them Scotty's way. What the hell. None went to Jerry. Not until Carmine asks me to.

I was waiting for a double order of fried shrimp and chips. When Jocko took out the kitchen in favor of a dance floor, he kept the deep fryer. It's in a small room off the walk-in fridge. It's not much, but you can cook a lot of stuff in a deep fryer. As a bonus, fried foods coat the stomach so people don't get drunk as fast, and teenagers can come in to buy sodas and listen to the live music.

Jocko was making a run to the bank which left Marni tending bar. She was just setting the basket of butterfly shrimp in front of me when Jocko came through the front door. I could smell him and watched his reflection move in the mirror behind the bar. He got a startled look when he saw me. His scent changed to anxious; fearful.

He stopped next to me and looked around him nervously. "What are you doing here, Tony?"

I looked at him in the mirror. I felt my brow furrow in confusion. "Eating lunch. Why?"

"Sommers was in here looking for you earlier." That gave him my full attention!

The bats were back in my gut. "Any idea what for?"

He motioned me to the back booth and I followed him with my shrimp and beer. If I was going to be bolting fast, I wanted it to be on a full stomach.

When I was seated he leaned toward me. "I don't know for certain but he was looking real cocky. Janice heard Sommers's partner mention on the way out that he was looking forward to nailing your ass."

Yep, definitely bats.

"They have a warrant? What'd you tell them?" I bit one shrimp off at the tail. No time for sauce.

Jocko shrugged. "I told 'em the truth—that I hadn't seen you in days. They waited for a while and talked to some of the customers before they left. They questioned Janice on the way out. She asked what they wanted you for. They wouldn't tell her anything but she overheard something about some lady who had picked you out of a photo line-up."

Shit. I knew I shouldn't have let that woman leave. I should have eliminated them both.

I heard tires screech outside and glanced out the window to see Sommers' car, followed by three squad cars. Doors opened. They had weapons drawn.

"You got a back door?" I already knew the answer.

He nodded. I gulped down the last of the shrimp, burning my tongue in the process. I took a final swallow of beer as I stood.

Thoughts not my own overwhelmed me just then. Who are you? What do you want?

The sheer power of Sue's terror engulfed me. I was suddenly on my knees and couldn't remember how I got there. I couldn't breathe past the fear.

Jocko turned when he heard the thud. I looked at him as though through gauze. I was in two places again. I was Sue. Rough hands pulled at me. There were walls around Us. Metal. A van. I heard a female scream in the background and knew it was Bekki. Sue was being abducted and I was along for the ride. I smelled a familiar scent but couldn't place it. The connection wasn't perfect yet. I was only getting pieces. Sweat. Fear. Menace. Something else. Nope. Can't remember.

Jocko was shaking me. "They're out front, Tony. Sommers! What's wrong with you?"

I tried to focus. I realized that I hadn't been breathing while I was with Sue. I filled my lungs and it burned. Panic of my own now. I had to get out of the bar. The connection dimmed for a moment.

I pulled my Sig from the waistband as the door to the bar opened. "You'll thank me later." Then I stood and moved slightly behind him and grabbed his ponytail to put him off balance. I put the gun to his head.

"What are you, nuts?" He didn't move. Probably a good plan. I had one in the chamber. "Drop it, Giodone!" exclaimed Sommers as he and three of his men entered the bar and fanned out. All guns were pointed at me.

"I will pull the trigger, Bob," I said calmly. I wasn't in my body completely. Nothing really mattered yet. "Put them down."

No officer likes a hostage situation. The bar patrons had either dived for cover or were too scared to move. One of the uniforms—he looked like a rookie—moved his thumb toward the hammer of his revolver. I put a bullet into the wall next to his head with preternatural speed. The gun immediately returned to Jocko's head.

Everybody froze.

"I *said* to put them down." I was still amazingly calm, but that's because I was too spacey to be scared. I hoped they wouldn't realize that I couldn't kill Jocko. It was best to let them think I was unstable. Hell, maybe I was unstable.

Sommers lowered his gun first and raised his opposite hand to order the others to follow suit. "I've got a warrant, Giodone. Even if you make it out of here, one call will put up roadblocks for fifty miles in every direction. Put the gun down now and we'll forget about you resisting arrest."

I smiled and it wasn't pleasant. I didn't have time for this shit. I had to get to Sue. I started to back away and pulled Jocko with me. To his credit, he followed smoothly. He didn't trip or dive. Others might have.

"We're leaving here," I said. "If you follow, you'll be picking up a body along the way. Maybe more than one. I've got nothing to lose."

Jocko blocked me as I backed behind the bar, through the employee break room and to the back door. I poked my head out to check for guards and then we slipped out the door into the adjoining building. It's not truly a dead-end inside the other part of the building—there's a locked door. Jocko has a key. I doubt the cops know about it. We were suddenly inside the upholstery shop. Faces looked at us but I wouldn't remember them later. I normally would, but I was with Sue again.

Her emergency was *not* helping right now. A wave of recognition hit me with a leaden thud. Oh, *shit*! Leo had her. Not good. Really, *really*, not good! I had to get to her.

I tried to focus on where I was there in her head. Tried to impress how important it was to give me some clue. Some way to find her.

I felt her mind center slowly as she understood. She opened herself to me and I followed, setting my fear aside. She looked around her slowly. Tried to fix names to people. She didn't know most of them. She did know Leo. He was in the front of the van. Bobby was there too. Damn it! I trusted him! I should have known better.

What direction? I asked in my head. There were no windows in the back of the van. She looked out the front, just as Jocko and I exited the upholstery shop. Nobody was waiting out front for us. I tried to position the sun that I could sense in Sue's mind with the sun that I was seeing. I pivoted my head until there was a spark of recognition. East. Yes! East but slightly north. She was traveling in a van—a black van—heading northeast.

"You with me, Tony?" Jocko asked. Again I was faced with one thing at a time.

"Northeast." I cleared my throat and then strengthened my voice. "We have to go northeast. Sue's in danger." I looked at Jocko in panic. "Can you drive me northeast?"

I was glad that Jocko has a reserved space. I opened the passenger door of his powder blue Lincoln Towncar and got inside. I automatically reached for a shoulder belt but remembered that it was old enough it only had a lap belt. He got in the driver's seat and started the engine. He glared at me with a mixture of confusion and anger. "What the hell was that about? I would have helped you. Why the gun?"

I tried to focus on his question. I blinked repeatedly. My tongue was thick and hard to move. "Hostage." I stared at him, willing him to understand my train of thought. "You're a hostage now, not an accessory. They won't do anything to you after you get me to Sue."

His brows rose and his jaw dropped. "You can barely walk, much less talk and you thought all that through while they were coming through the door? I mean, I know it's what you do, but wow!"

He pulled away from the curb and then hit the gas. He checked the rearview mirror more than once. "They'll tail us, you know."

"Then we'll have to lose them. You know Leo Scapolo?" He looked at me like I was whacked.

"Only by reputation. It's not a particularly rosy one."

"He's got my lady. I have to get her back."

"Your lady? The one you told me about? Shit." He thought for a moment and shook his head with a worried look. "Man! Leo Scapolo." He muttered under his breath. "Damn straight I'm a hostage. *Nobody* shoot the hostage."

Another glance in the rearview brought a string of curses.

He turned sharply down an alley. "Where do you need to go? You know where she is?"

I shook my head. I didn't know. Road? I asked. What kind of road? Highway? Dirt?

I felt her raise her body so she could see out the window. Highway. I heard as though she was in the car with us. Then fear stirred the adrenaline in my blood. For a brief flash, I saw through her eyes. I recognized another of the men. So did Sue. Vinny was back, and pleased to be there. I'd put odds that when Leo had looked for local talent, Vinny had jumped at the chance. Vinny is such a whore for money. I saw him through her eyes. He looked at her warily when he realized that she was being too aware. Noticing too much.

"Leo," I heard him say. "I think we ought to put her out." I felt Sue's panic as We watched Leo turn his ugly head and fix beady eyes on her.

One of the other men in the van spoke up. "Not yet. I want that case back. Where is it?"

Sue shook her head and I could see through her eyes as Leo raised his nose to sniff. "I don't know. Tony has it."

"I don't want the girl hurt until we get back those papers, Scapolo."

Leo snarled. "Don't tell me how to run my job. This is as much your fault as it is mine."

"Mr. Prezza is not pleased with your work so far, Scapolo. I've been sent to make *sure* you don't mess this up, too."

He growled low and deep and I could see Vito's boy blanch a bit. "Fine. We'll give her a little shot that will make her *talk* instead. Will that make your boss happy?"

The goon's eyes were still wide. He swallowed hard and nodded.

Leo motioned to Vinny. Sue turned as Vinny removed a syringe from a black bag. Oh no! Not a needle. No way! He removed the cap as though in slow motion. Hands grabbed Sue. One pair of hands was Bobby's. Traitorous bastard!

"No problem, pretty lady. We'll get the case back from your boyfriend. But until then, we'll have a little *fun.*"

Someone's hand pushed up her sleeve to expose bare skin. My panic added to hers. I couldn't let the needle near her—I needed her awake and alert if I was going to find her.

We started to struggle and the hands holding her tightened. Fingers dug in hard enough to bruise. I didn't care. No needles! I was panting, hyperventilating. Adrenaline rushed through muscles that weren't mine and supernatural strength followed. I felt the connection between us blow open another locked door.

My power added to hers and Sue broke free from her attackers. She kicked and punched and fought like a wildcat while I pushed her on. She knocked the needle from Vinny's hand and she punched Bobby hard enough that I felt the bone in her middle finger crack in a flash of pain.

The van swerved to knock her off balance. Leo shouted instructions, keeping out of her way all the while. Bobby re-entered the fray but I got the feeling that his heart wasn't in it. He grabbed for her and missed. It was Vinny who got fed up after she clawed manicured fingernails across his cheek. Blood dripped down and landed on his clean white shirt. He reached a hand up and it came away red.

"Fucking bitch!" he yelled. We watched as he hauled a fist back. My skills couldn't move her out of the way in time to avoid taking the punch full in the face. Her body wasn't trained to fight.

Pain erupted in Our brain. Her head snapped back and then hit the wall of the van. She sunk into unconsciousness; the connection broke.

I was in Jocko's car again, shaking and sweating. He was driving intently and trying not to watch me.

"You having some sort of seizure, man? Do we need to get you to a doctor?"

I could breathe again with Sue unconscious. I shook my head and tried to center where I was. "Is anyone following?" I asked shakily. "How long was I out?"

"I've been watching. I'm pretty sure I lost them." He glanced at me. He smelled curious and a little nervous. "You were 'out', as you call it, for about five minutes. What's up with you? I've known you for years and I've never seen you like this."

No doubt. *I'd* never seen me like this. Trouble was, I couldn't explain it without going into detail.

My cell phone rang. The abrupt sound startled us both. I stared at the number on the screen. I knew that area code, but I couldn't give away my hand.

"Tony here." I forced my voice to sound normal for those first words.

"Hey, Tony!" said Leo jovially. "I've got a friend of yours here in the car with me. I'd let her talk to you, but she's a little *unconscious* right now. If you want to see her wake up again, you bring me back my property."

"Where are you, bastard?" I could yell now. He would know it was bluster.

"I'll let you know." He hung up.

I stared at the phone long and hard for a moment and then turned to Jocko.

"Things are too complicated to explain. Can you live with that?"

I was concentrating on waking Sue. For the first time I was *trying* to start the connection.

Annoyance edged his voice and scent. "Fine. I'll keep my mouth shut and drive. But when this is over, I want to know what the fuck you've been up to."

I didn't respond. I didn't know whether I could ever tell him. I wasn't even sure I could explain it.

Whisper. Nudge. I reached out to Sue and tried to jump start the link. I pushed harder, then harder still.

Suddenly I began to feel her heart beat. Like it was part of me. I felt each throb in her body as though it were my own. As though I could control it. Then I saw it in my mind's eye. A thread, no thicker than a spiderweb, floating in the blackness. It glowed softly, like a tiny fluorescent tube and pulsed with each beat of her heart. Her heart beat slowly. She was safe. Not drugged. I was happy for that but felt guilty that my personal phobia caused her injury.

I could feel her blood flow, feel the pain in her hand. It was abstract. I knew that it wasn't my body hurting but it felt like it. My right hand started to throb as though I'd been in a bar brawl.

I whispered into her mind but it wasn't enough. I couldn't wake her. I pushed just a little more and was suddenly aware. There in the van, smelling blood from Vinny and surprise from Bobby. I was in her head and I was alone there. She was still out.

I couldn't move her. I simply had one or two of her senses. I could see and smell but I couldn't hear.

"Take the Interstate," I instructed Jocko. My own voice came to my ears from a distance. Vaguely I knew that he was still in the car and had heard me.

He glanced in the side mirror. "The cops are behind us, Tony. I'll have to lose them first. Hold on!" He accelerated the Lincoln hard enough that it threw me back into the seat.

At the same time, there was a sudden jolt in Sue's body as the van turned off onto a dirt road. The road was deeply rutted. The van slowed and swerved to avoid the deeper potholes. But which dirt road? There are a thousand of them outside of town. I closed my eyes to limit the input from where *my* body was. I felt Sue start to wake and she knew I was there. I begged her with a thought to stay quiet, to let me concentrate.

Now fully awake, she added her senses to mine. Input flooded my brain. Sounds. I could hear now. Scents were stronger. Vinny was flat pissed and smelled like blood and pain. He smelled like *food*. Sue was startled as that thought swirled into her mind. I fought back the need and she settled. I smelled Bobby react abruptly, felt his surprise, his pleasure. Pleasure?

I heard something through Sue's ears. "Pull over."

"Can't right now. I haven't lost 'em yet." We took the next corner on two wheels. A part of me wanted to watch and make sure that they were gone but I had to trust Jocko for that. I felt the car slow suddenly and move at a more sedately speed.

"Lost them." Part of my brain heard him. Part was still with Sue. My eyes opened there in the car and Sue was with me. She hadn't been in my body before other than the night at Linda's and she didn't know how to react.

I saw as we got on the ramp to the Interstate and headed north.

I removed Sue with a thought and stared into space. Jocko started to open his mouth but I held up a hand to silence him. He closed his jaw without a word. I listened through two brains and could hear sounds from both. One sound was a high pitched intermittent pulse. I knew that sound immediately. We had a tracker. The cops had *let* us go, but why did they follow in the first place? Maybe they figured that we'd get careless if we thought we lost them.

Jocko switched lanes abruptly to go around a semi. I opened the door of the car and leaned out. Wind blew back my hair as I strained against my belt to reach under the car.

Jocko glanced my way when he heard the door open. "What in the *hell* are you doing?!"

I ignored him. I had to lean out even farther to get my arm under the car. The seatbelt was cutting into my gut. My knuckles hit the speeding pavement briefly. I felt the pebbles embed into my skin. Jocko moved to the far left of the lane and one hand reached out to grab my waistband.

Damn it! I could hear the signal but where was the transmitter? I patted my hand all around the underside of the car and finally found it. The powerful glue was no match for my strength. I leaned back in the car and shut the door.

Jocko glared at me. "Are you *nuts!* You trying to get us both killed?"

I held out my prize. He looked at the small electronic tracker held in my fingers and swore. "Okay. Never mind. Get rid of that damn thing!"

I crushed the tracker in my fist, rolled down the window and tossed it over the car into the opposite lanes. With that distraction gone, I returned to finding Sue. I closed my eyes once more and pushed into her head.

I fought to place a new sound. Rumbling, whining. A

motor. But what kind? I closed my eyes again and let instinct take over. I breathed slow and deep and just let the sound filter into my head. Let my mind recognize it, place it.

It was more work than I thought as I tried to filter other sounds from both places. Speeding cars along the Interstate, rattling metal from the bouncing van. I calmed and drifted. Sue relaxed along with me and let me lead. I heard the sound again. Thup, thup, thup, then a vibrating rattle that grew to a roar. Propeller! Airplane!

I snapped my head to Jocko, who was staring at me out of the corner of his eye and looking nervous. "The old airport! At the edge of town. Can you get there from here?"

Somehow he was starting to figure out what I was doing and he could grasp it. Just. He kept muttering to himself, "This is weirder than shit! Nobody is *ever* going to believe this!"

I didn't comment on his discourse. I was concentrating on my own. I'm afraid, Tony, came a plaintive voice inside my mind.

I know you are, Sue. I'll be with you soon.

I tried to soothe her so they wouldn't know she was awake but her heart was beating faster. I could smell Bobby. He realized that she was awake. I felt him put a hand on her shoulder. He pushed down slightly. He'd done it to me more than once. Stay down, I commanded.

Sue slid along the floor slightly as the van came to a jarring stop in a swirl of dust. I could smell the dust irritate Sue's nose, irritate my heightened senses, and she sneezed before I could stop her.

"Good." said Leo's smooth oily voice before she opened her eyes. "You're awake. I want you awake. I want you *afraid*." He got out of the van and opened the sliding side door. Sue's eyes opened and I could see his face. His black eyes glittered brightly as he stared at her.

"You're going to tell me everything you know, little lady. And then *I'm* going to tell you everything I plan to do to you. Before I do it." He leaned over Sue. He ran his nose from her hair down her body and ended near her crotch. I felt her shudder.

He sneered. "You smell like that bastard Tony. I'll take care of that." He leaned over and licked slowly up the side of her face. She screamed and he laughed.

My vision bled red and I growled low and deep as we turned onto the road to the abandoned airport. Jocko's hands were fidgeting on the steering wheel, not sure whether to stop the car or drive faster.

Deep furrows had been cut into the dirt by the last heavy rain. Jocko was forced to slow the car to nearly a crawl to avoid ripping off his oil pan. I felt Leo lift Sue out of the van. She struggled but even with my added strength it wasn't enough. Leo held her effortlessly, then set her down. He released her and just stood there waiting. His eyes were smiling; amused. The other guards started to move in closer but he waved them back.

Run! I screamed in her head. She obeyed—she turned and ran at top speed—but it was a futile effort. Leo just stood there for a moment and then suddenly was in front of her. Like magic. She ran right into his outstretched arms. He had moved faster than the eye could follow.

"Hi there, baby!" He slapped her hard across the face with the back of his hand. She dropped to the ground, stunned. "Ready to play? I've got the knives all sharpened."

He bent down and touched her nose with each word. "Just . . . for . . you." He smiled evilly.

I could feel heat on my cheek from where Leo slapped Sue. Anger coursed through my veins.

"Move this damn car!" I exclaimed viciously to Jocko. "He's going to kill her!"

I could see the airport in the distance but we weren't going to get there in time if he didn't speed up.

It was Jocko's turn to be angry. "If I move this *damn car* any faster, we'll break an axle. Then we won't get there at all. You think you can do better, get out and walk."

I knew that I shouldn't be taking it out on him. This mess

wasn't his fault. He was trying to help. But that didn't rescue Sue. I felt her being dragged along the ground by her feet. She kicked and squirmed but Leo just kept on pulling her closer and closer to a metal shack at the edge of the runway. Her head hit a rock and We saw stars.

"Don't wait up, boys," Leo called over his shoulder as he pulled her along the ground. Through Sue's eyes, I saw the other men. Bobby looked positively pissed, and the rest just looked nervous—but nobody moved to stop Leo. Nobody wanted to get involved.

I wasn't going to be in time. I was going to lose her. Feel her torture. My leg was tapping nervously on the floor of the car. I couldn't concentrate on anything but the buildings in the distance.

Right about then, my tapping leg started to spasm. Twitch uncontrollably. I felt hot; feverish. It was a familiar sensation. But the full moon wasn't for more than a week yet! And it was the middle of the day!

I had to get out of the car. "Stop the car!" I screamed, but Jocko just kept driving, concentrating on avoiding the next huge hole. From my side of the car you couldn't see the bottom of it.

In a panic, I reached out and turned the key. The engine died and the steering wheel locked. Jocko didn't even have time to bitch at me. The left front tire immediately dropped into the hole that he was trying to avoid. Clear up to the axle. Metal screamed against unforgiving ground as irresistible force met immovable object. I heard the oil pan go and felt the frame twist as the axle bent. The scent of hot oil filled my nose. No gas, though.

Jocko slammed forward into the steering wheel. His head bounced backwards once against the headrest and then he slumped forward heavily, unconscious. He wasn't wearing a seat belt. I was. He's always been against the concept of belts. This is what that gets you.

With what I knew would be my last remaining thought before I turned, I reached out to make sure he wasn't dead. I didn't want to have his death on my conscience along with everything else. His pulse was steady. He did have the beginnings of a lump forming on his forehead. Good thing we hadn't been driving any faster.

Jocko was going to be pissed when he woke. The car was his baby; the only thing big enough to fit him. Finding parts would be a bitch.

I threw open the door and fell to the ground, thrashing in pain. I wouldn't scream. They couldn't know I was coming. White flowers erupted in my vision as I felt Leo and the goon stop dragging Sue long enough to open the door to the shack. Sue was terrified now, and unable to convince her muscles to move.

She felt cloth rip as my old body disappeared and new muscles appeared that didn't fit the shape of the shirt. For the first time I was *aware* during the change. I watched as color bled away from the world, to be replaced by brilliant whites and blacks and all shades of grey. I felt a thousand pinpoints of light and heat explode through my skin and watched long thick fur appear over my skin.

The change took only moments. Then I was running full out. I ran so fast that I couldn't even see the scenery. It whizzed by in a blur. I was to the airport and across the runway before Leo's hand left the doorknob. He looked at Sue and his confident look was replaced by a startled one.

He looked up just as I leapt into the air, not soon enough to get away. I crushed him into the wall of the shed. The corrugated metal screamed and bent from the impact.

Voices erupted around me as I tore at him with my mouth. Hot blood gushed from his arm where my teeth sank to the bone. He snarled, and it sounded like an animal. He grabbed my ear and pulled until I released his arm. Then he threw me aside long enough to get behind the shed. I followed, intending to finish the job. From the corner of my eye, I saw Bobby knock Vito's goon over the head. He dropped to the ground like a stone.

Vinny reached Sue before she could get away. She remained motionless on the ground. She was in the fight with me and couldn't seem to move her body at the same time.

Her anger and loathing fueled me as I stepped carefully around the shed. I fought to not let my heart lead my head.

I'd never before had human thoughts as a wolf. I could strategize, plan my next move. I stepped lightly and poked my head around the metal wall.

Leo wasn't there. In his place was a four legged animal. He wasn't a wolf. I'd seen a picture of what he was but it took a minute to place the picture with a word. Leo bared jagged yellowed teeth and it looked like a smile. It clicked the name into my brain.

A hyena! Leo was a carrion eating scavenger.

It fit.

The wound on his arm, now a foreleg, was healed. Only a rapidly fading scar showed where I bit him. He sidled sideways. I could tell that he had fought in this form before. He had a fluid movement to his muscles that I didn't. I felt gangly and clumsy, and I couldn't afford to be clumsy in battle.

A hot breeze cut across the sand. The airplane in the background was idling.

We moved back around the building. Leo was in reverse. I followed slowly. His blood dripped from my muzzle and I liked the taste of it. I licked it from my lips and Leo snarled at me.

I could see his black eyes dart from side to side, looking for an advantage. When we cleared the edge of the shack we were in sight of the others again. Nobody seemed surprised. Did everyone know what he was? Well, maybe he only brought people who knew. That made sense.

I rushed him abruptly but he dodged. People backed up quickly to avoid getting caught in the middle. Vinny had Sue's arm. He jerked it nearly out of the socket to avoid our fight. I felt a sharp pain in the same arm and I stumbled for an instant. Leo gave me that sickly smile again. His glittering eyes looked thoughtful and canny.

He jumped me and I only managed to get out of the way by a split second. He was aiming for a leg but only came up with a mouthful of fur. I took a bite at him on the way past and drew blood on his left flank. He yelped. I felt Sue smile darkly. She was getting a sample of vengeance. It tasted sweet.

Leo and I circled each other in the hot sand. The propeller on the waiting plane spun faster and faster, raising a sandstorm around us.

The men formed a circle. Vinny drew his revolver and tried to find an opening. I didn't have time to concentrate on him much but I managed to keep Leo between us. I saw a flash of light across the landscape, near the old control tower. My brief attention shift was what Leo was waiting for. He rushed me and I ended up on my back, holding his snapping jaws away from my neck with my legs.

What I had seen in the distance was the glint of light off a camera lens. I kicked Leo off of me and rolled over to gain my footing. A Channel 7 Action News van was parked near the control tower. Smile! You're on Candid Camera!

Leo dodged then and charged. But he wasn't aiming for me. He went past me. He ran full out past Vinny and then beyond Sue. He wasn't the type to cut and run but it happened so fast, I couldn't figure out what he was doing.

In the blink of an eye, he turned in a skid of dust. He aimed right for Sue. There was no way she could move out of the way in time. He went for her legs and bowled her over. Her body flew into the air. She landed on her back with a dull thud. The breath was knocked out of me so suddenly I staggered. Leo never took his eyes off me. When I reacted as I did, he gave me that sick smile again. He had figured out that hurting Sue hurt me. It hurt to breathe and I realized that he might have cracked one of her ribs. As he stalked toward me I tried to convince myself that I wasn't really injured.

Vinny was ignoring Sue now. He was concentrating on the fight. I felt Sue's pain, her anger and outrage. Leo had hurt my mate and he would pay for it.

With a deep-throated snarl I threw myself at him. I bit him; clawed him in a frenzy. He was unprepared for the ferocity of my attack and went down on his side.

I heard Leo's voice come out of that toothy muzzle and it startled me.

"Shoot the girl!" he ordered. Sue reacted in panic. Everything after that was in slow motion. Vinny turned to her. I felt her run, sluggish with an injured leg from the earlier fall. It wouldn't be enough. I tried to reach Vinny. Take him down. At least knock the gun out of his hand. Leo lunged at me and backed me away. I saw the gun raise and watched him aim. The gun barked as Vinny pulled the trigger.

Chapter 29

The bullet caught Sue in the right shoulder blade and spun her around. She was knocked off her feet. The shock and the pain made me stumble. I skidded on the ground in a tumble of dust and fur. I felt the wound as though it were my own. The smell of copper filled the air. Leo's lips pulled back from his gums in a predatory smile. He strutted toward me, lifting his nose to the scent. His tongue darted out and flipped across his muzzle. He knew he could take me now. It was just a matter of time.

I couldn't catch my breath. Sue's pain forced everything else from my mind. Blood. I could see blood when she looked down at her chest. There was a hole the size of a fist in the shoulder of her shirt, the flesh blown away by the Glaser round. She struggled to stay conscious I struggled with her. Her heart was slowing down from shock. The scent of it was overpowering; nauseating.

"End of the line, Tony," came Leo's voice from the foam flecked muzzle. Stiff hairs rose from behind ears set back far on his head. His heavily muscled, brown striped body was sweaty from effort. God, he was ugly. "All you would have had to do was return the case, Giodone."

I'd never spoken as a wolf. But I had to reply. "What? So you could *ruin* me and then have someone else kill me off — like you did to my father? You haven't even got the guts to do the job yourself, you goddamn *scavenger*!"

His eyes filled with hate and the fiery scent of jalapeños filled the air. He bared teeth. This was the end of the line all right. I tried to move, straining to raise myself to my feet. I wouldn't go down like this. I couldn't let Sue die unavenged.

I knew I was going to die with her—I knew my heart would stop when hers did. The connection was too tight.

It was actually okay. Better to die with her than live without her. But, by damn, he would go down with me.

He lunged at me before I was ready, always one to take unfair advantage. What's a fair fight to a hyena, after all? He was in mid-air when I heard the first gunshot and smelled fresh gunpowder. His body jerked sideways. He screamed and landed on his side. I could see the wound where the bullet entered him. The flesh was charred around the edges. It wasn't healing like the bites had.

Bloody bubbles rose from the wound and I knew the bullet had opened a lung. Fitting. He raised his head and the burning coffee of his anger filled my nose, stronger than the blood. He started to rise. Even mortally wounded he was in better shape than me. A second sharp crack split the air and his head slammed into the ground. His left eye disappeared in an explosion of fur and darker things.

I turned my head to see smoke still rising from the muzzle of Bobby's stainless steel 9mm.

Vinny looked as shocked as I felt. He raised his Browning .357 and started firing. Bobby moved like quicksilver and took cover. He returned fire and Vinny's body twitched with each bullet that entered him.

With bullets sizzling through the air over my head, I dragged my body to Sue's side. She was nearly unconscious. I couldn't feel her in my head.

I closed my eyes and felt for that little thread. That shining glowing line of energy that was Sue. I found it but it was dull and limp. It glowed weakly.

"Sue?" She fluttered her eyes open and looked at me. A weak smile warmed my heart.

"Guess . . . it wasn't meant to be, huh?" Her voice was a husky whisper.

"You're going to be fine." We both knew I was lying.

The air was suddenly still. The absence of sound startled me. When I looked up, only Bobby was still standing. He walked toward us. I turned to him and growled. I wouldn't let him have her. Not even though he had killed Leo.

Bobby was bleeding from a bullet to the shoulder. It was healing before my eyes like time-lapse. There were bodies on the ground. All of Leo's enforcers. All with multiple bullet wounds —one or more in the chest plus a head shot.

Even if he was involved with hurting Sue, I still owed him for getting us out of Vegas. He seemed to know who I was and it didn't appear to matter to him.

I coughed up blood. That worried me. "Camera crew—by the tower. All of this . . . on film." I couldn't stand anymore. I dropped to the ground and felt my heart slow as Sue's life slipped away. I smelled his surprise and saw him move in a blur when he spotted the television van and reporters. Two more bodies would soon be in the dust. I didn't care. I only cared for the woman on the ground in front of me. My mate was dying.

"Don't go." I felt my eyes beginning to water. "I don't want you to go."

Sue whispered with eyes still shut. "I hoped that we could go somewhere exotic." Her voice was breathy and her body shuddered as she fought to get each word out. "Somewhere with white sand and palm trees."

I rubbed my hand against her skin in frantic gesture. "We'll go there! I promise I'll take you. Just don't leave!"

She smiled brilliantly and opened her eyes for a brief moment. "I love you." Then her eyes shut again and I couldn't feel her anymore.

I reached inside my mind. Felt for the thread. I tentatively reached out to touch it, to feel what was wrong.

It was as though a zoom lens focused. I was suddenly standing next to the thread. Except it wasn't a thread. It was a cord as big around as my hand with smaller cords connected and twisted to make up the whole. It was a living thing. You could tell. But it was injured. I could see that strands of the larger cord were snapped and broken. As I watched, more threads snapped. The glow faded even more.

I didn't know what to do. I hesitated to touch it, to make it worse. Her wounded heart beat slower and slower.

Suddenly it snapped fully. Instinct took over. I reached out lightning fast and grabbed one end before it disappeared into the darkness.

A wind rose up that became a hurricane-level gale in milliseconds. The cord I held tried to pull away from me. There was a weight to it like it was caught in the storm. It whipped back and forth and started to drag me toward the darkness with it. I looked for something to hang onto and saw the other end of the cord.

The moment I reached out and grabbed the other side, it happened. The force of the contact blew me away. It raised every hair on my body. I felt electricity, power, whatever it was, accelerate between us. Lightning bolts of energy raced from me to her.

I was part of her. I felt my power tear through her body. I think I screamed. The magic touched every cell, every neuron, seeking . . . something. Each time the energy found what it was looking for, it tripped a switch. Surprised light blazed in long-darkened rooms. I saw strands of the cord expand and lengthen. They re-connected with their counterpart on the other side of my body. I felt her body heal. Felt flesh rebuild itself.

"Don't leave me." The wind caught the words and threw them into the darkness, tried to rip the mended strands apart. The whisper became a howl that cut through the cold night and warmed it. I felt her pain and helplessness as the wind got stronger. I fought back by sending more energy, more warmth, more . . . love . . . to her. More switches were thrown. More receptors turned on with each new burst of energy.

Every human has dormant DNA. Strands of us have been unused since the dawn of time. Some believe that people who have certain receptors turned on have psychic abilities—telepathy, empathy, and other stuff. I don't know if I believe that. I know that studies have shown that some of that dormant DNA has to do with human sexuality.

Rather, not sex precisely, but mating. Marriage rituals are

fairly recent developments. What happened before rituals to bond people? Was it body language or body chemistry? Can we smell and sense things that can't be seen?

Each switch that flipped brought Sue closer to me. I could feel it. 'And the two shall become one.' What if those aren't just words?

I pressed harder and faster. The energy found each piece of the puzzle and put it together. When the last piece slammed home, I felt it. My eyes were closed, both in real life and in my mind. The wind died at last.

Suddenly it was absolutely still. Absolutely peaceful.

When I opened my eyes in my mind, the cord in front of me was whole. It glowed softly in my hands. I released the strand and it instantly dimmed. I touched it and it glowed— released it and it faded. She was still in danger. She needed my strength to *make* her live. I moved myself closer to the strand; it reached out to me, and wrapped itself around me.

I opened my eyes in the real world and looked down at her pale, drawn face. I tried not to look at the wound in her chest. It was a killing injury, and I didn't want to think about that.

Long dark lashes lay against those pale cheeks and her hair stirred in the hot breeze. Her mouth was open slightly and even the lips were pale. She was unconscious from loss of blood. She couldn't hear me, but she knew I was there. I touched that cool porcelain skin and was surprised that I was human again. I didn't remember changing back.

Tingles raced through me, just like always. Even now I couldn't bear not to touch her.

I heard a noise and I turned my head. I knelt, naked, by Sue's side. My head was foggy. I could only manage to keep Sue alive. A man dropped to one knee beside me and I recognized him. Carl Jenkins. *Dr.* Carl Jenkins, a noted neurologist and an old Family friend.

"Jesus!" He opened a black satchel and removed instruments and bandages. "She's lost at least half her blood supply. I can't imagine what's keeping her alive! She should be gone."

I would have answered but I was too tired. All I could get out was, "Can you fix her up?"

"The wound's bad." The thick fog of worry added to his seriousness. "But if she'll stay alive long enough to get through surgery, I think I can save her. It's a miracle she's still with us."

Nice to know I'm a miracle. But he voiced the trick. Could I keep her "with us" long enough for Carl to stitch her back together?

I looked at her again as Carl started to clean her shoulder enough to see the internal damage. Carl's a terrific surgeon but I didn't know if he was good enough to save her in a field setting. We didn't have time for a hospital.

The smell of ozone found me and a low clap of thunder filled the air. A wind came from nowhere. Carl looked up in a panic and stripped off his shirt suddenly, using it to cover Sue's wound as sand began to swirl.

"We need to get her somewhere protected. God, I hate to move her, but . . . Carmine!" He draped his body over Sue, trying to keep the wound clean. I saw Carmine, Jerry and Mike head our way. Where had they come from? Who called them?

"We need to move her into the hanger," instructed Carl. "Gently. She's in bad shape."

I watched from where I was as the sand blasted my bare skin. Jerry and Mike each took one of Sue's legs and Carmine eased large gentle hands under her spine. Carmine's face was level with mine when he looked at me for the first time. "Christ, Tony, you look like hell! What did Leo do to you?"

I didn't respond. I couldn't respond. He stared at me long and hard. "We'll take care of your lady. Carl will fix her up." He reached into his pants pocket and dropped a set of car keys on the ground in front of me. The movement registered in my brain but I didn't stretch to pick them up. It was too much effort.

"I've got some coveralls in my trunk," he said. "They won't be the best fit but you need something. That storm's going to be here any minute."

I glanced down at myself. I looked like shit, but I felt worse. I was nearly catatonic. All I could concentrate on was internal CPR. Beat, beat, breathe. Beat, beat, breathe. Nothing else mattered. Just keep oxygen pumping to her brain—keep her alive long enough to doctor her. It was a conscious effort.

They lifted her in one smooth motion as though it was practiced. I was breathliss and panicked as they moved her. I felt the blood drain from my face from the effort of keeping her calm. She could feel it and it hurt. God Almighty, it hurt. She shouldn't be able to feel. But if I could feel her, what was she getting from me?

"She's waking up," I whispered. I looked to Carl with pleading with my eyes. "Give her something for the pain before you start, huh?" His eyes grew wide and he flicked a light across her pupils and swore. He took off for the hanger at a dead run.

As they moved her, I was forced to ask a question. It slipped through my mind before I could stop it. Was I willing to risk my life for this woman? Because that's what I was doing. If Carl couldn't heal her, she would drain me dry. Take me into that black nothingness with her. I was breathing for her, making her heart beat as though I were a life support machine in a hospital. The effort would exhaust me little by little. It already was.

I barely knew her. All I had to do was let go. Just hold my breath and not make her heart beat. A few minutes is all it would take. I could go back to my life if I survived.

No. I didn't want to make this decision right now. Not until Carl had a chance to look at her.

I stayed where I was on my knees as they moved away with her. I could only concentrate on the beating of her heart. I didn't want to distract myself with any additional movement. But as she moved further from me the effort became more; having her near made the life support easier. I stood in the hot sand. My legs were shaky and I felt stings of pain as the superheated quartz blasted my body. It didn't matter.

Bobby watched silently as I dragged my weary body toward the hanger, following like a dog on a lead.

The boys laid Sue down on a table that Carl cleared off with a sweep of his arm. It was dusty in the metal framed building, but it was also cooler and out of the weather. It seemed odd it was cool. There must be some insulation in the walls—it should have been an oven.

Carl immediately went to work. He ripped the tatters of Sue's shirt away from the wound and turned to the waiting men. Scarlet blood stained her snow white bra. Nobody looked. It was somehow too personal.

"Jerry, congratulations! You've been promoted to nurse." He kicked the black bag on the floor toward the men. "Carmine, you get some water. Clean, please. Find some way to heat it up. Mike, get the rest of my stuff out of the car. Jerry," he continued, as I slumped to the floor in the corner. "Get two pairs of latex gloves out of the bag and one of the large alcohol pads." None of the men argued. Carl's the doc. He's in charge. Otherwise, the next time one of *them* needed patching he'd just watch them die. His Hippocratic Oath has a vindictive streak.

Carl dropped to his knees and pulled a small glass vial from the black bag. He inserted a syringe into the top. He inverted the works and slowly drew the clear liquid into the needle. My heart beat faster and Sue reacted to my panic by moving towards consciousness. I watched Carl remove the air from the syringe by squirting out a small amount of the fluid. One hand held the needle while the other reached out expectantly for the foil square that was about twice the size of a condom. Jerry put it in his hand just like a nurse. He ripped the packet open with his teeth and I could smell alcohol in a sudden wave. He grabbed the towelette and shook off the wrapper. When he swabbed the crook of Sue's arm I couldn't look anymore. I kept telling myself that this was *good* clear liquid. I knew and trusted Carl. But my fists were closed tight and my legs drew closer to my chest.

I felt when the needle pierced her skin. I could feel everything with her now. The connection was locked tight.

I concentrated on keeping Sue's heart beating, keeping her breathing, while the needle spilled its contents into her body. I felt a warm soothing wave sweep through me as whatever drug Carl had injected started to work. No more pain. Sleep lapped at my consciousness and I had to struggle to stay awake.

A tap on my shoulder made me jump. I had turned to face the wall. Curled in a ball in the corner. Oh yeah. Big strong tough guy, that's me. I turned to find Mike staring at me. He was holding an armload of equipment.

Breathing was still an effort and Mike noticed. "You're not looking too good. Let Carl give you something to sleep." I had to admit that sleep would be a good thing right now. But not by needle.

"No!" came a harsh exclamation to my right. I turned to see Bobby walking toward me. He held a video camera in his hand with a 7 News logo on the side.

Bobby set the camera on the floor under the table where Sue lay. "No drugs for Tony." He looked me over as though seeing me for the first time. His brow furrowed as he looked from me to Sue and then back again. He gave an amazed shake of his head. "You need coffee," he said to me. "I've got some in the car. Let's go."

I shook my head. "I can't leave. I *really* can't leave." I didn't know if he would understand the reason but I knew that he would smell the truth of my words.

Mike saw the look on Bobby's face and shrugged. He dropped off his load and walked back out into the wind.

Carl turned from his efforts and looked at me for a brief second. "Do you know your lady's blood type? We've got to get some replacement into her or she won't make it. I've got plasma with me, but whole blood would be better."

I shrugged. I really didn't know. I couldn't ask Sue even in my mind. She was out. But he was right. She would die. "I'm O negative—universal donor." I held out my bare arm to him. "Just promise not to be mad if I hit you when you stick in the needle."

Bobby grabbed my arm suddenly and pulled me to my feet

in a burst. He dragged me off to the side. "Are you insane?" he said in a terse whisper. "You can't donate blood!"

"Why not? I'm universal. She'll die without blood!" Fine. If he could be angry so could I.

He gave a sharp exasperated exhale of breath. He hissed the words at me. "You aren't type O negative, stupid. You're W positive—if you get my meaning." He glanced at Carl who was ignoring us and starting to clean instruments. I had nearly forgotten. Beat, beat, breathe. Beat, beat, breathe.

Wolf positive. It hadn't even occurred to me. Hope surged through me. My blood could save her life. I glanced at her. Tried to imagine her awake and laughing again.

But then she'd be just like me. Sub-human. I really believe that. I'm not more than human, I'm less. Could I let her die when I could save her? Would saving her like that be a curse or a cure?

Curse or cure? Curse or cure? I shook my head while Bobby watched my internal struggle. No, I couldn't do that. Not even to save her life. Given the choice again, I'd rather have died. It's a curse.

There was pain in my voice. "Then she'll die. I won't do that to her. I won't make her an animal." It made me sad. Without the blood and unless by some miracle one of the others was universal Sue would die. I sat down on the floor right where I was, still naked. I brought my knees to my chest once more. She would die and I couldn't save her.

Fine. Then I'd go with her. We'll travel down the black tunnel hand in hand. I *could* live without her, but I didn't want to.

I understood suddenly. It was like sight. As if all your life you'd been able to see but had never seen color. Black and white had always served you until you got a taste of red and yellow and green. Then grey was never again enough. No sunsets, no Christmas lights. Sue was like that now. I'd had a taste of something incredible in my head. A never-ending technicolor sunset. Some magical something that I knew was special. One of a kind.

I ignored Bobby and concentrated only on keeping Sue

alive. I'd do what I could. Give Carl whatever chance he needed to save her. Right to the end. Bobby clenched and unclenched his large fists, but it wasn't his problem. This was mine alone. My decision. My choice.

Mike came in again. His arms were loaded with supplies. He paused nearby and juggled boxes. Then he tossed a pair of blue coveralls my direction.

"Get some clothes on, Giodone. There are ladies present." He beamed a confident smile at me. I forced a small one in return.

Bobby watched me, took a deep breath, and sighed. He left me on the floor. I made no move to put on the coveralls. It was too much effort. Beat, beat, breathe.

Out of the corner of my eye, I watched him walk over to Carl. He spoke softly but I still heard his words. Guess the ears were still working fine. It was just everything else that was slowing down. Grinding down with exertion. Beat, beat, breathe.

Carl was busy unpacking boxes and giving direction to Jerry and Mike. They were setting up tables and instruments like they knew what they were doing. Maybe they did. Carmine stood off to the side. He looked normal. Not anxious; not fretting. Just calm. Apparently he had found hot water. He was waiting for his next assignment.

"Do you believe in miracles, Carl?" asked Bobby.

Carl turned to him and gave him a long look. I brought my head up from where it rested on my knees and watched them. Jerry and Mike seemed to sense something was going on and moved a little further away.

"Let's just say that I've seen some things that can't be readily explained by modern science. If they were miracles, then so be it."

"Did any of them happen when you were actually *present?*" Where was he leading?

Carl gave him a brief smile, never stopping his work on prepping Sue for surgery. "I've noticed that miracles don't like an audience."

"Do me a favor then." His cold calm unnerved me a little.

"Leave the room. Go take a leak. Get a cup of coffee. Come back in five minutes."

That stopped Carl cold. "She'll die, Bobby. I need those five minutes." He continued working. He shook his head. "No. I can't."

"One minute then, Carl, just one minute for a miracle." He put a large dark hand on the doctor's shoulder, "Please."

Carl looked down at Sue, then at Bobby. He looked at me last but longest. I returned the look. He appealed to me with panicked eyes. Asking my permission. I was Sue's protector. It was my choice. Bobby didn't look at me, he just kept staring at Carl.

It was Carl's choice. He was the doctor. I gave a brief nod and then returned my chin to where it rested on my knees. One minute wouldn't matter but Carl didn't know that. I could probably last another ten minutes before my own strength gave out. Beat, beat, breathe.

I closed my eyes. So tired. Beat, beat, breathe. I heard but didn't see Carl, Jerry, Mike and Carmine leave the hanger. Bobby and I were alone with Sue. Whatever he was going to do, I wouldn't let him end her life. I would prevent that.

In my mind's eye I focused again on the spider thread that I held. I felt each beat of her heart. I breathed each breath with her. The cable continued to glow but only because of what I fed it. She lived because I allowed it.

It didn't make me feel cocky. I didn't feel like God. I felt very alone. Very tense. I concentrated but couldn't reach her mind because of the drugs. It was like a door was closed. Not locked. She slept behind that closed door. She felt no pain and that was good.

I felt Bobby. It was like standing next to a bonfire. Or a live high-tension wire. I concentrated on Sue's lifethread. I stood guard against whatever he would do. I didn't have the physical strength to fight him but I would watch over her life like Cerberus himself at the gates of Hell.

I heard a dark chuckle from Bobby. "Only *you* could manage to screw things up this bad, Giodone." He spoke softly but knew I could hear. He sighed and it spoke volumes.

"Mated to a *human*. Fiona will have a strip of my hide for this. I should not be doing this. Gawd! I should not even be *involved*. You'd *better* appreciate it."

I had no idea who or what he was talking about so I didn't respond. Bobby touched Sue. Me. Us. Placed his hands right over her wound and sealed it. I felt pressure but no pain. I held her life in my hands and guarded it. I mentally became a wolf.

Then the gloves came off. It was like Bobby had been holding himself in check. Not letting on who—or what—he really was. Power sang through the room and raised every hair on my body. I looked up with a gasp. Bobby was bathed in a silvery glow that came from within him. I blinked my eyes suddenly. Just for a moment I thought I saw him shift. Saw the form underneath his skin peek out and then slip back in. I couldn't tell what he was. It was just a flash. But whatever it was, whatever *he* was, didn't have fur.

The light that pulsed around him was too bright. I had to shut my eyes. Even after I shut them I could see echoes of the glow in the blackness. The image was burned onto my retinas.

Sue's lifethread began to shine brighter. Brighter even than when I first touched it. It pulsed more radiant with each passing second until it was as bright as a captive star. A tidal wave of power churned over us both. It enveloped my virtual body until I gleamed like a nova. I felt refreshed, energized. I felt Sue's body start to heal. He was going to heal her! He was doing what I *could* do, but his effort was like a bulldozer next to my ant.

Then it stopped and the silence was deafening. I looked up, startled. Sue was still bleeding on the table. But she was a little closer. She'd make it now. Her heart was beating on its own. She was breathing on her own. I could think for myself without that strain. But I didn't feel gratitude—I felt anger.

I stood in a flash and stalked toward him. He was standing over her, looking healthy and not the least tired.

I grabbed his shirt with both fists and pulled his face close to mine. "Goddamn you! Why didn't you finish? You could heal her. Why did you stop?"

He reached around me fast as a snake and grabbed my neck. He turned it sharply. Carl and the boys were entering the room. "That's why," he whispered sharply. "What I've done is bad enough! Now get your clothes on and meet me outside. She'll survive."

He pulled out of my best grip as though it were nothing and walked away. He spoke without turning. "Don't make me come and get you."

I looked down at Sue. She had color again. There was a pool of blood in her chest where there was none before. Her chest rose and fell on its own and she felt confident in my head.

Go. I'll be all right now. Then she drifted off to sleep again.

I didn't know if she'd be okay but at least she had a chance.

Chapter 30

I pulled on the blue coveralls. They were a little short and far too wide. But they covered me. Just as I was leaving the hanger to join Bobby outside, I heard the exclamation of amazement and delight from Carl as he reached the table. I could smell his astonishment.

"A one-minute miracle. Shit." There was a hint of anger from someone. I couldn't tell who. Carl and the others stared after me as I walked out. A miracle indeed—and I was walking outside to meet that miracle now.

The heavy metal door protested noisily as I exited the hanger. It slammed behind me with a bang. Bobby was leaning against the wall lighting a cigarette. He didn't look at me until I joined him. He walked away from me and expected me to follow.

I could think again. I felt almost like myself again. For that I'd follow.

We walked toward the plane. The bodies were all gone. The boys must have made them disappear. I didn't know to where, nor did I care. The sun was bright on the baked earth. I had to blink a few times to get my eyes to adjust. The coveralls were already making me sweat but it didn't matter. Nothing mattered except that Sue had a chance.

Bobby stopped suddenly when he felt that we were a sufficient distance from the hanger. He turned to me, his face cut in angry lines.

"Are you completely insane? What you just did is an automatic death sentence!" Smoke billowed out of his mouth as he spoke and the wind blew it right in my face.

I presumed that he meant attacking Leo. "He was going to kill Sue," I said in a quiet, equally angry voice.

The cigarette smoke was irritating my nose and I sneezed.

He pointed a finger at my chest. "And that is the *only thing* that is saving your ass right now!"

He plucked the nearly whole cigarette out of his mouth. He dropped it on the ground and pressed it into the dirt with a twisting motion of his foot.

"Mated to a human!" He smelled burnt metal annoyed and mildew amazed at that same time. "I'm going to have to inform your pack leader of these indiscretions." He crossed arms across his broad chest. "Which pack are you attached to?"

I furrowed my brow and felt a pressure on my chest at the same time. Carl was starting to work. He must be using a rib spreader. It was a very strange feeling. Not pain exactly, just odd.

"I have no idea what you're talking about."

He gave a little exasperated movement of his hand. It remained tucked under his other arm. "Okay, fine. Maybe you don't have a formal pack structure around here. Who do you hunt with?"

When I continued to look confused he twirled his hand, "You know, on the moon?" He waited expectantly but I had nothing to offer him. I shrugged.

"No one."

He suddenly looked startled again. "You really don't, do you?"

"Nope."

His expression grew both suspicious and tense. He licked his lips more than once. "If I said I was with Wolven, what would you say?"

"Who or what is Wolven?"

He closed his eyes and dropped his head. "Oh, shit! At least tell me you're a family member."

I shrugged. "You know I am. I grew up in the Patrone's house."

He gave a nervous chuckle with his head still bowed. One

hand reached up and covered his eyes. "Oh, this is not good at all." Bobby was no longer angry. He was worried.

He shook his finger in the air, thinking and murmuring to himself. I continued to look confused because I was still in both places at once. It was hard enough to concentrate on this conversation when I should be in the hangar with Sue. I knew there was nothing I could do but I needed to be close to her. It felt just *wrong* not to be near her. I reached for her, a tentative touch along the mental connection and felt her warm and loving in the background.

Loving. It's not something I ever thought I needed. Absolute acceptance and warmth. That was what I got when I touched her. Even this, having Leo take her, hurt her—it was all accepted as part of being with me. That was so completely unexpected and amazing.

Bobby's hand was waving in front of my face and I returned to myself.

"I'm sorry," I said. "Were you talking to me?"

He rolled his eyes. "Apparently not. Okay, fine. I accept that you're not all here. You're with your mate. But try to stay with me. I have to ask you some questions."

I felt my back go up. I don't willingly give information. "You can *ask*." He caught the meaning.

"I have the right to ask." He looked confident. I couldn't see any deceit in his eyes. I was starting to get a little sense of frustration, with the slight coffee smell of anger from him for the first time.

"Fine. I can tell you believe that. Now make *me* believe it. And while we're on smells, why can't I smell you? I'm picking up some emotions now but nothing else. What are you?"

That brought a sudden frown to his face. "Hmm. Must be wearing off." He reached up with both hands and used the fingers of one hand to pull down his lower eyelid. Then he bent his head slightly and removed a contact lens. When he looked at me again I actually gasped. His right eye was a solid dark brown with a black pupil. Perfectly normal for a South African male. The other eye, though . . . it was reddish-gold. Not just the iris. I could almost have handled that.

But his whole eye, including where the white should be, was reddish-gold. The pupil was a small black vertical slit. Then he blinked. I hadn't noticed it before. His eyelids blinked up! The lower lid covered the eye, not the upper.

He licked his lip just like always but now the movement seemed foreign; alien. What was he?

It suddenly occurred to me what I had seen in that flash as he stood over Sue. "You're a snake?" I asked, a little startled. "Are there other kinds of . . . creatures too?"

Lions and tigers and bears. Oh my!

He gave me a little smile. "You really are new at this, aren't you?"

I opened my mouth but no words came out. I tried again. "Apparently."

He looked suddenly amused. "Okay then. I'll give you the quick course. You know some of it already."

He bowed slightly. "My name is Robart Mbutu. I'm from Mozambique, South Africa. I am a Reticulated Python. I am the last of my kind." There was sadness and fierce pride in that statement.

"Collectively, we are Sazi. Your kind, the wolves of America, descend from the Anasazi of the Four Corners."

"The cliff dwellers?" I asked. It *would* explain why archaeologists never found many bodies. Werewolves stay in whatever form they die in.

Bobby smiled slightly. "Actually that isn't quite accurate. It properly translates to, *cave* dwellers."

That made even more sense.

Bobby lit another cigarette and took a long draw. "This is a pretty truncated version of our history, but you'll learn more later. For the moment, know that hundreds of years ago, a representative of each of the known were-species came together from all over the world. Humans were encroaching on our land and attempting genocide of our kind. We overcame our language barriers and our prejudices.

The first meeting was chaired by Inteque, the youngest son of the Great White Wolf. He, a powerful jaguar named Colecos and Sasha, a polar bear, used both reason and force.

By the end of the gathering, the delegates had formed a government and created a Council comprised of the greatest among us. We chose a name, Sazi, to include all of our kind. We remain hidden from the humans to protect us all."

I suddenly felt Carl working on Sue again. It seemed to come in flashes. I was with Bobby one minute and in Sue's body the next. He was cutting high on her thigh. Maybe a graft? There was a lot of flesh gone. Bobby must have seen my attention disappear because he put a hand on my shoulder. I tried to focus on him but it split my attention between the two realities and made me dizzy.

"You're making it difficult to carry on a conversation here. Let me help." I felt his power flow from his hand into my shoulder and up my shoulder into my head. It flowed like water and like steel. A wall grew up between Sue and me; his doing.

"Whoa."

"You need to learn to shield." His voice held a slight amount of reproach. "Many things will get easier after you learn how." He released my shoulder but the power remained like a tether between us. It was really strange, and it was making me nervous.

"You're scared of me," He flicked his tongue between his lips like a snake. He didn't even attempt to make it look like a human movement. I suddenly realized that the reason for all of his lip licking wasn't a human one. Snakes sense things with their tongues. I stepped back, a little weirded out.

He shrugged. "Probably not a bad thing. Most are. I am an agent of Wolven, the law enforcement branch of our government."

"So you're . . . a creature cop?"

He let out a low hiss. "Of a sort, and I really prefer Sazi. We're not *creatures*. I've been working undercover for a couple of years, investigating Leo."

Wait. Sazi. *That's* what Leo said when I visited his office. He called me Sazi. Then I focused on what Bobby had said. He's been undercover for years? I was forced to voice my surprise and outrage.

"Years? Jesus, Bobby, everybody knew he was killing people. It took you *years* to figure it out?"

He gave me a dirty look and crossed his arms disdainfully. "No, it didn't take me years to figure it out. It took years to get proof enough to convict him. He kept eating the evidence. It's hard to establish a murder without the body."

I grimaced involuntarily. "He ate the evidence? That is *sick*." But I suppose that would be a problem with a scavenger.

The warm sun beat down on us. It felt kind of nice standing there without feeling the pull of Sue's needs. But it was lonely too. I glanced at the hangar. I hoped things were going well.

Bobby noticed and rolled his eyes. "So now I'm going to lose your attention because you're *not* connected? Give me a break, Giodone!" I felt the wall he constructed thin in my head. It wavered until it was an invisible barrier. If I reached across I could touch her. It was enough. Bobby had such absolute control over his abilities. I was both envious and curious.

His tongue flicked again. He nodded. "Curious. That's good. Are you ready to answer some questions yet?"

My eyes narrowed. Friend or not, he's a cop. "I'll let you know when I hear the questions."

"Always on the defensive." He gave an amused shake of his head. "Probably why I like you. Pity you aren't more powerful— we could use you in Wolven." I wouldn't comment on that. But I had to admit that if Bobby was typical of the others in this organization, I wasn't up to snuff.

Carmine and Mike stepped outside. They ignored us and started to drag bodies toward the second hangar.

Bobby smelled nervous at their presence. He turned and quickly put his contact back in. He walked toward the plane, and twitched a finger for me to follow. He sat on the lowered steps where it was shady. The white nylon cord stretched with a high-pitched creak as the steps came to rest on the runway. I sat in the dust. It wouldn't hurt the oil stained coveralls.

He started. "If you aren't family, I presume you were randomly attacked." The tone implied a question.

Okay, I figured out that "family", as he meant it, were other Sazi. I had no problem telling him what happened. "It was an attack, but it wasn't random. She fully intended to kill me."

"You know who she was?" His voice was all business.

I nodded my head. "I do. Her name is Barbara Herrera, although you'd never guess the surname from looking at her. She's a green-eyed redhead. But she wasn't a wolf when she attacked me. She was just a woman I was hired to take out."

His jaw dropped slightly. I didn't think I could surprise him any more. "She attacked you in *human form*?"

I nodded again. The hot wind churned sand into my eyes; I blinked several times to shift the grains to the edge, then turned my body so the wind was at my back. The sand didn't seem to bother Bobby. I glanced at the sky. It appeared that the storm was going to miss us. Good. We'd probably need the plane soon.

"After she turned you, did she train you? Introduce you to a pack?" I shook my head each time. "Did she at least teach you to hunt?"

"I know how to hunt," I replied with a shrug. He just blinked. I leaned back onto my arms, extended my legs, and crossed one ankle over the other. The sand was cooler in the shade, but not by much.

"You were hired to kill her. Were you given specific instructions on the way to do it?"

"I don't take instruction. You know that."

He shook his head and moved his body so his long legs rested on the edges of the steps. "We can only be killed in a very specific way. You saw what I did to Leo and the others. Were you given instructions to hit her heart, then her head?"

I really don't want to discuss my techniques or my clients with an admitted cop. "I told you, I don't take instructions. Why does it matter?"

I'd never seen this side of Bobby before, the absolute authority. "Because it'll tell me whether it was just a disgruntled human or one of our own that wanted her dead. Did you finish the job? Who was your client?"

I couldn't answer right then. I literally couldn't. I tried but I was suddenly fighting for air. I couldn't breathe. Sue couldn't breathe. Something was very wrong.

I grabbed at my throat. I sucked air through my nose and mouth but it didn't satisfy the need. I couldn't tell Bobby what was wrong but he understood it.

"Now what in the hell is going on?" he asked. He pulled his weapon as I dropped to my side in the dust. He moved with lightning speed toward the hanger. I wished I could have followed, but all I could do was fight for air. Somebody was killing Sue and I couldn't stop it. I couldn't break free. When Bobby left he took the shields with him. Now we were dying together. The noose had finally closed and it was strangling me.

Couldn't breathe. No air. I started seeing spots and white bursts of flowers. I felt Sue's eyes open for a brief instant. Jerry stood above her, his face expressionless. He was blurry through the thick plastic sheet that he held over Sue's face. She couldn't fight. I couldn't fight.

I don't want to lose you, I thought at Sue. It was my last thought. The flowers collided and grew until my vision was white. Then the world slipped away.

Chapter 31

The air smelled like lush exotic flowers. The mid-day sun heated the cloud of mist over the porch where I stood into a golden blanket that was suffocating enough to even silence the insects. Imagine New Orleans in August.

This was worse.

I'm not good at waiting under the best of circumstances. I'm patient as all get-out but patience is a skill. Waiting, though . . . it removes choice. It's out of my control. Makes me tense.

Sue was still unconscious. Over a week had passed. Bobby saved her life and mine, but he could only do so much. They're not completely positive that she's alive. Her body is working but that could just be me. Breathing with her, my heart beating in unison with hers—it's become unconscious. I only know she wasn't in my head.

Carl has spent hours on intercontinental calls with top Sazi doctors, but there aren't enough mated pairs in the world for them to know—and I'm the only one to have ever mated to a full human. Naturally. Just my luck.

Of course we had to tell Carl everything because he went on the plane with us to the island. Bobby lost a lot of energy and had to feed. Carl's dealing with the knowledge. Kind of.

John Corbin arrived on the island yesterday with a psychiatrist from one of the big packs. Elizabeth Perdue, M.D., Ph.D. Dr. Perdue, Betty, is a specialist in "normalizing" the Sazi experience. Not for me; for Carl.

John is completely fascinated with the whole shapeshifter thing. He laughed that he has a couple of patients who *swear* that a dog once talked to them. Until now, he's just been tolerant and treated it as a mild psychosis. Even though he's sworn to secrecy, I'd be interested to watch his next session with *those* people.

He's been as excited as a kid at Christmas, being able to spend hours talking to Dr. Perdue. He told me that he's been on a waiting list for one of her seminars for almost a year. He said she's done some really cutting edge research papers about treating human trauma victims. Laura thinks he's *at* one of her seminars. We used the same story with Carl's people. He had to do some juggling in the office to be here. They'll even have seminar materials to bring home, from a talk that was already in the works a few months from now.

I didn't even know they *did* waiting lists for psychiatric seminars. Live and learn.

Bobby wasn't pleased at having to tell both John-Boy and Carl. He told me that telling them had been "approved" by the Council. If the approval hadn't come through, Bobby would have killed them. I reminded him that they've been Family for years. Nobody will talk.

He just hissed. He was in snake form at the time.

Later on he decided that having another doctor and psychiatrist who can keep their mouths shut could be useful to the Sazi. If Carl can get a grip.

I watched Bobby's multi-colored body slither down a mossy trunk toward an unsuspecting seagull. Loops of him were still draped like garland on the lowest branch. We measured—nose to tail, he's thirty-three feet long when he hasn't eaten. He loses some length with a full stomach. He can take down a full-grown goat as a single meal. I'm still fascinated by watching him hunt and hey, there's nothing better to do.

He's patience personified, but fast as a rattler. If he can get his teeth into prey, it doesn't escape. After he catches something, he wraps his body around it, and then slashes at it with a mouthful of sharp teeth and eats it by swallowing it whole in slow gulps. Like he had Jerry, except for the swallowing part. He has a vindictive streak too. Eye for an eye.

Jerry tried to suffocate Sue. Bobby wanted him to know what it felt like.

Wish I could have watched.

Bobby got a confession out of Jerry before he iced him. It apparently had nothing to do with Leo. I was simply competition. If getting rid of Sue would hurt me, Jerry would do it. He never figured there was anything wrong with doing it. He was more like Scotty than me. He wouldn't have lasted long though—Carmine had said no.

I'd found out a lot of stuff that happened during the airport incident. Like how Carmine and the boys got there: Jocko called them on his cell phone when he came to for back-up. Jocko always liked tag-teams.

Jocko still doesn't know anything about anything. He was hurt so he got a ride from Jake to a hospital. He'll be fine. Jake is unaware too, but Carmine had to be told since he's sleeping with Babs. One wrong scratch without silver and poof, insta-wolf.

Bobby moved a little too slowly this time. The seagull spotted him and jumped into the air just ahead of his mouth. It flew up into the canopy of trees and scolded him with a sharp piercing cry.

"Better luck next time," I called. He turned his head, still suspended in mid-air as though attached to a wire. His head is as big around as my fist and the middle of his long body has a diameter just slightly less than my waist. His red-gold eyes focused on me and he spoke. I still haven't gotten used to seeing that snake mouth move and hearing words come out. I keep expecting someone to step out from behind a tree and yell, "Gotcha!"

"You ssstartled it," he complained. "You owe me dinner." Burning coffee soared over the top of his jungle vine scent—almost indistinguishable from the surroundings.

"Excuses, excuses. You're just getting slow."

He flicked his tongue at me indignantly and lifted his body into the tree to wait for the next victim.

Snakes. They're all alike.

Wow. Suddenly I know how a snake thinks. I reflected

on all I had learned in the past few days. It made what I had endured over the last year seem so unnecessary. I leaned on the railing of the porch and stared into the jungle. The island belongs to Carmine and Linda. It's a good place to lie low, both from the cops and the crooks. Leo had friends, and I worry more about them than Sommers and Vito Prezza combined.

I wish Babs had told me things, given me some clue how to survive in this new world. I should have listened to what she *did* say. But she was running from what she did. She didn't want to admit her transgressions; she tried to pretend that it—that I—never happened.

Babs committed crimes but they weren't what I expected them to be. It was okay for her to use her abilities to defend herself. It was okay to kill me. She screwed up when I lived and became one of them. That violated the Sazi's equivalent of the prime directive. It's a death sentence crime, and Bobby is one of the executioners.

As Bobby tells it, any crime that a Sazi commits which would result in imprisonment in a human jail past any full moon puts you in Wolven's arena. They are judge, jury and executioner. No appeals. No second chances. The rule is simple. Break the law—whether or not you get caught by the humans, and discipline is swift and harsh. Either you are beaten or killed. And the beating isn't like a slap on the wrist. You get thumped on either by your pack leader or by a Wolven agent. The methods used depend on the type of animal doing the discipline. Could be claws, teeth—or, in Bobby's case, being crushed.

There's a bank of lawyers to defend a Sazi in human courts in case the crime is minor. If it's major . . . the Defendant won't be showing up. Ever.

Since Babs attacked me in self-defense it was the equivalent of a misdemeanor. For that Bobby would have just slapped her around a bit. But her dumb move was not to tell them I survived. Plus, she didn't mentor me. If you do accidently bring someone over, you're supposed to make sure that they are trained in the ways of the Sazi. She was supposed to teach me to hunt and instruct me on the use of my magical abilities—I didn't know I had any—to make sure that no humans ever see us. That's their second big rule. Bobby was impressed at how I handled not being seen, using the hotel room for my changes.

Babs's crimes got her a beating. It was bad enough that she's been laid up for almost a week now. Death and pain. Typical Family enforcement, although Bobby didn't like the comparison.

Bobby also did something that he called "claiming damages" on my behalf. Apparently, I was entitled to thump on her myself for making me a wolf. But I didn't know to ask and there was no family or pack to ask for me so he took the role of "concerned protector."

Babs didn't look real pretty for a few days, and still isn't quite herself. Bobby was thorough. But she was surprised not to be killed outright; she had expected to die. That's why she hid the truth. She was afraid.

He was lenient but didn't have to be. Wolven stands behind their people. Whatever decision the field agent makes is what goes. I would think that would lead to some abuses, but when everyone can smell lies I suppose that makes the thought less attractive. Bobby told me that he's in for a beating himself from his supervisor, Fiona Monier, a French cougar with a mean streak.

Wolven agents get full latitude when watching and enforcing, but aren't supposed to get involved. Helping Sue and me with Leo, and killing Jerry when he was suffocating Sue will get Bobby in trouble. He told me as much in the hangar but I didn't understand then. I guess the comment about taking a strip of hide is literal. Ouch.

Bobby's hoping to show mitigating circumstances. If he had done his job quicker, Leo wouldn't have been around to kidnap Sue. Of course, saying that he didn't do his job probably won't win him a friend, either.

I've been getting a crash course in the rules over the past couple of days while we've been waiting. It kills time. That's what I keep telling myself. On the plus side, it *is* fascinating.

I've also been getting biology lessons. I found out from Bobby that since I became Sazi, my body clock has slowed down to a crawl. We live decades longer than humans. Some Sazi have even survived centuries although that's rare.

Also, doctors are no longer necessary. Alphas can heal almost anything. I'm not that powerful, but I can probably drop the health insurance. Never did like the HMO, anyway. For serious wounds to non-alphas, the Sazi have "healers", who use magic to mend wounds—like Bobby had.

When I woke up in the plane hours after Jerry tried to kill us, I was healed but I couldn't feel Sue. I tried. I blew open every door, attached every connection I could, but nothing worked. Her body is living. I know. It's part of me now. I feel each breath, every heartbeat. But the part that's *Sue*, that indefinable spark of consciousness, is missing.

I left Bobby to his hunt and walked in the cabin. I laughed when I first saw the place. Calling this a cabin is like calling the Taj Mahal a bungalow. Forty-five hundred square feet on the first floor. The upstairs is the same.

Betty and John were earnestly talking at the kitchen table. Betty's dark blonde hair was in a bun at the back of her neck. She was wearing a white cotton tank top and shorts that stretched tight over heavy thighs. Betty tells me that she's a grey wolf, same as me, and I know she is because she smells like one. She doesn't strike me as a wolf though. It's hard to explain. She's supposedly the second most powerful female in the Colorado pack but she doesn't *smell* aggressive. She smells steady and warm, a calming presence. Like John-Boy. I'm having a hard time thinking of her running through a forest or ripping out a deer's guts.

I moved past them. Betty watched me out of the corner of one eye. I could feel it. She's been watching me a lot. She's tried to talk to me, tried to initiate some sort of therapy but I've avoided her. What's to discuss? If Sue lives, life is good. If she dies, I go with her. Not much else to say.

Good morning, gorgeous! I whispered into Sue's mind. She lay on a polished brass poster bed in a room with bamboo pattern wallpaper. A sea-soaked breeze ruffled the curtains on the French doors and caught the fan blades spinning overhead. The fan and the rustling lace were the only sounds in the large muggy room. It was only slightly cooler inside than out. I hate the heat but quiet is a nice change.

Betty and John both told me that a person in a coma can hear. They comprehend but can't respond.

I tried to ask Carl what might help bring her out of this—he *is* the medical doctor. He just snorted and said, very annoyed, "Why ask me? I don't understand a damn thing that's going on. Go ask the snake or the wolf in the next room." Then he took another swig straight from a nearly empty bottle of rum.

Okay then.

The teak floors creaked under my weight as I walked toward the bed. I sat down lightly on the edge. Sue still looked pretty rough, what with the surgery and then the near-suffocation. I watched her sleep. I keep telling myself it *is* just sleep. I moved a strand of hair from her pale silent face. The breeze pushed it back. Someone had placed her hands on her stomach, one over the other. Only the slow movement of her chest and the faint color in her cheeks reminded me that she's still alive. I touched her hand, slipped my own through it and squeezed softly. There was no tingle to the touch. Her scent was flat, like sterile soil with no breath of wind. That worried me the most.

"How are you doing today?" It felt strange talking to her like this. I'd rather be doing something—hitting a wall, screaming, fighting. Anything but just waiting. If I threw myself off a cliff at least I'd feel *something*. But I don't dare injure myself. She's too fragile.

My ears picked up sound from the next room and I looked up sharply.

"We interrupt our regularly scheduled programming for a special report," came a loud voice-over. I didn't even know that there was a signal to the island. I decided to listen in.

"This is Erin Stewart coming to you live from the 7 News Center."

Erin Stewart? She's from back home. I took my hand out of Sue's and stood. I walked toward the living room. I stopped in the doorway and leaned on the jamb. Linda was sitting on the couch, facing away from me. The television was on and the pretty black woman with poofy hair was speaking.

I heard Babs's voice from the kitchen. "Put it on pause for a second, Linda." Ah. It was a *tape* of a broadcast. I could watch it later.

I stepped back into the room with Sue, but heard Babs walk across the room and sit down. I glanced out briefly just as Linda hit the play button again, but then my eye caught the photo of a man and woman on the small box behind the anchor. I knew them from somewhere.

"We have just received in our offices a box which contained one of our Channel 7 video cameras. The whereabouts of the news crew who were in possession of this camera are still unknown. The footage that we are about to show you is very graphic in nature. We recommend that small children and those with limited tolerance to violence leave the room." The same wording was repeated at the bottom of the screen in type—I guess for the hearing impaired.

The picture changed to show a petite blonde woman with a microphone in a scene I recognized. I felt my heart in my throat.

The woman on the screen spoke. "This is Cindy Sigala with 7 News. We're here at the old airport where new development will soon transform this desolate scene into one of activity and progress." She motioned with her hand. "Several local construction companies unveiled plans today for a new factory outlet mall that will provide hundreds of new jobs for the area and give a needed economic boost to the region." Suddenly a scream sounded in the background and I felt panic tighten my chest. It was Sue.

"Shit!" I meant to say it soft but it came out loud. The girls started and turned toward me. The picture stopped as Linda hit the pause. The image of Sue, half out of the van with Leo gripping her hair froze on the screen and flickered.

Linda looked embarrassed. "Oh God! Tony. I'm sorry. I didn't know you were there."

"What's this?" I pointed at the screen.

Babs spoke as well as she could. Her mouth was still a mess. "'Armine put it togeth'r from the news coverage." I vaguely remembered the news crew; the sun glinting off the camera lens. It was just fragments of memory.

Betty was instantly beside me. I hadn't heard her move. "It's understandable if you don't want to watch this, Tony. If it's too soon just say so."

I didn't look at Betty. My eyes were glued on the screen. The look on Sue's face was part fear and part pain. It was suddenly hard to breathe. Could I go through this again? I glanced backwards at Sue's still form on the bed. Maybe there was a clue, something I'm forgetting that might help. No. I had to do this.

"Run the tape," I said in a flat voice. Betty watched me. Hell, everyone watched me. Betty glanced at John. He pursed his lips and then nodded. Betty must have agreed because she stepped back and gave me room.

Linda turned back toward the set but glanced over her shoulder at me more than once. She pointed the remote and pressed a button. Sound returned: wind and fast breathing.

The cameraman turned to the scream automatically. The reporter, quick on her feet, continued to report as though it was rehearsed.

"Ladies and gentlemen," she said with a hushed voice. "We are apparently on the scene of an attempted kidnapping. David, are you getting this? A black van has just pulled into the airport and a woman is being forcibly removed from it. She is obviously being moved against her will. Wait! Two men are opening doors on one of the hangers and a Boeing cargo plane is exiting. Can you get a close-up on that, David? Can you see anyone's face?"

The camera's view moved in closer and I watched again Sue's abduction—this time from a third person point of view.

"All of the men appear to have guns," said Cindy's disembodied voice. The scene played out just as it happened.

"The woman looks familiar; she might be a celebrity. One man appears to be the leader. He seems to be letting the woman go free. Okay, she's running now. Wait! Somehow he caught up to her. In fact he passed her by and caught her. He seems to be toying with her. Oh, God! He's slapped her to the ground!"

My eyes narrowed. Leo deserved everything he got.

This was about where I came in. Everybody in the room was glued to the screen, including myself.

"Now he's dragging her toward a small metal building. None of the men are doing anything except loading the plane. David, do you have your cell phone on you? We need to call this in to the police!"

I arrived in the picture in wolf form just then. I nearly knocked the cameraman over. Oops.

I'd only seen myself once before, on the video Babs made. I have mostly grey fur with a white star on my nose and a black and white neck ruff and tail. Pretty traditional markings. I must have run right by the news crew and not even noticed. Of course, I was a little preoccupied.

"What was that?" asked David.

"It looks like a dog. He's running right for the man with the girl!"

"All right! Attadog! Look at him go after the bad guy! Wow, that must have hurt. Think it's a police dog?"

Linda and Babs were echoing the cheers.

"Must be," agreed Cindy who had pretty much given up on reporting. "It's sure big enough. Oooh, look. There's another dog now!"

"*That's* a dog?"

I watched myself fight from a different angle. I felt my body move in reaction to the visual from the video and I split my attention between the images in my mind and the screen.

You fought wonderfully, I thought to myself.

Hold it. When did I start talking to myself in third person? I glanced sharply at Sue who was still inert on the bed.

Sue? I asked in my mind. There was no response.

"C'mon, big guy," muttered David. It brought my attention back to the video. He zoomed in on the dog fight. "Get the bad dog." Somehow they had picked sides and decided that Leo was the bad dog. Pretty astute of them.

"Look at that!" Cindy's voice was thick with horror. "They *shot* the woman! That man with the sandy hair. Oh my God!"

Time stopped. There was a buzzing in my ears. I watched the bullet spin her around for the second time. Watched her fall to the sand once again. A shudder passed through me.

"That was right through the heart," said David, appalled. "She'll never make it."

"Did you get that?" Cindy's blonde hair was in the edge of the picture now. "That black guy shot the second dog! Now they're shooting at him. He shot the sandy-haired man with the gun! Now he's taken a bullet. My God! This is a bloodbath!"

"Look at the dog." David didn't turn the camera to me and Sue. He knew where the bread and butter was. "He's going to the girl. Must have been her pet. They're both hurt pretty bad."

A pause. "—Cin, they'll never be able to use this on the air."

Bobby was the only one still standing when the bullets stopped. Suddenly he turned and looked right at the camera.

"Uh, oh," said David, moving the camera from his eye. The view turned sideways and most of the heads in the room moved with it unconsciously. It's instinct. "We've been spotted! Take off, Cindy. I'll hide the camera. We can come back for—" The picture went dead. There was a pause.

I wonder what Bobby did with the crew. I'd ask but I didn't really care.

The picture returned to the News Center. Erin was speaking again.

"That was the scene earlier today. Police arrived at the scene based on a tip from an unknown source. Perhaps the same source that returned our camera. Police have been unable to locate any bodies at the scene. Both the black van and the cargo plane have disappeared. However, 7 NewsCenter has learned the identities of several of the participants."

The screen behind the desk flashed a publicity still of Sue when she won the lottery. I smiled at the excited look on her face but then glanced again at her still form. Sadness won and the smile faded.

Then the screen split and showed a close-up from the video. "The woman apparently killed in a kidnap attempt was Susan Quentin. We profiled Ms. Quentin after she won the $268 Million Lotto jackpot last year. Her family has been unavailable for comment but we have learned that Ms. Quentin's sister, Bekki Meyers, reported her abduction from the Southside Mall parking lot earlier today,"

Another picture flashed. This time of Leo. It was a mug shot. One front, one side, with a number on his chest. "The man first involved that later disappeared is known to Las Vegas authorities as Leopold Scapolo, AKA 'Lucky Leo'".

He was? I never heard that one.

"He has been indicted on multiple counts of money laundering and racketeering. He is also suspected of being involved in the abduction and murder of several Las Vegas showgirls."

Next a fuzzy picture of me flashed. It was an older photo but I didn't know from where. "This man is known to local authorities as Tony Giodone. Sources at the police department have indicated that they believe this name is an alias." Good guess.

"Mr. Giodone recently had a warrant issued for his arrest for first degree murder."

Yeah, well, they would still have to prove it. Frankly it didn't matter anymore. Bobby warned me that if I didn't change careers, he'd be visiting me again, and it wouldn't be a social call. Guess I was going to be the one to bend after all.

Happiness suffused through me. Damned if I knew why.

Erin continued, "We spoke with Detective Robert Sommers of the Fourth Precinct Homicide Division." Bob appeared on the screen, live from the airport. He looks even worse on television.

"Detective, do you believe that we will ever find any of the bodies seen on the video?"

"Well, Erin," he said, "we've had forensic crews out at the airport since we received the tip about the shootings. There is definitely some evidence that matches the video. We have put out an APB for the van and have requested air traffic control to advise us of any radar anomalies during this time. If they're out there we'll find them."

"But will you find any bodies?"

He shook his head and shrugged at the same time. "I doubt that those who survived would carry the bodies with them. We plan to use infrared spotting from our helicopter as soon as the sun goes down. We believe if they're buried nearby we'll find them." If there had been anything to find that might work. I knew what Bobby did with the bodies. They won't be found. Bobby slept in the jungle for the first couple of days on the island because of *that* meal.

The screen went blue just then. "Okay, this is where we spliced it," said Linda. "Hold on."

The picture started and it was Erin again. New outfit, same hair.

"This is Erin Stewart. We're *live* at the Glendale Funeral Home where a memorial service is being held for kidnap victim Susan Quentin. We have been requested to remain outside during the service out of courtesy for the mourners. It appears that the service is just now ending and people are beginning to exit."

"They already had a memorial service?" I asked. "Sort of rushing it, aren't they?" I was abruptly angry at the callousness and the greed.

Blackened coffee filled the room. It emanating from Linda. "You don't know the half of it, sweetie. Watch and learn."

Erin moved forward quickly, forcing the cameraman to double step to keep up. She approached a young woman wearing black. Her eyes were red and swollen. Hey, it's Lee.

Wait. Lee who?

From where I used to work. The friend that I stayed with that night. Nice to know she missed me.

What?! Sue? I asked in my head. Are you there? I ignored the video and turned and walked back into the bedroom. Sue was still out. There was no movement. But when I touched her . . . tiny fingers of electricity. Faint as a dream.

Tony? said a voice in my head but then disappeared. I called again; nothing. Was I imagining it?

Immediately Betty was beside me. Power crackled from her and boiled over the top of me, and I began to understand why she was a big dog.

"Talk to me, Tony. What's happening?" She placed a gentle hand on my shoulder. She smelled concerned and curious.

"She was here. Just now. But she's gone again." I shook my head, fighting to think.

Intelligence burned behind Betty's hazel eyes. "The video," she said slowly. "Keep watching. Maybe it's breaking through."

I understood what she meant.

I strode back into the front room, crossing in front of Linda and Babs. They both suddenly smelled afraid. I ignored the grumble from my stomach at the succulent scent. I haven't been eating well lately.

I took the remote from Linda and hit the rewind button while it was still playing. I backed up the tape to the point where Lee came on screen. I sat down beside Linda on the sofa, my entire focus on the screen.

"Excuse me, Miss?" said Erin. "Were you a friend of Susan Quentin?"

"Suzi," she replied, which made Erin repeat, "Excuse me?"

"Her name was *Suzi*, not Susan. It was her given name. But she liked to be called 'Sue'."

"So you *were* a friend?"

Lee nodded. "I like to think so. We were real close a few years back but we sort of drifted after she won the Lotto."

Warm fuzzies ran through me. They were mingled with sorrow. I called to Sue again. No response. I knew it was her. It had to be.

"Stopped seeing all her old friends, huh?" prodded Erin. "Money went to her head?"

Lee look appalled. "Oh, god, no! Not Sue. Not ever!" She leaned close to Erin, who lowered the mike to chest level. Lee apparently forgot that she was on film, "It was that family of hers! Her mother just took over her life! Once her mom moved in, Sue couldn't even breathe without asking permission . . . and her sister! The money-grubbing witch! God, I could tell you stories!"

Erin's pretty brown eyes lit up and she tipped the microphone toward Lee. "Feel free."

Lee must have noticed the camera. She suddenly got shy. "No, no. This isn't the day for it. I'd better keep my mouth shut." Then she moved hurriedly into the crowd.

Erin picked a new target. Bekki was moving from the main crowd of family and heading toward the waiting black limos. She was wearing a designer black outfit and wore a small pillbox hat with a veil. She didn't look sad at all. Big surprise.

There *was* surprise in my mind at the cynicism.

Another search. Nope. Still nothing.

"Excuse me? Mrs. Meyers? You're Bekki Meyers, right? Sue's sister?" Erin poked the microphone directly in Bekki's path. No problem. I didn't feel any guilt at all for that.

"Can't you people just leave us alone!" Bekki said, slapping the microphone aside. She kept walking toward the limos but Erin walked in step with her. She voiced the question that I just had.

"I was just wondering. Isn't this service sort of soon after the alleged murders? No bodies have been found yet and police are still hopeful that some people survived. Your sister might still be alive."

Bekki stopped then. She turned and faced the camera. She was angry. "I watched the video. It was a direct hit. My sister is dead! Do you understand that?"

She suddenly looked startled. She took a deep breath and added more calmly, "It's time to get on with our lives. We need closure of this awful thing. I have my children to think of. They need to move on. Suzi would have wanted that."

Says who? came an angry voice in my head. I locked onto it, held it.

Don't go! I asked—begged—commanded.

I can't wake up, Tony! Why can't I wake up? Then she was gone.

I looked at Betty. She was watching me, not the screen. My face probably held the panic I felt. So close. Damn it! I hit pause again.

"She was here again." Only Betty understood what I meant.

"Don't fight it, Tony," she said calmly. "Don't fight her. Just watch the tape. Let *Sue* watch the tape."

I took a deep breath and then let it out slow. I punched the play button once more.

Erin Stewart's face took on a sly look when she asked Bekki, "What about the money? Your sister was a very rich woman. If there's no body, will your sister's estate ever be probated?"

Ah. There's the trick. No body, no money. Bekki's lips grew tight. Erin had struck a nerve. "Our attorneys have informed us that the law requires that we wait for seven years before we can probate."

"How do you feel about that?" She stabbed the mike in Bekki's face. She had scented blood. I wonder how many reporters are Sazi. I'll have to ask Bobby.

"No comment."

Abruptly, the microphone was pulled sideways by a slim well-manicured hand. I knew those fingernails!

"Oh God!" said Linda and dropped her head into her hands. Her scent changed to hot desert winds. "Here comes the embarrassing part! I looked like such a harpie!"

The camera turned to give a full face view of Linda. She was wearing a wide-brimmed hat with a veil. I couldn't see the dress but it was probably black. Although with Linda you never know.

Babs patted Linda's arm soothingly as she watched the screen through spread fingers. "s'okay," Babs said softly. "You 'ad erry 'ight to be angry." Linda turned to her and smiled. I smelled warmth and caring flow from Babs. Bread and sugar and musk.

"Well I have a comment!" Linda said sharply on the screen.

The camera stepped back, so all three women would be in the picture. Erin spoke, "You're Linda Leone, right? Owner of Carlin's Restaurant? Did you know Sue Quentin?" At least she picked up on the "Sue" the first time she was corrected. Some reporters never get the hint.

Bekki wanted to leave but it wouldn't be viewed well. I watched her eyes dart this way and that looking for an escape. Still, she seemed fascinated by Linda.

"Yes, I'm Linda Leone. Yes, I own Carlin's and yes, Sue was a very dear friend of mine." I felt Sue's happiness and gratitude at the admission.

"Sue says thanks," I said quietly to Linda. She gave me a startled look.

Just go with it, I told myself. Just relax. I leaned back into the soft cushions and watched.

"What did you want to comment on?" asked Erin. She seemed to have forgotten the question.

"You asked how the family felt about having to wait seven years to probate Sue's will. *Sister dear* here didn't have a comment. I do." Her voice rose until it drowned out everything surrounding her. Erin handed her the microphone and Linda addressed the assembled crowd. It wasn't big, probably thirty people.

"I've just spent the past two hours with Sue's friends and family. I've listened to the bickering, the sniping and the griping. This was *supposed* to be a memorial service for Sue. I came because I *thought* that I'd hear nice things about my friend. I did. From her other friends. But I guess it's true what they say. You can pick your friends but you can't pick your family." Bekki's eyes shot open and her jaw dropped. Myra looked furious. Her lips thinned just as Bekki's had earlier.

"All I heard from her family were complaints." She turned to Erin so suddenly that the reporter took a step back in reflex. Her brown eyes were startled.

"Know what her family thinks about waiting for the money? They're *pissed!* All of them." She imitated them one by one.

First Myra. She did her perfectly. Cold, with a whiny nasal quality. "'This is all Suzi's fault! What could she have been thinking? How am I going to get by?'" Linda glared into the camera. "Like she had a *choice* or something! She was *kidnapped!*"

Next came Bekki. A younger version of the same whine. "'Oh no! Seven years! Can you believe it? We should sue that attorney! The law should be changed. It's right there in living color. The woman is dead! I'm entitled to my inheritance!'"

Then another voice. "'How will I ever survive on the pittance that the trust gives me? I have a lifestyle to uphold. My children will be homeless in days!'"

It sounded just like Mitzi. I let the knowledge fill me because I knew it was Sue. I'd never met Mitzi. I felt Sue's thoughts swimming just behind my own. I felt angry and sad.

"That's what the family thinks about it! You people *make me SICK!*" She turned her back on the stunned group and tossed the microphone back to the closely following reporter.

Erin caught the mike on the fly. There was a scrambling hiss. She opened her mouth twice before she could speak. "Okay, then." She took another tack, "Um. Mrs. Leone. It's well known that even though you are married you have occasional . . . *relationships* with other women. Was Sue Quentin your lover?"

Anger and embarrassment filled me but I fought it down by being amused. Linda can take care of herself.

On the screen, Linda turned to the reporter with a look that could cut stone. "I *said* that Sue was my *friend.* If you know I'm bisexual, and in an open relationship, then you also know that I'm not shy about it. Nor am I embarrassed. If I had *meant* that Sue was my lover I would have *said* so!" Her voice rose with each word until it was a controlled yell in Erin's face. Small drops of spittle landed on the microphone. "How *dare* you even ask that! Sue's sexual preferences are none of your business! God! You're as bad as her family! Let the woman rest in peace."

Tears were rolling down her cheeks unchecked. Linda glared at the reporter until Erin's eyes dropped. Then she turned on her heel, slipped an arm through Babs's waiting one, slipped her other arm around Carmine and leaned into them, crying. Carmine put a caring arm around his wife while Babs turned and gave the reporter a look that could not only *cut* stone but should be able to turn Erin *into* stone. I found out after Linda arrived that Carmine hadn't said a word to them. They didn't know we were alive that day.

There was a stunned silence on the screen for a moment. Then Erin spoke. "Um, this is Erin Stewart, from Sue Quentin's memorial service. Back to you, Angela." The video clicked off. The entire group of us sat in dazed silence as the screen went dark.

Rage filled me and I let it. Homeless? Homeless! For God's sake! The trust gives her two hundred thousand a year. She's going to starve on that? What the hell is she doing with the money? I felt Sue's anger burn along my body like a flame. Her outrage and pain.

It's okay, I thought at her, You have the right to be angry. Tell me how you feel. Tell me all of it. I stood and walked toward the bedroom. Betty followed me like a ghost. My peripheral vision caught John and the others as they trailed in our wake.

I sat down on the bed, touched Sue's cheek with my hand. The tingles grew while I stroked her face.

"Wake up, Sue. Time to get up, sweetheart," I said to her sleeping form.

I can't! I can't wake up, Tony. Help me! I didn't know how. I looked at Betty. She was waiting patiently for some word. Her scent was masked by the sweet antifreeze curiosity drifting from the others assembled.

"She can't wake up. She's here." I tapped my temple. "But she can't wake up."

I looked to the group for any suggestions. Carl was out cold at a table in the corner. His snoring head was half underneath his left arm. His right fist was tight around the neck of a bottle. Still rum but the bottle was white this time. He smelled thickly of alcohol and sweat. Damn it, Carl. Why now?

Nobody understood what the problem was. How could I explain it?

Betty gripped my arm. She pulled me back. "Let me take a look at her." I moved aside for her. I shifted back a dozen steps. I felt Linda move up behind me. She rested cool hands on my arm and I let her. She laid her head on my shoulder and we watched the doctor work. Sue and I both felt comforted by her touch.

Betty leaned over Sue until I couldn't see her anymore. The room was strangely silent. Tough with so many people present. There was an air of solemnity. I felt Sue in my mind. She was worried. What if this was all? If she never woke up, never lived again.

I wouldn't consider that as a possibility.

A flash of light appeared over Sue's head. Trust a doctor to carry a penlight. The light flicked once, then twice. The white embroidered flowers on the pillow cover gleamed briefly.

Determination's hot metal filled my nose suddenly as Betty stood. Without any warning she slapped Sue hard across the face. What the hell!

Sue's head shifted violently sideways. Honeyed hair spilled over her face and her whole body rocked slightly. A vicious backhand brought her face back to where I could see it. The crack of the slap filled my ears and filled my mind with fury.

I broke away from Linda and was across the room faster than thought. A sound erupted from me—part howl, part roar. All rage. The third blow never reached Sue. I grabbed Betty by both shoulders and fiercely threw her sideways. She sailed across the room. Her back hit an oak and brass entertainment center that filled one corner near where Carl was slumped.

Carl woke in a flash as the cabinet disappeared in a rain of splinters, metal and broken glass. A shard of glass sank deep into her neck. I felt my eyes go. The beast inside was trying to lunge out. Betty's eyes glowed golden as she looked at me. Her lips pulled back and she growled low and deep. I didn't care. I answered with a growl of my own. She smelled confident and anticipatory. Her power raced over me; nearly as strong as Bobby. I think she intended to frighten me off.

Whether I was too angry or too stupid, it didn't work.

She would die for hitting my mate or I would die trying.

Thick orient spice crawled and clawed over the sweet copper blood. It urged me on, making me want the battle. I didn't need to look behind me to feel the fear from the humans. The tang was strong enough to make me salivate. The sound of the turning fan assaulted my ears. I was almost to her. My body tensed to fight. I saw her adjust her footing to spring.

"Tony?" came a tentative voice from the bed. Simultaneously, a burst of intense color exploded in my brain. Sunsets in the middle of the day.

I felt my heart stop. I turned in a flash. I had no words. Sue was sitting up with a slightly distressed look on her face. But her eyes were open. Her pale face was blushing. She smiled at me and I felt my eyes burn.

I ignored Betty. I hoped she wouldn't dive for me. In two steps I was at the bed with Sue in my arms. I hugged her tight. A pained sound reminded me that I could hug a little *too* tight. I eased her back and put pillows behind her so she could sit upright.

Long moments passed. I just stared at her. I couldn't keep a grin off my face. When I finally turned to the group, Linda had happy tears rolling down her face. Betty stood off to the side. Her arm was twisted at an odd angle. The shard of glass in her neck was pushed out by the flesh around it. When it was nearly out she reached up and plucked it away. She didn't admit the pain. She was stronger than I had credited her; I had underestimated her.

"Hey," I said to Betty with embarrassment, "I'm really sorry. I didn't understand . . ."

She waved it off with her good hand. "I forgot about the mating. You aren't an alpha so I didn't think you could hurt me." She looked at her arm with chagrin. "My mistake."

Carl narrowed his bloodshot eyes to stare at Betty. There was an injury and he was still a doctor—mostly. His voice was thick and slurred. "I think that arm's . . . um, unlocated."

She nodded seriously. "I could use some help." Actually, I didn't think she needed any help at all and *certainly* not from him. But maybe it's what Carl needed to hold on. Pretty good shrink. They moved into the other room where he had his black bag.

Sue smiled at me and then laughed. "Won't they be surprised when they find out I gave it to the geese?"

I frowned at her, unable to make the subject leap. It took me a moment to realize that she was commenting on the last thing she remembered: her funeral on the video.

"You gave your fortune to the geese?"

"Well, to the Department of Wildlife. I want them to tear down the house and make a preserve out of the grounds. I went to the attorney just before I had lunch with my sister. I changed my will and cut them all out."

Linda burst out laughing. The tears flowed so hard she couldn't speak.

"What's so funny?" asked Sue.

"Oh, God!" exclaimed Linda, gasping for breath. "They were so angry at the service because the lawyer wouldn't tell them what was in your will. He said until you were officially dead he couldn't reveal the contents. But your sister was so sure that you hadn't changed the will, because you told her that you *intended* to, not that you *had.*"

Sue looked chagrined. "She was so weirded out at even the prospect that I felt guilty. I fudged a little. I actually thought about going back to the lawyer and ripping it up. But I didn't get the chance. Vinny grabbed me right when we were coming out of the restaurant."

"They were making plans at the service about the things

they were going to do. Bekki is going to build a custom house and your Mom is going to travel. They plan to borrow and borrow and borrow some more against their future fortune."

She hooted loudly. "And it goes to the birds! Oh, Sue! That is priceless. Seven years of waiting and the *geese* get a new pond!" Linda laughed until tears rolled down her face.

Sue's mood changed and she smelled sad and angry. Her voice slid across my mind. They really didn't care. Didn't love me. I always knew it but part of me still can't believe it. I hugged her against me.

Then she turned her head to me, still snuggled against my shoulder. "Tony? Now what? I don't want to see them again, not ever. But where will we go?"

"What? You don't like the island? You told me *exotic*."

"But not forever," she said quietly. "Where will we live?"

I looked at her with confidence. "I don't know, sweetheart. But we'll find somewhere."

Bobby pushed himself off from the wall. I hadn't realized he'd come in. Sue looked at him and I smelled fear's tang rise from her. "It's okay. Bobby's a cop."

She nodded nervously and bit at her lip. "That doesn't mean that I'm not afraid of him." Okay, good point.

Bobby looked serious. Sweat beaded on his bare upper body. He was wearing faded jean shorts. That must be for Sue's benefit. Bobby is abnormally accustomed to going naked. Or maybe I'm abnormally accustomed to clothes. He tells me I'll get over it. "Wolven will relocate you, Sue. Tony needs to be with a pack—with other wolves. It'll take some time but we've got packs in Boulder, Minneapolis, and Chicago. There are packs in Anchorage and the Ukraine, too, but they're Arctic climates. You probably wouldn't like it." He sighed and it spoke volumes. "I'll do what I can but you might have to stay here for awhile while we sort it out. It's a slow process."

Longer? In this heat? Inside is fine, but outside is— well, a jungle. God, what I wouldn't give for a sudden snowstorm. Oh well. It was hard to bitch with Sue's hand solidly in mine and tingles racing through my body.

Betty and Carl came back in the room. Carl looked at little better. Maybe Betty could help him after all. Betty was carrying two white boxes. One big, one little. She came over to the bed and gave me the small package. The larger one was placed gently near Sue's feet.

"What's this?" I asked.

She shrugged. Her eyes were bright with curiosity. "I was told to give these to you as soon as Sue woke up."

Bobby frowned and it matched the one on my face. At least I didn't hear anything ticking inside the boxes. No smell either.

I opened my box first. Inside the plain white shirt box was white tissue paper. I opened the tissue paper and found a group of official looking documents. Without removing the documents from the box, I looked at each one.

Wow. Definitely impressive. "We apparently have different definitions of slow," I said to Bobby, amazement tinging my voice. "Okay, I admit it. I'm impressed." I shook my head. "Goddamn show-off."

He frowned and moved a little closer. "I don't understand."

I handed him the documents. There was a driver's license, worn-looking and ready to expire next March. It was from Illinois and showed my given name, J. Anthony Giambrocco, Jr. Giodone is my dad's name. I took it after my mom died. Dad rigged a phony birth certificate and everything. My real name is pretty safe because I've never used it.

There was a matching birth certificate. A certified copy of my real one. Quick work. I gave a little chortle at the matching license and certificate for Sue—oops, sorry, for Jessica Susan Giambrocco. I was betting from the condition of the license that there was a full dossier to match the names. Good identity people take pride in their work. The size and shape of the last paper made me nervous.

Bobby looked at each document in amazement. I smirked at him. "Guess I'm going to Chicago, huh?" Nice of him to decide for me. Probably best. He had told me about the various packs and their leaders.

Lucas Santiago is the alpha of the Boulder pack. He's strong, proud, and incredibly noble. Nope. I wouldn't fit there.

Minneapolis is headed by Josef Isaacson, a hard working Norwegian. Eh. Maybe.

Chicago, though—Chicago is led by Nikoli Molotov. I jokingly asked Bobby if he had an "explosive personality." I thought it was funny. Bobby didn't. "I wouldn't *ever* say that around him if I were you," he said solemnly.

"Jeez, I was just kidding. You know, Molotov cocktails?" I nudged him in the ribs.

"I caught the joke, Tony. I'm not stupid. But you don't understand. He's the *same guy*. He's been around since Czar Nicholas's court. He's Russian Mafia and runs Chicago with an iron fist. He's not a pleasant soul."

Ah. That's the one. My kind of world. I had no objection.

Bobby smelled sort of stunned. He kept shaking his head as he looked at each document. He turned each one, examined them, looked out the window at the muted sunlight through them. He handed them back to me with a seriously pissed off expression.

"Who in the *hell* do you have photos of, doing what?"

Sue and I looked at each other in surprise. "You didn't do this?"

He moved toward the bed and tried to grab at the box. "No! Hell, even I don't know anyone with enough stroke to get them. Was there a card? Anything at all?"

I shrugged. I hadn't looked. I let him take the box. He pulled the tissue paper out of the box and shook it lightly. A small note fell on the bedspread. Sue picked it up. The paper was thick and linen. The handwriting was masculine.

She read it out loud. "I've arranged for you to stay in Chicago. Nikoli will treat you well or answer to me. I've already paid your tribute. Don't let him tell you otherwise." She gave a little laugh. "It's signed Lucas Santiago." She looked at me with a curious expression. "Do you know him?"

I shrugged. I didn't. She looked at Bobby. His mouth had dropped as she spoke. The white box, brilliant against his ebony skin, dropped to the floor from his unexpectedly limp hand. Everyone else in the room was riveted to our conversation. Betty stared at us with a similar expression.

It took Bobby several tries before he could speak. "Know him? Yeah. *Every* Sazi knows him. He's a Council member. But how the hell do *you*?"

I had no answer.

"Why don't you open your box, Sue?" Betty suggested. I looked at her. She seemed as surprised as Bobby at the turn of events. The breeze blew through the open doors again, fluffing Sue's hair across her face. It blew her fragrance right at me. She smelled of summer forest and kitchen spices. I hadn't realized how much I missed the scent of her feelings while she was gone. Her every emotion was like sunlight off crystal; intense and startling.

She tried to pull the large box closer to her. Bending was still difficult. She gave a little grimace so I reached over and placed the box on her lap. It was heavy and about as long as a rose delivery box but wider. She lifted the lid. Taped to the white tissue paper was a note. Again, she read it to the group.

"If Chicago doesn't work out, you're always welcome in Boulder, Suzi. You and Tony both." She said it with surprise and amazement. "It's signed Lucas." She turned her head to me, her feelings mildewed with amazement. "I don't know him, Tony! Why is he doing these wonderful things for us?"

I didn't have an answer. I just shook my head. "What's in the box?"

Everyone moved closer as Sue opened the tissue paper. Under the tissue was a layer of rich green velvet. The thick antifreeze of curiosity overpowered my nose and I sneezed repeatedly. So did Babs and Betty. When we finished, the silence was so thick that I could hear every heart in the room.

I looked in the box. Inside was a plastic figure, a foot or so high, with red matted hair trimmed around a war-torn face. There was a ponytail at the top of the head. Green plastic eyes over a painted smile matched the stained and torn green velvet dress she wore. I smiled. The doll was ravaged as only a four-year-old could manage.

There were confused looks from those assembled. Betty seemed most confused of all. Why would someone go to the trouble to wrap this wreck of a doll like a treasure?

I wasn't going to spoil the surprise. It was Sue's story.

Sue's smile came slowly; recognition turned to joy. "Jessica!" She picked up the doll and hugged it to her tightly. Tangerines and cookie spices rose from her in a burst.

I'd wager two to one that Lucas has white fur.

Sue looked at me with shining eyes. She put the doll carefully back in the box and smoothed the dress reverently. She gently touched the red nylon hair. She was nearing tears. Happy and sad both. But her curiosity finally got the better of her. She reached for the papers I was holding. She looked at the picture on the license and smiled brightly at the listed weight. She cocked her head and looked at me, "I like Jessica and Susan but why Ge-am-brock-o?" She stumbled over the name.

I looked at her intently for a moment. "Because I'll share. If you want to use my name, I'd let you." I could see Linda grinning out of the corner of my eye. I swallowed hard. It had been thrust on me; hardly a choice. But how could I give up rainbows and sunsets?

"Oh, what the hell. I don't do subtle well. I love you, Sue. I *want* to spend the rest of my life with you. Will you come to Chicago with me? Be my mate? Be my wife? Please?" I held her hand and waited for a reply.

I stayed out of her head with effort; I had to let her decide for herself. No prompting. Plus, I was a little scared of what I would find if I looked.

Her face moved from confusion to astonishment and finally to absolute glee. She threw herself into my arms with a joyous cry. Her scent was tangerines and cinnamon and baked apple pie. Sweet musk and baking. Amazing how humans, even without being able to smell the emotions, find comfort in the scents of caring. The scents of love.

It was answer enough. I held her tight against me while

the others looked on smiling. I rolled in her scent. I let the sweet tingles fill my body. The Sazi looked on enviously. The others could only guess.

I was suddenly looking forward to a new life with a new love. Years and years of learning and being together. Sue didn't even look at the last paper. She didn't have to. She saw it in my mind. Sure, we're mated. But we were born human—and American.

It was a marriage license.

"An awesome new talent!"

–Sherrilyn Kenyon, *USA Today* bestselling
author of *Night Pleasures*

0-765-34861-6 • $6.99/$9.99 Can.

THE DARK LORD
PATRICIA SIMPSON

IN PAPERBACK JANUARY 2005

When a magical secret releases a dangerous and
powerful demon, one woman must find the strength
within herself to save the world, and her heart.

"Fans of the supernatural can rejoice as marvelous author Patricia Simpson delivers up another surefire hit."

–*Romantic Times Bookclub* on *Just Before Midnight* (4 stars)

If you enjoyed this book, you won't want to miss...

SHIFTING LOVE
CONSTANCE O'DAY-FLANNERY
IN PAPERBACK NOVEMBER 2004

Tor is proud to launch its Paranormal Romance line with a passionate tale of magic and love from *New York Times* bestselling author Contstance O'Day-Flannery.

"An author of incredible talent and imagination. She has the magic."
—*Romantic Times Bookclub*